Avoiding
Mr Right

Avoiding
Mr Right

Anita Heiss

BANTAM
SYDNEY AUCKLAND TORONTO NEW YORK LONDON

A Bantam book
Published by Random House Australia Pty Ltd
Level 3, 100 Pacific Highway, North Sydney, NSW 2060
www.randomhouse.com.au

First published by Bantam in 2008

Addresses for companies within the Random House Group can be found at www.randomhouse.com.au/offices

National Library of Australia
Cataloguing-in-Publication Entry
Heiss, Anita, 1968–
Avoiding Mr Right.
ISBN 978 1 86325 604 9 (pbk.)
Man–woman relationships – Fiction.
A823.3

Cover illustration and design by saso content & design pty ltd
Internal design by V J Battersby, typeset in Adobe Caslon Pro 11.5/15.5
Printed and bound by Griffin Press

Contents

one

Sydney vs. Melbourne

'I'm moving to Melbourne,' I blurted, and waited for the fallout.

'What?' My three friends chorused their disbelief, their voices echoing through Sauce Bar, which was uncharacteristically empty for a Sunday afternoon. It was a scorcher, so most locals were on the beach, and it was just us in the restaurant.

I'd known for three weeks I was moving, but wanted to wait until we were all together so I could deliver my prepared speech. I heard the umpire call 'Six!' from across the road as the local cricket match entertained the few spectators sitting under the thirty-degree sun. A drop of sweat made its way down my leg as I took a deep breath and began.

'I've been given the chance of lifetime – a job as a manager in the newly formed Department of Media, Sports, Arts, Refugees and Indigenous Affairs.'

'You mean DOMSARIA?' Liza confirmed, and sucked an oyster from its shell.

'Yes. With my policy-making experience, there's a real chance that I can move through the ranks quickly – and to be honest, there's no reason why I couldn't one day be the Minister for Cultural Affairs. We're always talking about how we never have Blackfellas managing our portfolio.'

'Wow, that's huge,' Alice said. 'But . . .'

'But what? I don't want to hear *buts* from my friends today. I want to hear *That's great, congratulations, we're happy for you.*'

'Of course it's great,' Alice said.

'And congratulations on the promotion,' Dannie added.

'And, yes, we're happy for you.' Liza lifted her glass in a toast.

'But . . .' they all said in unison.

'It's just that it's so sudden. We're a bit shocked,' Alice said.

'And why *Melbourne*?' Liza asked.

'I know, I know, it's not ideal, but this job is in Melbourne, so that's where I'll be. And besides, it's only for a year.'

'Don't be ridiculous, Peta, you hate Melbourne,' Liza said accusingly.

'*Loathe* Melbourne would be more accurate,' Alice said as she stuffed a hand-cut chip in her mouth.

'Actually, I don't believe I have *ever* heard you say a nice word about Melbourne,' Dannie reminded me. She was right – they were all right – but how could I agree with them now that I'd made the decision, accepted the offer and started packing?

'So, you're taking James with you, then?' said Alice. And there it was: the obvious question.

I tried to keep it light.

'Are you kidding? Taking a man to Melbourne would be like taking a sandwich to a smorgasbord.'

The girls looked at me in disbelief.

'I thought you were getting serious,' said Alice. 'Peta, he's totally into you. Surely you don't want to be single again?'

I had been in a relationship with James for eight months, but the more serious he got, the more unsure I became of myself and of us as a couple. He was already talking about moving in with me, and I felt pressured. He was a lot like Alice, wanting to get married and have kids by a certain date. He wanted it all done and dusted by the time he was thirty-five. He was thirty-three, but I was still only thirty.

'I actually liked being single before I met James. Remember? I used to have loads of fun. Of course I have fun now, but I'm just saying, being single wasn't a drag for me like it was for you.' Alice looked confused and I couldn't blame her. For the eight months I'd been seeing James we'd always been together on weekends and seemed very tight, but he was also one of the reasons I had to leave Sydney. At this point in my career, he was an albatross around my neck.

'Look at my track record – I've been in love so many times but it never lasts. Men never satisfy me like my job does, so I stay in the same work and just change the boyfriend, and somehow I'm always relatively happy and content, pretty much like you girls but around the other way.' As I said it, it made complete sense to me. I had finally worked it out: my best relationship to date had been with my job, not men.

'You know what you are?' Dannie said, waving her fork at me – something she'd rouse on her kids for doing at the dinner table.

'Tell me, oh wise one. What am I?' Dannie was getting a glow up and was about to throw some pearler at me.

'You're *love fickle*. Love fickle! That's what you are.' And the other two nodded in agreement.

'Do tell.' I was amused.

'You've had more crushes than I've had fights over TV on at the dinner table, and that's every other day,' Dannie said.

'That's a bit harsh,' I said. I'd had a few boyfriends, but did that make me love fickle? 'At least I'm not a relationship accelerator, thinking about getting married on every first date.' I didn't look at Alice but she knew I was talking about her. So did the other girls. We'd all been through Alice's ten-point plan to find her Mr Right, and in the end he turned out to be the guy who'd been emptying her garbage bin every day for years. Before meeting Gary every date she went on somehow turned into an interview for a potential husband.

I was completely the opposite. While Alice used to *say* she loved being single, I don't think she actually meant it. The difference was *I* did. I had never dreamed about the wedding and white picket fence – or in the case of Coogee, the car space outside the flat. That was Alice's dream. I dreamed about professional accolades and titles and an office door with my name on it. I wanted the power to make change through government policy. I wanted the high-flying career and a team of staff – and a pay cheque to match. I wasn't embarrassed to say I loved shopping. I was the Imelda Marcos of our group because I had an obsession with shoes. (Dannie, the only parent in our posse, always pointed out, 'You only have two feet, Peta. How many pairs of shoes do you need?') I didn't have that 'sacrifice-everything-for-your-kids' gene that married, maternal women had. I had the me-me-me-gene, and I was quite comfortable with it.

'Look, the reality is that I'm not ready to settle down yet, and I want to be completely sure when I do. I want to have my *own* life sorted out first and then I'll be ready to share it, properly.'

'But James is a great guy. A good guy. An honest, caring, generous guy.' Alice looked me straight in the eye. She'd be pissed off if I let him go. He was truly a rare find, particularly in Sydney.

'And he's gorgeous,' Liza added with a mouthful of salad.

'And he'd do *anything* for you. God, I can't imagine you'd ever have to nag him,' Dannie said, then sipped long on her wine. 'And you'd never have to work. He would make the *perfect* husband.'

'But I want to work. That's the point. I want to be out there doing it, making social change, not changing nappies.' I looked to Dannie. 'No offence.'

'And just because he'd make the perfect husband, does that mean he's perfect for me?'

'I reckon he's your soul mate, Peta, and you only get one of those,' Alice said.

'My soul mate is McDreamy, but I can't marry him,' Liza said and we all laughed. They were probably right about me and James. He certainly was a lovely bloke. Considerate, caring, wonderful, funny, sexy. I couldn't really fault him. But sometimes I thought he loved me too much. It didn't seem healthy. With James I couldn't do anything wrong, even when I did.

'You're all right, of course – we're getting on just fine. James *is* a great guy and he's perfect. And I do love him dearly, but this is the chance of a lifetime.' What I was doing was right for me and for James. I was being fair to both of us. I'd be a more complete woman when I returned in twelve months.

Alice just wouldn't let it rest. 'I know you always enjoyed the single life, but I thought maybe this time you'd met your Mr Right, just like I did with Gary.' I wasn't quite sure if it was friendly concern or something else in her voice. I tightened up my halter neck dress, and sighed.

'Look Alice, *your* holy grail might have been finding Mr Right, but mine has never been that. I've only ever wanted to enjoy my life, make some social change where I could through Indigenous education or whatever, and then, oh, I don't know, maybe one day settle down, when there's nothing else to do. Isn't that enough for now? I would've thought you'd be happy for me.' I delivered my words with a dramatic tremble in my voice and a quivering bottom lip, trying to make them all feel guilty. I could feel the alcohol kicking in and stood up for effect, not quite sure what I was going to do next. They all looked at me startled, as if to say, *What are you doing?*

'I'm going to have a smoke.'

I think they thought I was about to cry and if they kept humbugging me I probably would have. I tripped over my handbag, pushed my chair out of the way, turned towards the door and steadied myself. Guilt was good when used correctly. I'd got a lot of favours from whitefellas by suggesting that something be done for me 'in the spirit of reconciliation'. Couldn't pull that card with these girls, but guilt can come in many forms, and they were now riddled with it. As I walked off Alice sang after me.

'We are happy for you! Of course we are! We're delighted for you, sis, don't get upset. God, we've got somewhere to go for weekends away now and great shopping.'

'Excellent shopping,' Dannie said loudly.

'And great restaurants,' Liza bellowed. There were still no other patrons so we had claimed the entire restaurant as ours.

I stood outside rolling a cigarette. I'd really have to give up smoking when I moved to Melbourne. People always told me I had a beautiful smile, but the nicotine was starting to affect it. James had always hated me smoking, and drinking for that matter.

'Can you clean your teeth before you kiss me? Can you do that outside? Haven't you got better things to spend your money on?' His 'stop-smoking' nagging was relentless, but the girls never saw that. And as for drinking, he always counted how many I'd had, even when I wasn't driving.

When I went back inside, Liza was still stuffing her face. She could always pack it away in the past, but I noticed that she'd clearly gained some weight over the past few months since moving in with Tony. I'd read that contentment with Mr Right saw couples put on something like five kilograms in the first three years together. I certainly couldn't afford to do that. My skinny Murri ankles were flat out holding me up as it was, and when I did put on weight it went straight to my boobs. James being the architect used to say, 'If you were a building you'd be structurally unsound.'

When I sat down, no-one said a word. The mood was uncomfortable. 'Well, what now?' I asked no-one in particular. Liza immediately sat upright and grabbed a pen and pad from her bag, looking slightly pissed but nonetheless in control.

'No, please, not that. Anything but that!' I said.

two

The SWOT analysis

'Why don't we do a SWOT analysis about you moving to Melbourne, just to be *sure* it's the right thing to do?' Liza said.

'Oh, it's right for me, love,' I told her. 'Do you want to see if it's right for *you* girls if I go? Is that what this is about? Okay, I'm fine with that. Why don't we start with the fact that at least going to Melbourne means I won't have to keep doing bloody SWOTs all the time?

'Let's SWOT whether Alice should meet Mr Right. Let's SWOT Dannie having another child. Let's SWOT Liza moving in with Tony, let's SWOT which restaurant to try, let's SWOT, let's SWOT, let's SWOT. I feel like our lives are just one ongoing SWOT analysis! Sometimes I wanna bloody well swat you, Liza!'

Dannie was glassy-eyed from the wine; I could see that she agreed. Alice, on the other hand, was thrilled. Liza was unaware, tearing pages off her steno pad, writing headings, handing pages to each of us – the perpetual lawyer.

'Right, seeing as you are the *only* one at the table who thinks there is some strength to you going to Melbourne, perhaps you should start, Peta. Alice, would you like to do the weaknesses?'

Alice gave me a huge smile as she took her page. 'Oh, if I *have* to,' she said sarcastically.

'That will be sooo hard for you, won't it, Missy.' I could see she was going to try and slaughter me.

'Peta, you'll have a chance to rebut with the opportunities,' Liza said.

'Gee, thanks.' I was thinking I had better sober up quick smart.

'And Dannie, I know you're just dying to list the threats.' Liza had that look in her eye: she knew something entertaining was coming with Dannie in one corner and me in the other.

'Yes, as a mother I've become very good at threats.' And there was Dannie with the humour that I knew I would miss in Melbourne.

'More drinks, ladies?' The restaurateur was standing at the table rubbing his hands.

'Do we look like we need more, Andy?' Alice asked.

'You look gorgeous is all I know.'

'What? Have you been drinking too?' I joked.

'That's not very nice. I meant that sincerely.'

'Another round,' Dannie said. It was her once-a-month outing and she always made the most of it.

'Dessert, ladies?' We all held our bellies, as if to say, *I'm so full.*

Dannie succumbed first. 'I'll have the banoffee pie.'

'Me too,' the rest of us said, suddenly with room for more. We all watched Andy walk off.

'He's nice, eh?' Dannie said.

'What? You shopping are you, sis? What about George?'

'George says it doesn't matter where I get my appetite, as long as I eat at home,' she said as she started on her list.

We all put our heads down, determined to prepare our cases.

'Okay, Peta, I'm the judge and jury, and you can go first. I want you to present the case for the strengths. You have three minutes.' All of a sudden our boozy lunch had become another of Liza's life-changing workshops and it was nowhere near as much fun when the sides weren't even. It was three against one – against me.

'Well, the main strength is that this job will make me both professionally and personally happy, and I guess that should be enough, but clearly it's not for you ladies, so let me go on. I'll talk about the job proper in the opportunities category shortly, but there are other strengths. Melbourne has fabulous shopping – have you heard of Toorak Road, Chapel Street, Collins Street? Yes, I'm looking forward to going shopping for shoes and other gorgeous pieces of clothing, with my *pay* increase, but I do hope I can fit into my new clothes, because I'll be spending my nights trying out the fabulous food in Melbourne along Lygon Street and Johnston Street and, as I plan to live in St Kilda, will probably be eating a lot of cakes on Acland Street, too. Now, as I'll be working in the arts and culture, I will definitely be visiting the live music venues, Crown Casino, the galleries, the theatre and, of course, the numerous wine bars. All in the name of professional development, you know. As part of my cultural research, I'll also have to check out some sports, like the AFL, which is a religion in Melbourne. Doing that *will* be a drag – having to watch gorgeous men with long lean bodies and muscly arms running around for hours getting sweaty. Actually, why haven't we ever been to a game here?'

We all looked out the window at the rugby oval. In winter it was full of solid men wearing headgear and long-sleeve jerseys.

'Oh that's right, you gals prefer to watch league and union. That's okay, that's a very Sydney thing to do. Keep enjoying it next season.

'And finally, while I'm not looking for a man, as you know, I do think it's a strength to have more single men around. I honestly believe there's too much oestrogen in Sydney! And it's not all from the women.'

The girls looked startled by this diatribe, but they laughed. Andy had pulled up a chair at our table and gave me a round of applause.

'Alice, you can counter now with the weaknesses,' said Liza.

'Oh yes please, but let me preface my words by saying that I love you, Peta. I think I speak for us all when I say we *all* love you.' She looked towards the others, who raised their glasses in agreement. 'Here, here!' they toasted.

'So with that in mind,' she continued, 'I do need to point out that a weakness of your plan is that you'll be leaving behind those who love you and I don't just mean James, but us too. And that's not all you'll be leaving behind. Look!' She gestured over the balcony at the shimmering ocean of Coogee and we all knew she was right. My entire life, from Coolangatta down to Sydney, I'd lived with stunning coastline right on my doorstep.

'Next: you don't play or even like sport, so the AFL will be of no use to you, religion or not, especially given you're an atheist. As for entertainment, the last band you saw was a cover band at the Coogee Bay, and as for casinos, you're always bagging the aunts on the pokies. Since when have you become a gambler or even condoned such gambling dens? And as for food, we have Norton Street, and our own Spanish Quarter – correct me if I'm wrong, but didn't you have your birthday there last year? And that dress you're wearing today, wasn't I with you when you bought it? Yes, that's right, on Oxford Street, Paddington.

'And sorry for pointing out the obvious, lovey – Melbourne might have the MCG but Sydney has the world's number one best harbour and its bridge. We have the Sydney Opera House, remember? Home of the first recorded corroboree, Bangarra opening night, and the Deadlys, as you always point out to others. Sydney has great national parks, the Rocks, the world's best New Year's Eve fireworks and what about our beaches? Oh sorry, yes, I might have mentioned them already.'

'Melbourne has beaches!' I proclaimed and they all laughed, including Andy, who was a surfer.

'You can't swim at Melbourne beaches, Peta,' Alice said sternly.

'And you certainly can't surf,' Andy added, getting up for more wine.

'You'll have to travel way out of Melbourne to get a nice, clean beach. You could swim and surf three hundred metres from here right now if you wanted to.' Alice was on fire. 'And you'd have more sunny weather to swim in here too. Have you even considered the weather?'

I'd been waiting for that. Of course I'd considered the weather, it was one of the reasons I loathed Melbourne –

stifling hot in summer and grey and gloomy for too many months in winter. But I had some ammunition, or at least I thought I did.

'I have indeed. Did you know that Sydney gets more rainfall than Melbourne, so the idea of it raining in Melbourne all the time is a myth?'

'Actually, lovey, it's not.' Alice sounded slightly condescending. 'We might get more rain, but ours falls in one big hit usually, where theirs falls lighter and over longer periods, which is why it seems like it's always grey and wet down south. You're gonna have to do better than that. But while you're thinking of how to argue against me, let me remind you also that you have absolutely no friends down there.'

'Great rebuttal, Alice,' Liza cut her off finally. 'Now, Peta, you have the chance to put forward all the opportunities you'll have by moving to Melbourne. Time starts now.' Liza was impressive as a mediator. As long as I could get the lawyer onside, the others would be a pushover.

'The real opportunity is this job. It's an amazing, once-in-a-lifetime opportunity to play a significant role in a new department, managing a team, and getting the sort of direct experience which could one day lead me to holding the portfolio. I'll get to travel, especially to remote communities in the western desert where a lot of our internationally acclaimed artwork is coming from. You can't argue against that, none of you can.' They nodded because they knew I was right.

'The contract is only for one year, in which time I'll set up the team and oversee the introduction of some new systems, write policy and implement some groundbreaking cultural projects and programs. I reckon I can stay out of the local Black politics for a while. I can just be a Murri on loan and not be expected to have an opinion about who's Black, who's not Black, where the boundaries are, which land council I should join and so on. Actually, it will be a little holiday from Black politics – yes, that's what it'll be.' They all laughed, because they knew what a ridiculous idea that was.

'Yeah, you're right, not political at all,' Alice said. 'I reckon you'll be made a spokesperson before you know it.'

'Dannie, I think we need to move on to the threats before Peta talks us all into moving to Melbourne with her just for career opportunities and cakes and AFL players,' Liza said, hinting that I was doing well in the debate. My day was starting to lighten up a bit.

'Let me start by saying to you, Peta, that you need to be prepared for the Melbourne vs. Sydney argument when you head there,' Dannie said, licking the last of the banoffee pie off her spoon.

'What? You think the argument hasn't started here already? You girls haven't stopped since I mentioned the move.' Completely ignoring me, Dannie went on. 'Personally, I've never met a city suffering such low self-esteem. And that's because when you exist on the fringes of greatness, it's hard not to want to try and assert your identity.'

'Wow, that's a little philosophical, isn't it?'

Dannie was always trying to remind us that she had a degree – even if she had no use for it at home, pumping out kids.

'So that's your comeback is it, Peta? Well, I won't even bother.' She was offended but I didn't have time to repair the damage as Andy piped up.

'What about me?' he asked. 'Don't I get a say in the Sydney vs. Melbourne thing?'

'Girls?' Liza looked to the three of us, seeking our approval. We all nodded.

'Please, give us your five cents' worth, Andy, but if we don't like it, we're not paying for the last round of drinks,' she said.

'The last *hour* of drinks have been on me anyway, ladies, so I don't care if you like what I have to say or not,' he laughed. 'Look, Melbourne might be great for food, fashion and a wide range of moody, intimate bars for a single girl to haunt, but really, I prefer Sydney. It's much more like New York City, everything's open twenty-four hours, and Peta, you can't beat the harbourside glitz.'

Alice and Dannie looked at each other smugly, as if they'd just won the national debating competition in high school. Liza made a few notes, then looked up. 'Right, as judge and jury, and having taken into consideration all the arguments, I'd say the debate is a draw,' she said, to my relief.

'Please, can I have the pages as a memento of our last supper?' And I collected all the stray bits of paper. Truth be known I agreed with everything the others had said, but I could never admit it – it would kill all my arguments for going. I just hoped that I'd start to believe my own arguments over the next twelve months.

'Look, it's only for a year, anyway. I'll be back splashing in the surf and building sandcastles with you all again before you even learn to spell out the department's name in full. The only difference is when I come back I'll be able to move into a higher level in the department here, and I'm really looking forward to that.'

'Yeah, and then you'll be off to Canberra to be the minister of all things sporty, arty-farty, darky and reffy,' Alice said. 'Can I say reffy? Anyway, at least Canberra's only three hours away. Why don't you just go straight there? Then we could drive down there every couple of months to see you. Actually, seeing as there are no Spanish or Italian quarters in Canberra, and no Chinatown, and shit shopping and no sport, and it's bloody freezing, you'll have to be doing the driving back to Sydney to see us instead!'

'Jesus, I haven't even gone to Melbourne and you've already got me moving to Canberra too. Give me a break, will you?' I was exhausted.

Dannie was still stewing a bit and took a shot at me. 'You do realise, Miss I-Can-Do-Everything-and-Suddenly-Love-Melbourne, that you don't become minister by being department head. You have to join a political party.'

I pulled a card from my wallet.

'It's all under control, joined up a few months ago, and when I get back I'll be meeting with our very own local member here, Mr Garrett of the bald-headed variety, for some mentoring. I've got some years to go, but I'm on the right track.'

'Yes well, it will take years, because he's already the local Labor member so you'll have to wait till he's gone.' Dannie was being a bit catty, but I deserved it.

'Girls, girls, lay off sis here,' Liza said. 'We should be supporting her. It's her dream job, she gets a pay rise to do more shopping, and when we get bored we can go visit her and hang out.'

'Yeah, they probably sell some really groovy rain gear and galoshes so you'll be fine!' I said, and laughed – more at Liza saying 'sis' than anything else. It always sounded funny when whitefellas used our jargon, and talked about mobs and stuff, but I never said anything. I always wondered how the white girl with the Italian heritage came across at the Aboriginal Legal Service; I hoped they loved her as much as I did.

'I think we should toast the future Minister for Cultural Affairs who will one day be President of the Republic of Australia. To Peta!' Alice led the toast.

'To Peta!' Liza and Dannie echoed.

'To me!' I raised my glass to theirs. I'd miss the girls, Coogee and Sauce.

'Okay ladies, more drinks?' Andy asked, and opened another bottle at the table. I'd miss him too. He was young and gorgeous, and cheeky as all hell. 'I'm good for a spoon,' he'd throw into any conversation.

'Do we look like we need more, Andy?' I asked.

'Lots more,' he laughed.

'Then fillerup!'

'Peta,' Alice said, running a lip gloss wand across her bottom lip, 'I have a deadly young cousin in St Kilda. Her name's Josie and she's soooo cool. I'll hook you up with her and she can show you around, I know she'd love it. Just don't mention it to Mum, okay?'

'Why?'

'Trust me, just don't.'

three
NO sex, NO ciggies and NO-ONE calling me babe!

'So how's it going to work then, you in Melbourne and me here without you, all alone, with no-one?' James was half joking but in his eyes I could see he was heartbroken. We sat in my one-bedroom flat with dozens of boxes already packed, huge mounds of clothes in garbage bags waiting to be deposited in the clothing bin (if they survived Alice's rummaging), piles of recycling needing to go downstairs, and depressingly bare walls. I was going to miss my little piece of surfside paradise, and I knew that James would too. His own place was in the inner west, where the temps were always much higher and the air more stifling in summer.

I was taking a break from packing, watering the collection of small plants the neighbours and my landlord had given me over the years. I'd have to leave them behind and wanted to ask James if he'd like them, but it wasn't the right time. There were bigger issues to deal with than my orphaned plants.

'Firstly, you're not alone,' I told him. 'You've got all your mates, and Gary and Alice would love you to drop in occasionally, you know that. Secondly, it's just twelve months, which is nothing in the big scheme of things. Thirdly, we'll ring and Skype and email and text, and we can have weekend visits. I'll have work trips to Sydney. It might even be exciting seeing each other just once a month.'

'Once a month? That's enough for you?'

'Stop it, James, stop nagging me. I'm about to uproot my life to another state and I don't need all this emotional blackmail crap. For God's sake. I'm trying to be realistic about how we might manage it – both of us, not just you, but me also.' I started to cry. 'I'm leaving my friends and the place I've called home for ten years. I'm scared as hell. You're supposed to be the man, the strong one, and I feel like I'm carrying the load for both of us.'

'I'm sorry, babe,' he said and held me close.

I kept crying uncontrollably. 'You know I hate being called babe.' Everything was bugging me.

'But you *are* my babe, you always will be, until we have real bubs of our own, and sorry, but then *they'll* be my babes.'

'I hate children, they cry like this all the time. I'd never cope. And you'd never cope with me and them crying at the same time.' He just laughed and rocked me.

James wasn't emotionally crippled like most other men I'd known. He was good at being a manly man and knew what to do when I was upset. He'd just listen and hold me. That was what I loved about him.

He was an overachiever, though, and didn't do anything by halves. Even at his young age, James had already reached his professional goals and was a partner in a major architectural firm. That was part of the problem: now that he'd made partner, he was starting to think about his next goal: marriage and kids. He was always talking about other people he knew getting engaged. He'd already given me a gorgeous Ceylon sapphire ring for my birthday a few months back. James was romantic and not afraid to show it or spend money. Alice had always said that if she met James before Gary she would've married him for sure. But I wasn't Alice. I had always seen marriage as a threat to my independence, my individuality and my ability to party.

'You know you don't have to go,' he said hopefully. 'I mean, if you changed your mind, it's not too late. We could just move in together, now that most of your stuff is packed and everything.'

'I haven't changed my mind, James, and I won't. You don't understand, because you've got the career you want already. I haven't. Not yet.'

'But don't you want to settle down, too?'

'Of course I do, maybe, I think, one day. But not yet. There's other things I want to do first. I've got career goals, you know that.'

I'd managed to put off moving in with James, and for some reason he thought it was because I didn't believe in living together before marriage. I'd tried to explain that I just didn't believe in marriage itself, and wasn't even sure if I wanted kids, but he'd laughed and said, 'Don't be silly, *all* women want babies.'

'So, are you going to be dating other people, then, while you're *reaching your goals*?' The sarcasm in James's voice was uncharacteristic, but the jealousy was no surprise. The green-eyed monster was one of his flaws. I honestly gave him no cause – I flirted innocently at times, but did that mean I didn't love him? Mum had always said that when you were in a relationship it was okay to perve on other people, or in her words, you could look at the menu but you just couldn't order. That wasn't how James saw it. He didn't even like me talking to Andy at Sauce.

I started to roll a cigarette and James gave me a look of disgust.

'I know, I know . . . I'm giving up when I move, all right?'

'All right,' he said, and then there was silence.

I got up and walked out to the balcony and lit up.

'You haven't answered my question,' he said impatiently.

'Going to Melbourne is about my career,' I said exhaling. 'It's *not* about not seeing you so I can date other people. In fact, I've decided I'm going to be celibate.'

'Don't you mean faithful?'

'No, I mean celibate. The difference between being faithful and celibate is that being faithful is something that's *expected* of you when you're apart from your partner, while being *celibate* is something you *choose* to do for yourself. And I don't *expect* myself to be faithful – being faithful is just normal to me, but I will *choose* to be celibate because I am in control of my actions and my body. Does that make sense?'

'Kind of.' He took the cigarette from my hand and stubbed it into a pot plant on the balcony ledge, which annoyed me, but I didn't want to have an argument over a cigarette when the atmosphere was already tense. He started pacing. 'So, am *I* supposed to be celibate or faithful then? Because right now I haven't got a clue what you want from me.'

'To be honest, James, this isn't about you right now. I'm only in control of what *I* do. I don't know that I can ask a man as gorgeous as you and as sexy as you to go without sex for months on end. I mean, you'll be getting offers, there's no doubt about it. I'll just have to live with the consequences.'

'So you don't care whether I have sex with someone else or not?' He went red, covering his face with his hands to avoid the shame and the emotion of it all, hurt and angry at the same time. 'You're totally confusing *me* about *us*. What's really going on here? If you don't love me any more then just say it, but this argument or discussion or break-up or whatever it is that's going on here is doing my head in.' And James broke down. It was the first time I'd seen him cry and it pained my heart. 'I thought we were a happy couple,' he sobbed into his hands.

I put my arms around him but said nothing. I had never been the 'happy couple' kind of girl. I wished I could be, just to fit in, but I'd never even really believed in the concept of eternal love. I didn't really know anyone who was *truly* happy. You never know what goes on in someone else's home. All you see is the front they give you, even your friends. Still, with James I'd found something pretty close. I didn't get dry-mouthed and sweaty-palmed and my heart rarely raced when I saw him any more, like it had at first, but that didn't matter. He was kind and generous, mature and sensible and patient – even romantic.

I gripped him tighter. 'I do love you, James, more than anything in the world.' We stood still and silent for a few minutes, just listening to the dull sounds of the ocean, and then he pulled away.

'I have something to show you.' He walked into the flat and started rummaging through his work materials. 'I've knocked up some designs on a house for us,' he said proudly, unrolling the sheets and holding them under the light.

I stepped back into the room feeling defeated and exasperated. 'Will this house be in Sydney?' I asked.

'Well, yes. I don't think I could live anywhere else. Look, it's a four-bedroom, lots of space for when we're ready to have a family.'

James was so eager he was already too many houses and kids in front of me, but to say that now would make me sound ungrateful. Any other single woman in her right mind would jump at the architect and the house plans. I was a nutcase for sure.

I tried to keep it jokey. 'James, haven't you heard *anything* I've said? In case you hadn't noticed I'm not like most other women who want to settle down and have kids and all that. I'm Peta. I'm not even sure I'll have kids at all.'

'I know you're not like other woman, that's why I love you so much.' It was like he was there and watching my mouth move but not hearing the words coming out. 'I want to marry you. The only reason I haven't proposed is because I'm frightened you'll say no. At least there's hope if you haven't already said no.'

'Look, I'm just not ready for that kind of commitment yet.'

Even if I wanted kids and was ready, how could I know if James was the one? How could you tell when you'd met your soul mate? When the Melbourne job came up, it had seemed like an omen. I'd read *The Celestine Prophecy* and knew there was no such thing as coincidence. It would be a huge step forward in my career, of course, but it would also give me time out to think, to grow as an individual and to be sure James was the right guy for me.

'So, seems the plans didn't work.' James rolled them up. This time he was the one sounding defeated. 'I thought maybe if I showed you how serious I was you'd change your mind.'

He had to know that it wasn't him, that it was me, that I was the one who was frightened. I had to tell him, there was no other way.

'James, I've never told you this, but my mother was married three times and divorced three times. She had four kids to three men – a hundred per cent plus strike rate she called it. I'm frightened I'll be like her, and that's not what I want. The reality is I don't think I'd last five minutes with kids, and not much longer married. I honestly don't think married and maternal is in my genes.' And I broke down in tears again. I was exhausted from the to-ing and fro-ing, from the questions and the attempted explanations. I didn't want to have this conversation any more.

'I don't know your mother, but I think you're being a bit harsh on both of you.'

'I can't talk about it any more tonight, please. I'm so tired.' I wiped my nose on his sleeve like a child and smiled at him. 'Can we just love each other tonight?' I looked into his eyes and saw the warmth that I knew so well, that made me feel safe.

I pulled his T-shirt up over his head. 'I mean, seeing as it's going to be a few weeks . . .' I kissed his earlobe and whispered as I undid his belt and unzipped the back of my dress, '. . . a few *long* weeks before we'll be together again, can we just love each other tonight?' His pants got caught around his ankles and we both laughed as we fell on the bed.

four
Aunt Homophobe

A week later I went with Alice to see her parents and say goodbye before I moved. My own mum was up in Coolangatta and I rarely heard from her, so Aunty Ivy had always been a pseudo mother to me. She always fed me when I dropped around, and sent me away with a food parcel, which I appreciated as a non-cooker myself. And she always asked, 'When are you getting married, Peta?' whenever I visited. Aunt had taken to hassling me more since Alice hooked up with Gary. It was like it was her personal goal in retirement to make sure there were no young, single Koori women in her world.

'I don't think I'll get married until I'm about thirty-five, Aunt, when I've reached most of my professional goals. I might even go back and do some study before then.'

'So many choices for you young girls today, it's great, but it takes you away from what women are meant to do, have children, raise families, and be matriarchs.' Aunt was old school. Dannie loved her take on the world.

'Yes, well I'm sure I'd feel differently about the mat- riarchal thing if there was an adequate patriarch around, Aunt. But most men today aren't like Uncle out there,' and we both looked out the window and saw her long-time love mowing the lawn. I could see where Alice got her desire to settle down. Her parents were the perfect role models.

None of my mum's husbands had ever mowed the lawns, and in recent years she'd found it easier and better on the eyes to pay a young guy to tend her garden.

Alice walked in with a basket of washing. I couldn't believe she still got her mum to do it, but Aunty Ivy didn't seem to mind. It was that nurturing matriarchal thing she was talking about.

'So when are you moving to Melbourne, bub? Alice told me you've got a great new job.'

'I'm leaving next week, almost got everything organised.'

I was glad that Alice had made my move sound like a positive to her mum. I felt more supported as the time of moving drew closer.

'You know, I've read there are lots of men in Melbourne.' Aunty Ivy nudged me in the ribs and smiled; she was relentless. Alice used to tell us how her mum pressured her to meet a man, but I never really believed it until Aunt started pressuring me.

'I read that too, but that's not why I'm going. I have a boyfriend here anyway. But he'll just have to wait.'

'You sound pretty sure he'll wait for you, Peta. Be careful – a good man won't last long alone,' Aunt warned me.

Truth be known, I wasn't worried. I wasn't going to just settle for the first guy who wanted to marry me anyway. My mum didn't. Well, she didn't settle for the second or third either, but I wasn't planning on going to that extreme.

'Where will you be staying in Melbourne? At the Aboriginal Hostel?' Aunt asked. I didn't want to turn my nose up, but my days as a hostel or backpack traveller were long gone.

'Oh, no, I have family down there. My Aunt Nell, Mum's sister, is in the burbs. I'll crash with her and my cousins until I find somewhere of my own. I'm sure I'll make friends quickly too. I've got a few connections and Alice told me she's got a cousin there I should meet – Josie, is it?' I'd remembered the cousin bit, but forgot that Alice had told me not to mention her.

'What? No, you can't meet Josie! Alice, what are you doing?' Aunt looked at Alice, shaking her head, not happy at all. In a concerned voice she said to me, 'Josie's a lesbian. You're not a lesbian are you, Peta? Is that why you're leaving your boyfriend behind?'

'No Aunt, I'm not a lesbian.' Alice was rolling her eyes and mouthing *I told you so* behind her mum's back.

'Well, what do you think of them?'

I couldn't help having some fun with her. 'What do you mean, Aunt?'

'What do you think about, you know, what they do, as lesbians?' And she screwed her face up.

'Oh for God's sake, Mum.' Alice was embarrassed.

'Don't use the Lord's name in vain in this house.'

'Well, for Biami's sake, then, if you're going to be more worried about a white god than a Black one.'

Her mother just ignored her, and kept on at me. 'Peta?'

'Actually Aunty, I don't really think about what lesbians *do*, but if I did, I'd probably think that only a woman knows what a woman likes.'

'I'm not sure what that means, Peta, but I hope it doesn't mean you're a lesbian too. It seems every day there's more and more lesbians in Australia.'

'I told you so!' Alice said as she folded her washing and shook her head at the same time.

'Aunt, I think there are more lesbians because there's less and less men like your husband these days, and women are over settling for less than they deserve in a man. I'm not a lesbian but I can certainly see why some women are. Sometimes it's simply about companionship and equality.'

'Really?' I wasn't sure if Aunt didn't believe me or was confused by what I said.

'Yes, and regardless of her sexuality, I'm really looking forward to meeting Josie. She sounds like fun, and I think of you as family, and she's your niece, so she's my family right?'

'Yes, Josie's my niece, but she goes to *girls only* nights at the pub. She's *never* had a boyfriend, but her mum, my sister, won't admit it; she hasn't been to any family events for six months cos she's avoiding people. I can't blame her; I was beginning to think the same way about Alice before she met Gary. And he's so manly, drives the big council truck you know. A garbologist they call them these days. Yes, a real manly man, like men in the old days.'

'That's it,' Alice said. 'Come on, Peta, say goodbye to Aunt Homophobe.'

I hugged Aunty Ivy, gripped the food parcel she'd prepared for me and followed Alice, as ordered, out of the door.

five
Saying goodbye

The boarding call announcements distracted me as James was trying to say goodbye.

He held me tight. 'I love you so much.' He leaned into my neck and sobbed quietly.

I wiped a solo tear from the corner of my eye and grabbed my cabin bag. 'I should go through security now. No use you coming in, I'm going to the QANTAS Club.' I sounded cool, almost flippant, though I didn't mean to. I just didn't want to talk about it any more, or cry for that matter. We'd both done enough of that the past two weeks.

I walked off and left him standing there, shoulders sagging. I felt exhausted as I put my bag on the X-ray conveyor belt and walked through the barrier. It sounded off, and I had to take off the chunky choker James had given me as a farewell gift.

Once through security, I turned to see him still standing there, red-eyed but smiling bravely. He gave a weak wave. I blew him a kiss and he pretended to catch it, then I walked away.

I made my way down the concourse and up the escalators to the QANTAS Club, and suddenly I felt excited again. Going to the QANTAS Club was what all the bourgeois Blacks were doing these days. I'd even heard that a handful belonged to the so-called secret 'Chairman's

Club' as well. I didn't expect I'd ever be part of that, but I was certainly looking forward to the bar and to chilling out in peace before future flights. Work had made me a corporate member because of the travel I'd be doing. I showed my card and boarding pass and sauntered in like it was somewhere I was meant to be.

I looked at my watch: it was one pm. Somewhere in the world it was the right time to have a drink and that was good enough for me. I didn't want to look like a cheap lush, so didn't just go to the self-serve wine bar, but took a leaf out of Alice's old book – before she met Gary and could booze on – and ordered a gin'n'tonic from the nicely uniformed young man behind the bar.

Then I slowly passed by the food counter. Cold meats, cheeses, salads, rice crackers, nuts, corn chips, and an espresso machine. I was so confused and oddly anxious, I thought I'd grab a coffee as well, even though I hadn't found a table or had a sip of my gin yet. I stood perplexed for a moment, not knowing where to stick the cup, and a middle-aged man in a navy pinstripe suit gently moved my hand and cup under the spout for the burst of hot water and steam. I liked the QANTAS Club already.

Next I grabbed a magazine and newspaper. Anyone would've thought I'd never even flown before. I was like a child at a carnival who had to do everything at once, immediately. I found a table with four lounge chairs and only one taken.

'Do you mind if I share?' I asked a casual-looking guy reading the entertainment pages of the day's broadsheet.

I sipped my coffee and my gin'n'tonic – which didn't turn out to be as pleasant as having just one or the other – and pretended to read as I scanned the spacious lounge. Plasma screens with sports and the news and TV screens with flights departing, delayed, boarding and arriving. Businesspeople in suits with laptops and BlackBerries, couples going on holidays, a sports group of some description all wearing the same tracksuit, and families. Too many families. It wasn't as peaceful as I thought it would be, but I wasn't complaining. I was on my way to my new life in my new city and my new job.

I got up and roamed the NewsLink bookstore, thinking I should read more and get my finger on the pulse. With my background in the education sector I had some idea about specific books used in the classroom, and I was aware that more and more storytellers and artists were going into schools and doing workshops these days, but I really needed a better grounding in everything from the history of the Indigenous visual arts movement to the latest books released. I'd heard of the Miles Franklin Award winner Alexis Wright, but when I found her epic novel *Carpentaria* I was daunted by its size. With all the policy papers I'd read of a night in my old job, I hardly ever had time to read novels, and never read anything the size of this one. As I continued to scan the shelves with *Carpentaria* under my arm, I wondered to myself whether Wright's book would've been on the shelf of a mainstream shop if it hadn't won the award. Or would it have been relegated to the 'Australiana' section like other books by and about Blackfellas? I made some notes to myself in my diary to be followed up when I started work.

I went back to my table with another drink, my book,

and some food, certain I was about to drop something. The same guy was still there and looked at me with sympathy as I tried to crouch and set everything down at the same time.

'Let me help you,' he offered, taking the mags and paper from under my arm and placing them on the small, heavy table.

'Thank you. Looks a little greedy, doesn't it?'

'Not at all, I always have a little party for myself when I come here. This is the only place I get to read and have a quiet drink anyway, so I completely understand. My name's Mark.' He shook my hand and held it a few seconds too long to be just friendly.

'I'm Peta,' I said quickly, and withdrew my hand. James's tears were still drying on my collar. I pushed my sunnies down and opened my magazine, trying not to notice that Mark was still staring at me.

My flight was delayed as the weather was poor in Melbourne. I laughed to myself, knowing the girls would have gone to town with that information. I didn't care about the delay – I just had a few more drinks. The more I drank, though, the more I wanted to shove my entire fist into the lidded jar full of corn chips. And the plates were just too small to put anything of any substance onto them. They were smaller than a saucer. That would be my constructive feedback to QANTAS as a first-time visitor. Bigger jars and bigger plates for the nibblies.

I could probably have spent the entire day in the QC – which I decided was a groovier name for the place – and just hang out and chill. I could probably meet men as well, if that were my intention. I'd already met two in the course of thirty minutes. But my thoughts were disturbed by a noise, an annoying noise – a kid, no, two kids, whining, whining, moaning, and crying. I looked around to see if it was bothering anyone else, but it didn't seem to be. I thought the QC was a place for peace, for grown-ups, for businesspeople, and policy-making departmental types like me. Not kids and certainly not spoilt kids at that. Noisy, naughty, annoying brats who whine and moan even when they are in the QC and can have all the cold meat and soft cheese they want and an endless supply of gin'n'tonic, or Australian wine, or beer. Kids are so ungrateful. Then my mobile rang. It was James.

'It's me.' He sounded tired.

'Hi. Where are you?'

'In the car park.'

'What? Why? Flat battery?'

'Flat heart.'

My heart sank. While I felt sorry for James and his flat heart weeping in the car park, I didn't feel at all compelled to put down my very tasty gin'n'tonic or my soft cheese and go find him.

'Ladies and gentlemen, this is the first and final boarding call for QANTAS flight 433 to Melbourne. Your flight is now boarding through Gate 6.'

'They're calling my flight, baby, I have to go. I'll call you tonight.'

'I love you.' He said it with pain.

'You too.' And I turned my phone off.

Reality kicked in. I was on my way to Melbourne for

twelve months, but I felt like a kid going on a school excursion to the zoo. I picked up my bag and book, sipped the last of my drink and made my way out of the lounge.

I went to grab the first of my cases off the carousel and a young guy in black jeans and jumper grabbed it for me. He then leaned over and grabbed his guitar case as well. Chivalry was alive and well in Victoria. Musos too it seemed. I'd heard there was a healthy live music scene in Melbourne and I was looking forward to checking it out as part of the new job. I was impressed with my first few minutes in my new home.

At the taxi rank I turned on my phone. There were two messages from Alice, one from Dannie and one from Liza.

Miss u already, how's the weather? X A

P.S. It's gorgeous day @ Coogee, bout 2 go 4 swim. X A

Skype me as soon as you're set up. Miss u, LIZA

Don't light up cos ur homesick, Dannie

It was muggy and overcast, but at least the rain had stopped. This was Melbourne summer and I was just glad that the girls weren't there to see it. I would never live it down. I sent them a text:

Just landed, weather STUNNING, no ciggies, in touch afta shoppin, Luv ya, Px

six

Settling in fine, with vegan wine and a place that's mine

The Rialto building was the flashest office tower I'd ever seen. We didn't have the penthouse suite, but we weren't doing too badly for Blackfellas either. My view went right along Collins Street into the city proper and I finally felt like I was making it up the ladder – only a few rungs to go.

My first day in the office was spent meeting the other members of my team. My deputy was Sylvia, a policy development researcher who was also responsible for advising me on the Indigenous arts scene. Sylvia was about my age, with dyed jet-black hair, smoky kohl-rimmed eyes, big blood-red lips and olive skin. I wasn't sure if she was a Blackfella or not when I saw her.

'Hi, you must be Peta, welcome.' She handed me her business card and I read it immediately.

'Oh, Sylvia, thanks – great to meet you.'

'Actually, it's spelt Sylvia, but it's pronounced Sylv-eye-a.'

'Right, sorry.'

'No dramas, everyone gets it wrong first time. It's just that the pronunciation works better in the arts world.'

'So you're an artist, then?'

'Yes, I'm an eco-poet!' she declared proudly. 'I'm just working here until my first book hits the bestseller list.'

Although I was concerned to hear she was only working in the department to pass time, I was interested in knowing more. 'Excuse my ignorance, Sylvia, I mean Sylv-eye-a, but what's eco-poetry?'

'Eco-poets write about the natural order, or disorder, of the world. Our poetry is born out of a sense of impending disaster. It's about ecology, biology, conservation, philosophy. It's about the planet, the earth, the need for rebirth. Landfills, pulp mills, don't take pills.' She projected her voice like she was performing on stage.

'Of course, the name's fairly self-explanatory, isn't it? Thanks. And who's your publisher?'

'Well, my first book hasn't been published yet,' she said. 'But when it *is* published, I know it will sell big, and I'll be on my way to being part of the literati. No longer will Banjo Paterson and Les Murray be the only Australian poets taught in schools. It'll be Sylvia the Greek-Australian poet whose name will be on everyone's lips.'

'Is there a big market for poetry in Australia?' I asked. I hadn't read much poetry beyond Oodgeroo Noonuccal. Alice had given me a first edition of *We Are Going* in hardcover. The only other hardcover books on my shelves were textbooks from university, not nearly as enjoyable to read.

'I'm going to make it my personal mission to open your eyes and ears to the wonders of eco-poetry and the spoken word community in Melbourne, Peta.'

'Okay, but can you refrain from using the word *mission*, please Sylvia? Hasn't anyone around here told you that it brings back terrible memories of mission managers and mission life for a lot of Aboriginal Australians?'

'I'm just trying to reclaim the word is all. Like *Black* is a positive now and was a negative in the past.' Sylvia was confident in explaining herself.

'Yes, I understand, but to reclaim it, wouldn't *we* have to use it ourselves?'

'I guess so, good point.' She walked off, but I didn't think I'd offended her. She didn't seem the type to be overly sensitive.

I liked Sylvia immediately; she was passionate, original, eccentric and cheeky. And so different to Alice, Liza and Dannie, who in contrast I realised were a bit conservative. I was actually looking forward to the poetry readings she had promised to take me to, and glad to know I was working with someone who liked to 'manage upwards'.

I could handle an out-of-work eco-poet with a confused name. At least her holy grail was publishing a bestseller and not meeting men.

I spent the first week sleeping at my Aunt Nell's place in East Bentleigh. She had moved to Melbourne with her husband back in the sixties. They weren't married any more but unlike Mum, Aunt Nell didn't feel the need to try again, and again, and again. She was content with the six kids and the fifteen grandkids and another four on the way. It was great to be around family again and to meet more cousins. Aunt's house was always crowded, people coming and going, endless cups of tea, kids running and screaming and laughing, nonstop.

East Bentleigh was a long way from the city and the north side, where other relations were, but Aunt said she liked being the only Blackfellas in the street.

'I like being the only widow as well. I get a *lot* of attention from the ageing men, married or not. They like Joe's cooking too, especially his bush tucker biscuits.' Cousin Joe had just set up his own catering business and it was really taking off.

'I didn't know Old Mack died and that's why you were alone all these years.' It was the first I'd heard Aunt describe herself as a widow.

'Oh, he didn't. I just told people he died. It's much easier to be a widow than it is to try and explain to people that your fella left you.' She was matter of fact, my aunt.

'The verbal murder. I love it. You wicked woman.' Next time someone asked me about why I moved to Melbourne and where James was, I could tell them, 'James is dead.' I would never really do that, of course – James was too much of a nice guy to verbally kill him. I would just save that line for someone else in the future.

While it was great being around family and being loved and pampered with homemade meals, I was soon craving my own space and the coastline. With no ocean breeze or even a view of the sea to sustain me, the February heat was draining, and sharing a bathroom with my aunt, her teeth, my cousin Joe, his woman Annie and their two kids Maya and Will was just too much for me. I was used to a queen-size bed all to myself and my own bathroom and waking up naturally, not by having my eyelashes pulled at six in the morning by a toddler laughing hysterically. The sofa bed, the old crochet red, black and yellow rug thrown over me, and Aunt's cat Lola soon became all too much.

Aunt had a computer set up in the lounge room so at least I could send the girls and James emails after work. For the first few nights it was a group message, which wasn't the most personal thing, but I didn't have much time, as Annie needed to do the admin work for Joe's business while he bathed the kids and put them to bed. It wasn't till the end of the week that I finally had the chance to write more than a couple of quick lines:

> Hello all my darling friends, I miss you guys, and life here with the rels is soooo different to my little peaceful flat on the beach in Coogee. God I miss it. Aunt's place in East Bentleigh is a long way from the rest of the family, but hell, it doesn't stop people dropping in like a trail of ants following a line of something sweet. The attraction is always Joe's creations. Everyone raves about how he's a chef on the cusp of great things with his new marketable bush food. He doesn't just cater for local Koori events, but mainstream parties and even weddings. So the house is always full of the aromas of good, home-cooked, restaurant-quality food. Even the ageing bananas in this really old bright blue fruit bowl Aunt has end up as banana bread. And not just your basic banana bread – it's always sprinkled with wattle seeds or some other bush delight. Oh, by the way, I'm getting FAT! James, you won't want to look at me, I'm telling you! I'm going to have to walk to the city every day to shake off the weight if I don't move out soon. Even Lola, Aunt's very spoiled cat, has fresh kangaroo meat every night for dinner. I'm going to start looking at rental properties on Saturday and the closest thing I'm going to get to Coogee is St Kilda, so that's where I'm going to start. Luv ya, off to bed now, but email me back soon . . . Px

James emailed me back immediately:

> My precious babe, I miss you. I'm so glad you are safe there with your family. Joe's business sounds great; he could do our wedding

one day, perhaps. I will ask around at the office tomorrow and see who's got contacts in property management in St Kilda, might help. Real estate agents can't always be trusted. Be careful. I know you're in bed now, wish I was there with you. Will call you in the morning. Love you.

Your James

xxxxxxxxxxxxxxxx

PS Please don't send me group emails, I'm not one of your girlfriends.

I thought about emailing him straight back, but that would mean commenting on the 'our wedding one day' business, and I didn't know how to approach it. Then Alice emailed me back too:

Hey sistagirl, great to hear from you. We all miss you. I walked by myself last weekend from Coogee to Bondi because Gary was away with the boys. Liza's coming with me this weekend. It's not the same though without you. God, I miss the laughs. Your aunt's place sounds like a scream, can't wait to meet her when we visit. Look out for Acland Street, the cake shops will be problematic if you get homesick. Be strong. Love ya, x Missy

PS James rings me every other day in case I have any more news about you than him. He is so missing you!

PPS Don't forget to call Josie, she knows you're there already. I spoke to her yesterday.

I was a little jealous that Liza was doing the beach walk with Alice on the weekend, and annoyed that James was butting into my search for a flat, even though it would help me. I just felt like it was his way of having some control or hand in my life down here. I tried not to dwell on it as

I lay in bed thinking about the task at hand – finding a flat. If I was going to enjoy my twelve-month holiday from my normal life, from the Sydney office, from James, from the pressures of commitment, I needed to set up a strong foundation for my home life. Working life would take care of itself – it always had.

On Saturday morning I circled six or so units in *The Age* and headed out early, convinced I would have something by lunchtime. I had to. It was simply too hot to be doing anything other than sitting near the water. I was really missing Coogee for the sea breeze and the coastal walk and the Ladies Baths.

'Take my car, Peta – it's the quickest way to get to St Kilda.' Aunt handed me the keys to her faded red Cortina, a Blackfella's car if ever there was one. If the crocheted blanket in the back window wasn't enough, the stickers holding the back bumper bar together sure as hell gave it away: *Koori Radio, Reconciliation Australia, Land Rights NOW!, Stop Black Deaths In Custody, Moving Forward Looking Blak!* The slogans said it all. The tyres were bald, the car was dusty, but old Gemma was Aunt Nell's favourite family member. It was a tank of a car and I had no idea how the old girl manoeuvred it. It didn't have power steering and I was too scared to ask if it even took unleaded petrol. I was sure the car was as environmentally unfriendly as they came.

'Can I come with you?' Maya asked, looking gorgeous in her favourite purple dress.

'Oh darling, I can't take you today, it's for grown-ups. Maybe another day.' Maya was cute but I didn't have any problem saying, *No, sorry, not today.*

'Will you take me to Luna Park?' She was brazen at times, but maybe that's what kids were like these days.

Joe and Annie motioned and mimed behind her back: 'No, say no!' I couldn't understand what the drama was. She was a well-behaved little girl, and as I wasn't going to be staying with them much longer, I thought the least I could do was promise to take her to Luna Park one day.

'Of course, Maya, I'll take you and we'll have fun, won't we?' Joe and Annie shook their heads, but Maya ran off singing and clapping and I felt warm and fuzzy for doing something nice. See, I didn't need to have kids. I could just be nice to other people's kids, get lots of kid-cred, appreciation from the parents and family – and then give them back.

Not having a car of my own in Sydney, I wasn't confident driving down Centre Road, turning onto the Nepean Highway, then left onto North Road, but as soon as I saw the ocean in the distance and Brighton up ahead my spirits lifted, even if my forty-kilometre speed limit didn't. I was driving like the old lady the car belonged to. Even though other drivers were passing me and shaking their heads, I knew that Aunt knew every scratch on Gemma and I didn't plan on getting another one.

It was a steaming hot day and the area was crowded. I drove along the Esplanade looking for a park, finding one immediately outside the St Kilda Sea Baths, but there were coin-only parking meters and I didn't have any change.

There was no change in the ashtray, just too many butts. I was glad I was giving up smoking. It really was a disgusting habit. Scratching around the car and the bottom of my handbag looking for change, I was getting really frustrated, just as I did back in Sydney, where parking meters at some beaches only took credit cards. I recalled being outraged the first time I had to use one at Bronte, and thought it was a very strategic way of keeping Blackfellas off the beach, as most didn't have credit cards. Now I had a wallet full of cards, but no change. I didn't want to lose my spot, nor did I want to get a ticket, so I looked pathetic and desperate as I approached a man sitting in a white van nearby.

'Excuse me, you wouldn't have some change, would you?'

'Sure, what do you need, love?' he said in a friendly tone.

'I've got five in change, need another two – can you change five dollars?' I held out the note.

'Can't break it, sorry, but here's the two dollars to make up the difference.'

'Oh, really, thanks, that's very kind of you.'

'Pay it forward.' I turned to walk away, and he called back, 'Oh, and nice legs.'

It was going to be a hard task to avoid the men in Melbourne, they were friendly and cheeky, but were my 'nice legs' only worth two dollars? I was almost tempted to try again to see if I could do better.

I still had time before the first open-for-inspection, so I took a walk around the Sea Baths precinct. It was too early for a drink, so I got a green tea to settle my nerves and sat under an orange umbrella at Beachcomber Cafe and just looked out to the pier and the marina. I took a photo on my phone and sent a text to the girls and to James. He wouldn't know it was a group text, unless he asked Alice.

At St Kilda havin cuppa bout 2 find new flat. Wish u were here!
Luv ya, Px

I was starting to relax, feeling right at home among all the couples eating breakfast, the mothers and the fathers having time out together on the weekend, and then I heard him: a noisy, crying, whining, bawling, complaining brat.

I got up and strolled around the building reading the signs; there was a wellness centre, a tanning studio, a health club and a 'Day Spa Dreaming'. I was too scared to go in, just in case it was one of those places that tries to sell a 'traditional Indigenous experience' without any Indigenous involvement in the process at all. Like the Native Americans' dream catchers and medicine wheels, completely bastardised by hippies up the north coast who mass-produced them, probably believing they'd been Indigenous in a past life. I wasn't sure what 'dreaming' would be offered in the luxurious day spa, other than the obvious dreaming you'd do if you fell asleep during a relaxing massage.

As I walked along Jacka Boulevard, my phone went, and it was James.

'Got your message, how's it going?'

'I'm just walking towards the first unit and I'm laughing at the palm trees that line the street like an attempted Venice Beach.' I half expected to see some bikini-clad rollerblader zoom past me any minute. I didn't, but a red Golf passed me and I thought of Alice back there in Coogee and I smiled. 'I'm here now, gotta go, I'll call you later.'

'Love you, babe.'

'You too.' And I hung up.

The first unit I entered on Grey Street had a hot young agent in a pale linen suit showing people through. I liked the space as soon as I walked in. I wanted it. It would be perfect. One bedroom, newly renovated kitchen and bathroom, with a small shared courtyard out the back.

'Can I have an application form, please?' I held out my hand.

'Hi, I'm Max. You'd look great in this flat.' He smiled and handed me a form. Max was right. I would, and in fact did already look great in the flat. But there were about twenty other people looking at the same property. There were couples, single women, parents, and artsy-looking folk. No-one looked over forty, which I found interesting.

It was promising to see who wanted to move into the area that I'd decided I would call home for the next year. Problem was they all appeared on sight to be worthy applicants, so I had to think about what would set me apart, give me that edge that would mean *I* would get the lease over someone else. I needed to be original when I filled out the form. Could I simply write, *PS I'd look great in this flat*, just as the agent had suggested? Or had he said it to every single girl who walked in? James had warned me about real estate agents.

I put Alice down as a referee because someone employed as head of department at a private Catholic school would have to carry some serious weight for sure. I decided that putting Liza down from the Aboriginal Legal Service was an equally *bad* idea. I also put down my old landlord, who'd offered to keep my flat in Coogee on notice for when I returned. I handed Max the form.

'You have a good chance, Peta.' Max winked at me, and I thought, *You are way too cheeky and way too cute, Mr Max.*

seven

Manipulative Max

First thing Monday morning, agent Max called me on the mobile to talk about the flat. 'There are some things you forgot to fill out on the form. Do you have time to do it after work?' I was sure I filled everything out on the day, but if he said I'd left something out then I must have.

'Sure, but I won't be able to get there until six.'

'We shut at five. I can meet you at the George Hotel around the corner from the unit at six – do you know it?'

'I'll find it, and I'll see you there.' It seemed the George was going to be my local. I punched the air like a sports star who had just won gold in the 400-metre butterfly. It was obvious I'd landed the flat I wanted – why else would he need me to fill more forms out? Life was going to be very good in Melbourne.

'You look happy.' Sylvia appeared at my desk without warning. She was one of those phantom types, one minute there, the next gone, and then back again.

'I'm fairly sure I just got a great flat in St Kilda. I'm meeting the agent after work to go through the forms again.'

'Sounds great, congrats.'

'We're meeting at the George, do you know it?'

'Of course, it's also known as the Melbourne Wine Bar. But why are you meeting him there? Be careful, won't you.'

'What do you mean?'

'Now, Peta, I know you're an adult and everything, *and* you're my boss, but you do know that real estate agents deal in deceit every day, don't you.' She sounded just like James.

'Really?' I'd rented straight from an owner in Sydney and he was more like a father to me than a landlord. If only my mum had chosen him as one of her many husbands.

'Yes – and it's part of their job to tell lies to innocent, unsuspecting candidates, just like you.' Sylvia was adamant as she went through my diary and slotted in different events I had been invited to attend.

'Gees, that's a bit brutal isn't it, Sylvia?'

'I'm just worried about our new resident is all. Be careful, boss.'

'First of all, don't call me boss. I don't play the hierarchy thing. And secondly, thank you for your concern, but I'm not as naive as you imagine.' I liked that Sylvia was being a bit protective of me as the new person in town. It was exactly what Liza would do if someone from another state started work at the ALS in Sydney.

'Trust me, Peta, I know what I'm talking about. I'm not as old as you, but I've been around the block a few times, you know. I'm telling you, for every property deal he'll have a woman.' Sylvia was serious.

'Yes, and I can see why, because he's hot.' I showed her Max's business card with his photo on it.

'See, don't you think there's something conceited about someone who has a photo of themselves on their business card?' Sylvia said in an I-told-you-so voice, raising one eyebrow at the same time – something I always wished I could do.

'Hmmm, I don't know. I was thinking we should get them too!' I was joking, but she did have a point. I didn't know anyone else who had a photo on their business card.

I arrived a little early at the bar. It was dimly lit, so everyone looked better than they would otherwise, and I seemed even more gorgeous than usual. I didn't need a photo on *my* business card to prove it. I ordered a gin'n'tonic and sat, just looking at the shelves lined with bottles. I noticed their top shelf spirits were *really* top shelf, about ten foot up top, and wondered how expensive they must've been. Another whole shelf was lined with bottles of ouzo, and I pondered whether or not it was the Melbourne Greek influence that had done that. Was the owner Greek? George was a Greek name after all. It made me think of Dannie's George and I felt a pang of homesickness so I texted her as I waited for Max to arrive.

Hi D – just wantd 2 tell u I'm in bar called George! Made me homesik 4 u guys. Luv 2 ur mob. News on embryo??? Px

Dannie responded almost immediately, which really touched me, as it would be chaos in her house at that time of night, trying to feed kids and dogs and get homework done, et cetera.

Hi, lovly 2 hear frm u. Messy mob send luv. No embryo yet, will let u no 4 sure. Miss u, D x

I looked around the bar and noticed an extraordinary number of men – straight men, businessmen, grungy men,

men with men friends, men with women friends, men of all denominations. And then I missed James and sent him a text:

About to sign lease for flat. I miss you! Px

I turned my phone off because I knew he'd call and I couldn't really talk there and then. I smiled as I looked around some more and I knew this would be my local, even if I didn't end up living in St Kilda. Being faithful didn't mean being blind. The no-sex rule meant I'd have to at least be having a damned good perve.

Max arrived and kissed me on the cheek, which seemed very forward and unprofessional.

'Hi Peta, great to see you. Can I get you a drink?' he asked enthusiastically.

'Oh, okay, I'll have a gin'n'tonic.'

'You know this *is* a wine bar.'

Normally, I would have said, 'So what?' but I wanted the flat, so played the game. 'Right, well then I guess I might have a wine. Can I see a wine list?' Already I was thinking, *You're a knob, and you can stick the flat keys where the sun don't shine.*

'I'd suggest something from the Geelong region,' Max said, while I looked down the list of whites.

'Really, is their wine as delicious as the football team looks?' I thought I was funny, but he just rolled his eyes.

'Actually, I think I'll try a sauvignon blanc from the Yarra Valley.'

'Oh no, if it's a sauvignon blanc you're after, try the Kettle Lake from Central Victoria.' *It's just wine*, I thought to myself. This was getting too serious and too wanky and it had to end.

'Hmmmm, Kettle Lake, would that be to go with the Kettle Chips?' I couldn't help but laugh at my own joke, but Max didn't seem to think it was funny. The barman who overheard did, though, and laughed out loud.

'The lady will have the Yarra Valley Sauvignon Blanc,' said Max. And that was it. I couldn't stand it any more. He'd pissed me off. James would never have ventured to tell me what to drink. I wanted to get down to business and end the 'meeting'.

'So, have you got the forms for me to go through?'

'Oh, they're in the car. I thought you might like to go and look at the flat one more time and if you like it, we can seal the deal tonight.' A sly grin came over his face.

Something didn't feel right, but I wanted the flat, and only two sips of wine had lubricated me enough to chill and just go with the flow.

'We should go,' I said almost immediately. 'We can walk from here, can't we? And shouldn't we get the papers from your car?'

'Oh, we can get them on the way back.'

As we walked towards the unit I felt a little light-headed, but not drunk. I was excited about seeing my new home. I started dreaming about where I would put the few knick-knacks I'd brought south with me and momentarily forgot Max was beside me, so I was startled when he opened the door to the flat, slid one arm around my waist, spun me around and kissed me. I pushed him away.

'Get off me, you fucking jerk! What do you think you're doing? That's assault you know!' I yelled, and ran out of the building, frightened and shocked. 'I don't want the flat!' I shouted back at him, and kept going. James and Sylvia had been right.

I was relieved to be sleeping at Aunt Nell's that night, and let myself drift off without having to worry about renting for the next few days.

When I woke in the morning and turned my phone on there was a message from James asking about the flat. I sent him a text from the train on the way to work. I didn't want to fib, but I didn't want him to worry about me any more than he already was.

Owner wanted more $, can't afford. No worries. Call later on train. Px

He texted me back straight away:

I can help with the money if you like. Love you babe, x

That was generous James. And grammatical James: he always spelled everything out, even when he texted. Nothing was too much for his 'babe'. I could never take his money, though, it went against everything I said and believed in about women losing their independence when they hooked up with men.

eight
Getting cultured in Melbourne

As part of my enculturation into Melbourne, and my new job, I took the City Circle Tram upon the advice of some of the city's 'Melbourne Ambassadors'. Cute and cuddly looking retired men in red shirts, they were still young and feisty enough to make a pass at any gorgeous woman who asked them about their much-loved city. Coming from Sydney, where the greatest money spinner for the city each year was Mardi Gras, I almost keeled over laughing to hear the old fellas talk about the city's one main gay bar.

'Yes, it's for gays only. But there has been some legal opposition to it. You know, because other people want to go there on Saturday night.'

'Well, everyone needs to feel safe in their environments, don't they?' is all I said. These fellas were *real men*, like John Wayne *real men*. The kind of men that Alice's mum was talking about. I knew there was no point in trying to have the conversation about the 'gay bar'. Were they actually homophobic? Or was it just that homosexuality wasn't part and parcel of everyday life for their generation, like it was when you lived in Sydney?

I had to tell the girls about the tourist tram; it was fantastic. I sent the same email to James, but separately:

Hi there, just sending you my own personal blog so you know that
I'm still alive, have all my limbs and that life in Melbin ain't that

bad. Today I took the tourist tram from the corner of Spencer and Swanston streets and listened with interest to the running commentary from the tram driver, learning that Melbin has the largest tram network in the English-speaking world. Who'da thought? The tour was deadly. Can't wait till you come down, you have to do it for sure. Also saves walking!!! Have to tell you though that I smiled when I saw all the palm trees lining the streets, behind the Telstra Dome and along Docklands, just like at St Kilda. Like Melbin's some tropical paradise or something. Just an observation, I'm sure you'll have some of your own. Miss ya, P xxxx

Alice emailed back and cc'd the girls. I could hear them all laughing at my expense:

Hey yourself tidda, what's with the palm trees? Are they meant to convince Melburnians that it isn't that cold in winter? Are locals meant to forget the frost when they see the palms? Seriously Peta, can't wait to do the tram ride with you, sounds fabulous. Have fun. Skype soon? Girls? Miss you too, x Alice

At the end of my second week the department had happy hour drinks and I met some more of my new colleagues before Sylvia dragged me away. Warm-cheeked and light-headed from two glasses of cheap wine, I sat eagerly at a table at Pireaus Blues in Fitzroy scanning the menu.

'I've brought millions of Kooris here. They love it.' Sylvia enjoyed playing hostess and was right at home with the staff, calling them by their first names.

'Millions of Kooris, really? That's quite a lot given there's only a few hundred thousand Blackfellas in total.' Sylvia had a whole language of her own, and exaggerating for her really wasn't exaggerating at all. It was just the way she made her point known. I wasn't sure if it was a poet thing, a Greek thing or just a Sylvia thing. For her, everything was measured in millions, tasks were referred to as missions, and she'd always tell me she got up at sparrow fart, rather than saying she woke first thing in the morning. I wondered how she'd get on with Alice, Dannie and Liza.

'So, what's good on the menu?' My mouth was watering and I had that slightly pissed need to eat something urgently.

'Well, I'm a vegan, so I haven't tried any of the meat dishes,' Sylvia said, without looking up from the menu.

'Vegan? Is that like vegetarian?'

'Bit more than that. I don't eat eggs, dairy products, or any foods that are related to animals in any way.'

'What about honey?'

'Nup.'

'More to the point then, what *do* you eat?'

'Plenty! Grains, beans, legumes, vegetables and fruits.' She counted them off on each of her five fingers on her left hand.

'So no junk food, then?' The vegan diet sounded so boring.

'Well, I can buy vegan hot dogs and ice-cream.'

'Would you bother? I bet they taste terrible.'

'They do!' She laughed.

'Can you eat *anything* off this menu? I mean, we can go somewhere else if you want.'

'No, I love it here. I'll have the ladies' fingers, all the dips, and grilled vegetables. Peta, you eat all the chargrilled meat and octopus you like.'

'Hi Sylvia, great seeing you again.' The waitress Pires spoke to Sylvia like she was an old friend, and made me feel welcome too. I liked her immediately.

'Should we get a bottle of something, Sylvia?'

'You know I only drink because it helps me write poetry.'

'That's funny, I only drink because it helps me read it.' And we both laughed.

'Seriously, I try to only drink organic wine and beer which don't have animal products in them.'

'Beer and wine have animal products in them? Really?'

'Yeah, a lot of beers and wines are refined using something called isinglass, which comes from fish, and some are filtered with bone char.'

'Bone char? I don't know what that is but it doesn't sound like something I want to be drinking, that's for sure. But how do you know which wine is which? I've never heard of vegan wine before.'

'It's not called vegan wine – it's organic wine.' Sylvia seemed to be enjoying the cross-cultural vegan workshop she was giving me. Sitting opposite her I realised that the Greek-Australian eco-poet was going to be teaching me a lot while I was in Melbourne.

Pires was back at the table. 'Actually, Sylvia, we've just got some Robinvale organic wine. The owner agreed to order it in cos their cellar door is shaped like a Greek temple.' She smiled at being able to please her customer.

'Excellent, we'll have a bottle of your finest, then.'

When the food arrived, it was delicious and there was plenty for Sylvia to eat. I couldn't remember going to a Greek restaurant in Sydney where I'd enjoyed myself so much, so I just had to text the girls to tell them:

> Hi, havin best souvlaki this side of Athens, organic wine 2, deadly.
> C if u can find sum in Syd. Px

Then I turned my phone off, because I didn't want to be carrying on a debate via SMS over dinner.

I enjoyed hanging out with Sylvia, and was glad that we clicked immediately, but there were no boundaries with her, she said everything she thought – perhaps it was the artist in her, always challenging the audience. I was quickly exhausted by her dinner recitals, which included too much information on her bowel movements since becoming a vegan. I looked at my watch and it was only nine pm, but I was done.

'It must be time to leave, Sylvia, it's been a long day, a long week.' I wanted to call James when I got home if it wasn't too late and Aunt was still awake. I was using the sofa bed in the lounge room, in the centre of the house, so I couldn't talk if people were sleeping.

As we left the restaurant we bumped into one of Sylvia's friends on the street. Shelley was just on her way out, her night beginning as ours was about to end.

'Shelley, Peta, Peta, Shelley. Peta's going to be the Minister for Cultural Affairs, and Shelley's going to be the Chair of the Reserve Bank and save the working class from too many interest rate hikes.' Sylvia was the eternal optimist, and I liked that she believed in my dream, but I also knew by now that anyone who believed they were going to be a best-selling poet in Australia really did know how to dream.

'Nice to meet you, Peta.' Shelley had had a couple of cocktails by the looks of it, as she grinned a silly smile in her corporate clothes. She looked back at Sylvia. 'Hey, darl, I'm looking for a housemate, so if you know anyone who's happy to share let me know.' *I do, I do!* I screamed within, hoping that Sylvia would say something.

'Actually, Peta's looking for somewhere to live. You're at Albert Park, aren't you?'

'Didn't I tell you? I've moved into the family home at St Kilda. Mum and Dad have gone travelling around the country, which was perfect timing because I broke up with Josh the week before they left, and one of us had to get out of the flat. No such thing as coincidence, they say.' I already liked Shelley. 'They're doing that retiree trip they all do. So, I've got the place to myself, but it's too big just for me, and my brother refuses to come back home.

'So, the rent's cheap.' Shelley started talking directly to me, 'And we're close to bars and cakes if that's a drawcard at all.' God, Shelley was my Ms Right, or would've been if I were a bloke.

'Oh, sounds perfect – can I see the house?' I hoped I didn't sound too eager as we arranged for me to see it first thing in the morning.

I crept into Aunt's house as quietly as I could but she had one of those old seventies beaded curtains to keep the flies out that rattled forever. It was too late to make calls and I was disappointed but knew I'd speak to James the next day. The taste of taramasalata lingered even after I'd brushed, flossed and gargled, and when I collapsed onto the sofa bed, my head spun slightly as I burped the taste of garlic souvlaki, and fell into a drunken sleep.

I'm in a taverna in Delphi, and Miltos the waiter is filling my glass with retsina. I see the sun setting and Miltos is knocking off work and getting ready to go out. His friends arrive to go to the opening of a nightclub in town, and although I'm only in a dream, I'm invited. I don't have luggage because I've astral travelled there so I have to wear the clothes I've got on. Luckily I am in fashionable Melbourne black, as if I knew I was going to Europe in winter, but underneath my skinny pants and tight roll neck (because it is my dream I can be as thin as I like), I am wearing very ungroovy thermal underwear. Still, it's black, so that's a little sexy. It is winter after all, and Delphi has frost in the mornings.

The venue is Delphi-by-Night and it's the place to be. My friends say the disco is going to bring new energy to the olive-growing town. I'm dancing with Miltos for hours it seems, and then, as I make my way to the ladies, past the bar, one of his friends, Spiros, grabs me. 'Are you going to sleep with Miltos?'

I don't try to explain that I'm already asleep and that I'd need to wake up first to be able to 'sleep' with someone. I don't try to explain the concept of astral travelling either, because Spiros's English isn't that great, and my knowledge of astral travelling isn't that great either. All I can do is look shocked, which of course I am anyway. I mean what kind of guy asks you that, even in your dreams?

'I'm going to be sleeping alone, thanks anyway, Spiros. If you were worried about me or something.'

'I am not worried, Miltos is a fine man and it's your decision, but I can't do anything because Miltos saw you first.' Like I'm a bloody lobster being chosen out of the fish tank at a restaurant in Chinatown! I hate to admit it, but Spiros is gorgeous. He has big Moby Dick lips that you just want to kiss. He pulls me close and slips his hand up the back of my top, under my thermal underwear vest, and somehow undoes my bra. Greek men clearly have a better understanding of women's underwear than any Aussie man I have ever met, even in my dreams.

I return to where Miltos is sitting, because I'm loving the attention and I don't really want to wake up. As long as it's a dream, technically I'm not flirting.

'I'm not sleeping with you, Miltos, so if you want to go look elsewhere then that's fine with me.' Of course I don't mean it, it's not fine at all for a man to admit that he's only interested in having sex with you and then leave when you tell him it's not happening. But Miltos isn't an idiot, he's got his strategy down pat. He knows my line is a test.

'I'm not going anywhere, or looking elsewhere.' He kisses me. It's an all-right kiss, not an amazing kiss, but he didn't leave the booth, so he gets some points for at least pretending to be a gentleman. And then he whispers in my ear, 'Is there any chance you might change your mind?'

Oh my God, the man is cheeky and persistent and somewhat hilarious. I have to give him more points for trying. I mean, a man's got to at least ask.

The ouzo should be wearing off now, and I should be boarding my astral flight home to East Bentleigh, but somehow I am a teenager and I believe Miltos when he says, 'We can just cuddle.' Does a man ever mean that? Do other women believe them when they say it? How old are you before you recognise immediately that it's a lie, and cuddling never satisfies anyone unless it comes *after* sex?

The next thing I know I'm in a little hotel, flat on my back with a pair of big white Y-fronts in my face and Miltos is in them and I'm in my thermal underwear neck to ankle and I'm thinking this is not where I'm supposed to be, and what would my James think if he knew or God forbid saw this scene, and with Zorba playing in the background I lift myself out from under Miltos and off the bed, then grab my clothes, putting my pants on inside out, not even knowing how I get the zip done up. I want to travel back to East Bentleigh the way I came, but I'm waiting at a bloody bus stop and it's the middle of the night and I don't have a ticket or money because I didn't think to bring any with me. But then I'm on my way, leaving Delphi, Spiros, Miltos and their olives behind.

I astral fly over Athens and see the lights on the Acropolis, and it's beautiful, but I feel like I've missed the real tourist experience and I'm disappointed in myself for that as much as for my behaviour in Delphi.

♥

The next morning I woke up feeling almost jet-lagged, although I'd had a good eight hours' sleep. The kids were staying at their cousins' place so there was no lash pulling to wake me early. I felt strange about the dream but put it down to the wonderful time I'd had with Sylvia at the Greek restaurant. I channelled my energies into hooking up with Shelley before lunch and moving into a house in St Kilda as soon as possible.

nine
Two snow peas in a wok

As I walked down Eildon Road I liked the tree-lined street and the quiet of the area. It was peaceful, and when I saw the house I felt at home. I was so pleased to be moving to St Kilda, into a house that was close to cafes and the tram, and with a flatmate too, so I wouldn't get lonely. Everything had fallen into place. There was no such thing as coincidence, and bumping into Shelley the night before had proven that again.

She met me halfway up the driveway with a cup of coffee in her hand.

'Hihi, I've been waiting for you. So, this is it,' and she waved her hand around the garden.

'I love it!' was all I could say.

'Let me show you around, you might just like the rest of it as well.'

Shelley's family were obviously loaded and she offered me the room at a ridiculous price. Who was I to argue? I offered to do the cleaning and take care of the garden, ready to plant herbs as soon as I could. This was better than Coogee: I had a yard now, and could sit in it to read or sunbake or whatever, if I wanted to. It was much better than a balcony. I took a photo of the bird bath and texted it to the girls.

'Would you like a Pimm's, Peta?'

'Love one, thanks.' It was like the old days and having gin'n'tonics with Alice. It made me like Shelley even more.

She brought out our drinks and as we sat in the back garden with birds chirping away and the sun setting, we shared bits about ourselves as a get-to-know-you session. I had to confess I didn't know much about the industry she worked in and I'd always been a bit suspicious of stockbrokers.

'Isn't the stockbroking world very corporate and competitive and, sorry, but just about making money?'

'Essentially yes, but there are a few of us who are interested in corporate responsibility and do pro bono work with community organisations and so on. Most brokers aren't like that, though, and most of them are men, which means I'm around money-obsessed blokes all day who just want a meaningless shag of a night. But I'm not in it forever. I'll do some good work for some good people and then take my skills elsewhere.'

Shelley sounded okay, and when she told me she collected handbags and shoes, I knew we would get on perfectly. She also liked watching TV to relax, sleeping in on the weekends and food. Later that night, when I'd moved my stuff in, we went to a local Chinese restaurant for salt'n'pepper squid and talked some more.

Shelley was Australian-born, but her parents were both from Brunei.

'It's on the island of Borneo in South-East Asia. The official language is Malay.'

'I'm from Coolangatta,' I told her. I didn't tell her about my mother's three husbands and that I'd never met my father – it seemed too far removed from Shelley's perfect family. I told her about Alice, Dannie and Liza, instead, and the dramas I had with them when I broke the news that I was moving to Melbourne.

'Be prepared for more, Peta. I just ended a relationship with someone who was originally from Sydney, and he never let the childish discussions end if he could find someone to argue with about the two cities.'

Shelley had been single for only a month after breaking up with her long-time boyfriend Josh – he just wouldn't grow up – and she wasn't in any great rush to meet someone new. Shelley was the only female stockbroker in her firm and had endured male chauvinism and sexist remarks every day for five years, so admitted that she had all but started to dislike men altogether.

'It really was timely Mum and Dad went away because it meant I could have the warmth and security of my old room again. I feel like a bit of teenager.' She ate the last piece of squid and I was glad, I was totally full.

'That's so nice. I feel like I've found a home too. See, I've got a lovely guy, James, in Sydney, and we're trying to do the long-distance thing for the next twelve months. Well, he's really trying more than me. I'm trying to learn to be independent in a new city. And I already feel good flying solo down here. We're kinda like two peas in a pod really, you and me, aren't we?'

'Or, snow peas in a wok maybe,' Shelley said, and we both laughed. I liked her sense of humour.

We dropped into the George on the way home and it was livelier than the last time I was there – every table full and the bar crammed. When it was my turn to buy a round, I got talking to the cute guy behind the bar. When Shelley came to find me, we kept chatting a bit longer and he gave us our drinks on the house.

'He was into you,' Shelley said as we turned into our street, walking in the middle of the road.

'I've got James in Sydney, remember? Anyway, he was a barman.'

'What, so he's got a strike against him for being a barman?' Shelley sounded appalled, and stopped still in her tracks.

'Pretty much.'

'You're a snob, Peta. He seemed really intelligent and had interesting things to say about workplace reform and the union movement and he was a really up-beat guy.' We hadn't even had our first night in the same house and we were already having a fight about a guy that neither of us was interested in. I had to explain.

'Of course he was intelligent and insightful, and generous, too, given he shouted us a drink. But I'm serious about not wanting to meet anyone this year. I'm technically in a relationship, and besides, I'm completely committed to doing my job the best I can and making my way up the departmental ladder, which means I can't have any distractions. But, if I were looking for a guy, to be honest it wouldn't be a barman I'd end up with. I don't expect a man to pay for me, but I'm not going to cover the costs of a guy who's studying and doing bar work to survive. I'm over it. Been there, done that.' I sounded like a bitch but it was true. I'd done the bar work gig myself when I was going through university, and those were the days when I had my most fun as a single girl. I couldn't imagine that a barman going to uni would be chatting up women with a view to a relationship. He'd be crazy if he was.

'All right, hypothetically speaking, what about a barman as a one-night stand then?'

'Well hypothetically speaking, when I was single, I had a three-date rule anyway, so it never could really be classified as a one-night stand, could it?'

'Well if you just had sex once, then yes, it could. I'd classify that as a one-night stand.'

'Then I guess I was a slut when I was single.' And we both cracked up.

The next morning I woke up in my new room, no kids at my face, no cat calling 'herrow' at my door, no Aunt shuffling around in her slippers and talking to herself. Light poured in through the windows and I heard the sounds of the birds in the big trees in the garden. The olive trees out the back made me laugh as I remembered my dream about Delphi.

I knew Shelley would sleep late, because it was Sunday, so I didn't move. I just lay there and thought briefly about James and how we used to make love on Sunday morning and then go for a swim and brekky down Coogee beach. Then, as if he had ESP, he called me.

'Babe, where are you? You didn't call yesterday.'

'I know, I'm sorry, it was the biggest day. I'm in my new home already and it's a massive house in St Kilda, with a beautiful garden, and it's walking distance to just everything I want – bars, restaurants, cake shops, the sea, shopping and the tram. I love it.' I paused for breath, but not long enough for James to say anything. 'And my new flatmate Shelley is from Brunei and has the best taste in shoes, and she's funny, and likes a drink and we get on really well. I love it here.'

'Sounds like you don't miss me at all.'

'Awww, don't be like that. I'm supposed to be settling in and feeling safe and happy. I thought you'd be happy for me.'

'Of course I'm happy for you. It's just that I'm sitting here waiting for the phone to ring and you're having a party of a life down there.'

'Now you're being silly. I'm settling in. And don't sit by the phone, go out and have fun, catch up with your mates.'

'I thought I'd visit next weekend.'

'Oh right, well, I'll need to check that it's okay with Shelley, I mean I just moved in. I'll call you back later.' I wasn't sure how I felt about James visiting so soon. I felt like he was gatecrashing the chicks' slumber party. But I did miss him – and the sex.

ten

Painful piercings

James arrived at Shelley's at ten am on Saturday; she was out shopping so we had the place to ourselves. I hadn't realised how much I'd missed him until I saw him and we kissed.

We spent that day seeing *my* St Kilda. I wanted him to see the area the way I did, so he could understand how I loved being in Melbourne so much, and why I hadn't missed Sydney as much as everyone thought I would, including me. We walked along the pier and it was romantic; we held hands and laughed like we'd never been apart, like we were still a couple, like the couple he wanted us to be back in Sydney.

'It's so great to be here with you, Peta.'

'Mmmm, it's really good, eh?' I was truly content.

'We can have all this again you know, when you come home. I've started looking at some places for us in the eastern suburbs near the sea. I know that's what you like. I love it there too.'

'Why are you looking already? Twelve months, that was the deal.'

'What deal? It wasn't a deal with me, it was a deal you made with the department. I miss you. I miss us.' He stopped and looked me in the face.

'I miss you too, but I need this time alone to learn to fend for myself, to take care of myself. I need to know who I am before I come back.'

'And by then you'll be ready for us again, right?'

'Yes,' I said softly and as sincerely as I possibly could. I truly hoped that I would be ready for us by then.

'And kids and a dog and big diamond, right?'

Why did he have to go and ruin it?

There was a long silence.

'The water's really flat, isn't it?' James offered.

'Yeah, it's a far cry from Bondi and Bronte and Maroubra, eh? I really miss the surf beaches back home.' He squeezed my hand tightly.

'Yes babe, but they don't have piers to stroll down, do they?' Like me, he had begun making the trade-offs. Sydney had something, Melbourne had something else, but it was like measuring apples and oranges so there was just no point in even trying.

'Let's take a photo and send it to Alice and Gary,' he suggested. I felt like he was trying to prove something to them – that we were as happy as they were. But I did it anyway because I wanted to please him.

We watched lots of families making their way along the promenade, kids in prams and on rollerblades, babies screaming, spoilt kids throwing themselves on the ground having tantrums.

'That'll be us one day, sweetie,' James whispered in my ear.

'You think so? Whiny kids make me want to get my tubes tied.' James looked deflated, and I knew I had to do some damage control. 'Anyway, I don't want to share you,' I said, cuddling into him until he smiled.

We went to Chinatown for dinner, then to a bar called Eurotrash with a groovy red velvet Harem Lounge with chandeliers. James was too conservative to try the Red Light District for two because the bar was packed and everyone was watching who entered the confined porn booth.

It was nice to be around so many straight men, which was rare in Sydney, so without even knowing it I was ordering drinks with a certain girly spark.

'I'll have a Pimm's and lemonade, thanks,' I smiled cheekily.

'This one's on the house, love, for being so pretty.'

'Why thank you, sir, I do believe I might have to come back here.'

'Can you stop flirting with everyone?' James said with gritted teeth.

'What?'

'You seem to take their flirting personally – they probably give every girl a free drink like that to make sure they *do* come back.'

'I know that. What? Are you jealous?'

'Of course I'm jealous. You live in another city, I don't see you for weeks and when I do you flirt with men in front of me. What's wrong with you?'

What was wrong with me indeed? Maybe I was missing my single days and ways and Melbourne had made me realise that.

'I think you need to make a choice between us and this new lifestyle you've got. You can stay here or you can come home and let me make you happy in Sydney.'

'What? You're giving me an ultimatum? I'm already happy. My new job is making me happy. Haven't you heard a word I've said about my career and my goals?'

'Don't you love me any more? Is that why you're really here?'

And then I snapped. 'Of course I love you, as if I'd move states just to end a relationship!'

'Well, you want to be careful, or you'll end up alone.'

'Oh, for God's sake.' I put my glass on the bar. 'Let's go home.' I didn't have to ask twice.

It was icy-cold silence in the cab for most of the drive home until we took a sharp turn and I started playing corners, pushing right into James like I did with my sister Giselle in the car when we were kids. We both laughed and the ice broke. I started kissing his neck and told him I missed him. We made out like teenagers on the back seat, and I hoped the taxi driver wasn't getting off on my muffled moans.

Shelley was still out when we arrived at Eildon Road and fumbled our way to my room.

'What the—' I felt something metal in my mouth when I went down on him. 'You could've warned me!'

'Oh, yeah, I wanted to surprise you.'

'Well, you did. Why though?'

'I thought that maybe you thought that I was too conservative for you, or that maybe it would turn you on or please you more.'

'Why would you think mutilating your body by piercing your penis would please me or turn me on?'

'I read somewhere that women got certain pleasure from piercings.'

'Some women might. Did you also read that most women don't get any pleasure from straight sex at all?'

'I'm sorry.'

'There's no need to be sorry, and thank you for going to so much trouble and pain, but you really didn't have to. We're fine together, you and me. The best.'

'I thought maybe it was me who turned you celibate.'

'No-one turned me celibate. Anyway, how can I be celibate when I'm here with you? I'm faithful to you and celibate for myself. Does that make sense?'

'Not at all, but as long as there's no-one else I'm cool.'

'There's no-one else. Are we okay?'

'All okay, my princess.'

'Then can the princess and her prince go to sleep now, is that okay?'

'That's okay.' I realised then that James truly loved me, and he just wanted to make me happy. My happiness was his happiness. Oh, how we could all live happily ever after if I wasn't so obviously emotionally flawed.

I woke up about five am with my head resting in his groin. I was desperately dry but as I got up James yelled. My earring was caught on his piercing. Every time I moved it tugged on him.

'I'm sorry,' I said, but I couldn't help laughing.

'Don't move,' he said fearfully.

'Okay.' And so I stayed still. 'So, now what?'

'Just don't move,' he said determinedly.

'I'm not moving.' I squealed with laughter again. 'But I can't stay like this all day. We're going to have to separate ourselves.'

'Well, can't you do it? You're down there.'

'I can't see anything, my head's side-on, and my hair's everywhere, and so is yours for that matter. Thought about waxing?' And I cracked up.

'Oh, very funny. Let me see if I can get it.' He tried to find my ear through my hair but we both just got the giggles.

'This is ridiculous. Hand me my phone – it's near the bed.'

'What do you want your phone for?'

'Just give it to me,' I ordered.

'Not until you tell me what it's for.'

'James, just give it to me or I'm going to sit up right now really quickly and rip your dick right off and wear it as an earring.' He handed me the phone immediately, as any smart-thinking guy would. I punched the keys, laughing to myself the whole time. There we both were, naked, and not joined at the hip as the saying generally went, but joined at the ear and penis. What a sight.

I was embarrassed and nervous but there was no other option. What would my new housemate think, the one who'd only known me a week?

'Shelley, it's me. Sorry . . . I know . . . In my room . . . Long story . . . Can you come in, please, I'm in a bind . . . Yes he is, but he's in a bind too . . . Just come in, please, and be warned, it's not pretty.' I put the phone down on the bed.

'Are you mad? We're both naked.' James wasn't happy.

'What choice do we have?'

When Shelley entered the room she gasped loudly

and put her hand over her eyes. 'I am so not interested in a threesome. Sylvia never said that was your thing. This situation really isn't going to work, sorry.' And she started to walk out.

'No, no,' I called after her. 'I'm stuck, we're stuck.'

'What? What do you mean?' And she tilted her head to the side trying to figure out how we could possibly be stuck.

'Shelley, this is James. James, this is Shelley.' They both threw little embarrassed waves to each other. 'My earring is caught.'

'On what?' she asked.

'On his—' I paused, 'penis piercing.' She screwed up her face. 'We need you to uncatch us.'

'Are you serious? I don't want to see his – you know – and I'm certainly not *touching* it. Sorry, James, no offence.'

'None taken.' He had his hand over his eyes.

'Shell, if you don't come and unhook us I'm going to yell out to you all day, and pee in this expensive ensemble that your parents love. Now please do it – I'll cook and clean for the next two weeks, I promise.'

'Liar. I know you can't cook. And you're already supposed to be doing the cleaning and looking around this room I don't think you've been doing too much at all.'

'Well, I'll buy all the wine and Pimm's, then.'

Shelley walked over cautiously, mumbling, 'I must be freaking insane. I'm putting the rent up now – I need danger money living with you.'

When Shelley left the room holding in her laughter, I crawled up the bed. For some bizarre reason we were both suddenly horny as hell and all over each other, like my roommate was some crazy aphrodisiac.

I lay back and James went down on me. I was still thinking about what we were going to do about our relationship, and how I should probably just break up with him properly and completely, because I was almost certain that I was never going to be the wife and mother he wanted me to be. Having sex with him then made me feel like the jerk guy who has sex with a girl knowing she loves him even though he doesn't want the commitment. I felt guilty, but I couldn't bring myself to stop James. He seemed to be having a good time, and so was I, for that matter. I decided I should show him due respect and let him finish the job before we started talking about our future, or lack thereof.

James left on Sunday evening and I cried at the airport. Things between us were still uncertain, but I wasn't interested in being with anyone else while I was in Melbourne and nor was he in Sydney, so we agreed that we would just keep going the way we were going and would wait until we were living in the same city again to see what we would do. Well, that's what *I* agreed.

eleven
Toorak and tramlines

As the weeks passed, Shelley and I were like two snow peas in a wok, just as she'd predicted. I was loving food and drinks and cakes and the garden and living in St Kilda. Occasionally cousin Joe would drop by, whether I was home or not, and leave a sampling of his latest creation, which Shelley and I both appreciated. I wasn't that homesick because my family, Sylvia and Shelley had filled the void that Alice, Dannie and Liza had left. The difference with Shelley was that I wasn't squeezed in around the boyfriends. And likewise, I didn't have to check James's schedule to see when it was okay for me to hang out with friends. I was truly happy with my lot.

Towards the end of summer, Shelley took me by tram to Toorak Road and we spent the day drinking coffee and shopping. I never drank much coffee in Sydney, but it was a very Melbourne thing to do and it helped me get over the ciggies much easier, going from one addiction to another. I was down to having just the occasional social one and it was much easier of a night because Shelley wouldn't allow smoking in the house at all. Moving to Melbourne was a great detox of sorts, except that I was still drinking. On that front some might suggest I was re-toxing since I moved to St Kilda.

Sylvia had introduced me to soy milk, so I was enjoying soyaccinos, lattes and so on. As we sat and drank our coffees I spent the entire time with my mouth open, just watching all the men around Toorak Road. They got off trams, they were having coffees, and they were going into bookstores and clothes shops. They made me smile, and some of them smiled back. It was like a little hetero Mardi Gras just for me, and I loved it.

We strolled down the street and I was in awe of the space, the people, the energy, the sheer difference to Sydney. We went into a small boutique and I tried on a dress.

'Nice legs,' a guy said as he sat outside the change room.

'Oh,' I responded awkwardly. He was there with a woman and I had visions of getting bitch slapped then and there in this groovy little boutique in Toorak Road. 'I don't know how your girlfriend would feel about you saying that to a strange woman.' I knew exactly how James would feel about it.

'Oh, I'm his sister and he does it all the time. Generally, I just feel embarrassed, so apologies for my cheeky brother.' I looked sympathetically at her, cheekily at him, and hid in the change room until they were both gone.

'Gees, men are all over you,' Shelley said as I paid for the dress.

'Perhaps they know I'm from outta town and are just being nice.' Then I had a brainwave. 'Or perhaps they can sense that I'm celibate and they feel sorry for me.'

'Don't be ridiculous. They like the look of you.'

'I love Melbourne, Shelley, and before all my girlfriends got married up they would've loved it here, too.'

'Pity you're avoiding men.' Shelley nodded in the direction of a guy across the road leaning in a doorway, just waiting to be lured somewhere naughty.

'No it's not. I didn't get this much attention when I actually wanted a bloke. I'm having more fun not wanting one.'

'Here's my favourite shop,' Shelley said. 'A local designer, and the clothes are cut really well.' An hour later we walked out loaded up with clothes and bags and shoes Shelley would hardly ever wear. When she wasn't at work she only ever wore thongs.

I took a photo of us both on my phone and texted the girls:

Hi – Sat morn on Toorak Rd shoppin. You? Luv ya, Px

I knew Shelley must've made a packet working as a stockbroker. And the day's shopping was evidence that neither of us was paying enough rent.

'We *really* should be heading home,' Shelley said, trying to convince herself and me that she was done shopping, 'but I need to show you this one last shop called Shag.'

'Shag the shop – I like it, especially as it's the only shag I'm going to get while I'm here. Where is it?' Shelley laughed and grabbed my arm, dragging me round the corner into Chapel Street.

'Here we are,' she soon announced and pushed me in the door.

I spotted a coat I loved immediately and put it on.

'What do you think?' I said, doing a bit of a catwalk turn.

'It's pink!' Shelley screwed her face up like it was fluoro, when I thought it was a classy deep rose.

'Actually, it's watermelon,' the sales assistant said, 'and the buttons are original.'

'Yeah, it's watermelon!' I reiterated to Shelley, who was a proud member of the all-black drab Melbourne mass.

'And now it's time to go. Let's get a cab,' Shelley said. 'I can't carry all this on the tram then home from the stop.'

'No arguments from me, Imelda.'

We jaywalked across the road and I spotted a cyclist coming towards us. He was grinning and slowing down, as if to say 'hello'. He went to tip his helmet like a man would do with his hat in the past, in the days of *The Sullivans* or something. I giggled like a schoolgirl and he said 'Ladies' and beamed at us until his wheels got caught in the tram tracks and he toppled off his bike. I threw my bags at Shelley and ran over to him.

'Are you okay?' I felt responsible for the spill.

'That'll teach me to perve on a beautiful woman, won't it?'

'I guess so – where is the bitch?' We both laughed as I helped him to his feet.

'Thanks, my name's Allen, and you're Rachel Berger, right?'

'Actually no, I'm not. I'm Peta, and I'm avoiding men, Mr Allen, so if you'll excuse me.' I walked off and just left him there in his tight, tight bike shorts with his grazed knee and no doubt bruised ego. I hailed a cab and dragged Shelley in.

'You're an idiot, Peta. The man just falls off his bike for you on a main road in the middle of the day, and you can't even tell him your name.'

'He actually fell off his bike for Rachel Berger, not me. And even if it were for me, I didn't see the point in continuing any conversation. How long do you think I'll be celibate if I give my name and number to every cute guy I meet in Melbourne? They're fucken everywhere, like a bogong moth plague, except sexier and tastier.'

'You're an idiot.'

'Would you like to go somewhere, or did you just jump in for the aircon, ladies?' the driver said, winking at us both hot and sweaty in the back seat. We hadn't told him where we were going.

'St Kilda, thank you. Eildon Road,' Shelley said, slightly exasperated. All the shopping had worn her out.

'I'm not an idiot,' I said in a low voice, 'I'm just in control of my life for the first time in years, maybe ever. And I'm not here to play with men, Shelley, remember, and I need to be faithful to James. We haven't actually broken up. So technically, I shouldn't be flirting with other men anyway. And if I were, they'd have to do something more outrageous than fall off their bike for me. Like step in front of a tram or something.'

'You're an idiot *and* a bitch,' she joked, and shoved some of her shopping bags into my lap.

'Yes I am. Thank you very much.'

The taxi driver started to laugh.

'What's so funny?' Shelley asked him with a giggle.

'You young girls are funny. Whatever happened to a man just being a hopeless romantic, soft and sensitive?'

'Romantic, soft and sensitive is good. We like that. We also like clowns on bikes,' I said.

'So, if I was soft and sensitive and romantic, and showed up at the door with flowers, you'd go out with me?' he said, looking at me in the rear-view mirror. Shelley pinched me on the thigh.

'Well, I have soft and sensitive at home, and he can be a clown too. But it's about more than that, isn't it? It's about shared values and dreams and—'

'Just here on the left thanks, driver. I'll get it, Rachel,' Shelley said, giving me the eye to get out of the cab, and so I did.

Shelley had Skype installed on her computer – along with every other program known to mankind – and showed me how to set up my own account. I knew Dannie was on it regularly because it was free and her kids could talk to their friends and grandparents as often as they wanted to, so I thought I'd try Skyping her first.

'Hey, this is so cool,' I said as I watched Dannie on the screen trying to talk to me and shooing away her kids at the same time.

'Yes, much better than just talking on the phone, but as you can see I have absolutely no privacy whatsoever with this set-up. How's it going your end?'

'All great. Love my house, look . . . ' and I turned the computer screen around the room so Dannie could see how lovely and homely it was. Shelley was on the couch and just waved. 'That's Shelley, my landlady, I'm sure you'll meet sometime down the track.' At that Shelley got up and mimed, 'I'll give you some privacy,' and left the room.

'So, are you missing James heaps?'

'I've been really busy, but yes, I guess you could say I'm missing him an adequate amount.'

'You sound like a bloody politician, choosing your words carefully like that. So,' she whispered, 'how's the celibacy thing going?'

'Piece of cake really, and when I want some, I actually go and *have* a piece of cake, down on Acland Street.' I didn't really want to talk about it.

'Is James going to be celibate as well?' Dannie pressed.

'To be honest, I don't care if he's not. This isn't about him, it's about me. Anyway, can you expect a man to go without sex for months on end, if he has it on offer elsewhere?'

'Yes, of course. I'd expect George to go without sex if I wasn't around for whatever reason. Anyway George is pretty much celibate as it is and we sleep in the same bed.' She laughed.

'Why bother getting married if you're not going to have sex every day at least? I thought getting married was about not having to look for sex any more.'

'Marriage isn't about sex.' Dannie tut-tutted me like I was a child and looked around to make sure the kids couldn't hear her.

'Obviously not. Anyway, you're lying, Dannie. Aren't you and George trying to have a baby? You're not Mary Immaculate, so I'm guessing you're having sex – oh sorry, when you're married, it's *making lurrrrv*, isn't it?'

'You're so childish sometimes. And yes, we're *kind of* trying.'

'What the hell does that mean? *Kind of* trying. Does he

say, "Can I *kind of* put my penis in you tonight love and maybe *kind of* get you pregnant?" You know, like when you're teenagers and the boy says, "If it doesn't go all the way, it's not really sex"?'

'Sssshhhhh, the kids will hear you.' Dannie looked around nervously and covered the computer screen with her body, as if blocking my face might drown out the sound. She was right about a lack of privacy, and not even being able to have a grown-up conversation with her kids around. But she started it, so she was going to finish it.

'Well?' It was my turn to be pushy.

'Oh all right.' She leaned in as close as she could to the screen and whispered, 'We tried recently when we both had too much champagne at my sister's wedding and both of us got nostalgic. But we're not having endless nights of passion, if that's what you're thinking. When you get married you can measure your passion in minutes, trust me.'

I wanted to say, *And there's another reason not to get married* – because it was a passion killer – but I wasn't game. At least James and I had sex every time we saw each other.

When I'd told the girls I was planning to be celibate while I was down in Melbourne they'd shrieked so loud it startled the kitchen staff at Sauce, who came running out with utensils and wet hands and looks of horror on their faces.

'What's wrong?' Andy had asked.

'Oh nothing, everything's fine,' Liza told him. 'Peta has just taken a twelve-month vow of celibacy, that's all.'

'That's a waste of a good woman, I'd say.' He winked at me and walked off.

'What are you talking about, celibate. Celibate my arse.' Alice had laughed so hard she'd nearly pissed herself.

'Muuuuuummmmmmm . . .' I heard a cry on Dannie's side of the screen. I watched her push her chair back and yell like I'd never have imagined her do, 'I'm coming upstairs in five minutes and you two better have your homework done.' She looked back at me. 'I've gotta go, but keep in touch, okay? We all miss you. If you're not busy, let's have a Skype session on Friday with Alice and Liza too – it'll be fun.'

'Sure thing, catch you then. Now go and do their homework for them.'

We logged out and I just sat staring at the screen for a moment. Now that I lived in Melbourne, Dannie and I seemed to be closer than we ever had been while I was in Sydney – communicating via text and email had somehow helped us to understand each other.

I thought about never having privacy when you had children, and how marriage was almost a form of celibacy anyway. Neither commitment was at all attractive to me at that moment.

twelve
Lesbians, lattes and La Rambla

Hey Peta — what's news? Missed you on the Skype session on Friday. You would've loved it. Dannie told us about the planning committee for the school fete (yawn) and as usual Liza wouldn't tell us anything about any cases at the ALS — it's not like we'd tell anyone. We all miss you, and we're planning our visit to Melbourne, but the way we're going it won't be till you're ready to come home. When are you in Sydney next? And when are you going to call Josie? She keeps asking me when you're going to hook up. Okay, don't panic now, I didn't mean 'hook up', I meant catch up. She knows you're straight and married up. BTW, James is missing you heaps. Calls all the time. Missing his weekend visits to Coogee too. He's looking for property, but you'd know that, eh? Will be great when you're back and we can all hang out again. Speak soon, love Alice xoxoxoxoxo Gary says 'G'day' too! x

It was the end of March already. I'd been so busy at work during the week I hadn't found time to sit down to check my hotmail account until Saturday morning. I'd forgotten all about the planned Skype session the night before. I decided to call Josie straight away so I could at least tell Alice that we'd made plans.

I was glad I did. Josie was friendly, and greeted me like family. She was free that afternoon, and so was I, so we arranged to meet for a few bevies down at the Esplanade, a pub in St Kilda. Josie said I had to call it the 'Espy' if I wanted to sound like a local; it was apparently a rock institution.

'It's great to hear from you, Peta,' she said. 'Alice keeps asking me when we're going to catch up.'

That was so Alice, to be saying the same thing to both of us. After we'd hung up, I emailed her.

> Hello there Missy – funny you should email me just now, I'm catching up with cuzin Josie later today, and looking forward to it. I'm adding the lesbian parking cop to the Greek-Australian vegan eco-poet and the Pimm's drinking, thong-wearing stockbroker who are my mates here. I think you'd like them. Gees, wish I could've heard all about the chocolate wheel and face painting . . . blah blah blah, it makes me laugh when Dannie goes from something serious like censorship in the media to what she's making for the kids' lunches the next day. It really is great, though, isn't it? Give her my love, and I'll email her soon too. Just been really busy, still finding my feet at work and locally. All good though. Say hi to Gary, and I'll call you soon for a good goss.
>
> Luv ya, Px

I intentionally didn't mention James's property shopping. I was annoyed he'd been talking about it with my friends – I didn't want to disappoint him *and* Alice and Gary if in the long run it didn't work out.

Josie called as I made my way to the Espy. We wouldn't be hanging out at the pub after all, because she'd been offered an extra shift. She couldn't turn it down, so she invited me to walk with her as she did the streets of St Kilda. It was a gorgeous day and I was still getting my bearings so it would be a great opportunity to kill two birds with one stone – learn about Josie and the local geography.

Josie didn't *look* like a lesbian, just like people often said I didn't necessarily *look* Aboriginal.

'I'm a lipstick lesbian, that way I have both men and women want me. It feels good.' Josie laughed and I liked her straight away.

'Are you sure it's okay for me to walk with you?' I asked as we gathered speed along Fitzroy Street.

'Yeah, no worries, it's a public place – you can do whatever you want. Who's to know this is a date.'

'What? But this isn't a date!'

'I know, just gammin, love. Be sure and tell Aunty Ivy that one, okay? She'll expect a story like that.' Josie winked at me.

'Hey Josie, latte?' an old Italian man asked as we walked past Leo's.

'Maybe later, had three already, thanks,' she replied, and blew him a kiss.

'Three already, are you mental? How many do you have a day?'

'Depends on how many they give me.' Josie shrugged.

'They?'

'The shop owners. I never buy food or coffee when I'm working, and even when I'm not working and I'm in the area. Shop owners are always getting things delivered and blocking the road and driveways and footpaths. They feed me and I don't see a thing. I'm like the parking cop mafia, and coffee, cakes and pasta is my protection money.' I wasn't quite sure if Josie was joking with me but either way she had clearly had too much caffeine already.

'Watch this,' she said, as she went to a car parked in a disabled spot without a sticker. She started to write a ticket when a man carrying a coffee came running over.

'Oh no, love, please don't, I was just getting a coffee.' He was puffed.

'You think getting a coffee is an excuse for parking illegally? And parking in a disabled spot? It's not bad enough that someone ends up in a wheelchair but then they have to wait while you take your healthy spine propped up by two healthy legs and get a coffee. Sorry, that's not a legitimate excuse.' She handed him a ticket.

'Dumb bitch.' He spat the words at her.

'Actually, the name's Josie. Have a nice day.' And she walked back towards me slowly.

'That's unbelievable! He didn't even try and lie – say he was sick, or busting to go to the toilet or whatever,' I said, gobsmacked.

'Yeah, I know. No shame at all. But we're the bad guys; we're the scum of the earth because we ask people nicely not to park in spaces for people with disabilities when you can walk to get your coffee. You ain't seen nothing, though. It's Saturday afternoon – wait till we get on Jacka Boulevard.'

I remembered my first trip to Jacka Boulevard and the coin machines. 'Actually, I do have something to say about the coin machines on that stretch of road.'

'Go ahead. I'm sure you've got something to tell me that I haven't heard before.'

'It's fine to ask for coins if you have a bloody change machine nearby as well. But not everyone carries bags of change with them, so if you don't have the right money you have to ask strangers or not park or get booked. Ah! Is *that* the council's strategy? Now it makes sense.'

Josie shrugged her shoulders. 'It's a fair call. I don't know why we don't have change machines or machines that also take credit cards as well as coins. People suggest it all the time – but I'll note it in the office again when I go back.'

A motor bike was parked on the footpath blocking everyone's way on Acland Street. The owner was dressed in all leather, despite the stinking hot day, and having lunch with his mates. Josie started to write a ticket and he came over immediately.

'Hello gorgeous, what can I do to persuade you not to write that ticket? My pleasure is your pleasure.' I laughed to myself, *Oh I don't think it is, mate.*

'Is this your very macho bike, with the *very* big engine?' Josie asked. He puffed his chest out and I'm sure I saw his bulge grow in his black leather pants.

'Sure is, baby. You wanna ride?'

'Well, you're parked illegally.' And she handed him a ticket.

'Did you know that all this is Aboriginal land anyway?' He waved his arms along the street.

'Really? Are you Aboriginal?'

'No, but I'm an actor, and I played an Aborigine once, does that count?'

'No.'

'Bitch.'

'Thanks.'

As we walked off, I was surprised that Josie wasn't angry.

'How can you be so calm all the time? I mean with their stupidity and their abuse? You've been called a bitch twice already.'

'Yeah, but I've also been called love, gorgeous and baby. I love that men don't know I'm gay; they make passes at me all the time, look like fools and still get a ticket. You take the good with the bad.' I admired Josie's positive take on it.

'Hey Josie, strudel!' A stocky woman walked out of a cake shop I hadn't been to yet.

'Thanks, Sabina, but look at my love handles. There'll be too much to love soon. Maybe next lap!' If Josie didn't have a good relationship with the illegal parkers, she sure had one with the shopkeepers and maybe that was why she was so chirpy. Then she turned to me. 'Thank God my job is walking. I'd be a heifer otherwise.'

Between Spencer and Chaucer streets, outside Luna Park, we saw a gorgeous blue Citroën convertible, roof down, double-parked, minus a driver. 'I can't believe some people,' Josie said. 'Probably in having a ride on the ghost train.'

She walked over to the car, looked around the area for the owner and started to write a ticket. I stood on the footpath, just waiting for another dumb bloke to run up and offer sex or money and watch Josie shoot them down in flames. Instead two women strolled up to the car, denim and singlet clad.

'Hey darl, don't be like that. Let me buy you a drink at Girls Bar instead.' The taller woman grabbed her girl-friend. 'The three of us can sort it out together, whaddya reckon?' Josie just handed her the ticket.

'It's a seventy-five dollar fine for double-parking. If you've got any money left in your wallet after you pay the bill then, sure, you can buy me a drink at Girls Bar on Thursday night. Don't be doing it again – you're breaking the law.'

'Oh, we've been naughty gals. Can't you just spank us?'

'C'mon.' Josie gave me the head wave to move on, before it got too dirty, I think. I had never seen anything like it in my life. People everywhere offering sex to get out of a parking ticket. There I was trying to avoid men, and Josie had both sexes throwing themselves at her. What a nightmare that must have been – or not.

'It's hot, eh?' Josie adjusted her hat.

'I think it's just you, love, with all that sexual tension around you.'

'Hardy-har-har, I mean it's hot, must be thirty degrees. Let's get a juice.' We headed to a healthy juice bar on Acland Street and I remembered with a pang the days when I would show up at Alice's place with carrot and ginger juices and we'd debrief on the boozy night before.

'They do the best juices here. Should I order for you?' Josie asked, and went to the counter. 'Hi Mary, can I get a Vegie Power Juice for my friend and I'll have the Detox Juice.' She didn't pay a cent. Everyone everywhere who didn't own a car, or wasn't near their car, loved Josie. Actually she was quite lovable, and I couldn't understand how Aunty Ivy could be so nasty to her.

It was an hour before there was another incident. Josie had to book a car parked at the Sea Baths for twenty-four hours without a ticket.

'Someone's obviously been drinking and got a cab home, which is great, but would've been cheaper to get the cab both ways,' she said as she wrote the ticket and placed it under the windscreen wiper.

'Have you got your quota today, slag?' a guy said as he walked past.

'Is this your car, mate?' Josie said calmly.

'No, never seen it before.'

'Then fuck off and mind your own business.' And I knew Josie had had enough for the day. 'I need a drink. You up for one tonight?'

'Sure, but I don't really want to go to that girls' bar, if you don't mind. I'm avoiding men, but it doesn't mean I'm looking for women, if you know what I mean.'

'Oh for God's sake, you're starting to sound like my Aunty Ivy. I know you're not interested in women. Alice gave me the lowdown about your perfect man in Sydney. And how you're having an early midlife crisis and trying to figure out what you want to do.'

'It's not a crisis – I just want to be the Minister for Cultural Affairs one day.'

'I'd say a self-imposed sex ban for a gorgeous young woman like yourself *is* a fucken crisis. And don't panic, I'm not hitting on you.'

'Starving kids in Africa is a *crisis*. Now can we stop talking about me and start talking about tonight?'

Josie took me to Kanela on Johnston Street in Fitzroy for lots of sangria, tapas and flamenco dancing.

'This place is great!' I said as our paella arrived in a large cast iron pan.

'Yeah, it's run by two brothers – they're like two of the country's best flamenco artists.'

We watched the show and it made me want to dance, or try to dance or to have a dance lesson at least, and it wasn't because of the sangria. The rhythm of the music and the hard soles of the shoes hitting the floor was mesmerising and everyone in the venue was entranced watching the couple dance their song of love. The woman was truly beautiful and the guy was hot.

'How hot is that!' I said.

'Yes, she is,' Josie replied, eyes fixed on the flowing black dress of the flamenco queen.

When I got home Shelley was already asleep, so I tried to make as little noise as possible but I was really drunk and had started to feel sick. The fruit in the sangria didn't taste as good coming up as it did going down. I had a shower and felt a bit better, but took a bucket with me to bed. I couldn't remember how long it had been since I'd done that – at least as long as I'd been going out with James, and maybe even longer. He would have been appalled. I closed my eyes and the room started to spin and spin.

I'm at customs and the guy says I need a thirty-day visa and I explain that there is no way I will be there thirty days, maybe eight hours if I am lucky, and then I laugh and he laughs.

'What is your occupation?' he asks, because now I have to fill out entry forms.

'I'm the Minister for Cultural Affairs, on holidays,' I lie, because I can, and I know it doesn't really matter and he doesn't really care because he hasn't taken his eyes off my cleavage anyway. Then he takes me and my astral passport to a small room.

'What are you doing?' I ask, only a little scared, because I know that nothing bad is going to happen to me. I'm in a dream and I am, after all, the Minister for Cultural Affairs.

'I am going to strip-tease you,' he says and I laugh because I'm not sure if he means he's going to do a strip-tease for me, or that he's going to strip-search me, and I don't really mind which it is, because my self-promotion to minister has been an aphrodisiac, and I'm up for either because he's hot. And because I know I won't be there for thirty days and time is running out, we strip each other, starting slowly, unbuttoning clothing, undoing zips, unbuckling belts, but then getting faster and faster as stockings and boxer shorts are aggressively pushed down around ankles and our bodies are moving in time to the flamenco music and someone's clapping – not applauding, but clapping a dance – and one minute I'm on the plain table in the little room and then I'm walking along La Rambla in Barcelona and there are street performers doing acrobatics and flamenco dancing and busking. It's colourful and noisy and I love it. I walk and smile but soon I am frowning as I enter the Museu Picasso, which is like five large town houses joined together, all of them really old, 500 years old or more, and I'm walking in a bit of a maze and my confusion is exacerbated by the artwork; there's a portrait of a man in a beret and I get that painting, obviously, but I am not sure of others, like the Seated Man, who has a head like a horse but I read it's meant to be mask-like, it's supposed to be a symbol and fetish. No-one else seems to be struggling, rather they are talking about 'broad brush strokes' and 'a basic and brutal aesthetic'. I don't see it, though, and think Picasso must've been on some serious acid or something. But as the new minister I must try to appreciate the work; it is all part of my professional development. I step out of the Museu onto the street and I'm in Madrid but also Pamplona and there's bulls running and people cheering and I get caught up in the action and the red flags and matadors in the sexy outfits with tights and I'm thinking about the guy from customs and how I could strip-tease them but the thoughts subside quickly as I run past old churches and the cathedral into the Basilica de San Francisco, and ask for forgiveness from the God I don't believe in for my pornographic thoughts. I light a candle and hope for the best. I say a quick prayer for James too, because I feel I should.

A gorgeous beggar on the street is asking for pesetas but I think he says 'potatoes' and miraculously, I pull some from my bag. The Lord provides in mysterious ways. I want to make creamed potatoes with the beggar but I wonder if that's me being too community-minded and I just keep walking until I become bored with my astral dream because there's no men, and no more strip-teasing and I want to go home, and for the first time in my life I am glad that I am about to vomit because it wakes me up.

thirteen
Facebook friends and a fundraiser

It took me weeks to go through my hotmail account, my inbox was so full. I had a long list of emails inviting me to be people's 'friend' on Facebook. There were invitations from Alice, Dannie, Liza and even James. Apparently this phenomenon had been happening without me. I signed up and had too many friends in no time, all poking, super-poking, headbutting and kissing me. I was sent drinks and flowers and growing plants and invited to join causes and groups as my page had bling and bumper stickers added.

I posted photos of the house, of my office and of St Kilda so the gang could all see how things were going for me. Likewise Dannie posted pics of the kids, Liza put up pics of the basketball team she coached and Alice had photos of her and Gary down at Coogee. James sent me things constantly and got a bit annoyed when I didn't respond immediately, but Facebook had been barred at work as the department had calculated the amount of hours lost every day to the fad, and I had to set a good example anyway.

For about a month it was loads of fun, but also addictive and before I knew it I was spending hours every night responding to emails and aquarium gifts, vampire bites and likeness quizzes. It was a great way to keep on top of what everyone was doing, though, and better than trying to fit it all into three separate phone conversations once a week. We were all on the same Facebook page at the same time. I rationalised the time spent online by saying I was being sociable and maintaining my friendships, which could easily deteriorate in twelve months if I didn't make the effort.

Sylvia was on there as well and sent out an invitation to a fundraiser she was involved in for the Black Dog Institute, an organisation supporting people with depression. She really was a mixed bag. It would be great to go for a night out while supporting a worthwhile charity at the same time, I thought, so of course I accepted. It was at the Westin Hotel in the heart of the city.

'Wow, you look fantastic,' I said to Sylvia, who had lost the dark kohl look for something more conservative. I only found out then that she was on the organising committee and thought she should dress a little less poetically than usual.

We sat down at a table with some of her friends. Everyone was having little conversations in pairs, and trying to listen to the MC at the same time.

'The fashions are very different here, aren't they?' I observed. And as I looked around the grand ballroom, I noticed that everyone was wearing black. *Everyone*.

'Yes, Sydney's fashion has a more coastal influence, while Melbourne's is more diverse.' I couldn't see how everyone wearing the same colour was a demonstration of diversity, but I decided not to mention it, and changed the topic instead.

'Hey, why haven't you got a boyfriend?' I was curious that Sylvia, who was interesting and intelligent, had never mentioned a man. I'd been thinking that if she were gay, I could set her up with Josie.

'I have got a boyfriend,' she said, almost defensively.

'Oh, sorry, didn't mean to pry.'

'That's fine, I just don't let him out much,' she said with a sly smile. I could see Sylvia being in charge of the social calendar for both of them, like she was for me.

'Oh, you're hilarious. Why haven't you mentioned him before?'

'Well, Rick's a muso, and oddly insular and I'm really oddly outgoing, so we don't do a lot of things together that involve other people. We're great when we're by ourselves. He finds me a little too out-there when I'm with my friends.'

'I can't imagine why.' I smiled at her.

'You can meet him soon if you like. We might go see him play or something one night, if you're into it.'

'Sounds great.' I hadn't been to much live music for years, and only really ever saw bands at Klub Koori events organised by Koori Radio.

'I'm in charge of the silent auction, so I better go check out if anyone's bidding yet.' Sylvia got up and took me with her.

We strolled around the table and there were some interesting pieces to bid on: a framed pic of Kylie, a bronze World Cup Soccer trophy, a Russell Crowe *Gladiator* print, and a framed autographed pic of Jessica Mauboy from the 2006 *Australian Idol* final. I went to put a bid on

Jessica, but as my hand reached for the pen, so did another. I grabbed it first and wrote my name and mobile. I only bid a modest amount because I hadn't actually gone there prepared for an auction. The next person would easily beat my offer by at least fifty dollars. I put the pen down and the hand, belonging to a nicely cuff-linked wrist and even nicer looking guy, picked it up. I looked at him.

'Hi, I'm Lee,' he said, and offered me his hand to shake.

'Hi, I'm celibate,' I blurted, then cringed with embarrassment. I shook his hand roughly like a man and let it drop.

'That's an interesting name. Does it have a special meaning?'

'Actually my name's Peta,' I said, burning with shame, and not knowing where to look. He was so hot he was making me perspire.

'So, the celibacy is just . . . ?'

'A national crisis, obviously.' I was trying to be funny to take the focus off me being an idiot.

'You being celibate *is* a national emergency for sure. I'm in the SES, so maybe I can help you with it, if you like.'

'I'm sure you could, but you really can't. Thanks anyway.' I was tongue-tied like a teenager with a crush on the most popular boy at school, and just walked off.

Black tie fundraisers were clearly great places to meet men, for those in the market. Everyone there was supporting a worthy cause, they looked great, and the wealthy guys could always be found hanging around the silent auction table.

♥

When I woke up in the morning I had knickers on and nothing else. I threw on a T-shirt and walked into the mess that was the lounge room and saw my dress flung over the back of the chunky lounge chair. My shoes and stockings were just inside the front door, and my pink wrap was on the telephone table. My handbag was on the ground with coins strewn everywhere. My camera was in my bag, minus its cover, and the hundred dollars I had withdrawn at the pub we went to after the dinner was missing. It must have fallen out in the cab on the way home. I felt like I was still drunk as I jumped in the shower. I didn't bother using the four minute timer because I knew I probably wouldn't be able to stand up that long anyway, but I was hoping it would sober me up. I was supposed to meet Josie at nine to go shopping.

Dressed and feeling slightly better I went to leave the house. Shelley was in Sydney visiting friends so I didn't have to worry about tidying up with any sense of urgency. Then I realised to my horror that the front door was deadlocked, and the keys weren't in the lock, as they usually were. I searched the house, my handbag, under the tables, lounge, and telephone table. I panicked. I heard the neighbour's kids playing outside on the footpath but I was too embarrassed to ask them if the keys were in the door. How would that look? 'Excuse me, are my keys in the door? I'm locked in . . .' I had to find another way of getting the keys. They had to be in the door – I did get inside, after all. We never used the back door and Shelley hadn't given me a key for it. The only thing I could do was climb through the bathroom window. I'd need a leg-up even to reach it, and it was so tiny I was sure to get stuck. I started to cry with the stress of it all and called James.

'What do you want me to do about it, Peta?' He wasn't the warm, caring James I'd expected – the one who'd offer to ring the local locksmith to let me out.

'I don't want you do to anything. I just wanted to tell you is all.'

'Well, if you were so drunk you locked yourself in the house, what else were you drunk enough to do?'

'There were no men involved last night, if that's what you're asking me, James. Sorry I called.' And I hung up. The last thing I wanted was a long-distance domestic argument while I was suffering a terrible hangover and locked in my own house.

I took my shoes off, put one foot on the rim of the bath and the other foot on the toilet seat, hoping it wouldn't crack, then pushed myself up out through the window and fell into the bottlebrush plant below. There! I didn't need James after all. Dusting myself off, I got the keys out of the door, thankful that no-one had found them and robbed the house. Then I texted Josie to let her know I'd be late and ran to catch the tram to the city.

When I found her she was buying a dress for a hot date she had with some woman she'd let off a parking ticket. She even got a matching lipstick.

'This woman is hot, hot, hot!' Josie said as the girl at the make-up counter attempted to do her face.

'She must be,' I said as I watched Josie let her brows be brushed.

At lunch in the Melbourne Centre my mobile rang. I didn't recognise the number.

'Hi, I've got something of yours.'

'What?'

'Jessica Mauboy. You bought it, remember?' It was Lee, the cuff-linked SES guy from the fundraiser.

'Shit, did I? I didn't pay for it – I didn't hear them call it out. I must have left by then.'

'No, you were still there – it looked like you and your celibacy were having a great time.'

Fuck, I mouthed to Josie. I was so embarrassed.

'Well, thank you for picking it up for me. I should get it from you and give you the money.'

'No worries. It was no trouble, and it guaranteed I'd see you again.' He was going to be disappointed.

'Actually, how did you get my number?'

'You wrote your number next to the bid, remember?'

'Oh yes, of course I did.' I hoped he was the only one who'd made a note of it.

fourteen
Italy on eight hours' sleep

I met Lee in the early evening at Pellegrino's, an espresso bar in the city. At first it seemed to be an odd choice, with its bar stool service and very basic menu, given that Lee was a classy guy with plenty of cash, but apparently Pellegrino's was an institution, like so many places in Melbourne. Everything here seemed to be an institution or an icon, or a must-see and must-do. I wasn't overly impressed with having to sit on a bar stool at the counter, but the Italian food was as authentic as any I'd ever eaten, never having actually been to Italy.

'The minestrone is delicious, how's yours?'

'The spaghetti Napolitano is *bellisimo*!' Lee said with a mock Sicilian accent, kissing his fingers like an Italian you'd see on a television show.

'Thanks for bringing me here – it's like a little Italian cafe isn't it, very traditional.'

'Oh, someone would've brought you here on a date eventually.'

'I'm not dating,' I said. 'I have a boyfriend.'

'Where?' Lee looked around. 'Was he at the fundraiser? I thought it was just you and your celibacy.' He laughed and I cringed.

'Okay, so I deserved that. No, he's in Sydney. We're doing the long-distance thing.'

'So you're being faithful, not celibate.'

'Same thing.' I took another spoonful of soup, not wanting to discuss the difference between celibacy and faithfulness with Lee. He was too dangerously cute to talk to about sex, or not having sex, and I knew I would sound like a complete flip to anyone who didn't really know me. Even James had struggled with the concept and he loved me unconditionally.

Lee was staring right at me.

'What?' I asked.

'You've got some sauce just . . . there.' He wiped the side of my mouth and I went weak. Was that all it took to make me love fickle? A wipe of food from my grubby face?

I liked Lee. He was hot, and funny, and gentle, and single, and sitting there in front of me. It was a recipe for disaster on the celibacy front and I knew it, and knowing it meant I had to remove myself from the situation.

I looked at my watch. 'I think my tram's due shortly.'

'I'll walk you to Bourke Street, then.' Lee was also chivalrous, which made him all the more sexy. The men in Melbourne really were different to those in Sydney.

When we reached the tram stop we stood awkwardly and waited.

'Do you want to come back to my place for a nightcap?' Lee asked.

'A nightcap? Do people actually use that phrase any more?'

'Well, I did.'

'Yes, but don't you mean, *Do you want to come back to my place for a shag?*'

'Well, yes, I was trying to be a gentleman, but okay, do you want to come back to my place for a shag?' He raised his eyebrows and grinned, as if to say, *Say yes!*

'If you think you can trade a ten-buck pasta for my celibacy, you are so wrong. I'd have to have had some dessert as well for that.' We both laughed, and he leaned in and kissed me gently on the mouth goodnight just before the #96 tram arrived.

'You're wicked, Peta, but I like it. Now get on your chariot and stop teasing innocent men in the street. And take Jessica with you.' I'd completely forgotten about the photo I'd bought at the auction.

'The money, wait, here . . .' The tram's bells were ringing.

'It's a gift.' He *was* a nice guy. A guy who went to fundraisers, who dined in restaurants because he liked the food, not because they were fancy, and who was kind and funny and generous, giving gifts just for the sake of it.

I smiled all the way back to St Kilda, clutching Jessica tightly and wondering if I would see Lee again. I was still smiling when I finished taking my make-up off and went to bed. I closed my eyes thinking of Lee but knew that I shouldn't be. I remembered Lee's soft lips and the hot rush of blood that suddenly turns cold as I hear a countdown and everyone screaming and cheering, 10, 9, 8, 7, 6, 5, 4, 3, 2, 1, BANG.

It's midnight, New Year's Eve, but I don't know what year it is. I'm at Piazza della Signoria in Florence and everyone's throwing bottles into the middle of the cobblestone piazza, but there are no fireworks or 'Auld Lang Syne' like back at home. I turn to the guy next to me and it's Lee and I kiss him, because it's New Year's Eve and because he's there and because in my dream I'm not celibate, and there's no James, and I've been given a second chance and he looks good enough to eat.

'I'm Luigi and you are *bella*.' Lee-Luigi is there and I'm beautiful and everything is fine by me.

'Yes, *Luigi*, I am.' And we kiss again. In my dreams my self-esteem is good.

'I am a security guard and I must go check the city, you come with me, on my bike.'

'Okay,' I say, because I know I'm astral travelling and don't need travel insurance and I'll wake up in the morning and Lee-Luigi won't expect me to make him breakfast. But I know I'm doing things that girls should never do when they are travelling alone, things I would never do if I were awake travelling.

I put my arms around Lee-Luigi's waist and hold tight as we cruise the streets on his moped until we stop outside the Uffizi Gallery.

'I must check here, you come inside with me?' He helps me off the bike.

It seems less daring to go into the gallery than to stay out on the street by myself. Lee-Luigi flashes his torch into the darkness and I catch a glimpse of some Rubens posters and I'm tempted to ask for a complete tour, but just past the entrance he stops, and so do I.

I've heard about hot-blooded Italian men who love women and know how to romance them. Lee-Luigi is the kind of guy who loves women, who worships women, who wines and dines and does wicked things to women. I bet Lee-Luigi tells women all the time that he loves them. Lee-Luigi is love fickle for sure, and the only thing worse than one love fickler in a relationship is two love ficklers. But I'm dreaming, so who cares anyway, and we make out for hours. As he gently kisses my neck he starts to peel my clothes off and I just stand still, a willing participant in astral fornication, but then suddenly the lights go on and we rush out the door and when I go to step back onto the moped, my foot lands on the cold bathroom floor and it seems I've also been sleepwalking.

I met Josie for coffee on Brunswick Street the next morning feeling completely jet-lagged. I ordered a double shot soy latte and an Italian pastry.

'I need to tell you something.' I was bursting to tell Josie about my astral travelling experiences.

'What?' she asked, only half interested.

'I travel in my sleep.'

'What do you mean?'

'I eat a certain cuisine, and then that night I travel in my sleep to the country it comes from.'

'What? Like astral travelling?' She suddenly seemed much more interested.

'Yes, I think that's it. The dreams are really *real*, if you know what I mean. I'm what you'd call an international jet-setter,' I bragged.

'Oh my God, where have you been to then, in your sleep?'

'Greece, Spain and last night I went to Italy. I had New Year's Eve in Florence, it was fabulous.'

Josie pushed me so hard I nearly fell off my chair. 'You lucky bitch. You're seeing the world for the cost of a meal.'

'I know, it's weird. Actually, it's freaking me out. And I feel jet-lagged.'

'Don't complain. Hell, I want to go to Florence. How was it?'

'Amazing. I rode a moped with a local named Lee-Luigi, he was hot as.'

'That's a weird name. Is it Italian?'

'Well, it's what I called him; he looked like a Lee-Luigi.'

Josie just screwed her face up. 'And in Greece where did you go?'

'A gorgeous little village called Delphi.'

'I know it,' she said excitedly. 'They grow olives.'

'That's right,' I said. I was so engrossed in my own story that I didn't even ask how she knew of Delphi. I didn't know of it before I visited.

'So you had a good time? Met people?'

'Yes, yes, yes, I had a ball, each time. And the men are amazing when you're astral travelling, and it certainly beats backpacking.'

'You could write the astral travellers' guide to Italy. Or rather, *Italy on Eight Hours' Sleep*.'

'Don't be ridiculous. I'm not a travel writer. I'm not even a traveller really, and it's all just accidental.'

The bill arrived, and I realised I didn't have any cash.

'Can you take care of it, Josie, and I'll fix you up when we get to an ATM?' We had become good friends and little things like money didn't seem to get in the way.

'Sure thing, but if that little hottie Antonia comes to pick up the bill I'm going to offer to pay with the hairy chequebook.'

'The hairy what?'

She looked down to her lap.

'You are disgusting.' I threw my serviette at her.

'Don't blame me, I heard it from Alice, and she heard it from guess who – Aunty Ivy. It's an old saying.'

'Well, put your chequebook away, I've got a credit card if you haven't got cash.'

fifteen

Happy Easter

'Happy Easter!' We all clinked glasses. It was hard to believe that three months had passed since we'd seen each other. It was like a lifetime, so it was great to be back in Sydney with the girls at Sauce, sitting in our favourite spot in the corner.

'Hello ladies, you make this little love corner look lovely,' Andy said in his usual cheeky form, handing us our menus and walking off.

'So what's new?' I asked.

Alice and Dannie looked at Liza, who had dropped all the weight she'd put on at the end of last year.

'Tony and I broke up,' she said, and a dignified tear ran down her cheek. Dannie put her arm around her and Alice topped her glass up with wine as she began to sob.

'What? When? We spoke only three days ago! Why?' I was in shock.

'It happened last week but I couldn't tell you over the phone and I made the girls vow not to say anything.'

'Well, that's the only bloody secret *you've* ever kept,' I said accusingly to Dannie and Alice. I felt annoyed that I'd been kept out of the loop, but I knew the moment wasn't about me, so I tried to hide it.

'But Tony was Mr I-Can-Do-Everything. Wasn't he?'

'He was really Mr I-Can-Do-Everything-But-Won't,'

she sobbed. 'When we met he promised me he could cook and clean.'

'Yes, you told us he said he'd do it in the nude too.' We'd laughed when Liza told us that, but no-one laughed now.

'That's right, he did, but he never lifted a bloody finger to clean, naked or otherwise. In fact he never actually got completely naked, even for sex! And as for cooking, well spag bol was all he could manage. Spaghetti bloody bolognese. I'm Italian, for God's sake.' She sobbed some more while we three sat in silence, wondering what to say.

Andy appeared from nowhere and started rubbing her shoulders, and she seemed to appreciate the attention. 'There, there, you know I'm always good for a spoon, don't you, babe?' he said, and we all broke into laughter.

'What's so funny? I was serious,' Andy said, his hands still firmly on Liza's shoulders.

'Yes, we know, that's what's funny,' Alice said.

Liza gave us a weak smile. 'Every time we walked past a nice restaurant I'd say I'd like to go there, and he'd say "Done". But it never happened. When it was my birthday he just took me to Chinatown for yum cha.' And she cried harder.

'Ah yes, but did he moonwalk across the restaurant and then break into a hula?' Alice said. We all cringed. Alice had been out with some shockers before she met Gary. 'No? Then be thankful for a meal without a freak show is all I can say.' Dannie nodded in agreement.

Liza started to calm down, and Andy left to get us more wine. As soon as he'd gone, Alice dropped a bombshell.

'Gary and I are getting married.'

'What?' we all howled.

'When, how, WHY?' I asked. 'I mean why didn't you say something earlier?'

Alice gave Liza a quick glance.

'Oh God, don't let my misery get in the way of your happiness,' said Liza. 'You and Gary *should* get married; you're made for each other. What a story you'll be able to tell the grandkids about meeting over a garbage bin.' Liza was an amazing soul who always saw the best in every situation. But I was a little surprised she hadn't suggested doing a SWOT to confirm it was the right thing for Alice to do.

'Well, I guess that means a hens' night, doesn't it?' I said.

'Wait a minute while I refresh your memory, Alice. Let's see . . . ' Liza took a sip of her wine, blew her nose and took a deep breath. 'If I recall correctly, at the last hens' night we went to your exact words were along the lines of: *I'll probably have a girls' night in with pizza and good friends but if someone happened to order a stripper I wouldn't be offended.* Is that how you remember it?' Alice hung her head, giggling.

'Oh God, I did say that, didn't I? Shame!'

'What about a kitchen tea?' Dannie said.

'Again, not the kind of cultural activity Alice has been too keen to engage in in the past, is it my friend?' Liza was bouncing back well, but Alice looked almost disappointed at the thought of not having a hens' night or kitchen tea, although she had previously been appalled by both traditions. We all knew that women change as soon as they get engaged, wanting parties and gifts and girly things. Everyone says they won't, but they do.

'Oh, I know I gave those brides-to-be a hard time, but it's different when it's your own.' I couldn't help but roll my eyes. Thankfully, no-one saw me.

'But I don't need a kitchen tea, Gary and I have filled my place completely with his crap and mine combined, and we have everything we need. Trouble is I like nice clean white everything, and he keeps collecting bits and pieces from antique shops. He likes the eclectic look.'

'Or perhaps he just can't let go of his work, Alice,' I laughed.

'Yeah, I know. He comes home with rubbish all the time. Don't laugh about it. It's the one thing we argue about. He's a waste-not-want-not kind of guy.'

Dannie looked a bit disappointed too. 'So no hens' night? Then what? You realise I only get to go out when you guys have some romantic or career event for me to celebrate.'

'I thought I'd like to go away for my hens' whatever. Maybe the Gold Coast, cos it's cheap and we can do it in a weekend.'

'A hens' weekend, I like it.' I lifted my glass in a toast.

'And so do I. I like it a lot!' You could see Dannie's eyes bulge at the thought of being without George and the kids for the weekend. I couldn't blame her.

'Sounds good to me. When were you thinking of going? Would be a good escape out of the winter weather, wouldn't it?' Liza added, touching her glass to ours.

'The Melbourne winter, eh Peta?' Alice couldn't help but have a dig.

'Well yes, but Sydney has winter too, you know.' I always took the bait.

'I was thinking warmth, a pool, some cocktails, some laughs. I certainly miss our sessions, Peta, and a whole weekend should carry us over for a few months, don't you reckon?' Alice had obviously put some thought into her 'hens' whatever'.

We all got our BlackBerries out, and started to check our available dates.

'Why do you need a BlackBerry, Dannie?' I sounded like a bitch but I was curious.

'I've got the dates of school carnivals, canteen roster, ballet classes, swimming lessons, when George is away, dentist appointments, parent–teacher night, school assemblies and things like that. I do have a busy schedule, planning the lives of four people, you know. Three of them are children, and yes, I include George in that. Of course, I also put in when I'm ovulating so George and I can have sex.' They were still 'kind of' trying to have a baby.

'Can't you have sex on other nights?' Not having much sex myself I was obsessed with other people's sex lives.

'Of course, but we *have* to have sex on those dates if we want to fall pregnant.'

'Oh what a drag, *having* to have sex,' I said.

'Speaking of which, how's that going? Have you been completely faithful in Melbourne?' Dannie asked.

'Yeah, how's the drought?' Alice added.

'Hey, a drought sounds involuntary, something that's been inflicted on me and causing concern and worry and cashflow problems. None of which is true of my situation.'

'Yeah, yeah, just answer the question,' Liza pressed.

I sipped from my glass and smiled cheekily.

Liza's eyes lit up. 'Do tell.' She was chirpy at the thought of some juicy gossip.

'No, don't tell,' said Alice. 'I'm not going to be an accessory to your infidelity, not when I've got James calling me about you. If you've cheated then keep it to yourself.'

'Sorry, but I'm having the best sex I've ever had. And I don't have to say thank you, and I never get lockjaw.'

Alice rolled her eyes. 'In your dreams, Peta!'

The restaurant had all but emptied out so Andy sat and joined us. We were having too much fun to kick out or leave alone.

'Did you buy that gorgeous dress you're wearing down in Melbourne?' Andy asked, checking out my cleavage.

'Ah, well, this I actually bought in Paddington.' Liza and Dannie high fived each other and Alice fell off her seat laughing. Andy picked her up.

'Can't you tell?' I said, trying to remember what Sylvia had told me. 'Sydney fashion's so . . . coastal.'

'We're at dinner, not the beach.' Dannie was laughing through her words.

'I'm just saying that Sydney's fashion has a more coastal *influence*, while Melbourne's is more . . . diverse.'

'There's nothing coastal about that dress, it's by the House of Wong, and I don't think I've ever heard her work defined as "coastal". They're feeding you crap down there,

Peta,' Liza said. The girls were just having fun with me and I was taking it way too seriously.

'Okay spoon-man, I think it's time for us to go. Pass the bill this way, please?' I reached to grab it before the other girls did.

'Don't be ridiculous, Peta, you can't afford it.' I couldn't really, but I wanted to do it. I missed the girls and there was a little room left on the credit card.

'I might just pay with the hairy chequebook!' I said, then burst into laughter. It wasn't how I'd intended to deliver the line, but I couldn't do it with a straight face.

'Woo-hoo!' Andy punched the air. 'I knew that cocktail would do the trick.' He winked at me.

'You're going to pay with *what*?' Liza asked.

'The hairy chequebook,' said Alice. 'It means, you know . . .' and she looked towards her lap.

'That's hilarious, I love it. I am so going to use that.' Liza was impressed with the new phrase.

'Not at the ALS, I hope,' I said.

'Oh they'd love it there, I'm sure.' Alice rolled her eyes.

'Yeah, well I got it from your cousin Josie, but I know you won't tell your mum right, cos apparently that's where it originated!'

Just then James came into Sauce to get me and didn't look too pleased that I was tipsy and that Andy was sitting with us. He was quiet all the way back to his place, while I just rambled about Liza and Tony splitting up and Alice and Gary getting married and all the new places I'd been to in Melbourne.

'What's wrong?' I asked as we got to the door of his apartment.

'Nothing.'

'Come on, my big burly man, tell your princess what's up.'

'You told me it was just the girls going, and I'm happy for you to catch up with your friends. I like Dannie and Liza and you know I adore Alice. But it seems like it's always you and then that fella as well. I could've come earlier and sat and talked too. But you didn't ask me to.'

'Are you being jelly-bean James again?' I cuddled into him as we climbed into bed. I wasn't even really thinking about what he was saying. I was tired, but horny too.

'Don't make light of it, Peta. You're living in another state. When you're in town I don't mind you catching up with other people, but not other gorgeous guys.'

I crawled on top of him. 'Oh, come on, now you're exaggerating,' I said, peppering butterfly kisses on his forehead and cheeks. 'I wasn't catching up with Andy. He owns the restaurant. We spent quite a bit of money there tonight, and have always done. It's called *hospitality*. He's a good restaurateur, that's all.' And I kissed his mouth softly.

'If you say so,' he said, not sounding completely convinced.

The 'Andy issue' was resolved as all petty issues between lovers should be – with a night of sex.

sixteen

Poetic policing

I walked out of my office into the main area of our section. Even though there were strong fluorescent lights, the space remained gloomy as rain fell hard on the windows of the Rialto building. When I reached Sylvia's work station I stopped. 'Sylvia, what's this poetry reading you've put in my schedule?'

'You need to be up on all the art forms and Indigenous artists, right? Well, there's a reading every night in Melbourne. You at least need to be going to the ones with Blackfellas. Samuel Wagan Watson is in town from Bris-Vegas, so I put it in your diary. There'll be some poetry slammers there too, and some spoken worders. It'll be cool.'

'It will be much cooler if I know what a poetry slammer actually is.' I felt like I was truly out of my depth at times. It seemed I needed a whole new vocab for this job.

'A poetry slammer is just someone who participates in a poetry slam.' Sylvia thought she was making sense until I frowned at her. 'And a poetry slam is a competition where poets read or recite their work and are judged by members of the audience and given a score. It's a lot of fun, you'll love it.'

'I'm sure I will, but to help me love it as much as I can, could you please email me some dot points on the poet and any other Blackfellas on the program before we leave? I assume you're coming?'

'Of course, I'm reading too. It's about sense of place.'

I walked off, pleased that Sylvia was so on the ball. But who was this poet Samuel with the double-barrel name? At least I was up to date with music, listening to Koori Radio, and I'd been heading to events at the Koorie Heritage Trust Cultural Centre for visual arts, but there really wasn't anything too coordinated for literature, or new media for that matter. I'd have to get Sylvia to do me a program for every art form, and be sure that I attended all the openings and launches we were invited to. I had a meeting with the Australia Council in August and I wanted to be prepared.

I was surprised by the number of people in the pub for the reading. I wasn't sure if they were Melbourne poets or poets from elsewhere or just Melbourne locals, because they were all in black. They could easily have been musicians too, I supposed.

'This is Samuel.' Sylvia introduced me. They seemed to know each other quite well.

'Oh hi, you're Big Sam's son?'

'Yeah, Dad wanted to be here but he's doing community stuff back in Brissy.'

I was pleased that Sylvia had written me enough background information to know that there was a Samuel and a Sam Senior, otherwise referred to as 'Big Sam'.

The reading started and I sat at a small table with Sylvia and some of her mates, near a group of men who didn't appear to be remotely interested in poetry. They looked like it might be their local hotel.

When Sylvia read she spoke about the polluted winds of change. She seemed to have a big following. As one of the featured poets, Samuel read last. His material was about the urban environment around Brisbane's West End, and he ended with an insightful poem, a 'recipe' for Brisbane. I loved it. Whitefellas often expect Aboriginal writers to pen stories about place in a more traditional sense, even though many of us live in urban environments and have connections to country in those places as well. As the applause died away, I went to the bar to get drinks.

'Hi,' one of the local-looking guys said as he stood at the bar.

'Hi,' I said, and went back to listening to another all-dressed-in-black poet taking part in the open-mike section. I felt the guy staring at me, though, so I turned in his direction.

'I'm hot, you're hot, let's make fire . . .' he said with a wink.

'I'm hot, you're not, and you make me tired.'

'You're good. Are you a poet too?' He turned to face me front on.

'That's not poetry – that was a short response to a really bad pick-up line.'

'Oooh, you're fiery, I like that.' His blue eyes twinkled at me. I had to admit, he was cute.

'Are you enjoying the readings?' I asked.

'Oh, I'm not a big reader.'

'No, you're meant to be *listening* here, not *reading* – the writers do that.'

He laughed and touched my arm.

'Funny girl, can I buy you a drink?' He was seriously flirting with me, and I had to put an end to it.

'Thanks, but I don't take drinks from strangers – you know with all that spiking stuff going on.'

'Oh sweetie, no trouble there, I'm a cop,' he said, with his chest puffed out, proud as punch.

'Hah! Then you may as well give up right now. This,' and I pointed back from him to me, 'would never work at all.' I walked away. Even if I weren't with James, there was no point in pursuing anything of any kind with a copper. I sat back down at the table as a slammer took the microphone.

The cop came over to my table and planted himself next to me. I wondered if he had a gun strapped to his ankle, like in the old TV shows.

'What are you doing?' I asked, a little amused by his thick skin and determination.

'You must be an adverb, because you sure do modify me.'

'You're an idiot!' I laughed. 'Any more cheesy lines up your sleeve?'

'Oh, plenty . . .' and he looked up his sleeve. 'Is there a name behind that smile?'

Sure enough, he made me smile. I couldn't help myself.

'Mike,' he said extending his hand.

'Peta,' I said shaking it.

'Peta, I do believe you are beautiful.'

'Mike, I do believe you are right.'

'Okay, did someone turn on a fan, or is that you blowing me away?'

'That's enough now. Stop it, I want to listen to the poets.'

'Of course. You listen to the very exciting, engaging, not very good-looking poets, all in black.'

'Look, I mightn't be a huge fan of poetry either, but I'm less of a fan of the boys in blue,' I said.

'Well, I don't know why you feel that way, but I think we should have lunch or something to at least discuss your feelings.'

'I don't eat lunch.'

'Really?'

'Let me rephrase that. I don't eat lunch with cops. Blackfellas don't eat lunch with cops.'

'So, do you like stuffed animals then?'

'Well, yes.'

'Great, cos I just ate.'

'Okay, so I don't like stuffed animals then.'

'What about dinner, if you don't eat lunch?'

'Don't you get it? A Blackfella dating a cop is like a Jew dating a Nazi. It just can't happen.'

'I don't understand the problem.'

'And that's the problem. Excuse me, I need to speak to my friend.' And I walked towards Sylvia, who was bringing one of the poets over to me.

While we were chatting, I noticed Mike leave and momentarily wondered which venue he was going to next, but we'd decided to eat at the pub, purely for convenience sake. To my disappointment there was an unusual number of English-inspired dishes – like bangers and mash, ploughman's lunch and shepherd's pie. I ordered the shepherd's pie and wondered if Joe could do it as a fusion dish sometime using roo mince instead of beef.

When I got home Shelley was asleep on the lounge. I left her there and went to get some water from the fridge. There was a postcard from her parents, who were opal mining in Lightning Ridge. I smiled when I read it because they asked about me too – Shelley must have told them about me. It seemed she had a much better relationship with her folks than I had ever had with mine.

I went back into the lounge room, shook Shelley awake and waited to make sure she got off the sofa, because I knew she'd sleep there all night if left be. I dragged my weary feet into my room, tore my clothes off and collapsed on the bed.

I closed my eyes and I immediately find myself on a British Airways flight landing at Heathrow and I'm amazed at the size of the airport. As an astral traveller I don't have to wait at customs or at the baggage carousel and in no time I'm queuing outside Madame Tussauds.

'I hate queuing,' I say to no-one in particular, and an Australian tourist with a harsh Aussie twang says, 'Me too, love, but you know us, we're so easygoing and laid-back, no worries, eh?' I look at her 'I've climbed Ayers Rock' T-shirt and attempt to fly away, but I don't know how to. I haven't been in control of it before. Sometimes I'm on a plane, for long-haul flights, and sometimes I'm on a magic carpet, except it's the magic Aboriginal flag.

I'm being hurried into the museum as if they know I don't have much time and I'm drawn to a waxed figure of

Leonardo DiCaprio and I ask a stranger, 'Can you please take my photo with him? I'm a huge fan.'

The Australians I have been desperately trying to avoid are posing next to Kylie and for some reason Charles and Camilla, but I can't understand why – after all, we should be a republic already, don't they know that?

Next thing I know I'm kneeling in St Paul's. I've never been in a Church of England church before, only Catholic churches with Alice and Aunt Ivy, and I'm imagining Prince Charles and Princess Diana's wedding and that meringue dress she wore. I could never understand why she married him. She was so gorgeous, he was so not gorgeous. Kneeling now I feel compelled to pray for her spirit and memory. And I say a prayer for James because I think I should, and I pray to St Christopher the patron saint of travellers, just like Aunt Ivy said she'd pray for me when I moved to Melbourne, to make sure I got home safely.

I'm tired of flying, but I'm not sure why – I'm not actually doing anything physical to make it happen. I hail a black cab anyway and it's quite roomy, but expensive, and I wonder how I'm going to pay for it.

I don't really know where it is I want to go, but the driver takes me to Earl's Court, saying, 'You're Australian, aren't you? So this is where you probably want to be.' He goes on, as much to himself as to me, 'I can't understand why they'd travel across the world to hang out with other Aussies.'

'I agree totally – please keep driving,' and I'm not even concerned about the meter because I'm figuring whatever budget paid for my airfare will pay for ground transport also. But then he's gone, and so is the cab. I'm just floating, saying, *Don't stop, don't stop*, to whatever is keeping me in the air, in the atmosphere, in the universe, because I'm still not sure how all this works.

'STOP!' I shout as I see the Victoria Palace Theatre and the *Buddy Holly Spectacular Show*. I have to go. I'm wearing black-rimmed Buddy Holly glasses and I look hot! In the foyer I see James and I wave, surprised, because we've never had the same taste in music, and then I see Mike the copper and wonder if he's stalking me, and Lee from the fundraiser, too, and they're all wearing the same glasses and they walk in with me and we celebrate the 1500th performance together and then I have sex with one of them to the tune of 'That'll Be the Day'. I'm not sure which one it is because I don't open my eyes, but I hope it's James so there's no jealous rage to deal with. Neither of us takes our glasses off the whole time and the frames keep knocking against each other. Then I have a little baby boy and he comes out of the birth canal wearing the same glasses and it's all just too ridiculous and I desperately need to escape the absurdity and as Don McLean's 'American Pie' serenades me, I find myself entering a pub called Ye Olde Something-Or-Other and an arm reaches out to stop me as I work my way through the crowd. The arm belongs to a tall guy with sandy hair. He's cute, but the music is so loud it's too noisy to talk, and his cockney colonisers' accent is already grating on my ears, so I think it's a good idea if we just dance and while we're moving to music I've never heard before I'm thinking why do people even try making small talk with virtual strangers when trying to dance at the same time. So we don't talk, we just dance, and I sing along to the music, making up the words to the songs. Back at the bar, he tells me his name is Jason and he's clearly interested as he pushes the hair from my face and puts his arm around my waist, claiming me, as some young rugby players enter the bar.

'Last drinks,' a burly barman shouts to signal the end of the night. The music stops but my ears continue to ring.

'How long are you here for?' Jason asks.

'Not sure, playing it by ear.' I'm lying, I have no idea how many days or weeks my night's sleep could translate into.

'Wanna catch up again before you leave?'

'Sure.'

'Can I have your number?' He's never going to be able to call me, of course, because it's a dream, but I reach into my bag anyway and grab a business card. He holds it up and reads it aloud: 'Peta Tully, National Aboriginal Policy Manager, DOMSARIA' and he looks at me, then looks at the card, then looks at me again, obviously confused, and says out loud, 'Are you an Aborigine?' As if I'm a leper or some other highly contagious patient with a debilitating disease. I'm shocked and pissed off. One minute I'm gorgeous and worthy of dining with, and let's face it, he's a bloke, so I'm assuming I was shaggable as well. The next minute, I'm a thing, an 'Aborigine', like I'm illegal or even an alien being. I snatch the card from his hand.

'You won't need that now, will you?'

Wake up, wake up, I tell myself, but no, I'm not in my cosy bed in sheltered St Kilda, I'm still in Ye Olde Racist Arsehole Pub somewhere in London. I try to get away from him but the bar is cramped with 'last drinks' customers ordering three pints and four tequila sunrises, like I'm back in the eighties at a local RSL at home.

'You do realise that if it weren't for *my* people, *your* people would still be in shackles.'

'If it weren't for *your* people, *my* people would never have been in shackles in the first place,' I correct him. 'Do you think we shackled ourselves and then your mob came and let us out? Can you see how illogical that is?'

He looks at me like I'm some freak. I walk off, my card in hand, and my dream a nightmare. How could one word on a piece of cardboard make someone change their mind so quickly about another human being?

I leave the pub and walk into the cold English air and as it hits my face I wake up, agitated.

'It happened again last night.'

'What did?' Josie asked. She sucked hard on the frozen fruit at the bottom of her smoothie as we walked along Acland Street.

'I astral travelled.'

'No way. Where to this time, jetsetter?' Josie was ready for another sexy story, but I didn't tell her about the Buddy Holly stuff, just skipped straight to the exchange with Jason.

'I went to London, saw a show, took a black cab, had my photo taken with Leonardo DiCaprio at Madame Tussauds and then got in a blue with a racist arsehole in a tragic English pub where the barmen were fat and the music was too loud.

I hate the English and I don't want to *ever* go back there, let me tell you.' I was almost shaking as I remembered it.

'It was a *dream*, Peta, it doesn't mean that's what all the English are like. Sometimes you can be slightly irrational.'

'Is that right?'

'Yes, that's right. Have you told this to Alice or any of your other friends back in Sydney?'

'No, they've got plenty going on up there. They don't need to know absolutely *everything* about my life here.' Seeing as Liza and Alice were walking together and I assumed they were catching up without me, I felt that it was okay if there were some elements of my new life that I just kept here in Melbourne. I'd thought it was something that Josie and I could share, until she decided I was irrational. Maybe I was.

'So should we go to the Elephant and Castle for lunch, then?' Josie couldn't help stirring me. There was nothing more English than the Elephant and Castle chain of pubs in Victoria.

seventeen
The stalker cop

'Greetings and salivations,' the voice said down the mobile line.

'Who is this?' I had no idea who I was talking to as I walked along Collins Street towards the office.

'It's Mike, we met at the very exciting poetry reading a few weeks back. I've moved you up to the top of my "to do" list.'

I thought back to Samuel's words about dreamtime tabernacles and whitegoods sales, and then it registered: it was the cop.

'Well, take me off your "to do" list. And how did you get my number? You must have tracked me down illegally – that'd be right, different rules for you fellas, eh? You can do whatever you want. Well, I don't have warrants or a record, and I didn't even give you my last name, so you must have done something really underhanded to find me.'

'Oh yes, very illegal and underhanded. I'm from the FBI – the Fine Body Investigators,' he mocked.

'You're all so untouchable, aren't you? Why don't you go and punch a protester, or better still maybe try and lock up a criminal for a change?'

'Ooh, you're a fiery one, aren't you? I like it, it's sexy.'

'I'm hanging up. You have no right to be calling me. And how *did* you get my number? Tell me, or I'll . . .'

I was sounding slightly irrational, and I knew it. He was probably harmless. It was just a phone call, after all, and his lines were quite funny.

'Stop stressing. I saw Sylvia,' he said, suddenly serious.

'It's Sylv-eye-a,' I corrected him.

'Of course, Sylv-eye-a.' He pronounced it slowly, as everyone did when first saying it. 'At the reading last night. She told me where she worked and that you worked together. So I rang the switchboard, they put me through to your voicemail and your mobile number is on there. There is absolutely nothing illegal or improper about that process at all, is there? You've even got me doubting myself now, and that doesn't usually happen. I called you is all. It's not like I'm following you – but I do think you should be arrested.'

'What for?' I was totally confused.

'It's gotta be illegal to look as good as you do.'

'Where are you?' I started to look around me. 'You're a bit stalker-like, don't you think?'

'Stalker-like? Hell no. I just think it's the normal behaviour of a man who wants to take a very difficult woman out to dinner.'

'So a woman who's not interested in eating with you is considered difficult, is she?'

'A woman who constantly accuses someone of wrong-doing and claims she doesn't eat lunch because she's a bit, let's say, frightened of new friends, is pretty much being difficult.' I laughed – he was probably right.

'Ahah! I made you laugh! That's a good start,' he said, so I stopped laughing. I almost stopped breathing completely. There was silence.

'Are you there?' he asked.

'I'm here.'

'So, can we have dinner? Come on, be unique and different and just say yes.'

'Look, I'm just about at the office and I've got work to do. I'll think about it and let you know. I've got your number on my phone. I'll call you.'

'Don't call me too soon though, cos that'll mean you're interested in me. I know how you women work. Transparent as anything.'

'Goodbye.' I hung up with a smile that spanned my entire face and found I had an odd spring in my step.

'Do you think I could be friends with a cop?' I asked Shelley as she made a stir-fry for dinner.

'Do you want to be friends with a cop?'

I looked at the postcard her parents had sent from the Big Banana and frowned, wondering why Australians were obsessed by our 'big foods'. So far her mum and dad had been to the Big Avocado, the Big Prawn and the Big Oyster.

'Well, he seems nice and genuine. And he's funny. He comes out with these weird one-liners all the time. Really cheesy pick-up lines.' I grabbed a piece of broccoli out of the wok.

Shelley slapped my hand. 'Get out of it! Does the "cop" have an actual name? You think he's referring to you as "the public servant"?'

'Oh all right, let's give him an identity then. Constable Care, Mike the cop . . . whatever. He comes out with really bad pick-up lines. He's . . . kinda quirky.'

'You like him. I just saw a smile. You like Mike-pick-up-line cop.'

'I don't *like* him. I just think he's quirky. A quirky *cop*. Anyway, I can't like him, even if I wanted to. I'm in love with James, remember?'

'James, of course. Oh, there's a message on the machine from him. But check after, I want company while I cook. Which *you're* supposed to be doing, seeing as I unhooked you, remember?' and she grimaced at the memory. 'Now back to Constable Care . . . where was I? Right, cops are human too, you know.'

'You think so?'

'Yes, and sometimes my dear cultural affairs friend, you are not all that broadminded. Being friends with a cop might be good for you. You might actually learn something.' And Shelley raised her eyebrows, as if to say, *I'm trying to say this as gently as I can, but you're being a coppist!*

Hi, u free 2 skype? Px

Loggin on now, x Alice

I logged onto the computer in the living room and fixed my hair as I started to dial Alice's address. Skype was fantastic in that it was free and you could see the person at the other end, but it also meant you couldn't really talk in your underwear, like you could do on the phone. I tried to look as respectable as possible and only had the table lamp on so it wasn't too bright. I liked talking to Alice on Skype because she had a laptop from school and would move around her flat, and sometimes I could see the ocean behind her. It was almost like sitting in her flat with her. Gary the Garbo had Alice on a bit of a budget since they got engaged, and although she didn't admit it, she was doing it tough, not being able to do all the girly things, like going to the beautician regularly. The sacrifices women made for love sometimes made me wonder. Or maybe when you were truly in love they didn't feel like sacrifices?

'So, I met this, um, rather *interesting* cop at a poetry reading a few weeks back and he's asked me out for dinner.'

'I don't think it's a very good idea,' said Alice. 'I mean, if he's a cop. And what about James? Aren't you supposed to be celibate?'

I knew she wouldn't approve. 'Alice, it's not a date. It's just as friends.'

'Could you really be friends with a cop?'

'I don't know. He's funny. I kind of like him.'

'No way, Peta. Jews, Nazis, Blacks, cops. Get it?' Alice was using the same argument I'd used with Mike.

'You think too much, Alice. Reality is I have to eat, so I might as well eat with him.'

'Yes, but you'll have to talk too – can't just sit there and shovel food in your mouth and say nothing. It's the talking that's going to be the problem.'

'I don't have to talk politics.'

'Well, it's hard not to talk politics when you're Black and you work in policy.'

'Can't I just go, eat some food, and talk about the weather or Melbourne or poetry?'

'Poetry? Fuck, well that'll kill the night, won't it?' And she laughed.

'Yes, true, so I'll talk football or something, I don't know.'

'The problem will be the whole Black deaths in custody thing. You know that, don't you?'

I took a sip of the Pimm's that Shelley had brought in for me after dinner and adjusted the computer screen. Alice took a sip of tea. She didn't drink near as much gin'n'tonic since moving in with Gary.

'Why would I be talking about that at dinner?'

'Well, what's the point in having dinner or being friends if you can't talk about the stuff that's important to you? No point six weeks or months down the track realising that very significant aspects of the way you view society and the world are diametrically opposed, now is there?'

'Six weeks? Six months? I'm just having dinner with him, for God's sake.'

'Firstly, no guy *just* wants to have dinner, that's crap. It's always about sex, some just take a longer, less direct route, but in the end they're all playing the same game, and the ones who say they aren't are either lying to you and themselves or they're gay. In Melbourne, they're just lying.'

'I'll just have lunch, maybe. It can be my little bit for reconciliation. I'll be doing it to bridge the gap between our community and theirs.'

'You're mad. I've gotta go, I'll Skype you later in the week.'

'Okay, next time put some lippy on and grab a glass of wine and we can pretend we're out and about.'

'Excellent idea, see ya.'

eighteen
No pig jokes, no pick-up lines

After a restless night's sleep I decided that I'd call Mike. I'd suggest dinner, not lunch, so I could have a wine and relax properly and perhaps not be so uptight. When he answered the phone I simply said, 'It's Peta Tully.'

'My Koori rose, how are you?' He had a deep but playful voice.

'What? Where did you get that phrase?' I was a little surprised.

'You think you guys are the only ones to listen to Koori Radio here in Melbourne? I have it on in the wagon sometimes.'

'Whatever. I'm just ringing to say I'll have dinner with you this weekend.'

'Oh, no can do. Sorry, but I'm working nights this weekend, six pm till six am.'

'You're the one who suggested dinner, but now you can't go.' It was already too hard.

'I can go, just not this weekend. I'm off next weekend.'

I hesitated.

'What about Friday this week?' he said, but before I could respond he added, 'Shit, no, sorry – I just realised I can't do Friday. It's Anzac Day, I have to be out and about, it's a uniform thing.'

'So you'd rather drink with old men than a gorgeous young woman?'

'Peta, let me assure you that you'd be hard-pressed to find *any* guy who would choose a woman, as gorgeous as you are, over two-up on Anzac Day. Sorry, but it's the truth.'

'Actually, I did some research last year and you'd be surprised to know that when I polled one hundred men about whether they'd prefer to go to the pub and play two-up or make love to a gorgeous woman on Anzac Day—'

'But—'

'Sshhh, you know what I found?'

'But—'

'Don't interrupt; it was a rhetorical question – it doesn't require an answer from you.'

'I know what a rhetorical question is, Peta.' He laughed, which only annoyed me further.

I continued, 'My survey found that seventy-three men chose two-up, twenty-five chose the woman, and two were undecided. Eight proposed marriage, five asked me out for dinner, and three had to be asked to leave the bar because they tried to touch me. So, not *all* men, Mr Mike-the-stalker cop, will choose two-up.'

'Can I say something now, Miss Tully? Firstly, you didn't offer me a choice between two-up and making love, you said lunch or dinner. Of course I would have chosen that option had it been the question posed.'

'Well my friend, that's an option you're never going to be given.'

'Ah, but you just called me your friend, so that's a start. I'm going to lock in lunch for this Sunday before you change your mind.'

'But won't you be too tired after night shift?'

'Oh no, it'll be worth it. It's ladies' choice, so just let me know where you want to go the day before and I'll organise it.'

I was proud that I had agreed to eat with a policeman. It was the grown-up thing to do. Shelley was right, I might just learn something.

We met at what was commonly referred to as Melbourne's 'most famous restaurant on the beach', the Stokehouse. It was bustling with families and birthdays and young people in groups and the odd couple peppered throughout. It was unusually warm for April (at least that's what everyone told me) and I had a sleeveless dress with enough cleavage to be sexy but not saucy, and pair of brown boots. The space was large, open, with a wood-fired oven, and Mike was seated at a table in the middle of the room between the bar and kitchen. It was very beach-shack-meets-a-Californian-bungalow, or as they said in Melbourne a 'Cal Bung'. I studied the casualness of moneyed Melbourne and wondered what the Sydney equivalent might be. Ravesi's at Bondi perhaps? Nick's on the promenade at Cockle Bay? No, they were both flashier than the Stokehouse. It was more like the Clovelly Hotel. The full glass frontage could not hide the fact that St Kilda beach was dirty, and the wind was up so there was lots of white wash swirling around.

The wait staff were young and funky in jeans and white shirts. I stood at the bar just taking it in before Constable

Care spotted me and I walked over. He put one hand in the small of my back and kissed me on the mouth. Whoa, I thought, you don't lip kiss someone you've just met. I pulled back with a jerk, which he apparently didn't notice or chose to ignore.

'Damn girl, you've got more curves than a racetrack.'

'Okay, stop with the lines, please.'

'Sure, but you do look beautiful.' He seemed sincere.

'You look all right, too, I suppose,' I said with a smile. 'What else looks good, I mean besides both of us?' And I opened the menu as soon as I sat down.

'Well, I can tell you everything on the menu, I've been here a while.'

'Am I late? I thought we agreed on noon.'

'No, you're on time, I just got here early, to get the table and be waiting.' God, he was stalker material. 'I think the suckling pig looks good.'

'What, a whole pig?'

'No, it's just cut from a suckling pig.'

'So can pigs eat pig?' And as soon as I said it I knew I'd gone too far.

'Okay, are you done? Any more pork jokes you want to get off your very beautiful chest?'

'Okay, truce – no pig jokes, no pick-up lines.'

'Truce. But can I flirt with you?' He just never stopped; he was the perpetual comedian.

Flirting was technically acceptable, wasn't it? I could look but not touch, read the menu but not order, wasn't that right? I'd have to tell him I had a boyfriend sooner or later, but I didn't need to do it right away. It might look weird – and he might want to just be friends anyway, and I'd look like a right knob *assuming*, the way Alice did, that all men just wanted to have sex.

The waiter came and took our drink orders so the moment had passed anyway.

'Pimm's and lemonade, please.' I'd been terribly influenced by Shelley.

'Coopers, thanks mate.'

Just relax and be normal, I told myself. I'd always been the easygoing, happy-go-lucky girl in our group and now I was acting like a nervous schoolgirl, freaking out, thinking too much. Maybe Melbourne wasn't that good for my state of mind after all.

I decided I'd just jump straight in.

'So, give me your details, then. Siblings, birth date . . .'

'I'm twenty-nine and I have two brothers – PJ and Shaun – and two sisters – Lily and Patricia. We're a close family, so I'm lucky. With my schedule though, I hardly get to see them, even though I'm big on family and want to have one of my own someday. Yeah, life in the force means you need stability at home,' he said, as if he'd given it a lot of thought.

'The hours must make it hard to meet people, though?'

'Hey, I met you.'

'Yeah, that was just lucky!' I tried to brush off the compliment. I'd have to tell him about James soon, but I didn't know how to introduce the subject.

'To be truthful, the hours do play havoc with your social life. Sometimes it means having to hang out with cops all the time, because they're on the same roster and so on. Our happy hour might be seven in the morning, because we finish at six am. It's the kind of lifestyle that's not easy for most people to cope with.'

'I know what you mean. I travel a lot for my work, and it's hard to find someone with a compatible lifestyle. So you end up sometimes having to trade off one for the other. Most guys I've met can't cope with a career woman either. They seem to want attention exactly when they want it, and not just after the report has been finished or the field trip is complete. It's such a juggling act. I want to be able to manage both somehow, to have a balanced lifestyle.'

'And you should have it.'

'What about you? Do you have to date cops to have that compatible lifestyle?'

'Oh no, never date cops; don't dip the pen and all that stuff. Anyway, I do have a lot of other interests that make me attractive to all kinds of women, you know!'

'Really?' I laughed at his cheeky confidence. 'And what would they be?'

'I actually like hanging out in museums and galleries. I find them really soothing after long shifts on the beat. And don't laugh, but I love chick-flicks. That's what comes from having two dominating sisters I really like hanging out with. See, it's not all about cops and robbers.'

I could understand that; it was like people thought Blackfellas only ever hung out with Blackfellas and only talked about land rights and 'our' issues. I had friends from all walks of life and occupations. Shelley the stockbroker and Sylvia the eco-poet my two latest additions. My boyfriend was an architect and now I had the unlikely copper friend Mike.

When we were finished our meal, Mike signalled for the bill. He was turning his BlackBerry back on when I noticed a blue rubber band on his wrist, one of those charity bands that every second person wore to show their support for a particular cause: breast cancer, homeless youth, World Environment Day and so on.

'What's that for?' I asked.

'Oh, this.' He moved it around his wrist nervously. 'You probably won't like it.'

What wouldn't I like about a charity band? How could I possibly have a problem with MS or the guide dogs?

'It's in support of John Bush. Do you know who he is?' I nearly fell off my chair.

'Of course I know who he is! He's the policeman who killed a Black man up on Possession Island. How can you possibly support him?'

'I'm supporting due process.'

'Due process? What due process?' I was furious. 'The Queensland Director of Public Prosecutions was given a coroner's report that clearly showed that a Black man died at the hands of a white policeman, but she refused to charge him, and only after national outrage was there a special inquiry that led to charges being laid. Never at any time was the DPP's job under threat, though.' I took a breath. 'But at the other end of the spectrum, we had a Black man who spat at a cop on Redfern station – spat, not maimed, or stabbed or killed, just spat at a cop – and he was arrested immediately. When *he* went to court and the magistrate let him off, the bloody New South Wales Police Minister stepped in and the magistrate's job was under review immediately. So we have a policing and legal system that says it's worse for a Black man to spit at a white cop than it is for a white cop to *kill* a Black man and that's your fucken *process*.'

Mike just sat there for a moment, and then stood up, put his hand on my shoulder and said, 'You need to relax. I'll order us another round and we can talk about this.'

I was fuming. Relax? Relax? I didn't need to relax, I needed to be somewhere other than here, now, with him. I didn't know what to do, but relaxing wasn't on the top of my list of options. While he was at the bar I picked up my mobile and thought about calling Alice, but what would she say? *I told you so.*

Before I had a chance to punch in a number, Mike was back with a bottle of wine and the wrist band off. I didn't know where it was, but it wasn't in sight.

'I didn't mean to upset you. My intention today was to get to know you.'

'Do you want to be my friend?' I asked.

'Of course.' Of course he did, because he knew I knew my stuff and clearly I knew his policing stuff as well. I wasn't an idiot, and a smart man, even one who makes a poor judgement call in supporting John Bush, would want to see a smart, gorgeous woman again.

'Well, if you want to see me again, you have to read Simon Luckhurst's *Eddie's Country*. It will explain the history of relations between the cops and Kooris and then you'll understand why I'm so angry now. Can you do that?'

'I can do that.'

'You don't even know what it's about.'

'I don't care. You make me want to learn. If you think

it's an important book for me to read, then I'll read it.' He reached out and took my hand.

'I have a boyfriend,' I said. It was the right time to tell him.

'Really?'

'Are you surprised?'

'I'm surprised he's let you move down here all alone.'

'We can be friends, though. I mean, if you read—'

'I will. Friends is good.'

nineteen
Foot in mouth

The next day was so busy with the announcement of the cultural awards that I didn't have a moment to even consider my time with Mike the day before, which was probably a good thing – he made me feel uncomfortable anyway. There was no time for a debrief with Shelley, either, as her cousin Andrew was in town from Sydney for a week's work. She invited me to meet them both at a Japanese restaurant in the city one night, but as I walked down Collins Street right on seven pm, she called to say something had happened to the stock market. Not a crash, but not something I could understand either. I would have to entertain Andrew until she arrived. Shelley hadn't told me anything other than he was a podiatrist, and that he always had his head in a 'how to' book of some description. At the restaurant it was easy to find him: he was reading *How to Create Peace: Locally and Globally*.

As I walked towards him I scanned the room, looking at the tables lined up alongside the train of food making its way around the restaurant in a loop, as patrons pinched tiny plates and steaming baskets from it. It wasn't a chain-store variety sushi train: it was more up-market, full of businesspeople, some obviously talking work, others just unwinding; there was the odd couple, and one or two people sitting alone.

'Andrew?' I asked, and he stood, putting his book down and extending his other to shake.

'Hi,' he said and I sat.

'So, Shelley tells me you're a podiatrist.' I remembered what it was like to have James suck my toes – God, I missed that. And I missed sex.

'Yes, I've loved feet since I was a kid. You probably think that's weird.'

'Not at all, I can totally relate.' And then Andrew somehow morphed into James on the other side of the table, and I imagined him sitting there with my leg resting on the table and my freshly painted toes in his mouth. I wondered if Andrew was thinking anything similar.

Was toe-sucking technically sex? Would that kind of action break my celibacy rule? Then I remembered Liza's words of advice: 'If one of you has an orgasm, it's regarded as sex.' But perhaps I could – we could – have an orgasm-free toe-sucking session. That might be nice. Then I realised I'd been having a conversation in my head for a few minutes: the silence was a little uncomfortable. I looked across to the table next to us and there was a Japanese guy and an Anglo woman and their gorgeous kid, and not knowing why I even thought it, let alone said it, I came out with a line that surprised me:

'I love Eurasian kids, don't you?'

Andrew just looked at me oddly. Was that a racist thing to say?

'What I meant was that mixed kids are so much more interesting looking than standard vanilla-flavoured kids.'

'Vanilla?'

Was that also a racist thing to say? God, I could never be the Minister for Cultural Affairs when I couldn't even get my own act together.

'You know if an Aboriginal and an Asian had a baby it'd be called an Abrasion.' And I laughed at my own joke.

'Look, I'm only twenty-five, I'm not really thinking about Eurasians or Abrasions just yet.'

'Oh no, I wasn't thinking you were. I'm not thinking about kids either, I don't even like kids, I was just thinking, or not thinking, perhaps.' I was so embarrassed I just stuffed more sushi in my mouth, skolled some sake and watched the train of little dishes pass us by again. The food was great; it was a shame things were going so badly.

As I put a piece of tempura in my mouth our phones beeped simultaneously, and we dove for them as if expecting the message of a lifetime. It was Shelley, saying the same thing to both of us:

So sorry, lovelies, can't get there, emergency at work. Eat something yummy for me. Speak later. xx Shelley

Andrew looked relieved. 'Well, I'm done if you are.'

'I'm done too,' I said, as he waved the waitress over for the bill.

'Never again! How could you do that to me? I made a complete idiot of myself, and he must be wondering what's wrong with you, sharing a house with someone like me,' I said as Shelley walked in at ten pm.

She flopped onto the lounge and kicked off her heels. 'Why? What happened?'

'I hope he talks to you again, cos I'm sure he won't be talking to me.'

'What did you do?' Shelley asked, taking a sip of my wine.

'I think I'm racist.' I slapped myself on the forehead.

'You're not racist.' She got up to get herself a glass.

'Then I must be an idiot.' I lay down flat with my head on the armrest of the lounge.

'But a likable one.' Shelley threw a cushion at me.

'Thanks a million. I think I should go to bed, and then maybe when I wake up in the morning I'll find that tonight was just a bad, bad dream. See you in the morning.'

I could still taste the sake as I closed my eyes.

Within minutes I'm in Japan but it's not Tokyo, which is where everyone thinks of when they think of Japan. It's Kyoto, the old capital. I'm the Australian Minister for Cultural Affairs, and I'm treated like a rock star. A limousine arrives to pick me up and as we drive off I wind down the window and sign some autographs. It's early morning, but the city is bustling. There are people everywhere: 'small dog' walkers; students looking very proper, the girls in their pleated sailor-like tunics, and the boys in suits; office workers on their bikes, riding to work and not breaking a sweat, just sitting upright – helmet free – like being in a convertible car with the roof down. Almost everyone is busy punching keys or talking into tiny flip-phones. People are smiling and hospitable, but I am kneecapped, stifled, choking on my inability to speak. The only Japanese I know is *konnichiwa*, *sayonara* and *hai*. Why didn't the astral dream booking agency give me some intensive language lessons before they sent me here?

My driver, who is hot, hot, hot as wasabi, suggests that to make small talk I should always tell my hosts that I'm really enjoying Kyoto, that I haven't tried eel yet and that I think Japanese rice is the best in the world. He guarantees that if I do, people will love me, and of course I want to be loved. He tells me his name is Yoshi, and teaches me to say, '*Hajimemashite, Peta desu. Dōzo, yoroshiku.*' It means, 'My name is Peta, please be nice to me.' I rehearse it a few times, then he stops the car, gets out and climbs in the back seat with me.

'How nice do you want me to be?' he asks, and I'm wondering if that's a nori roll in his pocket or he's just glad to see me. He kisses my neck and whispers in my ear, 'Would you like to try some eel tonight?' and I'm thinking that Mike and the driver would get on really well.

He tells me about hotels you can rent by the hour. We should go to one, he tells me. I'm celibate, I say. 'Then you probably *need* to go,' he says, and laughs, but he agrees to take me sightseeing instead.

Our first stop is a Buddhist fertility temple and I panic because I don't particularly want to be fertile, but then I calm down – the temple grounds are really peaceful and lush, and the cherry trees are blossoming, and I'm thinking more westerners might go to church if it were so interesting and tranquil. The only harsh note is struck by crass Americans, talking too loud in this place of peace. I worry that people probably think I'm English or American too – I'm in a business suit, so they're probably never going to imagine that I'm a Blackfella from Down Under. Perhaps a T-shirt with the flag on it would do the trick. But would they recognise it?

Yoshi takes my hand and leads me to a massive wooden phallus which has just returned from Nagoya and the fertility festival.

'March is fertility month, you have just missed it.'

'Oh well,' is all I can say. I don't think astral travelling with a kid would be any fun anyway.

'Pregnant women stroke it for good luck, for easy childbirth,' he tells me. 'Do you want to stroke it?' He grips my hand tightly.

'Yes, I want to stroke it,' I whisper in his ear, loosening his grip and sliding my hand in his pocket.

We both know it's going to be 'on' now, but this is a religious place, a place of respect, and we have to wait until we get back to the city.

On the way, Yoshi tells me he's an eco-poet. He's impressed that I know anything about his genre of work. I pretend to recite one of Sylvia's poems but make most of it up as I go along.

'Could you send me a copy of this Sylvia's book, please?'

'Of course,' I say, which is okay, because even though it hasn't been published yet, commitments made in dreams don't have to be kept.

In Kyoto we rent a room by the hour. I pinch myself, trying to wake up, and then I pinch him and he pinches me gently back and even in a dream it hurts.

He tells me there's no time for foreplay in astral sex, or where you're paying by the minute, but I want to check out our room. The toilet seat has all these buttons that I'm not sure what to do with, but one is designed to warm my arse, which makes me want to sit there longer. I check out the mini-bar too: I can't read any of the labels, but I choose something that turns out to be sparkling chardonnay in a can. I wonder what Max the real estate agent wine connoisseur would say.

Yoshi is sitting on the bed, agitated, but waiting patiently, because if anything the Japanese are polite.

I turn on the telly, searching for the sumo wrestlers I must see before I leave Japan. Yoshi says I should stop being such a westerner. But I'm not a westerner, I'm Aboriginal – how can I be a westerner? I'm an 'other'. When I find them, they're serving tea to each other, not wrestling, and they don't look nearly as big as I thought they would, of course, on a fifty-two centimetre TV screen. I wonder what I'd look like in one of those G-strings, and decide that at least if I dated a sumo-dude I'd look petite, and that couldn't hurt.

Yoshi is polite, but he's horny and he's paying by the minute, so he turns the telly off and makes me stand up. I take one more sip of my can of chardonnay because I am nervous like a virgin. But I don't have time to think as he stands behind me and quickly removes the kimono that I've only just realised I'm wearing. When he turns me around he looks so much like Mike that it takes my breath away, but I can't stop what's about to happen because the nori roll is out, everything is happening fast and furious and I'm on fire like my body has been smothered in wasabi, but my astral flight to Tullamarine is being called and I have to go, I want to wake up alone and not with Yoshi the eco-poet and especially not with Mike the cop.

I'm the only westerner who doesn't want to be a westerner on the plane. I come out of the toilet and someone asks me for a blanket. They think I am an air hostess. I laugh and get them one.

My mobile rang and woke me up.

'Good morning babe, did I wake you?'

'Kind of, what time is it?'

'Seven-thirty, thought you'd be up already.'

'Oh, I'm running a bit late. What's up?'

'Thought I might come down this weekend. Would that be okay?'

'That'd be lovely,' I said, with thoughts of some serious toe-sucking flooding my mind.

'So this is Girls Bar, eh? I like it. It's got a nice groove.' I smiled at Josie and looked around the bar: it was full of all kinds of women, and a couple of brave men.

'So you think you might make this your regular hang from now on, then?' Her eyes lit up. 'If you do I'll have to call Aunty Ivy straight away. God, how I'd love to do that.'

'You're evil.' I toasted her.

'Yes, it's that evil lesbian gene I have.' And we laughed hysterically.

'James is coming down on the weekend.'

'Are you looking forward to seeing him?'

'I am actually, because in one night I managed to have waking thoughts about a podiatrist sucking my toes and then Mike the cop – or a guy who looked quite a lot like him – appeared in my latest astral travel dream to Japan.'

'You didn't tell me he was Japanese. That's interesting, I mean him being in the force. I don't think I've ever seen a Japanese cop in Australia. Or should I say someone with Japanese heritage, in case they identify as Australian? Gees, all this political correctness stuff gets a bit boring, doesn't it.'

'STOP! You're raving. He's not Japanese. He was just in my dream, and I was in Japan. It freaked me out a little. We were in one of those famous hotels you rent by the hour, specifically for sex.'

'What? Were you a prostitute in this dream?'

'God, you make it hard sometimes, Josie. Never mind. So, back to James. It will be nice to see him. I do miss him, at times.'

'Not constantly?'

'No, not constantly, I'd never get any work done if I was missing him constantly. Does *anyone* miss *anyone* constantly? I mean, except when you're a teenager?'

'I've missed girlfriends pretty desperately in the past – mind you, we usually moved in together on the second date.'

'Yes, but desperately and constantly are two different things.'

'You're right, I guess. You can miss someone to the point of almost stalking them but still get your work done . . . in the other two hours of the day.' Josie laughed.

'Back to me, all right? As I was saying, I haven't missed James constantly because I've been flat out since I got here. I haven't had the time to miss him. And I'm still learning the ropes at work. The twelve months will be up before I know it, and I won't even have started the job properly – I'll have to stay longer. But there's no way he'll cope with that.

'Maybe I'll just become a lesbian, it seems like it's easier than being with men.' Then I looked around the bar. 'Actually you know what, I don't think I like this place. I've just realised we've been here two hours and no-one's made a pass at me. I must say I'm a little disappointed that no-one here finds me attractive.'

'They all think you're with me, that's why.' Josie winked.

'What? So now you're cramping my lesbian style.'

'Sorry to burst your bubble, love, but you are soooo hetero, there's no dyke style going on with you at all.'

'Orright then, I think we've exhausted that conversation, let's take my hetero style and get some food. What do you want to eat?'

twenty
The first serious argument

On Saturday morning I took Shelley's car out to Tullamarine to meet James. He was already tired when he arrived because of the four-thirty start he'd had to get an early flight. He could only stay for one night.

James put his hand on my thigh as we pulled out of the airport car park and a rush of hormones flooded my body, blurring my vision. 'There's no more jewellery, is there?' I said to him. 'Cos Shelley's away for the weekend and she can't rescue us.' He cringed and laughed at the same time and I pushed down on the accelerator, aiming to get us back to St Kilda as soon as possible.

We spent the morning in bed – it was the natural way for us to catch up. It was how we always caught up. When things were tense between us, everything was always better after a good night's sleep or a good shag, or both.

We went to Circa at the Prince for lunch. The decor was crisp white, with kangaroo paw in pink glass vases, silver-grey chiffon curtains and wicker lights throughout.

'So, babe, I've been wondering if . . .' and he paused. Oh God, he was going to propose.

'Wondering what?' I didn't feel ready to deal with this.

'Wondering if you wanted to see other people while we're apart?'

'What? No. Why? Do you?' I was confused: this certainly

wasn't the proposal I was expecting. I was relieved, but also, I realised, disappointed.

'No I don't, but someone suggested to me that I should give you some freedom.'

'I don't need freedom; I need support for my career. Why don't you listen to *me* and not to *someone* – whoever *someone* is.' I was really taken aback. Had James actually met someone else back in Sydney? Was it guilt that led to his last-minute trip to Melbourne?

If James was anything, he was an honest, straight-up kind of guy, and would tell me the truth if there was someone else – but I wasn't sure if I wanted to ask.

'There's no-one else, in case that's what you're thinking,' he said, as if he was reading my mind. He reached out and held my hand.

After a moment's silence, he grinned at me. 'You won't believe this. I've started surfing,' he announced.

'Really?' I was surprised. While James loved going to the beach with me, I'd never even known him to bodysurf.

'Yes. I thought it'd be good to surf when I finally move in with you beachside. Had a bad experience already though – I nearly drowned.'

'What? Why didn't you tell me? When?'

'Two weeks ago. I had a lesson on Saturday down Maroubra beach, and I surprised myself. I managed to stand up within the first half an hour. I think doing gymnastics as a kid gave me a good sense of balance.' I'd seen photos of James in his gym gear as a child and he was so cute on the balance beam – I remember falling in love with him even more at that moment.

'I was so chuffed with myself, knowing that surfing is a really hard sport to master and that I seemed to have a bit of a gift, so straight after the class I went and bought myself a board and went for a surf the next morning.' Oh God, I could just see my little 'chuffed' gymnast out there with the Bra Boys and I started to panic.

'And?' I was impatient, wanting to know about the 'nearly drowning' business.

'Well, I paddled out, feeling really confident, and rode a couple of waves in – shaky, but I did it. I was good at it, really.' As if he were trying to convince me. 'But then I attempted a really big wave, and I ended up getting wiped out and thought I'd broken my neck. I got swished around beneath the sea for what seemed like ages. I truly thought I was going to drown and all I could think was that I'd never see you again.'

'Oh baby, how did you get out?' I gripped his hand tightly, feeling guilty about not being there for him on the day.

'Lifesaver by the name of Mark came out on the jet ski and towed me back. I was so embarrassed. I was out of breath, out of pride and out $500 for the board.'

'No, the board's not a waste – you should keep trying, it sounds like you have a gift, and it was only your second day.'

'I don't know, it was really a terrifying experience.' James looked at our joined hands intently, as if he was somewhere else, as if back under the sea.

'I'm so sorry, I wish I'd been there for you.' I put my hand on his.

'So do I. I really missed you that night, I needed some of Peta's TLC.'

'Let's go back to Eildon Road and I'll give you all the TLC you can handle.'

We went for dinner at a new place on Fitzroy Street, so uneventful I couldn't even remember the name of it the next day. I ordered basic pasta.

'This food is fucken awful,' I said, spitting into my serviette.

'You know, I've never said anything to you before, but boy you swear a lot – I mean, for a princess.'

'Well, as Alice would say, the colonisers gave us a whole new vocab, which I might point out also contained profanities. So as far as I'm concerned, along with small pox, bad language is just another colonial intrusion.' I pushed the plate of tasteless pasta aside and just stared at him.

'I know colonisation has a lot to do with where your people are today, Peta, but you swearing is your own doing.'

'Oh, this is a first, you talking to me about where my people are at thanks to colonisation! If you know so much, what are you doing to make some social change for us, then? I mean, aside from dating a Blackfella?'

'What would you like me to do, Peta? What *can* I do? To make change?'

'James, why don't you ask *yourself* that question?'

'Because I'm asking you.'

'I'm tired of being asked questions like that. I'm not at work now, and you're not one of my clients. Do you know how many times a day I'm interrogated by whitefellas wanting me to have all the answers for them? Why do

Aboriginal people have to have all the answers *and* do all the work? I don't want to have a cultural awareness session over dinner with the man who is supposed to be my partner! I don't want you asking me what you should be doing to help.'

'But you always tell me you know what's best for you.'

'Exactly! I know what's best for me, Peta. I don't have all the answers all the time for the 400,000 other Blackfellas living right across the continent.'

'But you have a sense of responsibility to your people. I see it in your work. That's why you moved to Melbourne, isn't it?'

'This isn't about me, it's about you. You need to take some responsibility for *you* and *your* people. Expecting us to know everything about our people isn't perhaps the best way to go. I don't ask you about whitefellas, do I?'

'Well no, of course not.' He looked browbeaten.

'Look, I love you, James, but I'm not your personal tutor. You need to do more to educate yourself about these issues. I would've thought that a man who wanted to marry me would take more than a superficial interest in what I do, but you hardly ever come to events with me in Sydney. You've never even been to a rally!'

'You never ask me to go.'

'I shouldn't have to. I come along to lectures and things with you all the time, and it's not because I'm really into architecture! I do it because you love it, and it's your career, and because it's important to you – but it's not who you are. The issues I'm talking about are important to me, and not just because of my work. This is who I *am*. Do you understand that?'

'But I'm just an architect. I don't really have anything to contribute.'

'Let's say you were a businessman, then I'd say you could give some Blackfellas jobs and encourage other businesspeople to do the same. If you were a journo I'd say write a feel-good story, a positive story about Indigenous Australia, and try to do it as often as you can. Maybe there's nothing you can do with your skills as an architect but you can still write letters to MPs and the newspaper and so on. I bet you've never done that, have you?'

He just looked at his food and pushed it around on his plate.

'Look, I'm not having a dig at you,' I said, a bit more gently. 'I'm just trying to make the point that whitefellas have to start looking at themselves and thinking about how they fit into the world and can make change.' I sipped my wine.

'You know, our office did hire a Blackfella but it didn't quite work out. He kept going walkabout and the partners couldn't bring themselves to hire another.'

'What the fuck! What are we doing here, Aboriginal Studies 101?'

'Don't swear at me, Peta.'

'Don't *make* me swear. See what I mean? In all the time we've been together you haven't learned even the basics. Don't you hear me when I talk to other people about this stuff? Blackfellas go *walkabout* for a purpose. Ceremony, trading, food, water, sorry business. Blackfellas in the city don't go walkabout. Whitefellas just say we do. We drive cars, catch buses and trains when we've got business to do.'

'Why are you getting so angry with me?'

'Because white Australians like you point out *my* responsibilities but don't recognise your own, or the fact that you benefit every day from the dispossession of Aboriginal people. You mightn't be responsible for the past, but you benefit from dispossession every day. And you sit here asking me, *What can I do?*'

James just sat there stunned. We had never had a confrontation about political issues before. In the eight months we had been together back in Sydney he had always been so lovely and kind and nice that we'd never had a full-blown argument. We hadn't talked politics at all, really. It wasn't his fault. We'd both been working hard, and at the end of long days and weeks we went to movies and chilled out and I tried to recharge my batteries. What we did together was fun, but not deep or intense. I did talk about issues that had come up at work sometimes, but he didn't challenge or correct me and I just assumed he agreed. The argument just proved Alice's point: it was best to get the important stuff out of the way on the first date, not eight or nine or ten months down the track. But it wasn't even an argument: James didn't disagree with me. He just hadn't thought about the issues before.

After a long silence, both of us just staring at our dinner, James said, 'You're going to think I'm an idiot, but I still don't know what you want from me.'

'Sometimes I just want you to listen, James, that's all. Right now, though, I want to get the bill.'

Reconciliation Week kicked off that night with a reconciliation football match between the Swans and

Essendon, but even though I'd been looking forward to going to my first live AFL game, it seemed more important to spend some time alone with James. I didn't even mention the game to him, as football was nothing that either of us had been keen on when I was back in Sydney, and the last thing I wanted him thinking was that I was only interested in looking at the long lean bodies in tight shorts – and knowing James, it was something he would think, even if he never said anything. So I decided that we'd spend the night at home and I made a kangaroo curry with a recipe Alice emailed me as a joke. It wasn't as good as hers, but it was okay.

I got up early the next morning and called her. 'You should have heard me at dinner with James yesterday. I behaved like a bloody lunatic. If I were him I'd give up on me for sure. I was a crazy woman. If he still wants to marry me I should just do it, because no-one else will ever have me. I don't even know why he puts up with me. I must be *his* reconciliation project and he doesn't even know it.'

'You're not crazy or mad. You're a passionate, feisty, gorgeous, intelligent Black woman,' she affirmed. 'Who cares about her community and doesn't suffer fools easily.'

'But James isn't a fool – he's a nice guy who's trying hard just to keep me right now, I think.'

'Then crawl back into bed and apologise for your tone, or your manner, but not what you said, okay, because you're not sorry for what you said, are you?'

'No, not at all. I meant every word of it. But it wasn't really intended for him. He just wore the brunt of what I want to say to some of the bureaucrats I work with, and probably a few members of the police force.'

'Right,' Alice responded. 'So it wasn't about James at all, then?'

'Well, some of it was, he needed to hear it. We need to be able to have discussions like that. But mostly it was about other people.'

'So tell him that, tell him it was a dress rehearsal for the people who really need to hear it. He's the forgiving type. He'll be cool for sure.'

'You're right, it'll be fine.'

'But if that fails, just give him a blow job!'

'God, now you're sounding like me. I'll call you later in the week.'

So I crawled into bed and all was forgiven.

We had a late lunch down at the Stokehouse, which felt a bit weird as I hadn't been there since the episode with Mike. We got a table at the window and just sat staring at the sea. It was an overcast day and cold.

'You're beautiful.' James moved closer and put his arm around my shoulder. It felt safe and good and normal, like it did back in Sydney when there was no pressure on us.

'I know I don't know everything about you and your politics and everything you want out of life, but I do know that I want to be with you. To be around you. To love you.'

'I love you too,' I said easily.

'And I know with all your passion you'd make a great wife and mother, and you'd make sure our kids were the most socially aware students in their classes.'

Oh God, why ruin it all? James just couldn't see that I would make a bad wife and a shocking mother. There he was acting like Muriel again – or Alice, anyway.

twenty-one
Babysitting

Reconciliation Week came and went in the blink of an eyelid. It was the most jam-packed week I had ever experienced. I'd been busy every day and night since James left with morning teas and launches, an event at the Bunjilaka Aboriginal Centre at Melbourne Museum, the launch of Archie Roach's new CD and a fabulously funny night seeing Tammy Anderson's play *Itchy Clacker*.

Each event did much to bring the Indigenous and non-Indigenous communities of Melbourne together, and I was glad for all the invitations to attend, but I was exhausted, too, because every event generated more work. Sylvia kept giving my card to people and then emails and phone calls came flooding in. But I was in my element.

'Sylvia!' I sung out like a command from my office. She came promptly. 'Right, what's left to do today?'

'One more event at the Koorie Heritage Trust Cultural Centre and then you can rest.'

'We can *both* rest,' I corrected her, as we'd been working strongly as a team since I arrived and she had to be as tired as I was. 'What's the event?'

'Opening night of a new exhibition; a local artist working in metal. But before that you have some guests from the Assembly of First Nations in Canada arriving. I thought we could walk down together and then they can get some local culture and we don't have to organise catering or anything – there'll be a spread on there.'

'God, I love the way you think. Thanks for that.'

From the moment I arrived at the centre I was avoiding people: one of my mother's ex-boyfriends who was still an alcoholic womaniser; a married man who kept following me around; a cousin who always bit me for money; and three or four potential clients who wanted to know when funding decisions would be made.

I was so frightened of bumping into someone I didn't want to speak to that I refused to head up the wooden stairs to the main exhibition. To look busy, and to show my interest in the artist and his work, I put a deposit on a blue metal sculpture worth three weeks' wages. I didn't even really know what it meant, or have my own space to put it in. It was titled 'Untitled', which I thought was just lazy of the artist. I'd always been mesmerised by dot paintings from Papunya and the stories they told, but there was no story attached to this sculpture to help me understand it. Of course, I could never say that out loud, not in the job I was in, but it was true. I only bought the piece because the artist saw me eyeing it, but he didn't realise that the look on my face was confusion, not admiration.

I was very drunk when I got home and started texting, first to Alice:

Belated Happy Reconciliation Week, miss ya, Px

Then a return text to Liza. She'd sent a message for Sorry Day on 26 May but I hadn't had a chance to get back to her:

Thanks sista 4 the msg. Been hectic here, will call soon, promise. Love ya, P xxx

Then to James:

Hi, sorry been quiet, was BIG recon wk, haven't stopped, just home now, exhausted. Will call soon. X P X

I stayed home every night for the next two weeks, played on Facebook, sent a backlog of emails, even wrote a letter to Mum. I had to save some money for the 'Untitled' piece I would eventually have to pay for, but I also needed to cleanse my system after a huge week of functions. I offered to babysit for Joe and Annie when I heard it was their wedding anniversary and Aunt had gone away with her line-dancing group for the weekend.

I rocked up to their place with lots of kids' movies and plenty of lollies and chocolate, which was the advice from Sylvia. However, Annie told me sugar only gave them more energy and their son Will needed Ritalin, not sugar.

Joe and Annie were going to dinner and then to Klub Koori – they were still young enough to enjoy the bar scene. I was there at six pm to help feed the kids.

'Now, Aunty Peta is going to look after you for a while tonight, and I want you to be on your best behaviour, okay.'

'Okay,' Maya said as she sat up to the dinner table.

'Kay,' Will echoed, looking at his big sister.

'We'll be right, you go get ready,' I said, and I shoved Annie out of the room. 'Right, let's eat.'

I took a seat next to Will, and started on my own take-away Thai while the kids played with and occasionally ate some of their food. Then Will poked me.

'Don't do that, Will, I don't like it.'

He poked me again.

'I said, don't! Okay?' I stared him right in the eye. 'I'll poke you back.'

He just stared at me until I returned to my dinner. Then he poked me again, so I poked him back really hard. He burst out crying, wailing uncontrollably until Annie and Joe came rushing out.

'What's going on?' Annie asked.

'Eeta poked me!' Will cried.

'He poked me first! I warned him if he kept poking me I'd poke him back. Eye for an eye, isn't it?'

'No, Peta, it's turn the other cheek in this house. Maybe you shouldn't have kids.'

'Oh really? You think I hadn't figured that out myself yet? Thanks for the advice. We'll be fine now – just go, we'll sort it out.'

'I'm worried DOCS might come and take the kids away from the babysitter,' Annie laughed.

When we'd all finished eating, I was pissed off to find more food had landed on the floor than in Will's mouth. Joe had prepared a yummy meal, but Will just kept saying 'cheese, cheese, cheese'.

Annie had left strict instructions that no ice-cream was to be served for dessert unless they ate their meat and veg, and I was determined to stick to the orders. After all, as a child I wasn't allowed to have sweets if I didn't eat all my dinner. But as a child, I also knew that while you might be too full to eat the brussels sprouts, you are *never* too full to eat ice-cream.

After dinner I sat them both down in front of *Madagascar* and we watched it together. Maya and I got Will to repeat the names of all the animals as they appeared on the screen.

'Monkeys . . .'

'Keys . . .' Will said enthusiastically.

'Giraffe . . .' Maya said slowly.

'Rarf . . .' was all he could manage.

'Racoon . . .' I said clearly.

'Coon . . .' And as hideous as the word was and sounded, there was something funny about this two year old innocently mispronouncing the word 'racoon'.

'Okay, so maybe we don't bother trying racoon for a while then.'

They were both still awake at eight-thirty and I was sure it was too late for them to be up, but when I suggested they go to bed Maya said she wasn't tired and Will just started to scream. I didn't want a screaming child, nor did I know what to do with a screaming child, other than perhaps smack them, but I also knew that there was probably some law against smacking other people's kids, so I just let them stay up and gave them more ice-cream, not thinking that the sugar might be contributing to their unusual energy levels.

At ten-thirty Will was so tired he could hardly move, so I carried him to his cot. He was asleep within seconds of me covering him over. Maya helped me get him settled and then took herself off to bed.

'Goodnight, lovely, see you soon, eh?'

'Oh yes, we still have to go to Luna Park, remember?'

'Of course, how could I forget?' Kids never forgot promises adults made to them.

It was only eleven when Annie and Joe arrived home, but I was exhausted. I was almost positive motherhood and I should never meet.

twenty-two
Stock market cum meat market

After two weeks of working long hours and staying in at night I was desperate to go out again. On Friday evening I felt like going for a drink and being sociable. I was still trying to make as much as possible out of my twelve-month stint in Melbourne, and to see as many bars and restaurants and venues as possible. Even if I had a boyfriend back in Sydney, I still liked to party. I asked Sylvia if she was up for some bevies, but she already had plans with the boyfriend I still hadn't met. I briefly considered texting Mike, but that was beyond ridiculous, given our last encounter, and even I knew that. Shelley always had drinks after work on Friday with her colleagues at a place called 'Comme', so I gave her a call on her mobile, thinking perhaps we could hook up. Typically, I got her voicemail – she never seemed to have her phone switched on – so I left a message.

'Hi love, I'd really like to go out for a drink. Maybe I could meet you at Comme bar? It's six pm, I'm still in the office, call me.'

But by seven, when I'd finished off my emails, I still hadn't heard from Shelley, so I got the tram home, wondering why she'd never invited me along to meet her workmates, and decided to confront her about it.

She stumbled in the door at twenty past nine, slightly pissed. She kicked off her heels and flung her grey suit jacket on the couch next to her as she placed both feet on the coffee table.

'It's sooooo good to be home.' She rested her head back and closed her eyes.

'How were drinks?'

'Same, same.'

'Is that a good same or an average same or a bad same?'

'Just same, same really. I only go because it's expected of me. Have you noticed I'm home at the same time every week?'

'Yes I have actually, and I've also noticed that you go every week and never invite me along. I'd like to check out this Comme bar with you and meet your colleagues sometime.' I couldn't have been any more up-front than that.

'Oh no, I don't think you really do, Peta.'

'Oh, yes, I think I really do.'

'I just don't know . . .' She sat upright and put both feet flat on the ground.

'What? Why? Aren't I good enough for your hoity-toity stockbroking mates?'

'Oh no, it's the other way around, Peta. I can tell you right now that you will hate Comme bar, and loathe the men who go there.'

'But I wouldn't be going there for the men. I hate to have to keep reminding you of it, but I have a boyfriend.'

'That's right, I forgot.' Shelley was drunker than I had originally thought.

'I just want to see what it's like in *your* world – you know, outside of our little salt'n'pepper squid and Pimm's existence we share here at St Kilda.'

'Well, okay, but don't say I didn't warn you. Come next Friday then.'

'Great, now put those heels back on because someone by the name of George is waiting for us on the corner of Fitzroy and Grey Streets, and I do believe he has a drink there too.'

Friday came and I was looking forward to my initiation into the Comme bar after-work soiree. I pulled out my obligatory little black Melbourne dress, fishnets and heels. The evenings were really cold by now, so I wore my pink coat, too. It made me stick out like a sore thumb, but I didn't care. I looked hot and I knew it. The black-clad Collins Street crowd would just have to cope.

Shelley was there when I arrived but it was hard to find her. I waded confidently into a sea of drab suits and made my way around the left of the bar, assuming if I did a loop of the oval space I'd bump into her eventually. It was jam-packed and I had to brush up close to everyone I passed. Squeezing as elegantly as possible through the crowd I was chest to chest with two guys talking about a woman on the other side of the bar.

'She's got the biggest tits,' one of them said, gesturing across the room. He proceeded to describe the woman's cleavage and exactly where she was positioned at the bar, no shame and no concern whatsoever that I could hear everything he was saying. Shelley was right, the FTSE, the Nikkei/Dow and the sharemarket were not discussed after work. It was a market of a different kind: the meat market. The wanker banker meat market.

I found Shelley eventually and we both looked at each other with relief. She was sitting with a few other people, and introduced me to them: there was a young gun in a suit who immediately excused himself to go to the bar; Ollie, around forty, with a completely shaved head; and Shelley's assistant, Casey.

'Ollie, this is Peta, my housemate. Ollie specialises in offshore investments with the firm.'

'Nice to meet you, Ollie.' I extended my hand.

'Yes, it is.'

I also shook hands with Casey, who generously offered to take my coat to the cloakroom.

Ollie leered at me as I slipped it off. 'Peta, just some advice, best you dress like you work in the city,' and he looked at my gorgeous watermelon coat like it was a housecoat. 'Loud colours like that scream you're from the burbs *and* desperate.'

'What? I bought this coat on Chapel Street, and I wear it all the time. Anyone with any spunk knows it screams *style*.'

Shelley pushed her chair back further, recrossed her legs and rested her drink on her knee like she was settling in for the show.

'And what's wrong with the burbs anyway?' I asked.

'I was just looking out for ya, love.'

'Well, don't bother. I don't need anyone looking out for me. And who's desperate? I'm doing my best to *avoid* men, actually. I'm not looking for one. Anyway, I don't give a rat's arse what a Melbourne—' I looked at his card. 'A Melbourne *whatever* thinks of me. I'm from Sydney and going back in a year.'

'Well, that explains it then.' He looked me up and down one more time, stood up, said, 'See ya, Shells,' and walked off.

'What was that? What a wanker! Surely they can't all be like that.'

'Not all of them, but a lot of them. Maybe you can teach them a thing or two, Peta. Who knows, we might actually have some fun tonight.'

After a couple of drinks Casey said she had to go home, and headed off. Then Shelley had to take a call from a client she'd been waiting to hear from. I was surprised she even had her phone on, but there were still deals to be made on Friday night, apparently. The place was really loud, much louder than the George, so she went outside and I was left to fend for myself. She was gone a while, and I made my way to the bar to order a drink. While I was waiting for my change, someone lurched into me. It was Ollie – and this time he had a mate with him.

'Hey, Peee-taah! This is Jake, he has too many girlfriends. Jake, this is Shell's housemate, Peee-taah.' Jake extended his hand, but without much enthusiasm. He checked out my cleavage then looked around the room for his 'too many girlfriends'. I wasn't sure how Jake had so much female interest, as he was packing a few pounds. With a paunch like a middle-aged married man content with home-cooked meals, I was surprised to learn he was only twenty-six.

'Where's the girl with the nose?' he said to Ollie. It was clear to me that women at Comme were only referred to by parts of their anatomy – breasts, noses, legs – but never by name, and rarely with respect or warmth. I needed Shelley back and fast. It was approaching nine pm, her usual escape time. I couldn't see her anywhere, though, so I thought I'd hide in the loos for a while.

When I came back, I took a seat at the bar. I still couldn't see Shelley, but was glad just to sit down again. My feet were killing me in heels. I wore them so rarely since moving to Melbourne – with all the public transport I was constantly paranoid about tripping on a tramline, or getting my heel caught getting on or off a train. I ordered a glass of water because I was already imagining the hangover due next morning.

Jake and Ollie were still there in the corner of the bar, but they didn't seem to feel obliged to talk to me. I was glad of that, and just sat and listened to their conversation.

'There's no-one here worth shagging,' Jake said to Ollie as he sipped his beer.

'Nah, and too many blokes, nothing worse than cock soup,' Ollie replied.

'Yeah, ya right, or a sausage factory.' They both sniggered like teenage boys.

'Hey, check out that woman there. She looks like a forty-year-old mother from the suburbs trying to find a boyfriend.'

'Yeah, it ain't gonna happen. She should be at home.'

'Absolutely, why doesn't she just try Lavalife or something?'

'That's right. It's half past nine. If she was a self-respecting woman she'd be home by now.' And they both looked at me as if to say, *And so should you, because you don't fit in either*. I was gobsmacked. I looked at the woman they were referring to and she just looked like a normal, well-dressed woman like me, perhaps a little older. Was I supposed to be at home too?

'Hey, check out the two sad cases behind us,' Ollie said, motioning his head towards the women at a high table nearby. I couldn't help but look too, because I wanted to know what a 'sad case' actually looked like in their eyes.

'Fuck, old and trashy, sitting there with their bottle of wine. Tragic.' I wasn't quite sure what was tragic about them – the wine, or the fact they could be there, willingly, among all the judgement and criticism. I'd had enough. I sent Shelley a text:

Meet u out front ASAP, ova this. Px

I went to the coat check and got my loud coat and put it on proudly. It was warm, it was stylish, and no snotty-nosed bloke was going to tell me I couldn't wear it. I came from the suburbs in Sydney and was proud of it.

Shelley soon followed me out, and we grabbed a cab home.

'What's with Jake and Ollie just standing in the corner and bagging everyone out all the time?' I asked, resting my head on the window. I was sure I was going to throw up at some point. I was just hoping to be able to get home in time.

'Oh, no-one takes them seriously. Everyone knows Jake's got a tiny dick and Ollie is a premature ejaculator, so they often have threesomes because it takes two of them to get one job done. All that judgement stuff is just projecting their own sense of self-loathing onto others. Left here, thanks driver.'

'Next time I invite myself to one of *your* events, can you remind me again why you didn't invite me in the first place?'

'Should I say it?'

'What?'

'I told you so.'

twenty-three
Luna Park

I was hung-over the next morning and the last thing I wanted to do was to go to an amusement park. I had policy papers to read for Monday, I felt seedy and I needed more sleep. But young Maya had made me promise – again – before I left their house a couple weeks before.

I picked her up in Shelley's car, and just as driving bomby old Gemma covered in land rights stickers was embarrassing, so was driving a brand-spanking-new Alfa among Blackfellas. I knew they'd be thinking I was uptown. 'It's not mine!' I'd have to explain over and over again, like it was a crime to have a nice car.

Maya was waiting out the front excitedly when I arrived. 'Look what I've got in my purse,' she shouted as she struggled to show me all the money her grandmother and parents had given her.

'It's my treat, darling. You can save that for Christmas maybe.'

'But Mum said I have to give it to you.'

Annie and Joe were smiling big, as if there was something they knew that I didn't.

'What's so bloody funny, then?' I wanted in on the joke, even though my head was pounding and the mere thought of laughing made it hurt.

'She's a chucker,' Annie said.

'A what?'

'I chuck a lot,' Maya said, nodding her head in agreement with her mother.

'Chuck what?' I was confused.

'Chuck up?' She pretended to spew.

'Excellent,' I groaned, and nearly threw up myself. 'And just so you know, there's a good chance I might chuck today too!' I rolled my eyes at Annie and Joe and mouthed the words *Help me.* Maya just laughed.

'Okay, let's go. Quicker we get there . . .' I started.

'The quicker we get on the rides,' Maya said.

'And the quicker we get home,' I said softly.

The drive from East Bentleigh to St Kilda was worse that any ride I could think of going on as Maya continued to talk about chucking and how many times she'd chucked and what was in it. It was turning my stomach. When she was bored with that conversation she wanted to ask and tell me things. 'Can I show you something? When can I spend my money? Which rides can we go on?'

All the chatter was compounding my headache. I couldn't for the life of me understand how parents coped – even if they didn't even have hangovers, which I assumed they didn't. There's no way you could party like I did and then have to feed, clothe and entertain kids the next day. Maya was helping me with my celibacy gig: the mere thought of getting pregnant was turning me off sex.

When we got there I insisted that she hold my hand. What would be worse than something happening to your own child? Something happening to a child you were looking after. We bought our ride tickets; I was astounded that it cost more to entertain a six year old for the afternoon than it did to go out with stockbrokers drinking.

Maya was excited and struggled with deciding which ride to go on first. I tried not to be too impatient. I was glad she was under 119 centimetres, so our ride choice was limited. The Big Dipper roller-coaster, which for some reason was called the Scenic Railway in Melbourne, was closed. *Thank you*, I mouthed to the skies.

'Right!' I had to take charge. 'We'll go on the Red Baron, the Magical Carousel, Silly Serpent, then the Arabian Merry, okay?'

'Okay,' Maya said, clapping her hands.

And so we did, and I found myself screaming and laughing and, amazingly, keeping the drinks from the night before down.

'What about the Ghost Train? It's my favourite,' I said, trying to enthuse her into a tamer ride.

'I'm scared of ghosts, Mum says you've gotta smoke the ghosts. But I know that smoking's bad for you, it'll kill ya. And ya can't smoke ghosts anyway. You smoke durries and Dad's always getting angry at Grandma for smoking, especially when me and Will are in Gemma with her.' Little Maya made me laugh, and for a moment I understood that having kids could bring joy to one's life. Were there enough of these moments, though? I just didn't know, I wasn't around kids enough.

I really wanted to sit down and not be churned around for a while, so I persisted.

'Maya, if you come on the Ghost Train with me, I'll buy you some fairy floss afterwards.' And that's how bribing kids with sweets and crap starts.

'Oh, I love fairy floss, okay, and I don't even think it will make me chuck.'

'Excellent, okay, let's get in the queue then.' Standing in line I watched the young teenage boys in front of me go twenty minutes without speaking to each other, while the pubescent girls behind me didn't seem to *stop* talking: about their clothes, about girls who weren't there, about the boys in front of us.

The ride went for all of two minutes and Maya loved it. A hot dog, hot chips and the promised fairy floss later, and we started to walk towards the exit.

'I'm gonna chuck,' Maya said, starting to cry.

'It's okay,' I said, picking her up and running to the toilets. I held Maya's sandy-coloured hair back as her little body leant over the bowl and threw up pink fairy floss and bits of hot dog – and then it was my turn.

'Look out lovely, Aunty's not well either.' Up came my hot chips and numerous drinks from the night before. I wiped tears from my own eyes as well as Maya's, washed both our faces and finally left Luna Park.

By the time I dropped Maya at East Bentleigh I was exhausted and fragile. I was stopped at the lights on the way back to St Kilda when James called.

'How are you, princess?'

'I'm so tired and hung-over, I feel like crap. I wish you were here to look after me.'

'And you know I would, don't you, baby? So, who were you out with last night?' Oh God, not again. I just didn't have the energy to deal with his insecurity right now.

'Just Shelley and some of her workmates. We were home by nine-thirty. I just drank too much too quickly.'

'Oh right.' I could hear the 'James-isn't-happy-with-me-going-out-partying' tone in his voice.

'Okay, well I better go – I'm in the car, and the lights are about to change. I'll call you later in the week. Love ya.' And I went home and slept.

twenty-four
Finding the answers
for myself and others

The department was hosting a national cultural information forum with academics, arts workers, funding bodies, policy makers and intellectual property lawyers. One of the keynote speakers, Dennis Droll, was a linguist attached to the languages department at the University of Australian Culture in Canberra. He came into the office to meet with staff to talk about a project proposal, and to suss out the department's funding for the national language strategy.

Sylvia had booked a small meeting room for us. It was just me, Sylvia, Dennis, and our new program assistant, Rodney. The walls of the room were lined with books by Australian authors, no doubt funded by DOMSARIA grants.

'I'd like to work in the Kimberley on a language project,' Dennis said eagerly after we'd introduced ourselves. We all sat listening intently. Sylvia took the minutes.

'Sounds interesting,' I said. 'What kind of project did you have in mind?'

'I'd like to record one of the local languages. Some of them only have a handful of fluent speakers left and we don't want to lose the languages altogether. Most of the speakers are very old so it's urgent that we get the grammar and vocab recorded orally as soon as possible and then translated into dictionary format.'

'Yes, of course, we understand that issue only too well, and language reclamation and maintenance does come under our mandate.' I attempted to be affirming of the idea.

'It's great you want to do something so significant for them,' Rodney said, his eyes wide.

'Yes, it's great for everyone. The language gets recorded, and I can add the dictionary to my publications list. I'm working towards being department head and eventually dean of the faculty, so a major language dictionary will score me a lot of points.'

'So, the project is really about *you* and *your* academic career, is it?' Sylvia said accusingly. I was disappointed to hear her sound so unprofessional, but we were definitely on the same page.

'What Sylvia means is that the project's main aim should be cultural maintenance.'

'The community get their language recorded. Isn't that enough?'

'Well, not quite. There are many other issues that need to be taken into consideration when we support a project. We need to discuss protocols and methodologies for working in communities, who gets the royalties, public lending rights, educational lending rights, and most importantly, who retains copyright over the material.' I'd learned a lot about copyright and intellectual property since being with the department.

Rodney suddenly lost his beam and pushed back his

chair and folded his arms across his chest, like a scary CEO of a major mining company.

'Well, I need to be paid for my work,' Dennis said.

'Haven't you applied for an ARC research grant?' asked Sylvia. We were working more and more on shared responsibility agreements with other agencies these days, so she was on top of all the other funding opportunities available. 'And what about your salary, are you still on staff at the university?'

'Well, part of the research will be covered by a study grant, and ARC have approved some funding as well.'

'So you're double-dipping, then?' Sylvia asked without looking up from her notepad.

'I think it's fairly standard. There are other costs involved with publication and so on that aren't covered under my grants.'

'Let's talk about income from the project, then,' I said. 'From the publication of the dictionary, for instance. Who will receive the royalties? I assume they'll go to the community?'

'Well, it's hard to split royalties among a large group of people.'

'Ah, but you *can* split royalties with one language centre. You will be working with a language centre, won't you?'

Dennis squirmed in his seat. I sighed as I uncrossed and re-crossed my legs. He really didn't have any idea what I was talking about.

'You have contacted the Wangka Maya Pilbara Aboriginal Language Centre, haven't you? I mean, you can't be working in the community on a project like this without their appropriate support and input. That's essential, it's protocol. The ethics committee at your university should've made that clear to you.'

'And what about copyright?' Sylvia asked. 'I hope the community as owners of the language and the intellectual property retain the copyright over their own words.' She'd done a lot of research to prep me for the meeting.

Dennis jumped right in. 'Oh no, the copyright in the work would have to rest with me. You might not understand that the Copyright Act of 1968, in lay terms—'

'Stop right there.' He was talking down to me, and I just couldn't have that, especially not in front of my staff.

'I'm the National Policy Manager for Aboriginal Arts and Culture, so I do know the Copyright Act. In lay terms, as you said, it states that the person who records a story or takes a photo retains copyright. But that doesn't mean you can't actually have a contract designed to give copyright to an organisation, one body. In fact, I don't see the logic in a non-Indigenous person legally owning the rights over a language that is not their own – or the morality of it. Why should anyone have to seek *your* permission to reproduce the material once it's published?'

He didn't respond.

Rodney leaned forward, pushing his glass of water aside. 'I'm new here, but it sounds a lot like some linguists are much like many anthropologists I meet. And I can tell you, I've met quite a lot since I started working in Indigenous cultural affairs. It seems like there's at least one anthropologist for every Aboriginal person in the country.'

'Why do you think there are so many anthropologists?' Dennis asked him calmly.

'It's not rocket science, it's because we're really deadly people. And we're very interesting.' He gave me a grin. 'And of course, there's a lot of money to be made off us. I mean we're a research industry, aren't we.' I was glad that Rodney was on my team: he'd been a slow and quiet starter, but was obviously smart.

'Anthropology is the study of behaviours, of social relations, of the physical, the social and the cultural development of human beings – of all human beings,' Dennis said a little defensively.

'So not just Aboriginals and other so-called primitive societies?' Sylvia said.

'Yes, you're right. But what's your point?' Dennis looked confused.

'Why don't we ever meet any anthropologists who study white people?' I asked. 'That's the point.'

'There are anthropologists who study white people.'

'Really? I've never met one, and trust me, I've met some anthropologists in my time.' And I had, at university, working in education and at a number of Aboriginal organisations I'd been part of over the years.

'Well, there are. Perhaps they just don't move in your circles. You make it sound like it's bad to be interested in other societies, other races, and other people.'

'I love that word, *other*,' said Sylvia. I was frightened she might launch into an eco-poem about 'otherness' so I quickly stepped in.

'What you need to understand, Dennis, is that your people are *our other*, but most of us aren't preoccupied with trying to understand what it's like to be *you*, to be *white*, to be the majority, or how it might feel to assume the superior role.'

'And we never ask whitefellas what it's like to be non-Indigenous, or what it's like to have the freedom to choose to be politically active or to choose to participate in the reconciliation process,' Rodney added.

'We don't ask whitefellas to tell us the entire history of white society or the customs of their ancestors, or why *their* people – *your* people, that is – can't seem to agree on major issues, the way you expect us to,' I said with gentle authority. 'And we don't ask these questions not only because they make people feel uncomfortable, but because it is important for us to determine our *own role, our own place* in this world that we share.'

'I understand, but there are a lot of good people working in the area of anthropology,' Dennis said.

'Yes of course there are, and we respect the work they do, but one of the reasons there are so many is because Blackfellas don't have access to western power and our voice is limited. And except where anthropologists are working to assist native title claims, there's a real risk that they're limiting our voice even further. To be honest, I've learned more from listening to elders who grew up under the Protection Act than by reading texts written by non-Indigenous academics.' It was true, and it was important to me, personally and professionally, to say so.

I was a bit concerned that Dennis had been working with mobs of old fellas who had English as a second, third or fourth language and may never have challenged his ideas or words before, possibly because they were unaware of what he was saying, or his motives for 'helping' them.

'I suppose it's all a matter of epistemology really, don't you agree?' Dennis just wouldn't give up.

'A-pissed-a-what?' said Sylvia. I was glad that she didn't know the term, it almost made her more normal. I hated the word, and how academics like Dennis used it to isolate people.

'Indigenous epistemology is just our ways of thinking and theorising, and knowledge via traditional discourses and media,' I told her, and looked back at Dennis. 'As a linguist, Dennis, you should understand that Blackfellas who have had the good fortune of education – and in our communities people like Rodney and I are completely privileged because we've had an education – we understand there's a whole language that westerners use to describe, define and locate Indigenous peoples into a particular static place.'

'What do you mean exactly?'

'For example, westerners are allowed to evolve and change, but when we do we're told we're assimilating. Westerners can become cosmopolitan but we're told we're losing our culture. When westerners intermarry their communities become multicultural, but we're told our bloodlines are being watered down. See how the language is different for the two groups? But it's not language that *we* use, it's language that's used *for* us.'

Dennis just looked blank, as if it was all too much to consume in one sitting. And perhaps it was.

'Rodney, can you please go and grab copies of the department's cultural protocols for working in Indigenous communities and give a set to Dennis?' Rodney jumped up straight away.

'Can I suggest you have a good read through these before you submit an application for funding? Rodney will be more than happy to discuss the application process with you when you've thought about how you want to proceed with the publication side of your project. And of course we'll need support letters from the local community to show they endorse the project concept and plan.'

I stood up and extended my hand. 'Thanks so much for coming in and meeting with us. It was an important conversation for us all to have, don't you think?'

'Yes, it was, thanks. I've got a lot to think about – a lot.' He seemed sincere, and I thought perhaps there was a chance I'd got through to him.

'Sylvia, can you escort Dennis to the lift? I can see Rodney waiting there with the protocols.'

And at that moment I knew that working in policy was what I wanted to be doing with my life. Marriage and kids seriously had to wait. I had a different purpose for the next few years and that was to educate those who worked with Aboriginal people as part of their daily lives.

twenty-five
The art of seduction
or seductive art?

I went to the Pissarro First Impressionist exhibition at the National Gallery of Victoria because I needed a break from everything Indij for a while. I wanted some peace, too – the phone hadn't stopped ringing since the latest Clifford Possum painting sold for a record amount at a Sotheby's auction.

I left the Rialto building and went to Degraves – the archetypal Melbourne laneway cafe – then just sat drinking a soy latte. I deserved the break. It was a surprisingly mild June day. I needed my coat, though, and smiled at the blanket of blackness that surrounded me, as I sat there brightly watching people. I felt like I was the only one alive.

Over at the gallery there was a long queue, but because of my position in the department I was able to walk straight in. There were definite benefits to the job, like getting invitations to events and books and CDs to read and listen to.

The gallery space was large and open and its bright white walls were hung with more than a hundred of Pissarro's works. The air was filled with the sounds of dozens of teenage male school students, joking and calling out to one another. They were all carrying clipboards and checking out the artwork – and their female counterparts – with enthusiasm.

I viewed the paintings slowly. Somehow this was different to any other exhibition I'd ever been to. I was held in a trance by two paintings in particular: *Woman and a Child at a Well* and *Woman Hanging Laundry*. They made me stop and think about what my life could become if I married James and had the family he so desperately wanted. Not that I'd be fetching water from a well, or hanging sheets on the line – I'd put them straight in the dryer – but it did make me consider my potential alternative lifestyle.

I read that Pissarro had met the love of his life at the age of thirty, married and spent the rest of his life with her. I wondered if I might also find that kind of love. Was James my own Pissarro? Could I break the curse my mother had cast on me?

I tried to focus and walked on. I looked at paintings from the late 1880s, done in a style the artist called 'romantic impressionism' and was shocked when I felt a hot rush from the knees up as one of the high school boys stood too close behind me.

Suddenly I missed James horribly – and physically. Making love can be taken for granted when you've got sex in your life. It seems to become so much more important when it's no longer just a part of your daily routine.

I'd never reacted to a gallery space like this before. When Alice and I had backpacked in our early twenties we'd walked the floors of the world's most acclaimed and glamorous art galleries – the Tate, the Louvre, and the Uffizi – but here I was in the NGV on St Kilda Road of all places, feeling almost uncontrollably aroused. I was surrounded by old paintings and young school boys and as horny as hell: something was wrong. I wondered if anyone else could tell.

Looking around, I realised that the teenage girls in the room were sending the young men's hormones soaring, infecting the room with unadulterated adolescent lust. It reminded me of when I went parking when I was young, with exploring teenage hands and bodies in front and back seats of borrowed parents' cars. I was just an innocent bystander here, attempting to wade through it.

I left the exhibition and went to have a cold drink. There were no spare tables in the busier than usual cafe, so I shared one with a young guy reading an art book.

'Hi, I'm Thomas.' He extended his soft hand with lean fingers towards me.

'Peta.' We shook gently.

'You've just been to see Pissarro?'

'Yes, I found it an extraordinary . . . well, an emotional experience, actually. I'm a little surprised by my reaction to the work.' I still had some tingling in my loins.

'I know. A lot of other people seem to feel the same way. I believe it's the work and the space and the history of the artist that have made this exhibition so popular.'

'Do you work here?'

'No, I'm an artist and curator for a small gallery at St Kilda.'

'I live in St Kilda, I should come and check it out sometime.' I sounded like an eager schoolgirl. 'That is, because I work in the arts. Is there a particular kind of art you specialise in?'

'Installation art.'

'Really?' I'd never understood installation art, and Sylvia hadn't briefed me on it yet. 'What exactly *is* installation art? I'd be interested in hearing a curator's perspective on it. You see, I was in an Aboriginal gallery in Sydney once when someone delivered a load of boxes and just left them in the middle of the room. People started hovering around, hands on chins, trying to determine what the artist meant. It wasn't an artist, it was a bloody courier, and ever since then I've been frightened to stand still in one spot at a gallery in case I get roped off as an exhibition.'

Thomas laughed.

'I know what you're saying – sometimes it's just hard to understand the concept. Installation art is about how an object is positioned, so that it becomes more than, well, just a pile of boxes, say. It's about what the installation is saying, its statement and its story. And installation artists use all kinds of media – sound, video, computers and so on. Does that make sense?'

'I guess so, but what about the artist who won the UK prize for the light switch that flicked on and off?' I remembered reading an article about it in the newspaper a few years ago.

'You mean Martin Creed, who won the Turner Prize in 2001.'

'That's right. It was just a bare room with a light that switched on and off. Apart from it being really bad for the environment, how would you, as a curator, define that as art? I'm curious, because some might say that a two year old could turn a light switch on and off.'

'Ah, but a two year old didn't.' He didn't answer my question at all.

'Right,' I said, none the wiser. 'Yes, I definitely think

installation art has a lot of explaining to do.' Thomas raised his eyebrows.

'What do you do, Peta?'

'I work for DOMSARIA. My area of expertise is Indigenous policy.' I handed him my card.

'That's cool. You should come to the gallery sometime; I'll give you a personal tour.' And he smiled a wicked, Pissarro-induced lustful smile. He was all of about twenty-two.

The following week I took Sylvia with me to Thomas's gallery, wanting to build on the connection while it was still fresh. I knew Sylvia would be able to determine immediately if there were any real opportunities for events or projects we could collaborate on – and she could also act as a chaperone. The space was compact, but uncluttered. Thomas was there to greet us and looked as sexy as he had at the NGV. He was dressed in a suit this time, no tie, but fancier than your average starving artist.

'Hi Peta, I'm glad you had time to drop by.' He was more formal now.

'It's part of my professional development, remember? This is Sylvia, my colleague. You look swish.'

'Yes, well, I actually own the gallery so there's some expectation I dress like a grown-up. I'd prefer to be in jeans, trust me.' He *owned* the gallery. Seeing the look of surprise on my face, he explained, 'Family inheritance – my parents died a few years back and my older sister looked after the gallery until I finished my fine arts degree.'

'Sorry to hear about your parents, Tom, and I'm glad you get to keep up the family tradition.'

'It's Thomas actually, not big on Tom. Another family tradition I have to keep on top of.'

'Right, sorry.'

He led us into one of the exhibition rooms, full of beautiful glazed bowls and vases made by a local pottery artist. Sylvia raced through, checking out the venue itself rather than the artwork, but I took my time, regarding each piece individually.

Thomas came and stood beside me as I was looking at one of the vases. It was gorgeous: two foot tall, metallic blue and purple, with a pierced neck and matte glaze finish. I knew James would've bought it for me if he were there. 'This one's beautiful,' I said, pointing.

'It makes a powerful statement, too,' said Thomas.

'Sorry, Thomas, visual arts aren't my strength, as you know,' I said. 'Can you explain to me what the artist is saying?'

'Oh Peta, no I can't really, or rather shouldn't. It's one of those things you need to decide for yourself as a viewer – what the artist is trying to say, how the work speaks to you. You need to listen to the artist's voice.'

His response left me none the wiser. James would always take the time to explain things to me, especially when it was related to his work. He'd never have given me some ambiguous, wanky bullshit like Thomas just had. It made me doubt if he knew what it meant himself.

'So what's the link between pottery and voice?' I asked.

'Art gives voice and voice gives freedom, Peta – that's

why it's so important, particularly for those in our society who don't enjoy freedom in other aspects of their lives.' That much at least was true. I wondered how much Thomas knew about Aboriginal artwork, and how it gave Blackfellas a voice in a country where we essentially remained voiceless.

When the tour was over and Sylvia was writing her details onto the mailing list form, Thomas said, 'Would you like to have dinner sometime soon, Peta, to discuss some of these issues in more detail?'

'Sounds good, let me check my diary and get back to you.' I didn't want to be going on a *date* with Thomas. Even if I weren't being faithful to James, he was too young for me anyway. But I *could* learn a lot about art from him.

On the way back to the office Sylvia didn't stop raving about Thomas.

'Well, he works in the arts, has money and sounds like he's got good politics too, which is important – for us, anyway. He's also got a bookshop in the gallery where I can sell my poetry. I could organise a reading there at some point, in the future, you know, when my book's out.' Sylvia was all over the thought of Thomas as a contact, and as usual was straight to the point. 'And I'm sure he'd give me a deal, just for the opportunity to see you again.' She winked at me.

'What are you raving about now?'

'What? You didn't notice how into you he was? He didn't take his eyes off you. He sounded like he was talking to us both, but he only ever looked at you when he spoke. I just hung around in case you needed me to comment on the funding programs we have.'

'Don't be so bloody ridiculous. Apart from the fact that I'm with James, Thomas is way too young for me.'

'Whatever you reckon, boss.' Sylvia smiled out the cab window.

'And don't call me boss.' I smiled out my own window, remembering Thomas's piercing eyes.

'You should check out this gallery when you're on your beat. The owner is really cool, and smart, and sexy too, I'd have to say – as an outsider just making an observation.' I handed Josie a card from Thomas's gallery as we sat in the Prince of Wales later that afternoon. I'd become used to having a drink of some description every day after work. Giving up the ciggies and sex was enough – I had to maintain some vices.

'Does he have a sister?' Josie laughed looking at the card. 'I mean, it's the first thing you straight fellas ask, isn't it? Has he got a brother?' She was absolutely right. It was the most commonly used phrase in the single girl's world. But in Sydney it was extended to *Does he have a brother, cousin, friend, uncle or unhappily married father?* The single straight-girl community really was quite pathetic. It was enough to make someone heterophobic.

'Actually he does have a sister but I don't know him in a personal capacity so I'm not going to suss it out, before you even dare ask me to.'

'By the spark in your eye right now I'd say you want to know him in a personal capacity.'

'Oops, look at the time! Shelley will have dinner on the table.' I shouldn't have mentioned Thomas to Josie and I knew it.

Her phone went as I stood up to leave. It was Alice.

'Say hello for me and tell her I'll Skype her after dinner,' I ordered Josie, as if she was one of my staff. When I left she was gossiping about Aunty Ivy.

I Skyped Alice later that night and told her about the Pissarro exhibition.

'You seriously need to see Pissarro, it's amazing. It will change your life.'

'Sounds fantastic. I'd love to get to Melbourne for it, but we're saving for the wedding, you know how it is.'

'Well, no, I don't, but okay – I'll see you soon anyway for your hens' thing.'

'Anything else you want to tell me?'

'About what?'

'About Thomas? He's cool, smart and sexy, I hear. Which is saying something, when it comes from a lesbian.'

'Josie can't help herself, can she? It's because I won't hook her up with his sister. He's just an interesting curator of a gallery down the road. He's asked me out for dinner.'

'You're not going are you?

'Of course I am, for work.'

'What do you think James might say about that? Or should I say, how would he *feel* about it?'

'What are you going on about? Thomas is a great contact. I'll take you and James to his gallery when you visit and you'll see. So have you decided about the Melbourne Cup yet? Bring Gary, I know he won't let you come by yourself. I also know he likes a bet.'

'Melbourne Cup, maybe. I'll ask if it's okay – I mean I'll check what he wants to do. I can come without him. We're not joined at the hip, you know.'

'Okay, I didn't mean anything by it, Missy. Don't get all defensive.'

'And as for dinner, I don't think you should tell me about guys you're wining and dining with. I know you too well, Peta. You've still got a bit of that naughty party girl inside you.'

'What does that mean?'

'It's me you're talking to. I've known you for a decade and for the most part you were a serial dater. I don't know what's going on with you and James, but I've got him here every other week, telling me how much he misses you, so if you're cheating on him, I don't want to hear even a hint about it. That's not something I'd feel comfortable with, okay?'

'Back up a bit, Alice. No-one's cheating on anyone, so stay comfortable.'

twenty-six
Dinner at Jacques Reymond

I kept telling myself that dinner with Thomas wasn't a date, because it couldn't be. I loved James, and I was faithful or celibate, whichever one was going to keep me from giving in to any urges, but Thomas had suggested Jacques Reymond in Prahran, which even I knew was a bit too flash for an arts-related business meal. Shelley dropped me off, threatening to push her face up against the window during the meal. I wore a black dress and boots and I looked hot, although I knew I shouldn't have gone to so much effort. As I walked up the side of the building I adjusted my bra and was then surprised to find the door open just as I got to it.

'How did you know I was here?' I asked the fresh-faced waiter.

'Camera, ma'am.' I was mortified that they'd seen me adjusting my bra through the security camera.

Thomas was waiting, looking at the menu and sipping on what I imagined was a scotch. It was a nice, bright space with orchids above the fireplaces. There were a few couples, two small groups and one table of eight with AFL legend Ron Barassi as the star.

I read the menu and there wasn't much that I fancied at first glance: lamb sweetbreads and tongue, young pigeon and saddle of venison.

'What do you feel like?' he asked.

I hesitated. 'What about the degust—'

Without letting me finish, he cut in. 'Degustation menu . . . it's just a way of getting to sample a wider variety of dishes. They're only small serves though.'

'Thank you, Thomas, but unlike installation art I did know what it meant. Just hard to get the tongue around sometimes.' I kept reading the menu, course after course, but there was nothing that really screamed out at me, and I had to stop and read twice the 'ten-hour suckling pig'. It reminded me of the terrible meal I had with Mike. I hadn't thought about him for a while.

'Who wants to eat a pig that's only ten hours old? That's just not right, it's almost cannibalistic.' Thomas smiled at me; the waiter standing by our table smirked too.

'What?' I wasn't prepared to be sitting there looking hot but being mocked.

'The pig is actually about three weeks old, not ten hours old. It's just slow cooked for ten hours,' Thomas said.

'Ten hours, three weeks – same thing really, and anyway, that's not how it reads.' I was repulsed by the thought of eating a piglet.

'I'll give you some more time to decide, shall I?' The waiter walked off.

'You're sexy when you correct people, and you're absolutely right, it does read that way.' Thomas was back-pedalling.

'I don't care how it reads, I'm not having that disgusting – I mean degustation – menu.'

'What about the vegetarian menu?'

'Hmmmm, yes, that looks tasty.'

'Do you want the matching wines?' I thought hard before I responded. Seven courses, seven wines, seven deadly sins and seven reasons why I could sleep with him – he's hot, young, fit, generous, smart, loaded, and here staring at me.

'Why don't we just order a bottle to share and see how we go? I don't feel like drinking much tonight.' I was lying, of course. It was Friday and I wanted to unwind but I needed to keep my wits about me and my knickers on.

He ordered a bottle of Dom Pérignon to start and then a Merlot to go with the first course, a French raclette – a dish of vegetables smothered in a creamy, strong-smelling Alpine cheese.

He smiled at me as he poured me more wine and lifted his glass. 'To beauty,' he said, and I knew we were in dangerous territory.

'So, raclette. I've never heard of it before,' I said. 'Which part of France does it come from?'

'It actually originated in Switzerland, but the French have truly mastered the art, don't you think?' Thomas said knowingly, and put a boiled potato covered in melted cheese in his mouth. He chewed and swallowed luxuriantly.

I was about to ask what 'raclette' actually meant when he changed the subject completely.

'Someone should paint you for the Archibald – your beautiful smile would bring any canvas alive.'

'I wasn't a fan of this year's winner, but I thought the portrait of Cathy Freeman had soul,' I said, nervous.

He kept going, course after course. Was he just young and brash, or was he seriously flirting with me? Either way, he made me feel agitated – hot, bothered, weak and wet.

It was not the business conversation I should have been having.

When dessert arrived, he picked up his spoon and smiled at me. 'Have you ever posed nude?' he asked, as easily as saying, 'How are you today?' and I nearly choked on my food. The meal had to end.

'Actually, Thomas, I'm feeling a little unwell. I'm sorry, but do you think we could head off?' He looked surprised, but got the bill, insisted on paying, then drove me home. I lied and said Shelley had her folks around for dinner so it probably wasn't a good idea for him to come in. He simply couldn't and shouldn't and I wouldn't let him, so we sat in the car awkwardly, like teenagers. There was chemistry that both of us were ignoring. Obviously it was normal to be attracted to more than one person at a time. And chemistry can't be controlled. All we can control is how we respond to it. And that's where being faithful came in. You can look at the menu but you just can't order off it, as my mum would say.

'I better go, thanks for dinner. I'll have Sylvia send you a funding guidelines booklet and some application forms for exhibitions, in case you want to do something collaboratively with one of the local artists.'

'I'll call you,' Thomas said through the car window as I started to walk to the gate. I was pleased that he found me desirable, but I didn't want him to call me – not socially anyway. I couldn't be friends with him, given the chemistry between us. I'd let Sylvia handle all his calls and requests.

Inside Shelley had crashed on the couch with a half-glass of Pimm's on the table and an empty packet of chips on the floor. There was a postcard from the Great Barrier Reef on the coffee table from her folks. I shook her, turned the telly off and told her to go to bed before I hit the sack as well.

I was dozing within minutes of my head hitting the pillow and before I know it I'm in a cab, driving wildly around the Arc de Triomphe in Paris. I'm screaming and the cab driver is laughing but he seems to know how to manage the chaos of the traffic. He takes me to the Eiffel Tower, and there's a group of young musicians playing brass instruments and singing and having lots of fun. There are security guards everywhere but I avoid them because I've already tried that in Italy and anyway I'm not really looking for men, even though I know that monogamy is not a priority to the French and celibacy is probably punishable by law in Paris-the-city-of-love.

I want to shop and I instruct my crazy driver to take me back to the Champs-Élysées so I can buy beautiful French things. And I do. I go into Louis Vuitton and Yves Saint Laurent and Chanel, and buy a gorgeous bag in Hermès but I know it will never come out of the satin bag it is in because back in Melbourne I can't really carry off the style. I keep walking and I'm looking at the gorgeous French women who apparently never get fat but I don't know how they do it because they eat all those buttery pastries – or maybe it's because they chain-smoke and don't eat – but they have tiny waists and fancy shoes that somehow manage to support them even on the cobblestoned streets.

The men whistle like Aussie blokes on building sites, but it's a refined, sexy, classy, we-know-how-to-please-women whistle, not the 'you root?' kind of whistle you hear back home.

I go to the new Musée du quai Branly to see the
Australian collection and there's a Koori there looking at his
own exhibition. Visual artists are so vain, I think to myself.
I go and say hello anyway, because it's my job. He hugs me
immediately, glad to see another Blackfella when he is so
far from home. But he holds me and won't let go.

'It's good to *see* me, yes, but touching me is another
thing,' I say because he has both hands firmly on my arse,
like we're together. 'You've got a wife? And kids?' I ask,
because I can't see his hands for a wedding ring.

'Yes, but old way I could have many wives.'

'Yes, and old way you'd be living under law, and not here
in Paris, so get your hands off my butt.'

He grins and morphs into the Mona Lisa and I'm
wondering what mystery is behind her smile? Was she
celibate? Or did she crave men like chocolate? Tourists
are flooding the Louvre and taking photos of the famous
painting which I think is sacrilege and I want to say
something but all of a sudden I'm in another room, exploring
the 'Americans in the Louvre' exhibition, and people are
speaking in twangy American English all around me. The
tourists all look the same till I see a brown person and I
think he's Koori so I follow him. He's cute, with long black
hair and beautiful dark skin. I haven't actually seen any other
astral travelling Kooris before today and I tell myself it's not
like an Aussie hanging out with another Aussie in Earl's
Court, because Blackfellas *have* to say hello to Blackfellas
they see in foreign places – it's protocol. Anyway, he might
be one of my mob so I need to see he's all right. But I get a
bit closer and I'm not totally sure he's Koori, even though

I'm perfectly positive he's drop-dead gorgeous. We'd make beautiful children if I were at all maternal, but I know that I could never go out with a man who had better hair than me.

He smiles as we leave the glass pyramid building and offers me a cigarette. I take one and suck on it hard because it's been months since my last one in waking life. 'I'm giving up next Toosday,' he says.

'Oh, you're American,' I say.

'No! I'm Mohawk, a Native from Canada,' he says proudly. Of course, Canadians hated getting mistaken for Americans and vice versa, just like back home Indigenous people didn't want to be confused with non-Indigenous people either. Everyone wants their rightful identity.

He tells me his name is Geronimo, and I start to tell him all about life in Sydney and then remember I live in Melbourne but just keep raving. He smiles. 'I have no idea what you said, but gee it sounded good. What is your blood quantum?' he asks. But before I have the chance to tell him we don't measure Aboriginal blood as a percentage – either you are or you're not – I can feel myself slipping away, and I grab onto one of his plaits. 'I'm not ready to leave yet,' I say out loud. 'That's okay,' he says, 'but can you let go of my hair?' And he takes my hand off his plait and holds it in his own as we walk.

I'm trying not to have preconceived notions of Indians, or Natives, or First Nations People as they say in Canada, but I can't help thinking about living in a tepee, wearing beaded and fringed dresses and braids, or at least a ribbon shirt, with long houses and sweat lodges, and arrows flying through the air. I'm like those tourists who come to Australia and expect to see lap-laps and didgeridoos.

We find a cafe in a street lined with tiny Fiats packed bumper to bumper. I choose a piece of Céline Dion's wedding cake from the menu and order a house wine, L'Auberge Notre Vin Maison, because even in my dreams I'm on a budget and can't afford the Moët.

I want to stay here with the gorgeous Geronimo. I want to go back to Canada with him and wear a jingle dress and eagle feathers and I want to eat moose meat and dance at the powwow in summer, even though I know I'd need a bloody good sports bra.

It was as I started to tell him this that I woke up in Eildon Road with the rain pouring down outside in typical Melbourne fashion. I tried hard to go back to sleep to get back to Paris, or maybe Mohawk Territory, but then a wave of nausea overcame me and I wanted to throw up and it wasn't from the wedding cake I'd eaten in my sleep, or the cigarette, but the realisation that I was hung-over on three glasses of champagne, and that Thomas was in my head and I couldn't get rid of him. No, I couldn't fall for him; it wasn't possible, anyway, after one meal, one guided tour and an exchange on installation art. Who could fall in love talking about installation art? I hated installation art! Anyway, I was already in love with James and falling for someone in Melbourne was not my plan. It would only substantiate Dannie's claims that I was 'love fickle'. And Dannie can't be right ever. I must have been dreaming like this because I missed James, that's all. So I texted him:

I miss u. Can u come down next w/end? Px

twenty-seven
It's nice being a couple

The following weekend James arrived and it was great to see him. The breaks between visits made me value him more. I missed his touch and his smile and his kisses. And God, I missed the sex. So many women said it was important to have it good in the bedroom. I'd never thought that way; I'd always believed shared politics and laughter would make it all okay in the bedroom anyway. But then again, I'd had some dodgy lovers who had great values and political views. I'd been lucky with James; he was a nice guy with good values *and* a generous lover.

As he went to get us some coffees, I sat and watched people getting on and off the #96 tram to and from the city, and I wondered if they were tourists or locals. There were a lot of young, funky types. The sun was hot, and there were more palm trees shooting up among the tramline wires overhead. I heard the Scenic Railway roller-coaster rattling in the background and kids screaming. A guy walked past holding a bottle of wine and I imagined he was rendezvousing with his lover, perhaps going for a picnic. Fish'n'chips on the pier maybe. As I started to think about how nice it was to be a couple, James snuck up behind me and gave me a big, noisy smooch on the neck: 'MWAH!'

I jumped. 'You scared me half to death,' I said, swatting at him. 'Are you ready? Let's go. The markets are this way.'

We strolled the upper esplanade at St Kilda with the masses of others out enjoying a mild Sunday afternoon. There was a lot of scaffolding along the beach front and next to the Palais Theatre. A sign said Suzi Quatro was playing, and I thought of Alice. 'If You Can't Give Me Love' was one of her favourite songs. Alice and I had very different tastes in music – but then, so did James and I. We never went to hear live music together back in Sydney, and we listened to different radio stations. He was into ABC Classic FM and I was on 93.7FM Koori Radio. Neither of us liked rap music, though, so we had that in common.

We stopped at a stall selling bangles created out of stainless steel cutlery.

'He's the original Fork Man. No piece of jewellery is the same as another,' I said.

'Would you like one?' James asked me.

'Oh, I'd prefer to use my cutlery to eat, but thank you.' I was trying to be funny, but James and the artist both looked affronted.

The next stall had kitschy name bracelets for girls and they reminded me of when I was a child and all the crap we used to collect.

'We have one that says "Rachel" if you like,' the stallholder excitedly offered me.

'Okay, but my name is Peta.'

'I'm sorry, you look exactly like Rachel Berger.'

'Yes, so I've been told.'

I ordered one for Sylvia as a joke and spelt it 'Sylv-eye-a'. I knew she'd appreciate my humour if no-one else did. I bought one for Maya too.

I could smell the next stall before we got there. Beautiful natural scented soaps made with peppermint oil and other yummy delights. I was too embarrassed to buy some in the shape of cupcakes, though. It seemed too daggy to do that. So I just kept walking, taking in the glasswork, the Japanese calligraphy, magnets with inspirational messages on them, the silver jewellery, and the wooden chopping boards and, to my surprise, the stalls with eccentric cat and dog collars.

Towards the end of the stretch of markets there was a memorial in honour of Carlo Catani, 'a great public servant of Victoria, 1876 to 1917'.

'Melbourne must be the only city to have monuments to public servants,' I said, 'but I don't see any monuments to Blackfellas along the boulevard.' I started visualising a monument to Peta Tully, 'a great national public servant', but James interrupted my thoughts, pointing towards the monument.

'Carlo Catani was an engineer and landscape designer. I read about him at uni. The Catani Gardens are around here somewhere. It would be good to check them out. Might help with some ideas for a project we've got at the moment.'

'That's a great idea,' I said. 'But I'm a little buggered, do you think we could go to the Espy and sit a minute first?'

James pushed his bottom lip out like a child. 'Isn't that a grungy band pub? You know I'm not big on live, loud music.'

'Of course I know, but there's no music – loud or otherwise – on just yet. Let's just have one drink and then we can go look at your Catani hero's work, okay?' I took his hand and led him across the road and up the front stairs of the pub.

'I'm going to the loo, I'll grab drinks on the way back. You choose a table outside.' I made my way through the dark, beer-encrusted hotel, through the poolroom and entered the ladies on the left.

On the way back I stopped at the bar to get a glass of chardonnay for me and a Corona for James. We sat outside and looked out to sea. I liked the grungy feel of the Espy and imagined all the old rockers of the past who'd played here now sitting back at home with their guitars hung on walls. I smiled as I looked across the table at James. It was nice to be there with him.

'It's not the Icebergs, is it,' James said, looking around the courtyard, then at me.

'No, it's more like the Coogee Bay,' I laughed.

'Yes, and you'd never be at the Coogee Bay at lunchtime on a Sunday, would you babe.'

'No I wouldn't, but I'm in Melbourne, and my life is different here.'

I decided to let the argument go. He'd be gone the next day, and what had come to feel like a series of weekend holiday romances would be over again.

twenty-eight
Woodford Dreaming

The department had become a major sponsor of the Dreaming Festival in Woodford and I was looking forward to going north to escape the cold in Melbourne and to get an across-the-board look at what was new and innovative in Indigenous arts. I was also excited about catching up with cousins and mates.

The program had great local theatre and dance and some international films as well. I couldn't move five metres without bumping into someone I knew through family, or my old job in education or my new role at DOMSARIA. I loved the vibe and seeing everyone having a good time. The only disappointment was that the bitter cold I'd hoped to leave behind in Melbourne had made its way to Queensland and my toes were constantly numb.

I hadn't been to Woodford for about six years and didn't remember there being so many hippies in the past. I thought their claims to be living an 'alternative' lifestyle were confused, to say the least. If there were so many of them living the same way, could they be regarded as alternative? At Woodford they were the majority.

The hardest thing about being a government rep at any event or festival, though, was that I was considered to be the 'cashed-up Koori'. Compared to the performers, I probably was. Some locals took shots at me for not camping on site and choosing to stay in a motel in Caboolture.

'A motel eh? You're not Black, you living like a whitefella,' one local artist had to say when she heard I was staying in town and not camping with all the Murris.

'Well, you can be as Black and cold as you like in your tent tonight,' I began, 'but I'm going to be warm in a bed with an electric blanket and doona and heating.' I watched her face squirm at the thought of the absolute discomfort she would be in compared to me.

'Anyway, my mum was born in a humpy – you fellas are going backwards instead of forwards. God knows, Mum would never sleep in a tent now, and I know she doesn't care where I sleep as long as I'm warm and safe.'

'Yeah, you just don't wanna rough it. Too good for the bush, aren't ya.'

'That's right, I don't want to rough it, but I'm happy for you to and I don't expect you'll be asking to use my hot shower then, will you? I mean, that's too white, isn't it? No, you enjoy your freezing cold in the morning and queuing to get a wash,' I said.

'But what about sleeping under the beautiful stars, babe? You don't want to sleep under the stars?' asked a young dancer with bulging biceps.

'Yeah, cuz,' I said, to stop his flirting. 'I wanna sleep under the stars – *five* stars would be my choice if I had my way!' And I walked off to find Sylvia, before I attracted any more crap.

'Sylvia, please, can you stop telling people we're staying in a four-star hotel? They'll wanna come shower and then sleep over when they realise how fucken cold it gets at dark. Anyway, four stars in Caboolture are about two stars in Sydney or Melbourne, so you're making us more flash than we really are.'

Back at the hotel my phone was back in range and there were numerous text and voicemail messages from James. I hadn't spoken to him for over a week and he was fretting.

Where are you babe? Are you OK? Call me.

I was still in work mode, and I was too tired to deal with James after the ribbing I'd had at the festival. I was ripe for an argument and didn't want to take it out on him. The problem with being apart meant that every minute talking or together had to be conflict free, which was enormous pressure. I sent him a long text instead:

J — sorry, range poor, weather cold, work hard, mood crappy, won't share misery. Call when back in Melbs. Love u! Px

Shelley had also texted:

Hihi, cuzin Joe dropd in sum roo Bolognese. Called it kanganese. I'll save sum 4 u, maybe! X Shelley

I was so cold at that moment that I wished for the yummy bush-tucker-Italian dish to warm me up.

twenty-nine
Saltwater, spas and steam rooms

Before I knew it three weeks had passed and NAIDOC Week had arrived, along with the bitter July weather. I'd hoped to get to Darwin for the NAIDOC ball and some warmth but Sylvia had managed to build me a tight schedule of events right around the state. James offered to fly down and come with me, but there was no point – I was simply too busy and had no time to play.

'Well, don't say I didn't try, Peta.'

'Trying once in the busiest week of the year shouldn't be the end of all your effort, James. You get some points but you're not in the black – no pun intended – just yet.' I tried to make a joke of it.

Sylvia travelled the week with me and we did a Thelma and Louise road trip, starting at the Kaawirn Kuunawarn Hissing Swan Arts Centre in Port Fairy and then driving east to Geelong for a local Indigenous tourism experience hosted by Narana Creations. Next we headed north-west to Ballarat to the Kirrit Barreet Aboriginal Art Gallery and then west to Brambuk Aboriginal Cultural Centre in the Gariwerd National Park, or what whitefellas called the Grampians. I suggested we take an extra half-day to visit the Johnny Mullagh Cricket Centre in Harrow, because I'd heard so much about the man who bowled Don Bradman out for a duck.

Travelling for the week was fun with Sylvia, and even though we were comfortable enough to have periods of silence, there was plenty of singing along to the CD she had made for us as well.

'Best of the 90s!' she said as she pushed the disc into the player and adjusted the volume dial. I couldn't believe the number of Mariah Carey, Céline Dion and Whitney Houston songs that we both knew the words to, and how soppy they were. All in stark contrast to the 'Macarena' we both tried to do in our seats.

'Can you take the wheel for this one?' Sylvia asked, as 'I Believe I Can Fly' started, and she pulled over. I got in the driver's seat and she restarted the tune and sung along to it with arms out like wings. We belted out Michael Jackson's 'Black or White' and then I went silent when Jewel came on, singing 'You Were Meant for Me'. It was the song that James had always said was *our* song.

'What's wrong?' Sylvia asked.

'Nothing, why?'

'You've gone quiet all of a sudden. Giving your vocal chords a rest, are you?'

Before I had a chance to answer, Britney Spears came on. 'Okay, that's it,' I said. 'We're not doing Britney Spears, have to draw the line somewhere. And there's a STOP REVIVE SURVIVE place up ahead, what perfect timing.'

'Good idea, my butt is a bit numb anyway – a stretch would do us good.'

'Yeah, and my butt is spreading from all the chocolate I've been eating along the way.'

'Don't worry about it, you need it for the sugar, to keep awake.'

'That's right, because you thinking you can fly in the car isn't going to do that for me, is it.'

We got out of the car and I noticed my skirt was tight in the waist. Our driving tour meant we were eating too much restaurant and fast food and sitting for too many hours without exercise. I could feel myself packing on the pounds every day.

We arrived back in Melbourne for the finale of the week at the Koorie Heritage Trust on Friday night, with soul and country performances by two young hot musos, Dan Sultan and James Henry, but I was almost too exhausted to enjoy it. I didn't think I'd ever be too tired to perve, but I was.

I woke up on Saturday feeling fat and frumpy and very, very unsexy. I'd have to marry James because I couldn't possibly take my clothes off in front of anyone else anyway. It's the ones who love us unconditionally who don't worry about love handles.

My weight gain wasn't just from NAIDOC Week, but also from eating date slices, plum cakes, cherry tartlets and other goodies from Monarch on Acland Street. The shop had been there for over seventy years and looked like it still had its original fittings. But my big weakness was Le Bon Cake Shop. Every time I went there I confused myself over what I would have because there were so many choices. Date slice, raspberry slice, rhubarb and apple slice . . . I reasoned that anything that had fruit in it was remotely healthy, but of course, nearly everything was full of sugar and fat. I had no rationale whatsoever for pigging out on the brandy, chocolate or caramel slices: they simply looked delicious and had to be eaten. I wished they could genetically modify carrots and celery to taste like *anything* I could consume on Acland Street.

Because of my indulgences I needed to get more exercise. I really missed swimming, and it would give me the best overall body workout, but winter in Melbourne had a chilly bite. Shelley had raved about the St Kilda Sea Baths, insisting that I should check them out; they were indoors, and heated, so I decided to take the plunge. At least my brown skin meant I'd look a bit better than everyone else. Fat and dark was better than fat and pasty white.

It was expensive to enter the baths, so I wasn't surprised that it was quiet and peaceful with plenty of lane room to swim. I guessed that most people like me would see the experience as a bit of luxury rather than part of a daily exercise routine. Shelley told me it had once been more 'working-class friendly' but from the moment I hit the change room, I felt it was a place for middle-class mums and retirees. And even though both groups of women had more stretch marks than I would ever allow myself to have, I still couldn't bring myself to undress in front of strangers. I laughed to myself, thinking that Josie would relish the change room experience, but I just couldn't do it so I took my cozzie (or my 'bathers' as the Melbournites called them) into the privacy of the toilet and got changed.

As I lowered myself into the pool I felt more relaxed immediately. I began doing backstroke in the salty water, watching the blue skies through glass roofing, then swapped to a slow breaststroke towards the horizon, watching the ocean approaching. In Sydney there was always competition to get a lane, but here there were only a couple of people in each, and none of them looked like they were here for a serious workout. I even managed to swim in the 'fast lane' as opposed to the slow or medium lanes I swam in back home. No, this pool was about relaxation and enjoyment, not fitness.

I shared a lane with an old man who should have been in the play area. I could hear his breathing, like an underwater foghorn vibrating throughout the pool. It was almost scary, like a whale was approaching. He swam so slowly that I caught up to him rather quickly, and copped an eyeful of his worn and wrinkled genitals floating around freely in his too-wide-legged swim shorts. At least Speedos kept everything packaged tight and close to the body. I couldn't swim another twenty-five metre lap with that in front of me. I considered stopping at one end of the pool and then kicking off in front of him, but then I felt weird about the thought of him swimming behind me and taking in my back view while doing breaststroke. The only thing worse than the idea of his wrinkled old penis was thinking that I might actually cause it to go hard. I couldn't have that, so I just kept going, but I switched to backstroke, focusing on the flags above the pool to make sure I didn't go head first into the wall at the end of the lane.

The pool was sea water, and so salty it reminded me of gargling hot water with salt out of the big white Saxa bottle when I was a child and my throat was sore. Even with goggles on my eyes were starting to sting. Not being able to take the salt or the wrinkled testes any longer, but determined to get my twelve-dollar entry fee's worth, I headed to the hydrotherapy heated seawater pool where even more old men played. At least their genitals were well hidden under the foam. They hogged the few spa jets in an attempt to cure their aches and pains. I had none of those, but I wanted to get the full experience, so while I waited I checked out a bald guy in black shorts. He was the youngest male in the pool and had a well-cut chest. A jet became free and I paddled over and pushed my back up against it, facing the main pool.

I turned around and rested my head on my hands, looking out to the bay and thinking how beautifully relaxing a space it was to be in. I could have gone to sleep but I turned my head left and read a sign that told me I should only spend ten minutes in the spa, so I got out and set off for the steam room, walking up the stairs as sexily as I could, aware of the cute bald guy still in the pool. I knew my legs looked good in my black Speedo, even though I often fantasised about wearing a red Baywatch cozzie like Pamela Anderson. I believed that kind of cozzie could help make anyone look good, or at least better. A good cozzie was a far healthier and cheaper option than cosmetic surgery.

A young life guard in a black and orange uniform smiled at me and I was hoping it wasn't because I needed a bikini wax. It was winter, after all, so I hadn't thought to prepare myself for public exposure.

The steam room was all white, with two levels of benches along three walls and eucalyptus vapours that cleared the throat and lungs. It was cleansing and refreshing after the salt in the pools, but in that hot, confined space I felt a particular energy as the only woman in there with two men. One was a young guy in long shorts who kept pouring water over himself from a Mount Franklin bottle. It was a very sexy thing to do, but I couldn't imagine myself doing it. There are some things that some people just shouldn't even try.

He was only about twenty, way too young for me, so I tried to focus on work priorities then, to block male thoughts from my mind. I started making a to-do list in my head: *edit the new music strategy paper; check staff are all doing the required amount of professional development* . . . But then I noticed that the other guy was staring at me. He was around thirty-five, dark, fit and cute, but hairy. I didn't really like hair. James didn't have anything other than three strays on his chest which he would never let me pluck out, even though they were worse than the comb-over on an old balding man. This guy was incredibly attractive, though.

I was suddenly horny and started visualising getting naked with my toy boy and the hairy older guy at the same time. I was so turned on that I scared myself and got up abruptly and left the room.

Ever since I'd decided to stay away from men because of James and my long-term career plans, all of a sudden they were everywhere, following me. Or maybe they weren't at all – maybe I just subconsciously wanted them to be. I emerged from the spa for the final time, grabbed my towel and sat on the white chair facing the bay. I started to dream about the Ladies Baths back at Coogee – serene, private, and women-only – and I wondered how Alice and the girls were getting on. Were they there right now, sunning themselves on our rock? A pang of homesickness consumed me, and it was easier to satisfy that pang than the horny one, so I headed back to Acland Street to Monarch and some chocolate guglhupf and sachertorte in honour of my friend Alice and her Austrian heritage. I sent her a text:

Missin u all, eatin cake 2 feel better. Ur fault if I get fatter! Pxx

I also bought a piece to give to Josie as she was taking me to my first football match that night.

thirty
A trip to the G

'Peta, you really have to learn to fit in, assimilate already.'
Josie just looked me up and down and shook her head.
We were manoeuvring through the masses of traffic
heading to the game. I was in black pants and polo and
my watermelon coat. I couldn't be all black at the football,
but I didn't own any footy attire and promised myself I
never would.

'What? I have to assimilate in order to be accepted?'

'That's right. They should make you do a bloody entry test
before they let you into Victoria – the Melbourne IQ test.'

'What? Like the national values test?'

'Exactly! And top of the list of values for Victorians is
commitment to football!'

'Right next to only wearing black, yeah?'

'That's right, unless you're at the football.'

'Right, got it, made a mental note. I'll pretend for now
that I'm completely committed and I'll act obsessed.'

'Good, now let me focus while I find us a parking spot.'

AFL was like a cult in Victoria. Even Shelley, the stockbroking, Pimm's drinking shoe and bag lady, was into it,
and said I *had* to go for St Kilda while I was in Melbourne.
This evening's game was Collingwood vs. Sydney Swans,
though, so I was barracking for the Swans. Josie was a Saints
fan, too, but even she was going for Sydney tonight.

'I'm confused – how do you go for the Swans when you're a St Kilda fan? Shouldn't you at least go for the local team and not the Swans tonight? Sorry, but I don't get it.'

'No, see, if your own team isn't playing, then you just go for the team playing Collingwood, doesn't matter if they're from Sydney or West Coast or Adelaide. No-one likes Collingwood, except for their own supporters, and they're mongrels.'

'Oh, I'm getting it. Like everyone hates Manly in the rugby league.'

'That's it, you've got it!'

'What about women? Are there many female supporters at these matches?'

'Oh, yeah baby, it's really the reason I go. About fifty per cent of AFL supporters are women, and they make up about forty-five per cent of the crowd at games.'

'Really? That surprises me.'

'That's because you come from a rugby league state, where female support is only about thirty-nine per cent.'

'How do you know all these stats?'

'Vested interest, love.' Josie winked at me.

There was an exhibition game with young lads before the main match, and as we walked past the entrance to the change rooms where the team was warming up we heard the coach berating the aspiring players.

'Look, there are kids your age in other parts of the world fighting for their lives, fighting for their freedom, and all you have to do is go out and win a fucken football match. Do you think you can do that?'

'Yes,' they responded solemnly.

'What? You can't even yell like men. DO YOU THINK YOU CAN WIN THE FUCKEN MATCH?'

'YES!' they roared, as much from fear of the coach as passion for the game. I didn't think I'd ever really understand the AFL psyche, but with sports in my department's portfolio I needed to get my head around it at least, with so many Blackfellas in the code and at the top of their game.

There weren't many Swannies there and as we made our way to our seats we were heckled by Collingwood supporters. One of the other parkies had given Josie tickets to the MCC Members Reserve. It was the best place to watch a game from, or so Sylvia told me. I didn't really care where we sat, I just wanted to see what all the fuss was about.

'I'm really excited about this, Josie. I've always wanted to go to the "M"!'

'What's the "M"?' she asked, screwing her face up.

'The MCG!'

'It's called the "G", you twit.' And we both laughed. I really had no idea.

'Are any of your other friends coming tonight?' I hadn't met many of Josie's friends, and wasn't even sure if lesbians were interested in AFL as a rule, or just the female spectators.

'Are you kidding? I couldn't get anyone else to go to a Swans game, especially when they're playing Collingwood. They're dogs, you just wait and see.'

Then the game started and it was all on.

'Carn the Woodies!' came the cry from an old fella sitting a few rows behind us.

'Right, what's a woody, apart from the obvious thing?'

'You heteros only ever think about that, don't you?'

'Pretty much.'

'The Woodies are Collingwood.'

'Of course, Colling-*wood*.'

Barry Hall missed a mark for the Swans and I heard a young boy no more than eight years old scream with the passion of a veteran spectator: 'Send them to hell, Collingwood!' He sat down and wrapped his 'Hot Pies' banner around his shoulders for all those behind to see. Then a boo from the crowd sounded throughout the stand.

'What happened there?'

'Holding the ball,' Josie said, looking straight towards the field, not even blinking an eyelid. She was completely into the game.

'That's not good, is it?' The Swans seemed to be down on the scoreboard.

'It's okay, Sydney are getting their groove back, watch,' Josie said, as Adam Goodes ran and kicked the ball further than I've ever seen a ball travel. I elbowed her hard with excitement even though I wasn't quite sure what was going on. I could see red and white bodies waving streamers and flags here and there around the stadium.

Three generations of Collingwood fans sat in front of us: a brother and sister, their father and grandfather. Their dad had his phone in his ear, listening to the game being called on the radio. The kids spent their time running up and down the stairs until the daughter fell and hurt herself. The father didn't fuss, though – in fact, he didn't take his eyes off the game while he rummaged through a backpack looking for a drink bottle to appease her. Later in the game I watched the boy clutching himself through his shorts, saying, 'Dad, I really have to go to the toilet.' The third time he said it, about fifteen minutes later, he finally got a response: 'Now's not a good time, son.'

'I hope he pisses his pants,' I said to Josie.

'No, you don't want that. It will be embarrassing for him, not the father.' She was right.

'Well, if he doesn't take him soon, I'm going to offer to take him. That's really bad parenting. Even *I* know you have to let them piss occasionally.'

I tried to ignore the potential pissy-pants boy, just like his father was. There was a cheer and the Swans got a goal.

'How many points for a goal?' I asked Josie, leaning in.

'Six if you get it through the middle posts, and one point if it goes between the outer posts,' she answered without looking at me. She seemed to be in a trance. After a while I started to understand how it all worked and got right into it: when your team was winning the game really was addictive – and so was looking at the long, lean, muscly, pumped bodies all over the field.

Sweat glistened on biceps and glutes filled out tight shorts and I imagined the joy of being a footy team physio or masseur. How did women control themselves in the locker room with all that testosterone and firm flesh? And how hard would it be to control sexual urges when you were rubbing the players all over? I was getting agitated at the thought of naked men I didn't even know, wrapped in very small towels with torsos rippling, loins in need of some deep tissue massage and tired muscles in need of liniment.

'I'd rub it in,' I accidentally said out loud.

'What?' Josie asked without looking at me.

'I'd rub the liniment in for them, you know, in the locker room, if I had to. If it was my job. I mean, I was just thinking that it would be a hard job, I wasn't perving or anything, you know, cos I have James, and he looks good in shorts too.'

'Oh God, stop rambling. It's okay to perve, everyone does it. Even I do.'

'You?' I was glad the emphasis had been taken off me.

'Don't be so surprised. Just because I prefer the female form to play with doesn't mean I don't or can't appreciate a good-looking male. And there are plenty of them out there. Which means there's plenty of females right back here.' She leaned back in her seat and looked around at the women in the crowd.

I continued to stare out at the players, dreaming about my new fantasy job as the Swans' team liniment applicator. Before I knew it it was half-time, and we headed to the Blazer Bar.

'Hey, I forgot to give you this.' Josie handed me a Swans beanie and I laughed.

'Priceless, thanks.'

'Well?' she asked, looking at the beanie in my hand and then at my head.

'Oh, you don't seriously expect me to wear it, do you? I spent ages doing my hair this evening. I don't want beanie hair.'

'At least put this on, then.' And she pulled a scarf out of her bag as well. It clashed terribly with my watermelon coat, but I wrapped it around my neck with as much glamour as I could.

'Cheers!' We clicked our Blonde beers in a toast. 'Thanks again, Josie, this is the highlight of my Melbourne experience so far.'

A pissed guy standing next to us decided to join our conversation. 'Where are you from?' he asked.

'Sydney,' I said proudly, ready for the onslaught.

'No you're not!' he slurred.

'Excuse me?'

'No, you're from up further north than that. Your tan's from up north.' I saw Josie step back in concern about how I might react. In her job she'd learned not to let losers get to her, and I knew she wouldn't want to deal with any conflict while she was out socialising, so I tried to take a leaf out of her wise book.

'I'm from Sydney, I just spend a lot of time on the beach.' That was all he was going to get from me.

'Hey, you look like that comedian Rachel Berger,' he said.

'Yes, apparently I do.'

'Okay, let's go over this way.' Josie dragged me away.

'Thanks for saving me from that guy.'

'Oh, I didn't, I just wanted to stand over here where all the hot women are. Watch this. I'll get that woman there.'

'Is she gay?'

'Probably not, but I reckon I can get her to come talk to me.'

'You're insane, but go on, I'm intrigued.'

I watched Josie concentrate in the direction of a blonde woman with an ample breast and arse. About the same height as Josie, she was standing with a group of friends and enjoying her beer. I saw her notice Josie and just go on talking. But Josie kept in direct line with her and just kept staring. I wasn't sure what she was doing, but sure enough, ten minutes later the woman sauntered to the bar, bought a couple of beers and walked over and handed one to Josie. I'd never seen anything like it.

'Don't I know you from somewhere?' she gushed. I noticed she was wearing a wedding ring.

'I'm a parking cop in St Kilda – hope I didn't book you.'

'No, it's not that – I always obey the law.' She threw a sleazy smile and touched Josie on the arm.

'Maybe I've seen you at Girls Bar,' Josie said.

'Oh no, I haven't been there.'

'Maybe you should.'

'Maybe I should.'

The siren sounded, signalling the game was starting again and everyone began moving out of the bar and back to their seats.

'How the hell did you do that? You knew her already, didn't you?' I couldn't believe what I had just seen.

'Never seen her before in my life.'

'Seriously?'

'Seriously. It's something my old people taught me, but sorry, I can't share it with you.'

Fair enough, I thought, but I was sure the old people would've been teaching her how to attract men and she'd just manipulated it slightly.

'So was wearing that sexy black top part of the strategy to meet women too? It's great, even though it's *black*.

Where did you get it?' I touched the sleeve – it seemed a bit thin for a wintry night out in Melbourne.

'Like it?' She ran her hands over herself. 'I bought it yesterday.'

'Weren't you working yesterday?'

'Yeah but I go MIA all the time.'

'MIA?'

'Missing in action. Don't they use acronyms in Sydney?'

'Of course they do, I just thought that maybe the "M" was for Melbourne something or other. So, how do you go MIA when you're supposed to be on duty?'

'Easy, we all do it. We need to do our shopping, pay bills, and check our email, MySpace and Facebook pages. We only get thirty minutes for lunch, can't get much done in that time.'

'But don't you get eight days off after each ten-day shift?'

'Yeah, but sometimes things need to be done before the next day off. Like I needed a new top for tonight.'

'Then I suppose you never get bored at work, do you?'

'Nah, if that happens we just issue tickets.' We both laughed, then settled back to watch the second half.

'Wow, that was great. I mean the atmosphere, not the fact that Collingwood won. I have to say I'm surprised the time went so quickly. I didn't think I'd manage sitting through an entire football match. It really is addictive, isn't it?'

'You mean the players are addictive.' Josie was right, I was on my first football high – I was starving, too.

'So, where do you want to eat?' I hoped she'd have somewhere groovy and tasty in mind, but she didn't.

'I don't care as long as I get fed.'

'God, you're rough sometimes, girl. What about just going to a pub?'

We went back to the Prince of Wales and it was busy enough to have a buzz to it, but not so busy that we couldn't find ourselves somewhere to sit and order food. Scanning the room for a table, I saw some Blackfellas sitting in a corner, laughing and having a good time. I recognised one as a local filmmaker and another was a photographer.

I groaned. 'Oh, God. They're my clients, they'll start asking me about funding opportunities and deadlines if they see me.'

'Yeah, and they'll ask me to get them out of a parking ticket. Let's eat first, and then head over.'

'I like your style, Josie.'

I watched her completely devour a huge porterhouse steak; I had the Moroccan chicken.

'Okay, let's go say hi to the 'lations,' she said when she was done, wiping her face aggressively with her serviette. 'Come on. You know we never bundy off as Blackfellas.' She was already on her way over to the table.

As we sat down, drinks were plonked in front of me: two pints of pale ale and a glass of red. I followed the hands up their arms and to the face of Constable Care, Mike.

He looked me straight in the eye and said, 'Honey, I'm new in town – dya think I can have directions to your house?'

'You're mad.' I giggled like a schoolgirl.

'I know you like me, I'm a likeable guy. That's me, Mike, Mr Nice Guy.' We hadn't spoken since the hideous lunch, but looking around I realised he couldn't be such a bad guy, even if he was a cop: he was sitting there with a mob of Blackfellas. But what was his story? Did they know about the blue wrist band too? I couldn't control myself and grabbed his sleeve, pushing it up to his elbow, and then, not satisfied, pushed it further up his biceps to see if the rubber band was there. It wasn't.

'What are you doing? You want to touch these puppies, do you?' He flexed his muscles. Now that he wasn't wearing the blue band any more he suddenly became more attractive. Perhaps he wasn't so much the Nazi in the Nazi/Jew scenario I'd imagined.

'You know I have a boyfriend.'

'And where is he then, this boyfriend you keep mentioning? Why isn't he here protecting you from potential suitors like me?'

'Because he doesn't have to *protect* me. And even if we weren't together he knows I would never kiss a cop,' I said adamantly, looking into the bluest eyes I had ever seen.

'Peta, how would you feel if I said that I wouldn't kiss someone who's Aboriginal?'

'I'd think you were a racist prick and probably tell you so.'

'And fair enough. I would be a racist prick if I said that. But it feels the same when you say to me that you could never kiss a cop. Can you see how discriminatory you're being?' And he was right. I didn't say anything. There were a few seconds of uncomfortable silence between us.

'I hope you know CPR,' Mike said, dodging the topic.

'Why?'

'Cos you take my breath away.'

'Okay, that's enough already. It's time to go. We've got a huge day tomorrow.

'What's on, babycakes?'

'The rally against the government's intervention in the Northern Territory. But I don't suppose that's anything you'd be interested in.'

'Why would you think that, Peta? Gees, you're so quick to judge and second-guess others, aren't you? Of course I'm concerned about human rights; my job is about protecting human rights. I'm not marching tomorrow because I'm on duty, but I would've.'

'Yeah, yeah.'

'Look, I'm just as pissed off as you are about the way the NT legislation was passed by suspending the Racial Discrimination Act. It was unlawful, and I'm an officer of the law. And of course it's immoral as well.'

I must have looked surprised.

'What? You think you're the only one who reads the newspapers? It's the first thing I do every morning. I've even been known to write a letter or two to the editor.'

'Of course, my apologies. It's actually getting late, we really should go.'

thirty-one
End the intervention!
Human rights for all!

I was supposed to meet Josie at Federation Square at ten am, ready for the march. It was difficult to find her as everyone was asked to wear red. I wasn't sure if it was because we were 'seeing red' due to the intervention, or if it was to connect to the red earth of the Northern Territory or if it was just for visual effect. Either way, it was great to see that even the Melbourne black was put aside for this one day. There were thousands of supporters there, hundreds of Aboriginal flags and loads of banners reading: *NT LEGISLATION = DISCRIMINATION* and *STOP THE INVASION OF THE NT* and so on.

There was a huge contingent of Greens supporters and even Bob Brown. He was such a great politician, he just needed a good Melbourne makeover. While I was scanning the crowd for Josie I saw staff from other sections of DOMSARIA huddled together behind one massive banner. I called James, knowing he'd be thinking of me. Sunday mornings we'd nearly always be together, out for breakfast or lazing in bed with the papers. Just as he answered Josie walked up to me, also on her mobile. We air kissed and just kept talking into our respective phones.

'Where are you? It sounds like a circus down there.' James had forgotten about the march.

'I'm at the march against the intervention with Josie and a mob of Blackfellas, and some staff from other sections of the department.'

'Of course, many people there?'

'Masses, it's a great statement.'

'You know it won't make a lick of difference, don't you?'

'What?'

'People marched against the war in Iraq, they marched against mining, they marched against the GST even, but the government will still do what they want.'

'So what are you saying? It's a waste of time?'

'Well . . .'

'Well, what? It's not a waste of time to the Elders who have travelled here from their communities looking for support when the government won't even meet with them. It's not a waste of time if lone individuals can take some sort of collective responsibility for the cause, and make a public statement about how they feel.' I sounded like I was in a meeting at work, talking to the linguist again. 'I've gotta go, there's some movement up the front.'

'Just don't get arrested.'

'So you won't bail me out?'

'You know I would, I'm just saying it's not worth a record.'

That was the difference between us: I thought the fight for social justice and human rights was worth whatever I could give.

We marched down Swanston Street past Bourke Street Mall and the chants were well timed and strong. I was straining my lungs with Josie and all those around me when

I felt someone grab my arm gently. It was Mike and he was in uniform.

'Hi!' He had to bellow over the chanting. I could see people around me looking worried, thinking I was in trouble with the law or something

'Hi. You didn't tell me you were on rally patrol. It's almost laughable. What are you doing, making sure we don't cause a riot?'

'No, I was meant to be at the station.' He was still bellowing – a guy with a megaphone was making his way along the line of marchers to keep us all in sync. 'But I swapped with someone so I could be here.'

'Why?'

'Didn't you hear what I said last night?'

'Right, but you can't march in uniform, can you?'

'No, I can't, but I can walk along the side and do my job and still feel like I'm part of it. Better go, I'll call you.' And he was off.

Before I had too much time to think about it a new chant began: 'End the intervention! Human rights for all!'

We all ended up soothing our sore throats back at the Espy. Josie and I found a table in the corner because we both wanted some quiet.

'So, Mike was there today, didn't know you had a date,' Josie teased.

'Don't be ridiculous, he was working,' I told her.

'Oooh, that was a bit defensive, Peta. Touch a raw nerve

did I? Like he touched your arm, eh? Yes, I saw the gentle move he made.'

'Now you *are* being ridiculous. And I'm not talking about him with you.'

'Keep digging there, sista, you'll bury yourself in a minute.'

'You really are a nut, Josie, but I like you.' I smiled. 'No, not *that* way, so stop grinning like the cat that got the cream.'

'But what if I buy you one more drink? Will you like me *that* way then?'

'I'm going home to put the pics up on Facebook to show the girls, and *James*. See you soon, eh?' I said as I pushed my chair in and left Josie with a mob of strangers who had made themselves comfortable at our table.

Shelley was out and I got busy uploading photos and sending emails. I especially wanted James to see the turnout, and how many people had rallied to exercise their democratic rights and try to do something to make the country more equitable for all. I sat at the computer for hours catching up on superpokes and snowglobes and hugs, and then my phone sounded a text message. It was from Mike:

Hi Peta, gr8 turnout 2day. Was good 2 c u. Hope 2 c u soon.
The Cop

The cheesy lines had gone, like we were real friends now. I drafted and redrafted my reply, and before going to bed finally sent it:

Hi Mike. Yes, a good response all round. Perhaps we cld do dinner?
Peta

Minutes later he texted me back:

I'll call u soon. Good nite.

thirty-two
Authentically, not!

I stayed at Aunt Nell's place in East Bentleigh on Monday night to babysit Maya and Will while Joe and Annie took Aunt out for her birthday. Maya greeted me at the door with a painting she had done at school for me.

'That's beautiful, Maya,' I said, not quite sure what I was looking at.

'It's you and Mummy and Nanny and me out shopping, without Will.' She turned her nose up as Will came crashing into me yelling, 'Eeta, Eeta!'

'Hello big fella,' I said, lifting his heavy weight off the ground. Will was chunky for his age, no doubt from Joe's cooking. 'What are you up to? Are you being a good boy for Mummy?' No sooner was he up than he was down on the ground again, running through the house bellowing 'Eeta, Eeta!'

I enjoyed hanging out with Maya and Will that night and even got them off to sleep without too much hassle. They'd become better behaved with me over the months and had learned that going to bed without arguments meant that Aunty Peta was a nicer and more generous aunty. My first babysitting stint had taught me the advantages of bribery as a strategy.

I pulled the sofa bed out and crashed in the lounge room and somehow didn't wake up when Aunty Nell and the others came in the door at midnight. The next morning I was awake early, expecting the kids to torment me, but despite the central heating even Will and Maya seemed to think bed was the best place to be in winter.

'Okay, cuz, if that's not a blanket keeping you warm in there then kick him out.' Joe stuck his head around the doorway and came in with some homemade muffins for breakfast.

'Oh, you're sooooo hilarious aren't you?' I pulled the doona up further.

'Or so he thinks.' Annie followed him with a freshly brewed pot of tea.

'Shouldn't you stay in bed and make the most of the kids not being awake?' That's what I would've done.

'Actually, it's much nicer to be up and have a quiet cuppa together while we can.' Annie poured me a cup of tea and Joe passed me a muffin and they sat on either side of the sofa bed and just ate and sipped. There was a sense of homeliness about being there again, and the relationship between Annie and Joe inspired me. They actually seemed to *like* each other.

Joe dropped me at the station about quarter past seven and when I saw people running for the train, I ran as well. Even though I had plenty of layers on, including my loud coat, I was numb from the low temperatures. There was simply no denying that Melbourne was a lot colder than Sydney.

I watched my breath as I exhaled into the cold air, and smiled at the well-dressed men who hurried beside me in their dark suits and scarves. Scarves were something I rarely if ever saw men wearing in Sydney, it never got cold enough.

As I waited for the train to pull out I laughed at the palm trees that made a weird backdrop to the station and the graffiti-adorned wall. It was like a fusion of Los Angeles and Western Sydney.

Sylvia and I had agreed to meet at the Vic Markets before work to buy some supplies for the after-work drinks that day. It was a farewell for one of the IT guys, Jeremy, whom we were all going to miss because he always managed to find the files we thought we'd deleted and lost forever.

As I mostly caught trams in Melbourne, I still didn't have my bearings on the train line, even though I'd been in the city for six months. I got off at Flinders Street station by mistake and was immediately caught up in a sea of pin-striped, scarved and stilettoed Melbournites on their way to work. Their dark strides were fast, determined and purposeful, and I was carried along with the current quickly. Everyone was well dressed, well groomed, well rugged up, but they all looked the same. Dark, grey, drab, dull. Black. I was in the so-called fashion capital of Australia, but everyone looked exactly the same. I felt like I was at some big fat city-wide Greek funeral. And then there was me, sticking out like dog's balls, in my watermelon coat.

It was obvious that the 'coastal' fashions and colours of Sydney were out of place here in the Euro-moody weather of Melbourne. I walked in step with the others, completely conscious that I did not fit in, yet feeling oddly good about it. I liked being an individual. I liked having some spunk about me, even though I felt other women in the street were smirking at me, as if to say I had no fashion sense whatsoever. I upped my pace until I reached the markets.

It was my first time there, so I'd planned to arrive early for an unrushed browse before meeting Sylvia. I strolled along each aisle, lingering at some stalls, ignoring others. I wasn't interested in leather jackets, running shoes or cheap jewellery, or a logoed T-shirt made in a Taiwanese sweatshop. I found a stall where I could get my name written in Japanese and framed, but couldn't think of one reason why I would.

Then I hit the stands selling 'Authentically Australian Souvenirs', where generic dot-painted *everything* seemed to be the flavour of the day. At one stall I picked up a tea towel with a map of Australia on it. Each state had its flower or bird or other animal, like the Tasmanian tiger. The Northern Territory, however, had a stereotypical Aboriginal man in a red loincloth, holding a spear. At the Vic Markets Aboriginal people were still considered part of the flora and fauna of Australia.

In another aisle the sign read, 'Extensive range of quality Australian souvenirs'. I had to ask myself how much *quality* you could actually buy for two dollars. At that moment the issue for me wasn't so much about the appropriation of Aboriginal cultural property but just how cheap and nasty most of the items were. But most people were ignorant of the value of Indigenous arts and culture and were happy with kitsch rip-offs.

I picked up a packet of ten clip-on koalas to see where they were made.

'Three packs for ten dollars.' The seller was excited as he worked two sets of tourists at the same time. I turned the packet over and looked at the label: China. I put them down without saying anything. What was the point getting upset about the quality and inauthenticity of the merchandise? There were dozens of stalls like his selling the same crap. My favourite was the one advertising boomerangs: 'guaranteed to return, machine-made, authentically Australian'. Obviously the marketing people hadn't seen the contradiction in promoting a 'machine-made' boomerang as authentic.

At the end of another aisle I stumbled upon the pièce de résistance. An Aboriginal statue in full chocolate brown, red loincloth, holding a spear and, just in case I didn't know what I was looking at, a bronze plaque reading: 'Australian Aborigine'.

'Fifteen dollars for you, Miss.' The seller didn't see how ridiculous it was to try to sell it to me. For him, I was clearly alive and there as a customer, but not as an Aboriginal person. It was so kitsch I was tempted to buy it – it would be useful in discussing stereotypes and identity in cross-cultural training in the department – but I couldn't bring myself to even pick it up, so I moved on.

'You tell me your best price, Miss, we can do a deal.' He winked as I walked away. He was cute, but I didn't want to engage in a cross-cultural awareness training workshop there and then – no time, and not for free, and not even for his very cheeky smile.

I was authentic-Australianed out, but kept walking and looked at ugg boots in pink and purple and wondered if anyone would buy them. The suited of Melbourne would probably never be seen dead in ugg boots, but they probably didn't shop at the Vic Markets anyway.

I kept wandering and was seduced by a stall with interesting ironing board covers. I bought the one with the Statue of David on it, believing it would make ironing less of a chore. I wasn't sure how Shelley would react, and we'd have to make sure it was gone before her parents came back. She hadn't said how long they'd be away, just that it was indefinite.

At nine I made my way to the coffee shop on the corner to meet Sylvia, who hadn't arrived yet. I ordered a soy latte, sat in the window and took in the surrounds, trying not to think about the cold. I sent a text message to the girls:

Hi – at Vic Markets, freezin, but coffee + barista hot! Miss ya, Px

The barista was handsome, European handsome, dressed in blue jeans and a black shirt and apron. When he turned around his arse was tiny and taut. I'd definitely become a bit of a perve since being in Melbourne – but checking out men when you were celibate was like staring into a cake shop window when you were on a diet.

Sylvia arrived puffed and apologetic for being ten minutes late, but I didn't really care. We'd both put in a lot of overtime over the past months so a ten am start was fine occasionally. We finished our coffees and headed in to buy the goodies.

'I don't go into the meat area,' Sylvia said, stopping still in her tracks.

'Oh, for God's sake, Sylvia, why didn't you tell me? I could've done it all already.'

'Sorry. I didn't think to mention it before.'

'And do I have to carry it all as well?'

'Not if it's all in double plastic bags and then in your environmental bag.'

'You're an idiot!' I laughed. 'You get the breads and I'll get the cold meats and some prawns.'

'Get ready for a carb explosion, then – there's about fifty different types of bread here . . . I might be a while.'

As I roamed the seafood area I couldn't believe the wonderful choices: raw prawns, tiger prawns, banana prawns, green prawns, peeled prawns.

'Good morning, beautiful lady, what can I get you today?' a chirpy fella greeted me.

'Two kilos of cooked prawns, please?' He handed them over with the flirtatious smile that all butchers and fishmongers seem to have when serving women. It's an art form. Butchers do it the best, guaranteeing that female customers come back time and time again.

I looked at my list: olives, prawns, pâté, cold meats. At one stall there were fifteen different types of olives; the next had hot cabana, mild cabana and a whole range of other sausages. I could've spent the entire day trying to decide, but I didn't have time.

Sylvia came back with a bag of continental and Middle Eastern breads and a mix of soft and hard cheeses. I put her in a cab with the food – including the cold meats – and sent her to the Rialto building while I raced down to the Koorie Heritage Trust and rummaged through the shelves for a gift for Jeremy. The shop had its fair share of dots and kitschy pieces as well, but I ended up getting a selection of bush chutneys and oils because Jeremy was a man who loved food. I also got him a tie because he always dressed well at work.

I bought James a book on Aboriginal Melbourne while I was there. I was going to Sydney the following week and then on to the Gold Coast for Alice's hens' night. It was probably a good thing. I kept wondering if Mike was going to call me about having dinner, even though it was probably a bad idea.

thirty-three
Virgin to Vegas

I couldn't believe August had come around so quickly, and so too Alice's hens' weekend and birthday celebrations on the Gold Coast. I was excited about going away for a few days not only to see Alice, Liza and Dannie, but also to escape the miserable Melbourne weather. Alice had Skyped me every day the week before, and counted down on her Facebook page the days to arriving at Conrad Jupiters. I knew that she was also bursting about her hens' night – the one she'd once vowed she would never have.

I was in Sydney for a meeting with the Aboriginal and Torres Strait Islander Arts Board at the Australia Council the day before we left, so it meant we could all fly together up the coast. I stayed overnight in a hotel in the city and James came and stayed with me.

We only had twelve hours together and most of it was spent sleeping – we were both exhausted from work. We made love, but it was sex you have when you're still half asleep, or mostly asleep, with no energy at all, just rhythm and grinding until the job's done. Neither of us said anything, but as James drove me to the airport I wondered if that was what married life was like for busy working couples. It wasn't how I wanted it to be for me.

'I'm glad you're having this weekend with the girls. Just behave yourself, all right,' he said as he patted my thigh, half jokingly, half seriously.

251

'Oh, I thought I might find myself a retired fella in a Hawaiian shirt and a really bad tan and move to the Gold Coast.'

Perhaps sleepy sex with someone you loved was better than no sex at all.

Dannie, Liza and Alice were all full of life and happiness, but I boarded the flight pissed off that we weren't flying QANTAS. I wasn't a frequent flyer for nothing. I wanted to sit in the QC and have my free coffee and raisin toast. But Liza was on shitty money at the Aboriginal Legal Service; Alice was on a teacher's wage; and Dannie had school fees, uniforms and excursions to pay for so it was a miracle she could even afford to come at all. I had to hold my sensibly single Black bourgeois tongue and get the cheaper ticket on Virgin as well so that we could all fly together to Coolangatta.

From the moment my foot stepped onto the Virgin aircraft and the yet-to-reach-puberty flight attendant welcomed me aboard by my first name, I knew it was going to be an inordinately long flight.

'Hi Peta! I just love that name – my best friend at school was Peta.'

Don't call me Peta, I thought. *Call me Ms Tully or madam or whatever. But don't be so bloody familiar. And I'm not the least bit interested in who your friends were at school. I'm not your friend – I don't even want to be your customer, okay?*

I didn't say it of course, but it sounded good in my head.

'Eight aisles down on the left, Peta.'

And I don't need you to point me in the direction of my seat. Obviously it's ahead of me somewhere, on either the left or the right of me, as there's only one aisle to walk down. I was already looking for the exit, remembering the nearest one might just be behind me.

'Good morning, groovers, welcome to flight 537 to the Gold Coast. If you're *not* going to the Gold Coast, then you're probably on the wrong plane.'

'Wow, he's a genius,' I said sarcastically to Alice.

'My name's Ryan. I tried out for *Popstars*, but didn't make it, so instead I'm going to be your singing flight attendant. I might sing you a song later, but first up let me introduce you to your crew today.

'Sandy likes dark chocolate, Georgia has just broken up with her long-time boyfriend so can you all be kind to her today, Alex still lives at home and his mother does his washing, blah blah blah . . .' Was I the only one getting the shits listening to nonstop commentary?

'We're very lucky to be led by our Captain James Cook.'

'*James Cook*? Hilarious!' Alice said.

'Yeah, and I'd like to know why we're so lucky. Are the other captains dodgy? Or are we lucky because he can't hear Ryan rambling and won't be pissed off or distracted from doing his job?' Alice had been joking, but I was deadly serious.

'Maybe we're lucky cos he's sober.'

'What's luck got to do with flying a plane anyway? I thought it was about skill and experience.'

Ryan still hadn't shut up: 'And in the middle of the

plane is Abbey. It's Abbey's birthday, so let's sing Abbey happy birthday.'

'Let's not,' I mumbled to Alice, but to my surprise a good proportion of the plane, including Dannie, started singing.

Then the safety demonstration began.

'Seriously, who needs to be shown how to do a seat belt up?' I mumbled.

'What's wrong with you?' Alice asked. 'You're such a grump today. Melbourne's turned you into a real whiner. I hope you're not going to be miserable all weekend and spoil it.'

'*You're such a grump.*' I whined some more, but under my breath, watching the cloned Virgins check and double-check that tray tables were up, seat backs were upright and hand luggage was stowed correctly; all of them identical in their camel pants and skirts, crisp white shirts and red jackets. Alice was right about me being grumpy, but no-one was going to accuse me of spoiling the fun of the girls' weekend on the Gold Coast.

I closed my eyes and started to count down to our eventual arrival at Coolangatta airport. I tried to sleep but couldn't, because even after we started along the tarmac to take off Ryan was *still* talking.

'Again, ladies and gentlemen, boys and girls, pimps and pros, you're on flight 537 to the Gold Coast . . .'

'Yes, we know that you knob, just shut up,' I said out loud and even Alice laughed.

♥

'Ladies and gentleman, it's Ryan here and we've just begun our descent, so please take your seats. The cabin crew will be coming through shortly to collect your rubbish, so to make turnaround time quicker at the other end can you please look under your seat and in the seat pockets, and help us with the cleaning?'

'What? It's not bad enough that we have to buy a bottle of water but we now have to provide the cleaning as well?'

Ryan just kept going. 'Please don't leave your ex-husbands or children behind as they are both hard to sell, and don't go well on the baggage carousel.'

Let me off the bloody plane, I was screaming to myself.

If Sydney had a coastal feel about its fashion, then the Gold Coast had a tropical island feel about it. It seemed like there were no dress regulations at all. The foyer of our hotel had everything from board shorts and miniskirts to canary-yellow slacks, hot-pink strapless frocks and no shortage of gold glitter T-shirts. The four of us in our tailored dresses and darker colours looked classy and high-end – and distinctly overdressed. I couldn't exactly say it felt great to be home, even though it was good to be back with my friends.

I'd decided not to see Mum or Gis or the boys while I was up. I didn't want to spoil my weekend with the girls trying to squeeze in a visit with the family as well. We needed more than a couple of hours to catch up, and I didn't have the time or the inclination right then.

We spent the day lying by the pool at the hotel. It was low season so there were hardly any tourists and, to my great joy, no schoolies. Hanging out with Will and Maya was one thing; teenagers were quite another. I delved into the novel Sylvia had lent me for the trip, *The Accomplice*. It was by a local writer, Kathryn Heyman, and told the story of a seventeenth-century shipwreck off the coast of Australia.

'You'll love it,' Sylvia had assured me as she put it in my attaché. 'Heyman's been shortlisted for the Nita Kibble Award and sells well abroad. A literary writer, does better than we mere poets.'

What she'd failed to tell me was that it was a meditation on evil. According to the jacket reviews it was a cross between *Robinson Crusoe* and *Lord of the Flies*. It was a brutal read for what was meant to be a relaxing holiday, but I really didn't care. It was so wonderful to feel the sun on my skin and build some of my tan back up.

On our first night we strolled along Broadbeach Mall and ate in an Italian restaurant, nothing like the standard of Lygon Street but I wasn't going to say a thing. I was hoping to get through the weekend without any cross-border debates happening.

None of us really wanted to go clubbing that night, because we were all too old compared to the bronzed, blonde girls out and about. We went back to the Prince Albert Pub at Conrads and listened to a covers band instead.

The food we'd had at dinner wasn't really authentically Italian, so I didn't think there was any risk of having an astral dream while sharing a room with Alice – and I didn't.

The next day we spent hours walking around Pacific Fair, checking out the shops, stopping for coffee and just taking it easy. I took some pics on the camera phone and sent them to James. He texted back:

I'm glad you're there with the girls. It must be like old times, hey babe? Love you. James

On our second and final night we decided to get frocked up properly, which made us really stick out. We had our hens' celebration dinner at the hotel's Charters Towers Restaurant.

'So, Missy, what plans do you have for the wedding? I do recall you said I could be "producer" and God knows you'll need me to coordinate the music. Remember your mum said you could have Archie Roach play? I could probably help with arranging that if you like.'

'Gary said we can only afford to play Archie's CDs in the background.'

'Right. Well, we can talk more about the music later.'

'I still want you to help me do all the planning, of course. It's just a bit harder with you down there, but you'll be home in January and the wedding's not till March. Dannie's still matron of honour and I'd love you to be bridesmaid.' She looked directly at me, but not Liza, and I felt uncomfortable.

'Well?' Alice asked, when I didn't respond immediately. I looked towards Liza, embarrassed. 'But what about—'

'Liza's already agreed. I asked her last week.' Alice beamed at Liza, who returned the same broad glow. Alice was my best friend, but I was the last to be asked, and the last to know. Our fabulous foursome seemed to have become the terrific threesome since I'd moved to Melbourne.

'I've offered to do a pre-nup for them, too,' Liza added.

'Of course Gary's got nothing to "nup",' Dannie threw in.

Alice grinned. 'Truly, without making you want to spew, I *know* Gary and I will be together forever. We don't really need a pre-nup.'

'What about dresses?' I asked.

'Well, we've already had a look at a few,' Alice motioned to Dannie and Liza. 'And we kind of decided that you girls should just wear whatever you want, but I thought maybe cocktail, to the knee, and then you should get some more wear out of it later.'

'Great!' I said, with as much enthusiasm as I could muster. My nose was really out of joint now, but I tried not to show it. 'There are some fabulous shops that I know Shelley can take me to in Melbourne. If you want we can have a look when you come down for Melbourne Cup.'

'Sounds like a plan! Let's toast to that,' Alice said, raising her glass.

'Now, what about your ring? When's that happening? I've seen some gorgeous designs in Melbourne.'

'Actually,' Alice said, reaching into her handbag, 'it's been really hard for me to keep it hidden. But here it is. It was Gary's grandmother's – we had it remodelled into a more modern design. I love it.' And she put the ring on and showed us all the most elegant diamond ring that sparkled like none of the diamonds today. Antique diamonds had something special about them.

'It's absolutely gorgeous. Why didn't you show us before?' Dannie asked.

'It's just that Peta is missing out on stuff, so I didn't want her to miss out being the first to see the ring also.' The girls nodded, and I gulped back a lump in my throat. I'd been a little selfish, I realised – tonight was really about Alice, not me.

'Thank you for thinking of me, Alice. I have been feeling a bit left out because I'm so far away, but now I feel lucky. So who's for the casino? I think I'll be a good luck charm for a high roller,' I said as the waiters cleared the table.

When Alice and I got back to our room that night, I couldn't stay awake no matter how hard I tried and no matter how much Alice kept talking. I think I fell asleep within seconds of saying, 'Goodnight, Muriel . . .'

thirty-four
The hairdresser with heavenly hands but a world view from hell

The winter months and mochas and heavy meals coupled with my weekend away to the Gold Coast had done damage to my liver *and* my waistline. I needed to do some exercise desperately. I wanted to keep swimming, but couldn't go back to the St Kilda Baths, it was just too relaxing for any real exercise and too expensive to be a regular part of my life. So I went to the Melbourne Sports and Aquatic Centre, or 'MSAC' as it was commonly referred to. 'It's where serious swimmers go,' Josie told me.

I loved MSAC straight away. The centre was massive and like nothing I had ever seen. There was an indoor comp pool, an outdoor comp pool, a leisure pool, stadiums for basketball, squash, table-tennis and more. I wanted to move in. The MSAC also had a hydrotherapy pool, but I told myself I could only use it *after* I'd done some serious swimming.

I started going after work and aimed to swim 1.5 kilometres three times a week. For the first week I stuck to the 'medium' lane. The workout would help me sleep soundly, which had been a problem lately. Alone late at night was when I missed James the most. It was the only time when my head wasn't in overdrive thinking about work.

I bought a red Speedo, the closest thing I could get to the Baywatch cozzie. My red pout matched my cozzie and the fitter I got, the more I felt like Pamela Anderson.

The downfall of a completely chlorinated pool, though, was that the chlorine stayed in my pores regardless of how much showering, soaping and moisturising I did.

The biggest problem was the damage the chlorine was doing to my hair. My hair had always been long, but now it reached right down my back. I was wearing it up most days, but my locks needed some attention from spending so much time in the pool.

I left work early one afternoon, around three-thirty, and walked into a salon just a short stroll from the office. It looked groovy and had a price list I could survive. A young, fit guy with biceps bulging through his black T-shirt looked at my hair, touched the ends, pushed it off my face and said, 'I'm Benny and I'd *love* to get my hands on your scalp.'

'That's one I haven't heard,' I laughed.

I sat in front of the mirror as Benny lifted strands up and down and fluffed the hair around my face.

'Do you want a new style? A colour and a cut?'

'I hadn't given it much thought. I really need a treatment, and probably a trim, but I think the colour's fine.' I had dark hair and didn't need to colour it. It was normally naturally shiny, but the pool had completely dulled it.

'What about just a couple of pieces, here—' he lifted some strands to the left of my face, 'and here?', indicating the opposing strands on the right. I thought it might be nice to have a change and so agreed. As he painted mahogany dye onto sections of my hair and wrapped them in foil, I read a newspaper article about the government's new immigration policies and the introduction of language tests. The hairdresser looked over my shoulder and tut-tutted.

'Look, I'm not racial, but why can't they just learn to speak Oz-tralian when they come here?'

'*Oz-tralian*? There's no such language. I think you'll find you mean English.'

'Yes, English of course, because that is the language of Australia, isn't it!'

'Actually, no. There's no one Australian language. Originally there were over five hundred languages spoken in Australia and about forty in Victoria. Immigrants didn't have to do language tests back then, luckily, or your own ancestors mightn't have got in.'

'It's not the same. My ancestors were British – they weren't *boat people*.'

'Sorry to be the one to break the news, but the First Fleet weren't planes, they were BOATS! The original "boat people", as you say, were British!'

Benny just stared at me with a look of dumb confusion.

'Look, I think I'll just read my book if that's okay?' And I opened the latest book sent to the department, one we'd funded as part of a literacy project.

'Sure, yes, read your book, go for it,' I heard him say, but I was already trying to bury myself in thoughts of something other than this ignorant man whose mercy I was at. The next thing I knew a foil flopped on my forehead and my hair hung right into my face. I didn't know if he had done it on purpose or not. I blew the hair out of my face and pushed the foil away, but it happened again, and again, so I just closed my eyes and waited for him to finish.

'The clock is on for thirty mins, love, you just relax.' I knew then Benny had no idea that I was pissed off with his ignorance. He continued to fluff around as if we hadn't even had a conversation at all, put the clock on and got started on the woman next to me. She was reading a trashy women's magazine, and while he applied her colour they chatted about Lindsay Lohan.

I went back to reading *The Papunya School Book of Country and History*. I loved that more and more kids' books were being published with Aboriginal people involved in the development of the stories and the artwork. I'd been researching illiteracy in Aboriginal communities and a lack of relevant reading material was a big part of the problem. Black kids needed to see their own realities on the page – urban or remote – and they needed to see dark kids on the page as well. Just as boys generally read books about boys, and the same with girls, Black kids wanted to read stories about Black kids. We'd never had books at home when I was a kid, and I was so glad times were changing.

'Over to the basin, babe.' God I hated being called 'babe'. It was such an annoyingly generic term. Men only used it because they couldn't think of something original or when they didn't want to use your own name. I knew that wasn't the case with James, but I hated him calling me babe too. There just wasn't anything special about it. I much preferred to be called by my actual name – except by Virgin airline staff or racist hairdressers, of course.

I rested my neck on the towel of the basin and enjoyed the lukewarm water rinsing the dye out.

'How's the temperature?'

'Perfect, thanks,' I said in a half-trance. I could've gone to sleep there and then. A shampoo was followed by the best head massage I'd ever had, as Benny worked and reworked the conditioner through my hair with his magical hands. It was so good I momentarily forgot he was a jerk. If I focused enough, I could possibly even orgasm from his hands massaging my head. Would it mean I'd been unfaithful to James? Again, I remembered Liza's advice: 'If either one of you has an orgasm, then it's regarded as sex.' I'd answered my own question.

'There, let's get you back to the chair for a cut.' He wrapped my hair in a towel and helped me out of the seat. I was still aroused from the head massage and my legs were shaky.

I looked in the mirror and even with my wet hair I could see the beauty of the highlights. I wanted this man with the hands and the hair magic in my life – as long as he remained mute. I could still pretend that I was celibate if there was no touching of genitals in any way. I could even just come for a wash and dry once a week, the cost of three glasses of wine. But I had that niggling feeling about him – I couldn't give my money to a racist, regardless of how magical his hands were.

'So, what do you do for a job?' Benny asked me.

Oh God. I could feel a cross-cultural training session coming on.

'I'm the national Aboriginal policy manager for DOMSARIA,' I said.

'DOMSARIA?' Benny had no clue. Seemed like the years of fumes from the perming lotion had damaged his brain.

'It's the Department of Media, Sports, the Arts, Refugees and Indigenous Affairs.'

'Really? Then can I ask you something?' He leaned in close and whispered in my ear. 'I'm not being racial, but why can't Aborigines handle their drink?'

'Excuse me?'

'It's just that I was at the pub the other night and there were two Blacks really pissed and they ended up causing havoc.'

'Oh, right, and so how many white people were there drunk?'

'About thirty probably, but none of them were fighting.'

'But have you ever seen pissed white people fighting?'

'Of course, all the time.'

'And how many times have you seen Blacks pissed and fighting?'

'Well, just the other night. But it's more obvious with them.'

'It's only more obvious to you because they're different to you. There's probably noisy, drunken white people, many of them hairdressers, around you all the time, but you don't notice them cos they look like you. Don't worry about the cut, I'm outta here.'

'But it's not even dry.'

'I don't care.' I tore the plastic cape from my neck, shook my head a little and ran my fingers through my hair. There were no knots, he had used so much conditioner and combed it at the basin, so I was pretty much ready to go.

'Did I say something to upset you?'

There was no point saying, *I'm Aboriginal*, because that's not why I was offended. I was simply offended as a human being with a brain. I put the cash owing on the counter and walked out.

I still needed a haircut so I called my hairdresser in Sydney as I walked back towards Collins Street from Bourke Street Mall. Prue suggested Paul in Melbourne Central and called him for me straight away. I did an about-face and headed right there. It looked far more bourgeois than I would normally feel comfortable with. It had sleek fittings and the customers were drinking glasses of wine and champagne. But Prue had said, 'He does good hair and good politics,' so it was a done deal.

I told Paul the whole story. He was sympathetic but said, 'Oh, love, it's worse for me, I get all kinds. But I've learned how to manage it. When one of my clients says something racist, I still do good hair for them, because I have my professional reputation to think of, but love, I charge them a racist tax. I up their total by about eighty dollars, because while I have integrity as a hairdresser I also have integrity as a human being.'

I left the salon looking and feeling better, about my hair and about my hairdresser. Paul became my new stylist, and he promised me a good deal: whatever he charged other clients in racist tax, he'd take off the cost of my haircut. And that suited me fine.

I raced to meet Sylvia at 3 Below. We'd agreed to meet up there so she could give me the afternoon's messages, but I also wanted to take my new hair out to a chic drinkery. I needed a glass of red to warm up anyway. It was a blustery August evening, and my gorgeous new hair was being blown everywhere. I had a huge black scarf around my neck which hung down the back of my watermelon coat, but the wind went right through me. I needed some of that thermal underwear that I'd worn in my astral trip to Delphi.

'Hello there, stranger. Not answering calls any more?'

It was Mike.

'What do you mean? You haven't called me! Behaving like a typical bloke, saying you'll ring then not delivering.'

'I've tried calling about a dozen times, but you never answer your phone.'

'Your name hasn't come up as a missed call once. And you haven't left a message.'

'Damn!'

'What?'

'I have "private number" set on my mobile, completely forgot. I don't know how to turn it off.'

'Well, that explains it,' said Sylvia. 'She never answers calls from private numbers, do you, boss? She usually makes me answer if I'm around.'

'Isn't it your shout, Sylvia?' I said. She took the hint and went for another round.

'Why didn't you just leave a message?' I asked Mike. 'You're not really the shy, retiring type, are you?' Two drinks down and the policeman was looking attractive.

'I just figured if you didn't answer the phone and you didn't call me back, then you probably didn't want to talk to me.'

'Not the case, Constable Care. Give me your phone and I'll fix the settings for you, and then you can call me tomorrow, I'll answer the phone, and we'll make a time to catch up properly.'

'You're not just a pretty face and hair are you?'

'No, she's not!' Sylvia said with a naughty glint in her eye, as she placed another glass of wine in front of me.

Mike grinned. 'I've got to go, but I'll call tomorrow. I'll be expecting either one of you to answer the phone. Okay?'

'Okay!' Sylvia and I said in unison, like two cheeky teenagers propped up on our bar stools.

thirty-five
Caring for Constable Care

'If you were one of the seven dwarfs I'd call you sexy.'

I knew who it was but I asked anyway. 'Who is this?'

'It's your Mike.'

'You're not mine, and vice versa.'

'Crunch time, Peta, we've gotta make a date for dinner. I've been doing my homework and reading. You promised.'

'I don't recall promising anything, Michael, but I do have to eat at some point every day – three times a day actually – so I suppose I could be sitting at the same table at the same time as you, if we happened to be in the same vicinity.'

'I like a woman who plays hard to get.'

'I'm not playing anything.'

'Then I like a woman who's just hard to get.'

'Well, with the pathetic lines you use, I'm not surprised you find it hard to get women.'

'Yeah, I think you might be right.'

We went to a place called Il Duce Si Diventa in Carlton. It was the strangest, most eclectic drinking hole I'd ever walked into, but cosy too, which was good. Sydney had usually started to warm up by mid September, but the nights were still chilly here. I looked around the room and was fascinated by the cube seats and glass-topped gilded Egyptian-styled tables. There were sculpted busts and torsos throughout the bar under red ceilings and low lighting, and pictures of everything from Rubenesque nudes to posters of Sophia Loren. It was Greece meets France meets Italy, but somehow it worked. The candelabras and chandeliers told me that anything went there. I liked it. I couldn't help imagining what my architect would think of it, though. James liked clean lines, sterile white spaces, uncluttered and formal environments. Although he loved my place and said it had a warm feeling about, it used to drive him nuts that nothing matched, and he often rearranged things to put them where they were aesthetically more pleasing. This bar would have sent him into re-design overload – but I didn't really think it fit the macho cop profile either.

Mike seemed happy to sit silently while I just sat and looked at all the paraphernalia in the upstairs bar, mesmerised by the colour and contrasting fixtures. We were comfortable, like friends should be, or so I thought.

'I like it here,' I said.

He nodded. 'Me too.'

'So anyway, Mike, I still don't know all that much about you. I don't even know where your family are from. Did you grow up in Melbourne?'

'No way – south coast of New South Wales. Ulladulla.'

'I love the coast down that way. Great beaches.'

'Yeah, I really miss the beach, being in Melbourne.'

'Oh God, tell me about it. I used to see the surf every day.'

'Me too!' Mike said enthusiastically, like we'd been connected by the sea. 'Actually, I'm fourth generation from Ulladulla,' he added with Aussie pride, and I laughed.

Most whitefellas didn't realise how ridiculous they sounded when they talked in such short time frames about their connection to a certain place or country. But I liked Mike, and whitefellas were really only ignorant if they'd been told the truth and still said ridiculous things. If we were going to be friends I couldn't lecture him every time we met, so I tried to tread lightly but honestly.

'Well I'm 4000th generation Coolangatta, or as we call it, Bundjalung Country.'

'Wow, 4000th, that's a lot eh? Fourth generation doesn't really rate then, does it?' he said with an embarrassed smile.

'No, it doesn't really count in the Koori world, Mike, and to be truthful, most Blackfellas laugh at the way whitefellas talk about their so-called looooong histories on the land.'

'Really?'

'It's just that Aboriginal people have been here through ice ages, and whitefellas talk like the First Fleet was the beginning of any human existence here.'

Mike was just looking at me all doe-eyed, and his blue, blue eyes were just staring into mine, and before I knew what was happening he had lunged in and kissed me on the mouth, and I took longer than I should have to pull away, and I felt like I was astral travelling but I wasn't. It wasn't earth-shattering but it was nice, and I remembered how exciting kissing could be and thought about how the passionate kiss gets passed up these days. Did anyone still kiss for hours on end any more, or was that something you only did as a teenager, because you weren't supposed to be having sex? I missed kissing. I liked kissing, I wanted to kiss more.

'What are you doing? I have a boyfriend!' I said, pushing him away. I hated myself, I had never cheated on James. 'You *know* I have a boyfriend. And infidelity is one thing he wouldn't cop. No pun intended.'

'This so-called boyfriend of yours – where is he? He's never here when I see you. I'm beginning to wonder if he even exists.'

'He exists, and he would never forgive me if I let this go any further. I'd never forgive myself. I should go.' I stood up and steadied myself.

'Wait, I'm sorry, please don't leave. I never meant to upset you, or disrespect you in any way. It's just that I thought this was a date.'

'What? Why? I can't go on dates, I have a boyfriend.'

'So you keep saying, but I've never seen him, and you left him in Sydney for a job eight hundred kilometres away, and you're out with me, so I thought perhaps you weren't that serious about him, and that if I charmed you enough with my very witty repartee, I might be in with a chance.'

He paused for breath. I was stunned into silence, and he knew it.

'I know I'm just a cop and you're a high-flying bureaucrat, but I like you. And you make me think about things I *should* be thinking about. And you were there right in front of me being really smart, and dangerously sexy, and I just couldn't help myself, and believe me I'm not in the habit of kissing women like that, I just thought—'

'It's okay, I'm sorry too, I should've been much clearer from the outset. I *am* in a relationship and I *am* faithful to James.' I didn't want to explain the celibacy business – we were already on shaky ground. 'Look, I should go.'

'No, please don't, sit down, let's just finish talking.' Mike was half out of his seat, urging me to stay. I sat back down but kept my bag in my lap. He looked relieved, but still a bit nervous that I might up and leave at any moment.

'Now we know where we stand, I'd still like us to be friends. I need people like you in my life – I've got to have someone to go to chick-flicks with, don't I?'

'Are you sure we can do this, the friendship thing?'

'Absolutely, and I even promise I'll sit on my hands when I get an urge, and I'll only wrap my lips around my drink.'

'Me too then!' I put my bag down on the seat next to me.

'Deal! So let's talk about you then, Ms Peta.' He seemed genuinely interested. 'Siblings, family life, marriage, kids?'

'Two brothers, Benjamin and Matt, and a sister, Giselle, one mother, one absentee father and two step-fathers. So as you can see, as dysfunctionalism goes my family has the monopoly. I'm in no real rush to get married or have kids – I've got a defective marriage gene.' I meant it as a joke, but it sounded truer as I said it out loud and there was a tone of sadness in my voice.

'That's a bit harsh, Peta.' He reached for my hand, then changed his mind and picked up his drink instead.

'Look, my mum's been married three times and she's still alone. What's the point of all the heartache when you can skip all that and stay single and happy, and not screw up other people's lives by also having kids?'

'Is that what you seriously think?'

'If I were truthful, I'd say no. I've seen some very happy and stable families. My cousin Joe and his wife Annie are made for each other, and so are my best friend Alice's parents. So are Alice and her boyfriend Gary, for that matter. So I do know it's possible. I just don't know if it's possible for me. I'm pretty much married to my career goals if that makes sense. Marriage and children would just hold me back right now.'

'I totally understand what you're saying, because my sisters talk about this all the time. All their friends got married young and started families, and there's a lot of pressure on them to do the same, but Lily says she's too young to have kids at twenty-two. She's not even sure if she wants them at all – says she doesn't have the patience. She wants to go back to uni and do her masters in creative arts – her boyfriend goes to uni so they have similar goals. And Patricia's just become partner in a cafe in Ulladulla and is working sixteen hours a day, seven days a week, and reckons she'll be doing the same for years to come, so she can't even contemplate kids. My sisters know their own minds – they want careers and independence, and peer pressure just isn't going to change them at all. I love them for taking a stand and believing in themselves. I just listen and then tell them to do whatever makes them happy, but I'll kill any bloke who hurts them. That's a brother's job.'

Finally, a man who seemed to get what I wanted from life: a career and independence!

thirty-six
The 'too cute' guy

Come Friday I was anxious to finish a ministerial briefing paper on moral rights for Indigenous artists and communities, and an overdue performance management report. As I hit the send button the report went to the director, the brief went to the minister's office, and I breathed a sigh of relief. 'Happy hour!' I yelled. 'Anyone still here?'

Sylvia had worked back late too, and was getting changed to go out. 'I'm meeting Rick at Revolver for the launch of the Charcoal Club's new album,' she said. 'They're a local Koori band. They say their music is for "burnt-out Blacks and singed whites". That's you, right? Do you want to come? Richard Frankland's the lead singer.'

'Isn't he that bald-headed Greek-looking Blackfella who once worked in a Chinese restaurant?'

'That's him!'

'I saw him on *Message Stick*. He was a scream. I didn't know he was a muso, though – they were interviewing him about his latest film. God, we're just so deadly, us Blackfellas, aren't we.'

'Yes, you are. And you're often late, too. Let's go.' Sylvia took me by the arm and led me out of the office.

As we set off for Flinders Street station, I felt good. October had a different smell about it and the days had finally started to warm up.

I was in a black skirt, a tight black tee and red shoes. Sylvia gave my outfit a quick once-over and nodded her approval.

'I'm so glad you didn't wear your coat.'

'Why? Are you telling me how to dress now as well as managing my diary? For God's sake, I am so over this rude Melbourne right to comment on people's attire.'

'Calm down, boss. I was just thinking that the place is going to be full of rockers and tatts and not a lot of pink is all.'

'It's *watermelon*.'

'Yeah, and that's worse. You'd be smacked for sure if you argued that it's watermelon.'

When we arrived, I spotted Josie at the bar and waved. She pointed at her beer and then at us, then held up two fingers. *Yes*, I nodded. It was a massive turnout, and loads of Kooris were there to support the band.

'Here you go, gals.' Josie handed us a beer each.

'Thanks. I'm Sylv-eye-a, nice to finally meet you,' Sylvia said, shaking Josie's hand formally. I could see Josie giving her the once-over and I frowned at her to stop. We found some space on a sofa to sit and claimed it all for ourselves.

As I scanned the room I noticed that most of the crowd were wearing black and while they looked different in a quirky way they somehow looked the same. When I spotted a guy wearing make-up who wasn't a drag queen I couldn't help myself. 'I thought I left guys in make-up behind in Sydney!' I joked to Josie.

A young guy walked past me sporting a blonde Mohawk and he reminded me momentarily of Geronimo. Next to me Josie was stretching her neck, desperately trying to find some hot women to hang with. The next thing I knew, she'd disappeared. I looked around the crowd for a moment, but I couldn't spot her.

'Everyone here has really skinny legs,' I said to Sylvia.

'Yeah, they're really skinny all over. Drugs probably,' she said, as if she knew all about the drug scene.

'No, it's not drug skinny, it's body shape skinny. Look, they're also really tall. It's not normal. Look around,' and I motioned my head around the room, 'there are all these extraordinarily tall people with long skinny legs. See?' And I pointed to about ten really skinny guys in long black jeans with skinny legs that went right up their backsides and almost up to their armpits. I felt like taking my black skirt off to prove I had good legs as well, but that wasn't the point these people were trying to make. They weren't trying to make a point at all.

'It's a really interesting crowd here, don't you think?' Sylvia asked, looking around while she spoke.

Then I saw a hot young Koori guy in black jeans and a yellow T-shirt adorned with the face of some waif-like model. He made me catch my breath. That hadn't happened since I'd first met James in Bondi Junction one Saturday morning when we took a number at the deli counter at the same time.

I assumed this guy was a muso because he had that cool, grungy look about him. The look you either had or didn't have but certainly couldn't create by choice. He had a wholesome face, with a tiny ginger goatee and kissable mole on his upper lip. I tried not to stare when he turned in my direction.

Sylvia stood up and took my hand. 'Hey, come meet some people,' she said, and led me to the back bar where the guests were mingling. Loud music was playing over a sound system in the background, and a band was setting up.

'Who's that guy?' I asked Sylvia, throwing my head in the goatee's direction.

'Oh, that's Timmy, he's a drummer, and a session muso. He's a friend of my boyfriend's. Stays with us sometimes. Nice guy. Why? You interested?'

'No, of course not. I'm with James, remember?'

'Good, cos he *is* a drummer.'

'What does that mean?'

'You know all the jokes about drummers, don't you?'

'No, what jokes?'

'You've *never* heard a drummer joke?'

'No I haven't. Obviously I've been living under a rock.'

'What do you call a drummer with half a brain?'

I just looked at her.

'Gifted.' She went on, 'What's the best way to confuse a drummer?'

And still I looked.

'Put a sheet of music in front of him.'

I frowned. I couldn't read sheet music either.

'Why is a drum machine better than a drummer?'

'Why?' I was already over the drummer jokes.

'Because it can keep good time and won't sleep with your girlfriend.'

'Hey, I've got one,' a guy said as he stopped and stood in between Sylvia and I.

'Why do guitarists put drumsticks on the dash of their car?'

'So they can park in the handicapped spot,' both Sylvia and he said in unison, and laughed.

'That's appalling! They're just like blonde jokes.'

'Did you hear the one about the blonde drummer—?' he started.

'Stop, I can't listen to any more.' We were supposed to be making policy to support *all* artists in all art forms, drummers included.

'Relax, Peta! This is Rick, my boyfriend.' She cuddled into him as he offered me his hand to shake.

'I'm Peta, I work with Sylvia,' and I handed him my card.

'Nice to meet you. You government types all flash with your cards and everything, aren't you? Bet you think I can't read.'

'Why, are you a musician?'

Rick laughed. 'Something like that. Time for another beer, see you later.' And he kissed Sylvia on the cheek and walked off.

'Those drummer jokes are a bit cruel aren't they? I mean, why are drummers different to other musicians?'

'They're just jokes, Peta. Why are you so worried about jokes and drummers? I thought you weren't interested.' Sylvia had a smile on her face.

'I'm not interested in the drummer or humour, clearly. And anyway, guys like that never choose girls like me; they choose swimsuit models or young girly groupies, don't they?'

'What?' Sylvia said.

I couldn't stop. 'No, my best bet is to stay right away from guys like that, because he is cute, isn't he? I mean too cute for someone like me.'

'Oh yeah, he's cute all right. Every woman at the gig probably thinks he's cute. He could have most of the women here and probably has. You know, it's that kind of industry. I think a couple of the boys fancy him too. But I'm pretty sure he's not gay. He doesn't say much when he stays. He seems pretty laid-back. Rick reckons he's the best drummer this side of the Queensland border.'

'Maybe he's a thinker.' I kept staring at his mole.

'Maybe.'

'But he's too cute.'

'Stop saying that. He may be too laid-back for someone like you, but he's certainly not too cute for you. That's just ridiculous.'

'What? Are you the big relationship counsellor now? I didn't even know you had a boyfriend till I'd been here for weeks.'

'So, we just like to keep it low profile, that's all. But I do love him, and he's my soul mate and that's all that matters.' We both looked over towards Rick, who was deep in conversation with one of the guys from the Charcoal Club.

'He's obsessed, you know. All he talks about is his music and CDs and new bands.'

'That's it?' I asked seriously. 'Nothing else?'

'Oh, and the Saints. Loves the footy of course, but he *is* a bloke.'

'He sounds really lovely.'

'Yeah, he is, I've learned to live with him being in the studio till all hours and having no money. We'll probably never own our own house. But we love each other.' At that moment, Rick looked over and motioned to Sylvia to see if she wanted a drink. 'I'm right,' she mouthed back.

'I don't know if loves me more than his music, but I know I can tell him anything and he'll always be there. And he reads my poetry.'

'Well, that must be love!'

'Yeah, that's what he says.' And then the band walked on stage and people started moving from the bar towards the front. Sylvia went off to talk to Rick and I found myself a spot up the back near a massive wall fan. It was already hot and I hadn't even started dancing.

A few songs in I found the drummer standing next to me. One hand in his pocket, the other holding a beer.

'Hi, I'm Peta,' I said over the music.

'Hi, Timmy.' He offered nothing more.

'You a local?' I asked.

'Nah, Bundjalung, a Jones from Iluka, up Grafton way.'

'Me too. Bundjalung, that is. I'm a Tully from Cool-angatta. The Joneses are a big mob, I hear.'

'Yeah, pretty big.'

'So what brings you down south?'

'I'm just here gigging for a week, doing some studio work, then back home.'

'So, you're a drummer?' And he looked at me as if to say, *How did you know that?*

'Oh, sorry, just . . . a guess.' Could he tell I was lying? 'What do you play?'

'Yeah, I play the tubs. What about you?' I didn't want to kill the conversation by saying I was a top-ranking departmental bureaucrat with aspirations of being Minister for Cultural Affairs. Would a drummer even understand what that was?

So I massaged the truth a little. 'I work for the public service, in cultural affairs, so I know a little about music, but learning more every day. So, do you sing also?'

'No way! When I do, I sing like a bee.' He laughed and took a swig of beer.

I wasn't sure if he was kidding or not. Trying to be funny, I said, 'Oh, kind of like Muhammad Ali?'

'No, sis. I'm pretty sure those song words are "floats like a butterfly and *stings* like a bee".' Shit, he was right, and bigger shit, I looked like a complete knob.

'Of course, clearly I know nothing about song lyrics *or* boxing.'

'But Ali *is* Black, so I can see how you might confuse us.' And he flexed his muscles.

I laughed; he was funny. Then a younger girl asked him for a cigarette and they headed outside. I was a little jealous – I wanted to talk to the muscly bee-singer some more. Then I suddenly thought about James and felt guilty. I went into the dimly lit ladies' toilets and sent him a message.

Just 2 say hi, hope ur well. Miss ya, Px

We left Revolver as the groovy younger crowd started to file in, long legs and all. As we stumbled down the stairs and out the door onto Chapel Street, I saw Mike across the road and immediately caught my breath. I'd bumped into him too many times now and it was just getting weird. It was too much of a coincidence – especially when I didn't believe in coincidence. I didn't know if I should avoid him or go and say hello. He was with another cop and I was with Josie and Sylvia. But it wasn't my decision anyway, as Mike saw me and sung out straight away. People in the street stopped to look and Josie had a sly look on her face.

He waved to get my attention and jogged across the road. 'Hi. Do your parents know you're out this late?' he said in his usual cheesy way, then kissed me on the cheek, which made me feel uncomfortable and tingly at the same time.

'Hi,' I said awkwardly, not knowing what to say or do next.

'Hi Sylvia,' he said, with the correct pronunciation, and he kissed her on the cheek as well, which made me feel less special. 'Josie, nice to see you again. Good night, was it?' he asked the three of us.

'Excellent,' Sylvia answered.

'Deadly,' Josie added.

'Yeah, really good, but it's late so we should probably get a move on, eh girls? Been a long day – long week actually. So, guess we'll be seeing you round then.'

'Yes, hope so – you make the beat look much better, all of you.' The other girls laughed, while I rolled my eyes, wondering why he was flirting with them as well.

When I woke in the morning and turned my phone on there was a text message from Dannie:

> Hi everyone — we're having bub #3. Due April. Very excited. Love
> D&G

I couldn't believe it, Dannie and George had finally conceived. I was happy for them, because having a family was their thing and they were good at it, but I was really hurt and disappointed that she'd sent me a group text and didn't call. By my calculations she'd been pregnant for three months, which meant it was twelve weeks she'd not said anything. Was I now so out of the loop? First Liza breaks up with Tony and I don't know, then Alice and the girls make decisions about the dresses without me and now Dannie sends me a text to say she's pregnant.

I called her straight away to say congratulations and to hear all about it, but I got her voicemail and assumed that she was on the phone taking calls from other people.

'Hi darl, it's Peta, I am soooo happy for you and George. Great news. I'll see you next week for the Melbourne Cup and we'll celebrate. Well, you'll be on mineral water, of course, but we'll make sure it's the best sparkling we can find.'

thirty-seven
My Melbourne Cup floweth over

I was excited about the Melbourne Cup. Alice and Dannie were coming down, but Liza had to work. The girls had sent me pics of what they were wearing and I was looking forward to seeing them and their men. James was also meant to be coming, but at the last minute he couldn't leave the office as there was a problem with a job for Lane Cove Council. I was slightly relieved, though I felt bad about it – I'd gotten so used to doing my own thing and flying solo, and with just three months left on my contract, I didn't want to start thinking about going back to Sydney and into the same confused rut I was in when I left.

I was looking forward to my first Melbourne Cup as well. I'd bought a new dress, shoes and a hat. I'd opted for the hat because I didn't know what was so fascinating about wearing a fascinator.

The night before the race I took everyone, including Sylvia, to the Hofbräuhaus, a kitschy German family restaurant in the city. I knew the boys would love the beers and the schnapps, and I thought the girls would like seeing the male staff in their lederhosen.

Alice burst out laughing as soon as she entered the restaurant. 'This is so . . .'

'What, can't find the right adjective, Alice? That's not a good sign, what with you being a teacher and all.'

'It's a bit like Mum and Dad's place, is what I was thinking.' She scanned the room. There were wooden plaques with greetings in German, and flower boxes in the windows in true German countryside fashion.

'I thought you'd like a bit of European heritage – closest thing I could get to Austrian, but they're nearly the same anyway, aren't they,' I said, proud of my efforts to please my best friend.

'Actually, Peta, they're two different countries, like Australia and New Zealand, or should I say like Wiradjuri and Bundjalung?'

'Okay, okay, I get the point. No need for the history lesson at dinner, Miss Aigner.'

We were soon seated in heavy wooden chairs. Blue tablecloths overlaid white linen and Lufthansa posters lined the wall. Oompah-pah music wafted through the restaurant as the band dressed in traditional garb entertained us with the occasional yodel. Behind the stage two Australian flags rested against the wall as a reminder that we weren't actually in Bavaria, while steins of beer were delivered to table after table.

When Sylvia arrived minutes after us, she puffed as she sat down.

'Hi, sorry, got caught up with some rels in the street.' The Greeks were as bad as Blackfellas for community and family and having to stop and gossip.

'Everyone, this is Sylv-eye-a,' I announced.

'Like Sylvia,' George said, clearly not having been briefed by Dannie.

'Actually, it's Sylv-eye-a,' she said in automatic pilot mode.

The girls all smiled, friendly, but a bit wary of my new mate and how she'd fit in.

'So, is this your favourite place, Sylvia?' Alice asked, as if the choice of dinner venue might be her fault.

'Hell no, this is my idea of a nightmare meal – I'm a vegan.'

'I like you!' Alice exclaimed, and it seemed that Sylvia had immediately been let into *our* circle.

The waiter came to take our orders.

'So I guess you won't be having the giant Wiener schnitzel then, Sylvia?' Dannie asked.

'No, I'd prefer just the giant wiener.' The girls laughed and the men raised their eyes at each other as if to say, *We've got a live one here.*

'Look, if we're going to do this, we should do it properly.' Alice happily took control and looked at the menu, then the waiter.

'We'll have the *Frankfurter*, *Bratwurst*, *Weisswurst*, the goulash and some venison, please. And a side of *Kartoffel*. Enough for the whole table, except one. Actually, do make it for the whole table – Dannie, you're eating for two anyway.' I was impressed by her accent: she sounded just like her dad. Then we all looked at Sylvia, wondering what she would order.

'And you, *Fräulein*? What will you be having this evening?'

'Right, can you make me a platter of sides? I'd like the potato dumplings, sauerkraut, red cabbage, potatoes of the day – I don't care what they are – and the fresh vegetables. And I'll have the *Spätzle* without the pork gravy.'

She didn't look up once from the menu and rattled the order off like a woman who knew her mind, and her stomach.

'But it won't be *Spätzle* then,' said the waiter. 'It'll just be fried noodles.'

'That's okay, can I have that please?'

'I'll ask the *Koch*,' the waiter said, unsure, and walked off.

'What's a *Koch*?' Sylvia asked Alice.

'That's a man who can cook,' she said matter-of-factly.

'What? As opposed to a man who *can't* cook?' Dannie said, nudging George, who wasn't known much for his culinary ability. 'I really should just call you *Koch*.' She pinched his cheeks like a little boy.

'Yeah, well it beats you calling me *cock* all the time.' The table erupted with laughter, drowning out Dannie's protestations. 'I never say that word! I *never* call you names – not to your face anyway.'

When the laughter subsided, Alice said, 'You know, Sylvia, you shouldn't really bastardise another culture's traditional food. Let me guess, you're going to Aussie-fy it and add tomato sauce.'

'Actually, I was thinking I might Greek-afy it and flame it with ouzo.' And she continued to endear herself to my Sydney friends. I was glad, because it showed them I was doing all right in Melbourne and had nice, supportive people around me.

After dinner everyone was full of meat (except Sylvia) and potatoes. It was time for schnapps.

'The tradition my dad taught me was that either every-one at the table has schnapps, or no-one does,' Alice said.

'Is there anyone who doesn't want one?' Silence fell on the table; no-one was going to miss out, except Dannie.

'I'll have the Mozart liqueur, cos it's dark chocolate like me,' Alice laughed.

'I'll have the Killer Schnapps, cos it's extra strong like me,' Gary added, the two of them cuddling close and laughing at their own lame jokes.

'I'll have the Stonsdorfer,' Sylvia said.

'Because it's *herbal*!' I couldn't help myself, but she laughed and so did the whole table.

The band got into full swing and the men started slapping their thighs. We all clapped.

'I love the *Schuhplattler*. My dad would never do it at home.' Alice was enthralled by the cultural activity up front.

'A schu-what-ler?' Dannie asked with a glow in her cheeks. She wasn't drinking but she said her hormones were going crazy.

'It looks like Bavarian aerobics to me,' Gary laughed, slapping his thigh, then Alice's. For some reason I thought briefly of Mike: he would've fitted in really well with the group, with funny one-liners and lots of laughs. I should have asked him along.

We stayed at the restaurant until stumps and the happy couples went to their hotel, where we agreed to meet in the morning for a pre-race bevie before heading to Flemington.

♥

Back at St Kilda, the house was empty. Shelley was at a pre-race ball with friends from her firm. One thing they knew how to do well was party. I didn't expect to see her home before sun-up, so I put a bottle of water next to her bed, knowing she'd need it, and crawled into my own. I was thinking about all the meat I'd consumed and wondered if it would appear on the scales in the morning. I laughed when I remembered George and Gary trying to yodel and do the *Schuhplattler* and I suddenly find myself skiing on the Katschberg mountain in Austria. I've never actually skied before and I'm terrified of breaking bones and my skinny Murri ankles are in really big boots and I'm glad that there's heaps of padding so people can't see how scrawny my legs really are.

Little skiers are going right through my open legs with no fear at all. And there's something called a black run, and I wonder if it's especially for Blacks, because most of the people here are white — actually, they're nearly all white, probably because it's such an expensive sport and Black-fellas can't afford it. And I look at the black run and it's whoa, really steep, and I'm chanting, *I ain't goin up there, I ain't goin up there.*

My ski instructor Gerhard is dictatorial like Hitler and he hates me. I don't know if it's an Aryan thing or because I can't ski or because I'm a woman or because he seems to hate everyone. He watches me fall over time and time again and refuses to help me get up, not once, and I'm crying with the frustration of it all. 'This is bullshit!' I say, but Gerhard just laughs at me.

Where's the schnapps and gluhwein and schnitzel and where are the sexy ski instructors I can be love fickle with?

I can hear the oompah-pah music; I know there's a party somewhere and I'd be happy to have pork gravy *Spätzle* and to eat as many potatoes as they give me, just to get out of the skis and the cold. It's freezing, and I don't have thermal underwear, but really I should.

The desire to get my arse out of the snow gives me a burst of inspiration and I lean uphill and get myself to my feet. Gerhard says, 'See, it's not that hard after all. You need to not be so much the princess.' *Fuck you*, I want to say, but I don't know if he knows who I am and what department I work for in the waking world and I don't want to risk a complaint to the director, so I just smile a pathetic, I-can't-ski smile.

I find the party and enjoy the après-ski, but I'm partying in my ski gear, because it's the only outfit I have with me. Everyone else is in ski gear as well, though, and as the Austrians aren't renowned for their fashion anyway, I needn't worry that I've got little edelweiss flowers embroidered on my beanie and I'm in red and white rather than black, but I laugh out loud at what the Melburnians would say.

I'm still in my snow boots as I land in Vienna at the Prater fun fair, and I'm on the Riesenrad. The guy working the ride says, 'This is one of the world's biggest Ferris wheels, *Fräulein*. It has fifteen cabins,' and he lets me have a cabin all to myself for three spins until a blonde-haired, blue-eyed Viennese man gets in. He looks too much like Timmy the drummer, but with an accent.

'I am Erik,' he says, and kisses my hand, as if to say, *We Viennese are very chivalrous*. I want to ask if he's Viennese from Iluka but I can't speak, as the Ferris wheel is going around and around, and my head is spinning and the lights of the city are beautiful and Timmy-Erik leans into me, and I feel a hot rush, and he says 'I eat you,' which I think is incredibly forward even for a chivalrous Viennese, but not for a drummer.

'Um, excuse me?' I'm not sure I've heard him correctly.

'I eat you,' he repeats.

'Oh,' I sigh, not sure if he means there and then or for dinner or later, and I must look confused, because he says, 'Is it wrong? When someone looks sweet enough to eat, you say, "I eat you", no?'

'Where I come from that phrase means something very, um, personal.' And I can feel my face is hot and red – even for a Blackfella the blushing is noticeable.

'Oh, I am sorry. Please, tell me what it means where you come from. I want to learn the cultures of other people.'

I don't think *cunnilingus* is a word that he will know in English, and it's not the kind of word that comes out easily for me either, let alone with a complete stranger, but the situation needs some clarity, and it's only a dream, so I'm safe to do whatever I want. I lean in close to his ear and gently touch the lobe with my tongue and say, 'It means doing this . . .', and I grab his hand and slide it up my skirt, 'Down here.'

'Oh,' he says, 'I like your meaning much better.'

'Mmmmm, me too,' I moan.

♥

Alice looked great, and there was only the tiniest bump on Dannie's belly. They both had huge fascinators on, and I couldn't help touching them constantly like a naughty child. At the racetrack we met up with Josie, who was frocked up like the prissiest girl I'd ever seen, and even Sylvia had traded the kohl eyes for spring colours. The boys were all decked out in suits and looked very handsome. I wore my soft pink silk dress and black hat with matching pink flowers.

'You look like Rachel Berger,' George said.

'Yes, apparently I do.' And as he walked off and I stood there watching a race, a woman came bouncing up.

'Rachel? Rachel Berger?' I'd had just about enough of being mistaken for Rachel Berger. I'd never even heard of her before I moved to Melbourne. I watched Josie high five George like a bloke at hearing the comment, as if they were old mates, and so I just said, 'Yes, sorry, do we know each other?'

'Oh no, I just love your work is all. I've read *Whaddya Mean You're Allergic to Rubber?*'

'Oh, great, I hope you liked it,' I said, thinking that I had just made myself a comedian and an author in one fraudulent swoop, and that I was getting myself into some serious illegal shit.

'Oh, my sister is going to be so disappointed she didn't get to meet you. But hey, I'll get my friends!' She went to turn around but I grabbed her as quickly as I could.

'Actually, I'm trying to have a quiet day here with my friends watching the races.' I looked at Josie, who was motioning that the Berger fan was a hottie. Sylvia was just shaking her head in disbelief, and Dannie was busy fixing Alice's fascinator.

'Of course, of course, I completely understand. Nice meeting you.'

As she walked off the race began and the crowd went crazy. The boys and Sylvia started hollering. Alice and Dannie were jumping as high as their heels would allow them on the grass, and Josie was standing next to me trying to read the numbers on all her tickets and the numbers on the horses at the same time. She'd had too many already.

'And coming round the bend is Chaotic Camilla followed closely by Chuck's Revenge, but closing in on both of them is Piccaninny.'

'Did he just say Piccaninny?' I asked angrily.

'I thought he said Truganini,' Josie slurred.

'Don't be ridiculous – it's the Melbourne Cup, not the Tasmanian Cup.'

'And Royal Rudd looks like he has taken out the honours today, ladies and gentleman, followed closely by Green Principles and Democratic Desires. As soon as Howard's End crosses the line, we'll have the photo finish to confirm the placings.'

Some people were cheering and hugging each other, while others were throwing the losing tickets on the ground. The Rachel fan appeared again and said, 'I just wanted to say what an honour it was to watch the Melbourne Cup with Rachel Berger,' and shook my hand earnestly. When she walked off I felt incredibly guilty and said to Josie, 'I have to tell her, I can't let her think I'm Rachel Berger.'

'You can't tell her now – she'll feel like a fool and you'll look like an utter bitch.'

'But I am a bitch.'

'Yes you are, but we like you. Let's go home. I've had enough, and it looks like you have too,' Josie said, linking arms with me in an attempt to keep us both balanced.

'Are you hitting on me?'

'No, I don't sleep with drunk women, it's highly unattractive.'

'So I'm a bitch *and* unattractive.'

'I don't know why you're worried about trying to be celibate or faithful or whatever it is you reckon you're doing. You're such hard work I reckon most men would give up on you pretty quickly anyway.'

Shelley was still out partying when I got home, but there was a note stuck to the fridge:

Cousin Joe dropped in some croc-cakes. They're for the first drunken dame to find them. Hope you backed a winner!
Shelley xxx

As the first drunken dame home I had the croc-cakes for dinner. Microwaving bush tucker was a bit sacrilegious but it didn't stop me doing it, or enjoying Joe's gift.

After eating I ran a hot bath, lit some candles and soaked my weary feet, unused to standing in expensive high shoes for any length of time. My calves were burning too, and by eight pm the hangover had begun to set in.

While I soaked and listened to the sounds of Sharnee Fenwick singing 'Kiss That Boy', I thought about how nice it would be to kiss a boy right then, but I suddenly remembered what Josie had said about me being hard work, and started to think that perhaps no-one would ever want to kiss me again. Did James think I was hard work or high maintenance? Was that why he hadn't come down this weekend? Maybe I *was* hard work. I didn't think so, but I hadn't heard from Mike for some weeks, either, so perhaps I was too much hard work even as a friend.

I lay there with my eyes closed and thought that perhaps I needed to make more of an effort. Since moving to Melbourne I'd become stressed, uptight and lost my sense of fun. Back at home I'd been a party girl without a care in the world, an easygoing, reliable friend. I made an effort to channel the old Peta, and sent James a text:

Hi darl, did u hava win 2day. R U free 4 yarn? Px

I waited for ten minutes and there was no response, which was unlike James, so I called and got his voicemail. I didn't leave a message – I didn't want to seem too desperate and I was convinced he'd hear a slur in my words, which wouldn't impress him.

I sent a text to Mike next, just for the sake of it:

Happy Melbin Cup. Did u hava win? Peta

He texted back immediately:

Back at ya. No gamblin means no losin. On duty, call u 2moro?

I liked Mike's mantra about no losing. I sent a simple text back:

Good motto. And OK.

When I went to bed that night, James still hadn't responded to my message.

thirty-eight
A day at the Guggenheim and the gardens

Mike called as promised and we met that afternoon at the NGV. It was a work day, but I'd decided to take the afternoon off and call it professional development: it was one of the perks of the job. As I walked down Collins Street I just couldn't figure Mike out. He was a cop with terrible pick-up lines, but he had a sense of culture too. There he was taking me to the Guggenheim exhibit and I hadn't even mentioned that I wanted to see it.

I saw Mike standing at the information desk before he caught a glimpse of me. He had a proud stance about him, even when he wasn't in uniform.

'Hi there, babycakes,' he said, planting a kiss on my cheek.

'Peta will suffice, Constable Care.'

'Oh, let's be formal then. Here's your ticket, Ms Tully.' He handed me my ticket and led me towards the gallery space.

'But—'

'But nothing, I think a friend can shout a friend to an exhibition.' He winked at me and I didn't have the heart to tell him I could get free entry because of my job.

As I walked through the collection I found it increasingly difficult to justify the money spent on some aspects of the arts. One 'Untitled' piece was simply yellow and green fluorescent lights. Eight orange cubes stacked on and around each other were also 'Untitled'.

'I've got a title for them,' Mike said, looking at the cubes.

'Me too.'

'*Eight Cubes*,' we both said simultaneously and roared with laughter until the security guard started to make his way over to us.

The portable wooden shed sitting on a platform and titled *Floating Room* was better than any Blackfella demountable I'd ever seen, while *Pink Corner Piece*, with two pieces of pink elastic cord stretched across a corner of the room, had us both asking the question, 'Why?' It was obvious that Mike and I had the same opinion of some objects in the collection. It was fine for Mike as a policeman, but for someone working in arts policy it was a bit of a concern.

'I'm over this, you hungry?' Mike asked, looking me straight in the eye and rubbing his belly.

'Me too, and yes I am.'

'Right, I've got it covered – my car's parked in the Botanical Gardens.' He ushered me out with his hand just under my elbow, like he was protecting me.

Mike had a canary-yellow Ford Festiva that made me laugh out loud.

'What? You don't like my little tulip? I love this car, so don't make fun of it.' He ran his hand along the length of it as if stroking a prized racehorse.

'It's just that it's not the kind of car I expected the tall, rugged policeman would drive is all.'

'Like I said, I love this car. It reminds me of my grandmother, she liked tulips. Now, I've packed us a picnic.' And he opened the boot to a picnic basket with breadsticks and utensils and an esky with cheeses, cold meats and light beers.

'Wow! You're so organised – I'm impressed.'

'Thanks – again, growing up with two sisters trained me well.'

We sat and ate the food Mike had prepared, both hungry from looking at artwork we didn't understand. The afternoon sun was hot and I could feel sweat beading on my brow; not even the beer could cool me down. Mike took his shirt off and lay down next to me on the picnic rug. I immediately noticed a scar on his left shoulder.

'It's a bullet wound,' he said, as if he knew what I was wondering.

'Shit.'

'Oh, it's nothing, no real damage. A bank hold-up gone wrong is all.' He was blasé about it.

'Does it hurt?'

'Nah, it's from five years ago. Don't really think about it any more. And you shouldn't either.'

'I don't think I could date a guy who was at risk of being shot every day.'

'Lucky we're "just friends", then.' He did the quotation signs with his fingers. 'Anyway, I've only been hurt twice on the job in five years. Once was this bullet, which didn't do any real damage, and the other was walking into a spider web that went in my eye and caused an infection. I had more time off work for the spider web incident than the bloody bullet. Most days it's just a few tumbles. The bad stuff is rare – that's why you see it on the news.'

'Okay, if you say so.'

'I should drive you home, I'm on night shift tonight. Come on, sweet pea.'

'Can you not call me sweet pea, please? I really hate it.'

'Why?'

'I just don't like it. That's all.'

'You're a strange one, but I like you, babycakes.'

'No flowers or vegetables or other foods, okay? And especially not foods as fattening as cake! Peta will do fine.'

He laughed as he offered me a hand to help me off the ground.

I thought about Mike too much that night and the thoughts became torturous. Was there a chance that I was just being love fickle because Mike was available and clearly dug me?

The problem doing my head and heart in was that I was starting to like Mike, but I knew it simply couldn't go anywhere. I was in a relationship with James and would be going home soon. And at the end of the day Mike was still a cop, I was still a Blackfella. But at least I didn't feel that he was too cute for me. Not like the drummer. Mike had a different kind of look. He was a nice guy: casual and sexy rather than cute. I didn't think he'd be surrounded by bikini models or groupies. And he wasn't too laid-back or too cool either, he was completely the opposite. Right in your face Mike, with those ridiculously funny pick-up lines, who called when he said he would. Reliable Mike, that's who he was.

thirty-nine
The World Famous Fat Bastard Burger

Mike called me twice the next day but I just let it go to voicemail. I was behaving appallingly, like a bastard guy, but even though I beat myself up for not taking his calls I didn't do anything to remedy the situation. What could I do anyway?

He didn't call me the next day, or the next day. A week passed and we hadn't spoken.

Then my period was late. I counted back to the last time I'd seen James and realised that I hadn't had sex since August. I'd had a period since so it was unlikely I was pregnant, but it wasn't impossible, and I started to think for the first time about children. The last time I'd checked I didn't want kids, but spending time with Maya and Will, I'd started wondering if it just might actually be nice to have a baby. Anyway, kids would look after me when I got old.

I still wasn't convinced about marriage, but if I had kids I'd want to be married. Truth be known I had gained *some* inspiration from Alice's parents. I knew that a family structure was what kids needed. But with my genes, I'd end up a single mother on a bloody pension for sure, even though I'd never had a handout in my life. I decided it was pointless thinking about being pregnant, but for some reason convinced myself I was having cravings. That was one advantage of being pregnant, anyway: you could eat anything you wanted for nine months and not feel guilty.

I took myself and my imaginary cravings to Greasy Joe's down at St Kilda and sat outside. I knew it wasn't morning sickness I felt – just a hangover from the two bottles of wine Shelley and I polished off watching videos the night before. I was tempted by everything on the menu, but ordered the 'World Famous Fat Bastard Burger' with triple cheese, triple beef and triple bacon. As I bit into it I imagined Sylvia totally freaking out at all the animals I was consuming with every chew. There was music blaring and it hurt my head, but I didn't say anything as I'd already been warned in the menu: 'If the music is too loud . . . tough!'

I chewed slowly and watched a dog lapping water from a bowl at its owner's feet. I still couldn't understand why or how dogs had become part of Australian eating-out etiquette. I heard screams from the roller-coaster at Luna Park, and the caw-cawing of seagulls. I saw the street sign to Thomas's gallery and my heart sunk a little. I'd really stuffed up over the past nine months. Technically I'd been celibate, but James would be devastated if he knew how much time I'd spent with other men. I was starting to feel guilty about everything, even the massive burger I'd just ordered.

I looked at my phone and felt sick, not from my hangover but from guilt about James, about how I hadn't missed him enough, how I'd spent too much time with other guys, about how I couldn't even bring myself to call him then. I needed sympathy, but I knew I couldn't ask for it from him. He'd only be annoyed that I had a hangover anyway.

I couldn't finish the burger and hardly touched the fries because I felt so queasy. Walking out into the morning glare, I hoped that no-one I knew would see me and that Josie wasn't on duty. I didn't have it in me to talk to anyone. I needed to go back to bed.

My head hit the pillow and I didn't move. My shoes were still on but I didn't have the energy or inclination to take them off. If Shelley were home I'd call out, but I didn't even feel like I could speak.

As soon as I closed my eyes I found myself on a Continental airline flight leaving Tullamarine. I'm not even sure Continental exists any more, and I really want to be on QANTAS so I can use the QC and cos they have a really good safety record, but here I am on this American carrier and the staff are all lovely, but I don't have the energy to astral travel this morning, and at how many weeks are you allowed to fly anyway when you're pregnant? I'm not sure and there's no-one to ask, really, because they're too busy pointing out exits and oxygen masks and handing out colouring books. I like flying Continental better than Virgin.

My flight takes me to Vegas and I'm excited about the casinos even though I've never been a gambler. I remember Mike's text on Melbourne Cup day – *no gambling, no losing* – but before I have time to consider the evils of betting on anything I'm playing blackjack at Caesar's Palace and I'm in a red sparkling dress like they wear in the movies. I'm decked out in so much jewellery I'm wondering why

I'm even trying to win money because I look rich enough not to need any more, and I don't even know how to play blackjack as I've only ever played snap and go fish with Maya and Will. I don't know which cards I should keep and which cards I should fold, and I'm not even sure what folding cards means, apart from the obvious. And then there's a man next to me and it's a young Robert Redford and I'm thinking, *Don't bother making an indecent proposal to me, cos I'm celibate.*

'You are my good-luck charm,' he says in his sexy voice, and I just say 'okay'.

A woman comes around and offers free cocktails, and I'm thinking, *Wow, free drinks, a gorgeous dress and Robert Redford, I hope I never wake up.* This is the perfect dream.

Robert wins a lot of chips, which reminds me I'm hungry, but we don't have time for food, and my tight sparkly dress won't allow it anyway. He places his soft hand in the small of my back and leads me to a lift and to one of the three thousand rooms in the hotel. Will it be Roman, Centurion, Forum, Palace or Augustus, I wonder? But my chastity belt tightens under the dress and I take his hand off me. I can't do the deed with Robert, even though he looks as sexy as he did in *The Way We Were* decades ago.

I walk off, not really knowing where I'm going, and I follow two characters who look like Caesar and Cleopatra and we're entering some Roman-style pools where goddesses and gods are handing out frozen grapes to cool people down. I don't take one. I don't want brain freeze as it might force me to wake up and I'm enjoying this trip into Roman history in Nevada.

'Oh, you southern girls are full of virtue, aren't you,' Robert whispers in my ear from behind, as though I'm from a plantation in Mississippi or something.

'Why yes, sir, I do believe we are,' I say in the best southern belle accent I can muster. 'But you do realise that when I said I was from the south, I meant south of the equator.'

'Yes,' he says, leading me out of the front doors of the casino and into a stretch Hummer, which is not as elegant as I am, but it is the modern-day expression of manliness in America and I know that's why he has it.

We tour Las Vegas Boulevard and I am in awe of the lights, the people, the colour, the carnival atmosphere of it all. I almost need sunglasses it's so bright. We pass Treasure Island and Circus Circus and we turn around and come past Harrah's, Flamingo, Ballys and MGM Grand – and it is grand, so grand I can't believe the size of everything and wonder how in the middle of the desert all this building goes on. Robert slides his hand up the split in the side of my dress and splits it some more. I don't care, because I don't even know where the dress came from. I couldn't see it in Melbourne – or Sydney for that matter. Maybe it would make it on *Dancing with the Stars*. He kisses my neck and I am weak with desire at the thought of the Great Gatsby fondling me.

I see a drive-through wedding service chapel ahead and laugh.

'Should we?' he asks, jokingly, seriously.

'Oh yes, with Elvis too, please.' And I am laughing, jokingly, seriously. And the driver is listening to everything and is laughing too, jokingly, seriously, and drives us through the wedding tunnel, which has a starlit ceiling painted with cherubs. One of the cherubs whispers to me, 'Are you sure?'

'Why not?' I whisper back, and he fires an arrow through a heart for me and my astral husband.

We say 'I do!' as the car moves on and the glass window between us and the driver slowly hits the roof of the car. I don't know how old Robert is but it's clear that he has decades of experience of making love as he manoeuvres me expertly in the back of the car and without removing anything but my knickers we are moving in time to Marvin Gaye's 'Sexual Healing' and even though it's completely corny I don't care because it's so long since I've been touched, but he is in demand and has to be somewhere else, so we find the nearest drive-through divorce and we both laugh at the mockery Vegas has made of marriage.

Robert gets out at the Luxor, which is the shape of a huge pyramid. He has a charity dinner to go to, and I'm not invited. Another bride-to-be no doubt awaits him there. He tells the driver to take me wherever I want to go.

'I'd like to go to a show, please,' I say.

'Yes, ma'am,' my driver responds. And he takes me to the Las Vegas Hilton and I'm sitting there waiting for Barry Manilow to take the stage. Of all the gin joints in Vegas he brings me to this one, and it's perfect. Alice would love this place, she's always had appalling taste in music, but in my dreams it doesn't matter, no-one judges anyone. I'm having the time of my life, and I'm still glowing from the taste of Robert back in the car. And I know this is something I could *never* tell anyone back in Melbourne, where live music is at the country's best.

I've forgotten my five-minute husband already and I've left my knickers in the car, but I'm by myself and having a great time, until a photographer approaches me.

'Would you like a photo with your boyfriend when he comes back from the bar?' she asks, hoping for a sale.

'I'm here by myself,' I say without hesitation.

'Okay then,' she says, and walks off.

'Hang on,' I sing out, pissed off. 'Can't I have a photo by myself?' I feel like telling her that I have a boyfriend when I'm awake and anyhow, I've just had sex with Robert Redford in the back of a Hummer and divorced him straight after. And I want to tell her how rude I think she is to suggest that it would only be a meaningful photo if I had a partner in there with me, and anyway, what if I was a lesbian? I could just as easily have had a girlfriend at the bar. She shouldn't be so presumptuous. But I don't say any of it, just tell myself in my head, until she says, 'Okay, if you want one,' like it's a really bizarre request I've made, and no-one *ever* asks for a photo by themselves.

'Don't bother,' I say as I raise my gin'n'tonic cocktail to my lips and look up to see Barry walking towards my table singing 'Can't Smile Without You'. He stretches out to take my hand and suddenly we are flying together, leaving Las Vegas. I look down and it's just one bright light, and my mind's eye sees Al Gore crying over the amount of energy it must take to light up the city in the desert, because I'm sure no-one is using any energy-saving light globes.

Barry is serenading me as we leave Nevada and he hasn't once asked my name, but instead starts singing 'Mandy' as if it were written for me, and when I frown, he lunges into 'Copacabana' and I have to tell him my name isn't Lola either, and I'm not a showgirl, but I look at my dress and can see his confusion.

Barry takes me to Los Angeles and leaves me on a street corner all alone in my red sequinned dress and he astral travels off, singing to no-one but himself about writing songs that make the whole world sing, and I think that it's time to wake up, but then I bump into a guy who looks just like Mike, but he tells me to call him Monday, and just like Barry I start belting out a tune myself, 'I Don't Like Mondays', but Monday's never heard of the Boomtown Rats so he doesn't get the joke.

'My name's Peta,' I say.

'I thought all you Ossies were called Bruce and Sheila. And that you all have pet kangaroos.'

'Most Ossies are, but I'm Aboriginal, so we're really just sis and cuz. And we eat kangaroos.'

Mike-Monday takes me to Disneyland and we visit Fantasyland, Tomorrow Land and Critter Country, but I really want to go on the cups and saucers. That's what I've seen on telly all my life and even as a grown-up it's the main attraction.

'That's the Mad Tea Party,' Mike-Monday tells me.

I meet Mickey Mouse and nearly wet myself with excitement, then I go on the Matterhorn and the Bobsleds and my sled flies off the tracks and astral flings me across the USA to New York City and the Metropolitan Museum and New York cabs and Broadway and giant slices of pizza and Central Park and the Rockefeller Center.

I feel like I'm in every American movie and cop show and sitcom that I've ever watched. I go to Central Perk Cafe and see Monica, Chandler, Joey and Phoebe, but where's Ross and Rachel? I want to go to the Nazi Soup Kitchen and see Jerry, Elaine and Kramer, but I go to Katz's Deli instead so I can say 'I'll have what she's having!' and have a mock orgasm like Meg Ryan did in *When Harry Met Sally*.

I'm walking around Soho and the Diamond district and I can see why some women want to get engaged – the rings are beautiful – but I still don't want to get married and even in my dream I know I'm on a public servant's wage and can't afford a rock, so I just accept I'll never have one.

Someone on a street corner gives me some roasted walnuts and an American Express card, which I think is a particularly kind and humanitarian gesture, even for the Americans, who are still bombing the shit out of Iraq. But I take both and consider that I will at least do something positive with the Amex. And I do. I go shopping on 5th, 6th and 7th avenues. I buy boots and bags and clothes and I have big cardboard shopping bags with tissue paper sticking out slung on my shoulders and look like all the other shoppers travelling down the street.

I breathe in the city that never sleeps, which is weird, given that I am actually asleep, and I marvel over the crowds and the colour and the lights of Times Square, on all day and all night, advertising music and running shoes and Broadway plays.

What does Al Gore think about the electricity being used in New York City? Is it as bad as Vegas? I shudder to think how much energy is being consumed, but I know it's too much, too much, too much.

There are lots of cops, so many cops on the streets, everywhere, and I feel safe. I think of Mike momentarily but I remind myself that I'm kind of on a holiday so shouldn't be thinking about home, I should just be worried about how much shopping and sightseeing and how many Broadway shows I can consume in one astral dream.

I feel like Audrey Hepburn when I enter Tiffany's and I gasp when I see Mike-Monday standing behind a counter. Did he follow me from Disneyland? Is he astral travelling too? Or astral stalking? How does this work?

'Can I try on that bracelet?' I say, pointing to some white gold under the glass. He gets it out from the cabinet and puts it on my wrist.

'It looks beautiful. You look beautiful,' he says and I look down and I'm in a long black frock like Audrey's with a split above my knee. My hair is in a twist, I'm wearing black satin gloves and I've got a cigarette in a long elegant holder. And I do look beautiful.

'I'm celibate,' I declare at a volume that almost wakes me from my sleep and everyone in the store turns and looks at me with a frown, as if I've just farted really loudly.

'No, you're not,' he says and takes my hand and leads me into the plush Tiffany's toilets.

'Audrey wouldn't do this,' I say out loud.

'Ah, but you're not Audrey and I'm not George Peppard and we're allowed to do whatever we want.'

Mike-Monday carefully manoeuvres me up against a wall as 'Moon River' is piped through the building. He kisses my neck and it makes me crazy with desire. 'You are so beautiful,' he says and I know it's just bullshit but the moment's not real so it's okay to believe him. Mike-Monday expertly lifts my dress and removes my knickers, not once taking his eyes from mine, and I think maybe it's not bullshit, maybe this is making love and not just sex in fancy, expensively designed toilets. I get carried away because Mike-Monday is touching me just right and I lose count of how many orgasms I have because I've never really been any good at maths but it doesn't matter as we're both panting and he's saying, 'You are so beautiful,' over and over again, and I almost start to believe it and then I hear a phone ring, but I don't have a phone with me, just my little blue Tiffany's bag and my cigarette holder, but the phone is ringing so loud now I wake up.

'Peta? Are you okay?' James said down the line with concern.

'Hello?' I replied, almost breathless, still recovering from Mike-Monday and talking into my mobile with my eyes closed. 'Oh hi, yes, I was just sleeping.'

'But it's two o'clock in the afternoon. Are you sick?' He was worried and I knew it would be better to say I was unwell than to say I was hung-over from the night before and exhausted from multiple orgasms had in public toilets in my sleep.

'Yes, I've got a bug or something, just feel a bit weak – probably a twenty-four hour thing. I'll call you back later.'

I tried to go back to sleep, to find Mike-Monday, but I couldn't.

♥

That evening Cousin Joe dropped off another food parcel. This time it was mutton bird he'd had flown in from Tasmania. Josie came round to help me eat it.

'It's really fatty,' she said as she licked her lips.

'And salty,' I added, doing the same.

'But really bloody good,' we both said simultaneously.

'It happened again,' I said and made like a kid pretending to be an aeroplane.

'Fuck you.' Josie was starting to seriously get annoyed with my free international travel.

'You wish.'

'No seriously, where to this time?'

'Las Vegas, LA and New York. Where else?'

'It's not fair,' she sulked.

'Hmmm, what's fair anyway?' I was being a bitch, and kept going. '*And* I had sex with Robert Redford and a hot guy named Mike-Monday.'

'That's a weird name. Was he out of *Bold and the Beautiful* or something?'

'No, his name was Monday, but he looked like Mike, the policeman.'

'Oh, Mike the *policeman*, who used to be referred to as "the cop"? So you're having sex dreams about him now? Let's explore those.'

'Let's not. Monday, as I was saying, took me to Disneyland.'

'Did you go on the cups and saucers?'

'I did. And then he was in Tiffany's.'

'God, you got it all sewn up, eh? He knows what kind of jewellery you like, and he can protect you too, cos he's a cop. Sis, if only you could make your astral dreams come true.'

'My life's weird enough without living what goes on during my sleep. But let me tell you, not having much sex in my real life has been a bloody good idea, because it's been great in my dreams.'

'So what's news on the cop front anyway?'

'Don't you mean James front?'

'No, I mean cop front. You haven't seen James for ages, and you hardly talk about him any more.'

'I spoke to him this afternoon, so there, nah nah nah nah nah!'

'Well that was grown-up, Peta. I bet he misses your childish ways, eh?'

forty
Singing the Kimberley

The next week was so busy I didn't have time to think about James, or Mike, or Sydney vs. Melbourne or celibacy or any of it. On Monday I flew off to Kununurra in Western Australia for a forum coordinated by the department – 'Literacy, Literature and Living Stories' – and I'd had to do an awful lot of reading over the weekend to prepare for it. I couldn't believe the number of books by Aboriginal authors coming out of Western Australia. Representatives from publishing houses and writing programs and support staff from relevant government departments all travelled from across the Kimberley and as far away as Perth to the very top north-east corner of the state, near the Northern Territory border. Mum had always worried about me visiting communities in the Territory and WA where law and tradition were still adhered to and practised. I think she was worried about me falling under some 'love magic' and being sung by or to a Blackfella and then living my life too far away from her, but now I'd ended up all the way down south in Victoria anyway.

The week in Kununurra gave me ample opportunity to talk to writers and storytellers, as well as visual artists from Waringarri Aboriginal Arts and Warnum Art Centre. It was a non-stop hectic six days. In between chairing sessions and running client meetings with organisations from the region, I wanted to get a feel for the country and do some tourist sites as well. I only had time for a cruise on Lake Argyle in the hope of seeing a croc, and to visit the Zebra Rock Gallery. I really missed Sylvia managing my diary and hadn't realised until then how much of a task it must have been for her juggling my workload and obligations.

On closing night there was a concert with musicians travelling from Broome and One Arm Point to play for the tourists and locals alike. The Broome-based rock band Footprince re-formed for the occasion and Kerrianne Cox strummed her guitar, while local Peter Brandy played some country and western. But there was one acoustic musician with a velvet voice who really captured my celibate attention – when the last thing I needed was to fall for a local.

I sat up the back with the local Elders, who were all cooing over young Chad.

'Chad the lad, he's all right, hey daught,' one said, winking and nudging me in the side.

'Bet they don't make 'em like 'im down south, eh?' another prodded.

'Well, no Aunt, they don't actually,' I had to concede. It wasn't a Melbourne vs. Sydney thing now, it was a Kimberley vs. every other community thing. And the men here could really belt out a tune.

'He could sing to me anytime,' another aunt laughed, 'or I could just sing him to me instead.' And they all held their large bellies and laughed until tears streamed down their faces. It was so lovely to see elderly women enjoying a harmless and hysterical perve.

'Can you do that? Sing people I mean?' I said in my naive Murri way.

'Of course, we have to do it before the good Black men end up with white women.' And the Elders laughed some more.

'Or other men!' another chimed in.

'Ah, but can you sing him to me so he moves down south? Cos Aunt, I like it here, but I'm a concrete Blackfella with Westfield Dreaming. I can't live in the Kimberley, not enough shopping.'

'Ah daught, this fella here, he'll never leave his country. He too shy to go to big city. He'd wanna woman to stay and have too many babies. I don't think that's you, is it?' Somehow she knew. I wasn't likely to be a Kimberley bride, and the wisdom of my Elders never ceased to surprise me.

As Chad finished his last song and took a bow amid screams for an encore, a mob of women surrounded him, all shapes and sizes, all ages and shades. He'd find his woman, no worries, and no-one would have to be sung to anyone.

The flights home from Kununurra were tiring: first to Darwin, then Adelaide, then Melbourne. I spent the time thinking about my thirty-first birthday, which was the following week. James was coming down, so we'd probably just go out for dinner and have a couple of drinks. It would be nice. It would be romantic. I would be spoiled for sure. And it would be a lot quieter than my birthdays in the past, without Alice, Dannie and Liza to party with.

I'd have to work out when I could squeeze in Shelley, Sylvia and Josie because they'd all mentioned doing something too. Surely they'd understand that with James just there briefly, I'd have to spend the bulk of the time with him.

As soon as the plane landed and we were allowed to turn on our phones, the messages came through: two from Alice, five from James, six from Sylvia and one each from Shelley, Josie and Mike. I'd been out of range in Kununurra and didn't bother turning the phone on when in transit. I was too exhausted to deal with work and nothing urgent would've been coming through on a Saturday anyway. James and Alice were also on my voicemail, and I called James back as I waited for my luggage. It had been nearly a week since we'd spoken and he sounded anxious.

'Babe, God, it's been ages,' he fretted.

'I know, I know, had no range up there, sorry. I tried your office a couple of times during the day from the library but you were always in meetings.'

'I'm sorry.'

'Don't be sorry, it's your work. I understand completely – it's the same when I'm in the office. Are you okay?'

'I've got some bad news.'

My heart sunk, someone had died. Alice and Gary had broken up – I couldn't think of what else would make him sound so distressed.

'What is it? Tell me.'

'I have to go to Dubai next weekend.'

'That's so exciting! Wow, how wonderful.'

'I'll miss your birthday, though. I thought you'd be upset.'

'If you were missing my birthday because you were going

to the footy or something I'd be upset. But Dubai, I've always wanted to go there. Is work sending you?'

'Yes, we've got a small contract with the main firm doing the Islands of the World project.'

'Oh my God, not the one we saw on the telly, that's fucken huge! That's so cool, you're so lucky.' I was so excited it was like I was going myself.

'Yeah, it's pretty big. We're tendering to design the buildings on the Australia island. I'll have to leave next Friday, though, so I can't be in Melbourne. I wanted to take you somewhere really fancy. It's been ages since we've been out on a "date". Remember what that was like?'

'Yes, I do. But we can do it another time.'

'You don't sound upset.'

'I'm not upset – I'm happy for you! You're going to be working on the world's biggest project. Truth be known I'm a bit jealous!'

'But it's your birthday.'

'Yes, but I have one every year, it's not a big deal.'

'I'd hate you to put work before my birthday.'

'And that's the difference between me and you, James. I can see this is the chance of a lifetime, and I'm excited for you. I'm putting *you* first.' I hoped he might see how unsupportive he was earlier in the year when he moaned constantly about me following my career dream.

'What will you do for your birthday, then?' he said, contrite.

'Oh, probably go out with the girls and drink cocktails and eat food. Everything I like doing. Might get a bit messy, it's been a while.'

'I worry about you when you drink too much.'

'Oh for God's sake, I hardly ever do it any more, and if I do I'm at home. And you don't need to worry, I'm a big girl and can look after myself.'

'When you come home for Christmas we'll have a double celebration, okay? We can psych ourselves up for that.'

'My bags have just come out on the carousel, so I better grab them. I'm so tired I'll sleep like a baby. I'll call you on Monday. Congratulations, James, I'm so proud of you.'

I didn't have the heart to tell him we wouldn't be waking up together on Christmas Day. Mum had asked me to come home to Coolangatta for Christmas, as usual, and for the first time in four years I'd decided to make the effort. My brothers Benjamin and Matt and sister Giselle were going to be there with their kids, and I was looking forward to seeing them all. It had been so long my nieces and nephews probably wouldn't even recognise me by now. James was already flat-spirited about missing my birthday, though, and I didn't want him even contemplating not going to Dubai as a consequence of me going north in December.

On the way home in the cab, I called Alice. She was out for dinner with Liza and Tony, so couldn't talk properly, but she ducked into the ladies for a quick chat. 'Just wanted to let you know that it looks like they're sorting things out,' she said. 'We're on a double-date, and Liza looks happy.'

'So what changed?' I asked.

'Don't know,' Alice said. 'You'll have to ask her yourself.'

The long cab ride back to St Kilda also gave me time to return text messages to Sylvia and Josie about my birthday.

Hi, back in Melbs. B'day drinks next Sat night perfect. Speak soon, Px

Mike's message said:

Hi Miss Tully, long time, hope life's treating u kindly. The Copper

It had been a long time. I texted him back:

It's my b'day next Sat, thought u might like 2 buy me a drink.

He answered straight away:

Night shift next w/end but can u do lunch?

I texted back:

Lunch perfect, spk later. P

Lunch was a good option – it meant I could meet the girls that night for drinks. Having so much time to spend with friends was one of the best parts about living in Melbourne. I realised now how conservative my life back home in Sydney had become after I'd met James. I really only ever saw him on weekends, because of our work schedules, so I hadn't been out partying much. Now I was in my new job, I was working even harder and really relished having my weekends to myself to unwind. I was kind of glad James wasn't coming down, just so I could have some fun with the girls.

forty-one
Kissing cousins

I was excited about celebrating my birthday in Melbourne. I had a full day planned so that I wouldn't really miss the girls in Sydney and James in Dubai. Before I was barely awake, though, the doorbell rang and there was a massive bunch of long-stemmed red roses from James. They were James all over: classy, elegant, expensive. I loved them. I put them in a vase immediately, then crawled back into bed and read the card three times: *Happy birthday, babe. Sorry I'm not there. Love, James.*

Somehow I felt something was missing from the message, some part of James's love had gone, even though the roses suggested otherwise, and as I looked at the card again I couldn't blame him. I had been away for ten months and I hadn't been near as committed to keeping in touch as he had. I hadn't called him daily like a girlfriend should. Instead, the calls had given way to Facebook emails and late-night text messages when I had time. Not even I would bother waiting twelve months for me.

Shelley came crashing into my room at nine am. 'Haaaaaapy birthday, princess!'

'Do I really behave like a princess?' I was still worried about how Josie had said I was hard work.

'You *are* a princess, but that's okay, cos I'm a princess too, and this is our castle. You wanna go out for some brekky? It's going to be a scorcher,' she said as she pulled the curtains open and let the sun stream in. It was already hot.

'Yeah, but let's go low-key – I've got lunch and then cake at Aunt Nell's to get through . . . My birthday is all about eating, it seems.'

'Ah, to absorb the alcohol – speaking of which, I'll be back in a minute.' And she walked out of the room. My phone went and it was Dannie and Alice together, singing 'Happy Birthday' in their loudest high-pitched voices.

'I'm so glad neither of you took up singing as a career,' I joked, with tears streaming down my face from laughing so hard.

'So are we!' Alice said. 'Wish you were here, sis, the sun's beautiful, the ocean's glistening . . .'

'And I don't have the kids,' Dannie yelled with joy.

'Hey, don't have too much fun today – it is *my* birthday, remember.'

'Of course, but we're using *your* birthday to catch up and eat and shop. Liza's working, as usual,' Dannie said, as Shelley walked back into the room with a bottle of bubbly.

'Sounds like fun, but listen, I'll have to let you go. I'm off for breakfast with Shelley then a full day of indulgence. I might do the drunken dial tonight so turn your phones off.'

'Bye, say hi to Shelley, see ya, ciao!'

I thought of them up there together and I momentarily wished I was there too, but then Shelley handed me a glass of champagne.

'It's not French, but then neither are we. It's something

to mark the arrival of your good self on the planet. Happy birthday!'

'Happy birthday to me, then.' I sipped the foam that was about to spill over the rim.

Barely awake but already tipsy, we sat at the Espy for brekky. I knew I'd be having a big day and so wanted to fill myself with some carbs and protein for the celebrations ahead. I looked out to the sea and felt completely content.

'I could live here,' I said to the horizon.

'You do live here.' Shelley looked at me confused.

'I mean for longer, I've only got eight weeks left.'

'Oh, don't start on about leaving already! Our celebrations will turn into a wake, and that's an excuse for a drink we should save up.'

Mike took me to a funky Italian place on Chapel Street for my birthday lunch. 'It's Kylie's favourite,' he told me as we took our reserved table outside. I liked it the minute we sat down. The waiters were young Italian hunks and very friendly. Their service was effortless and efficient. They explained the dishes and the wine with obvious passion, but I couldn't understand a word they were saying: it was all in Italian. Mike's bilingual skills came as a complete surprise.

'What?' he asked, as I sat there mouth agape. 'I told you there was more to me than being a cop.'

'A Campari Prosecco for the *signorina*?' said Fabio the waiter, who was back at our table almost immediately.

'Um, yes, I guess so,' I said and shrugged my shoulders and smiled at Mike. As Fabio walked off I followed him with my eyes back into the restaurant and saw Campari bottles lining the walls.

We were still reading the menu when a man rushed to the doorway of the restaurant yelling, 'You're all drug dealers, stop dealing drugs to my wife!'

The whole restaurant – inside and out – stopped still. It was like a scene out of a movie.

'Shit,' Mike said, 'stay put,' and he got up swiftly and took the man aside, holding him gently but firmly by the arm. The guy was wearing grey tracksuit pants and a black T-shirt and I didn't imagine for one second he was packing a pistol or any other weapon, but he was agitated and really pissed off.

One of the cute waiters went over to them and asked, 'Is everything all right here?'

'Get him, go get him, I want to see him!' the guy shouted, craning round, trying to look for someone in the restaurant. 'You're all drug dealers,' he said, over and over again. I didn't know who 'him' was, but knew it was someone that I didn't really want to be seeing there and then. It was exciting, like an Aussie-style version of *The Godfather*.

'Get out or I'll call the police,' the waiter said calmly. I had to strain to hear him. Was he trying to defuse the situation because there was some truth in the man's allegations? I saw Mike pull out his badge and show them both. It was high drama. I grabbed Fabio and whispered in his ear.

'So, should I be nervous or afraid?'

'No, *signorina*, he has just found out his wife is having an affair, and he is angry and blaming someone who worked here some years ago.' He briefly rested his hand on mine. 'Please don't be worried. I think your boyfriend the policeman is sorting it out.' Before I could clarify that Mike wasn't my boyfriend, the waiter was gone and so too was the angry man. Mike was on his mobile. I just sat and observed the other patrons, who were all watching Mike with interest. Their eyes followed him as he came back and sat down opposite me.

'The waiter told me that guy's pissed off because his wife's having an affair with someone who used to work here – high drama for lunchtime, eh?' I said.

'Really? Do you believe that?' Mike went back to reading the menu as if nothing had happened.

'Yes, why wouldn't I?'

'A man who just found out his wife was having an affair would have been in there looking for the man who was shagging his wife. Why was he yelling about drugs, that's what I want to know. I won't ruin your birthday lunch by following it up now. I've called his details into the station, so I can check out the claims he made later and write a report this afternoon.'

'Can I get you a drink on the house, *signorina*?' The waiter was back, looking at my already empty glass.

'*Vino. Bianco, grazie.*' All of a sudden I spoke Italian too and I could order wine. It arrived with our bruschetta napolitano and carpaccio della casa and our meal finally began.

Just as our calamari was served four men in suits walked up to the entrance of the restaurant and my heart started to race – to my untrained eye they looked like drug dealers, the famous Melbourne's underworld, coming to eat lunch and make deals and plan cement shoes, right near my table.

'Don't turn around,' I whispered, which of course made Mike turn around immediately, which I didn't think was policeman-like at all.

'Oh my God, they're in black suits and everything. They must be,' and I lowered my voice, '*drug dealers*.'

'God, you make me laugh, the way you stereotype people. Haven't you noticed that *everyone* in Melbourne wears black, except you and me?' And he was right: Mike was always in blue jeans and a coloured shirt.

I wasn't convinced they weren't bad guys but I let it go, as Mike started writing on the paper covering the table.

'What are you doing?' I was giggly after just one drink.

'I'm writing down the only phrase you'll need in Italian, for today anyway.'

'How do you even know any Italian? Do they teach it at the police academy?'

'I'm not sure if you're being a smart-arse so I'll ignore that last comment, okay?'

'Okay.' I giggled some more.

'Remember my tulip grandmother? The one my gorgeous yellow car reminds me of?'

'Oh, how could I forget?'

'Well, her second husband was Italian and he taught her and she taught me. We only ever spoke Italian when I visited there. I really miss her, she died a couple of years ago,' he said, without looking up from the paper tablecloth he was still writing on. 'So I like coming here just so I can practise. There.' Mike put his pen down and smiled broadly. I was gobsmacked. Constable Care was also bilingual.

'*Io sono Australiana e non parlo Italiano*,' I read. 'Is that right? What's it mean?'

'Have a guess,' Mike said.

'I'm Australian and I don't speak Italian?'

'*Brava, signorina*. You are correct.'

I practised on the waiter when he returned. '*Io sono Australiana e non parlo Italiano*.' Fabio was impressed.

'That is very good Italian for someone who doesn't speak the language. What other Italian don't you speak, *signorina*?'

'None!' I laughed.

'That is such a shame! I could teach you Italian properly, and you know you could pass as Italian,' he said to me. 'Perhaps Sicilian.' He was flirting with me, but Mike just chuckled.

'Are you interested, *signorina*?'

What could I say? It would be rude to say no, and some Italian lessons would be great.

'Here is your first lesson. You say *sono interessata* if you are interested. And *non sono interessata* if you are not interested. But I think you need to also learn to say *interessante*.'

'Which means?'

'It means *you* are *interesting*.' I liked Fabio.

'Yes, she is,' Mike said, with a tone of ownership over the *signorina*. Fabio smiled and walked away, and we enjoyed the rest of our meal uninterrupted.

♥

Cousin Joe had baked me a beautiful birthday cake with wattle seed cream in the middle and Aunt had decorated the kitchen with balloons and streamers, mainly for Will and Maya's benefit. They had so much fun blowing the candles out. We kept lighting and relighting them again and again, and by the time they were done the icing had just about melted. I couldn't recall ever having a party like this as I grew up. Mum never made me a birthday cake, it was always shop bought. Having photos with the kids and Aunt overwhelmed me a little – it was one of the most moving birthday moments I could remember *ever* having. I looked at my aunt: she was completely different to my mum and I wondered how they could be sisters.

'Can I ask you something, Aunt?'

'Of course, but I mightn't have the answer.'

'Well, an opinion will do. When do you know you're supposed to get married?'

'Oh, that's a hard one, daught, it's different for everyone. Sometimes you feel it in your belly, sometimes you know as soon as you meet the person. Sometimes it's just easier knowing who *not* to marry.' How much did she know, I wondered. I hadn't really talked to her about James at all during my stay in Melbourne and, unlike my mum the neighbourhood gossip, she never pried for information.

'I tell you what I've come to know from looking at women around me, and not just my age but women of all ages, and that is that most women don't usually end up with the loves of their lives.'

'Really? That's sad. I mean, isn't that the person you *should* marry?'

'Yes, of course it is. But most women marry the man who will make a good husband and father and provide a lifestyle for them all. If you can find the man who can give you that and is *also* the love of your life, then you're one in a million.'

'And what about marrying your soul mate?'

'Well, if you meet your soul mate, dear girl, then you'll have the good husband and father and lifestyle because it will fall into place. And boy we will have a humdinger of a wedding. You can have it here in the backyard if you like.' I loved my aunt so much at that moment; she was so down to earth. No bullshit at all.

'Oh, I've gotta go meet the girls, Aunt. Thanks so much for the cake and the words of wisdom. You should have a column in the *Koori Mail* so we could write in and you could solve our relationship woes.'

'Oh, can't be givin' all my secrets away now, can I – I'll never get another date!'

Joe kindly drove me to the Prince to meet Sylvia and Josie on his way to cater a function at Albert Park.

By seven o'clock we were all pretty trashy, but having a great time. It was my birthday and I would get drunk if I wanted to. I started talking to a couple of Koori musicians, Warren and Jason, and their manager Rob, a rather odd, snobby bloke. Rob's only conversation was the boys or talking about other bands. When he did attempt to make small talk it was a disaster.

'So what do you do, love?' he asked me.

'I'm the National Aboriginal Policy Manager for DOMSARIA,' I said reluctantly. I didn't want to talk shop on my birthday, but I needn't have worried because being a public servant didn't impress Rob at all. He just responded, 'Right,' and with that he turned around and started talking to Jason again.

'Well, that was a conversation killer that one,' I said to Warren, who looked embarrassed at how rude his manager had been. 'What's his problem? Here's my card anyway, because there may actually be something that I can do for you fellas through my job.' Warren read it and nodded with approval. 'When I'm not here you might want to pass it on to your snobby boss.'

'Yeah, sorry bout him, there's this bullshit A-circle in Melbourne.'

'A-circle? Is that "A" for Aborigine?' I joked.

'You wish. It's the A-list for top dogs, and we're not on it. I'm on the D-list for sure. But old Robbo there, he likes to think he's on it. Doesn't realise he's not, but we just let him go.'

I liked Warren, he was cool. And tall, and hunky, and there, and James was in Dubai, and it was my birthday, and I was drunk, and time was moving on and I hadn't had a birthday pash, and knew I wouldn't be getting a birthday bonk, and it *was* my birthday, and at least he wasn't Mike the cop, so I just said, 'I think you should kiss me.'

'Do you?'

'Don't you want to?'

Warren looked taken aback. 'Only since the minute you

walked into the pub. But why would someone like you—'
and he looked at my card again, 'want to kiss someone
like me?'

'It's my birthday!'

'But . . .'

'But what? It's just a birthday kiss! I didn't ask you to
marry me. I would *never* ask that. Nothing personal, you
know, it's just I *never* want to get married is all.'

He leaned in and kissed me softly on the mouth.

'Happy birthday.'

'Thank you. It wasn't that traumatic, was it?'

'No, it was lovely, but if you're expecting another one I
really think we should do the family tree first.'

'Are you serious? Really? I have *never* thought about
doing that before I kissed someone.' I was from such a
small family there was no way Warren and I could be
related, and I knew the names of all the families I was
related to.

'Well, I'm a Tully from Coolangatta,' I said confidently
and his face dropped.

'I'm a McGrath from McLean and I'm pretty sure
we're related,' he said seriously. My face dropped too. I
knew the McGraths and he was probably right. Were there
any of the Bundjalung mob actually left up north?

'Ewwww,' I said wiping my mouth. 'No offence but
I've gotta go.' And I grabbed Sylvia and Josie, who were
standing at the bar in deep conversation.

'Let's go to Mink, NOW!'

Thank God it was just a flight of stairs away. I'd been
out and about since breakfast with Shelley and wasn't in the

best form, but it *was* my birthday, which gave me a sense of diplomatic immunity. But when I tried to get into the downstairs bar I was told it was full. I knew they didn't want to let me in because I was too trashy – Mink was a sophisticated, up-market sort of place.

'Pull the race card,' Sylvia whispered in my ear.

'Get her away,' I said to Josie, who had got a dose of the giggles.

'I'm luscious, and sexy, and dark, just like your bar,' I said to the doorman, but he didn't respond. 'Don't you know who I yammmmmm?' I slurred. The girls were in hysterics, holding each other up like drunken teenagers.

'Look at me, look at me hard. Or look hard at me, whichever is the most grammatically correct,' I said, and the doorman finally gave me a smile. 'Can't guess? I'll tell ya. I'm Rachel Berger. Now, I know I haven't been on telly for a while, so you can be excused for not knowing me straight away. I'll forgive you this time, just this once, but you have to let me and my gorgeous friends in, because in actual fact, it's my birthday.' And then I panicked. I had no idea how old Rachel Berger was. Should I be looking older or younger? But it didn't seem to matter as the doorman had changed his mind.

'Of course, now I recognise you. And happy birthday. Of course you can come in and celebrate, but there's some-one here who loves your work, so could you just wait one minute while I get them?'

'Of course, anything for my fans.' The girls burst out laughing again. The doorman walked away and the three of us just stood there waiting for him to return with my 'fan'.

'Ladies, I'd like to introduce you to Rachel Berger.' And there she was with the doorman, larger than life. 'This young lady is celebrating her birthday and just told me how much she admires your work, Rachel.'

'Well, it's like looking in the mirror . . . but with a spray-on tan.' Rachel was really friendly, and very pretty, and funny, and so I was pleased people mistook me for her.

'Peta – my name's Peta,' I said, ashamed.

'Let me buy you a birthday drink, Peta, and your friends.' And we all went into Mink – for just one drink. The doorman smiled as we walked past him. 'Thank you,' I mouthed when I looked back.

forty-two
New Year resolutions

It was December and the scorching Melbourne summer had set in. There was no way I was wearing black anything to anywhere. All of a sudden it wasn't the cold that bothered me, but the dry summer heat I had first arrived to earlier in the year. I missed Coogee more than ever – the smell of the ocean, the sound of waves and the afternoon southerlies. The countdown to returning to Sydney seemed manageable when I thought about swimming in the sea again.

First, though, I was going home to Coolangatta for Christmas.

James had been completely irrational when I finally found the courage to tell him I wasn't going to Sydney for Christmas. 'Are you punishing me for going away on your birthday? I knew it. I knew you were angry with me. I shouldn't have gone.'

'Don't be so bloody ridiculous. I was never bothered by you going away, and I told you, I had a brilliant birthday with the girls in Melbourne anyway. I was *happy* for you to go to Dubai – in fact, I've been hoping you brought me something gorgeous back.'

'I did, of course – I was going to give it to you when you came up for Christmas.' He was sulky and being too much hard work.

'Well, you can give it to me a couple of days later, and it'll still be gorgeous, and we can still celebrate Christmas.' I sounded like a parent talking down to a child. 'I just want to see my family this year. It's been four years since I've had Christmas with them.'

'I didn't know that.'

'There's a lot of things you don't know about me, James, and that's okay, but right now I'm telling you that I want to be with my family on Christmas Day, like you'll be with yours.'

He picked up on the stress in my voice. 'I'm sorry for being a sook, I just miss you.'

'I know, but we'll do our own delayed Christmas dinner with pressies when I get to Sydney, okay? And it will be wonderful.'

I flew into Coolangatta airport on Christmas Eve and there were millions of people everywhere. Tourists heading to the Gold Coast for holidays, family members greeting loved ones, kids running around with what looked like presents already opened. Mum was waiting with a huge smile and hugged me like a mother who hadn't seen her daughter for four years. It was the best welcome I could've asked for.

'The boys and Gis can't wait to see you,' Mum said, patting me on the thigh as she pulled out of the car park. 'And the kids have all made their aunty Christmas cards. It's so good to have you back, everyone's excited and looking forward to tomorrow. But tonight it's just you and me. I've got some prawns for us – I thought we could have some dinner, go and look at the houses all done up with lights and then go to midnight mass.'

'I can't believe you still do that. Why? You don't go any other time of the year.'

'There are some holy days that must be respected always, Peta.'

I smiled as we pulled into the drive. The family home looked just the same, like the place was in a time warp. Mum's blonde brick house looked like every other house in our street – they were all exact replicas. I could smell the frangipani tree immediately, and Kyla the family dog came running up to me straight away, like she remembered who I was after all the time away. I took my case into my old room, which Mum had turned into her sewing room, and then we sat down with a cuppa.

'Coffee, bub?' she asked as she got the jar out of the cupboard. I didn't have the heart to tell her I only drank barista coffee since moving to Melbourne and couldn't face the instant variety any more.

'I might have a tea eh, Mum, just black.' I also didn't want to say I'd moved on to soymilk and preferred my tea green, not black. She would think I was being too uptown. If I could get through the time on the coast without having a row with Mum, then my Christmas would be perfect.

'So, when you going to settle down and have a family of your own?'

Mum got straight to the point; it was one of the traits I'd inherited from her.

'Mum!' I protested.

'Okay, okay, then. How's James?' But talking about boyfriends with her was not something I had ever done or wanted to do. I had always viewed my mother harshly for having had so many husbands and leaving me so distrustful of men and relationships.

'He's fine, spending Christmas with his family. They have everyone over to their home and do the traditional Christmas thing, you know, turkey and all the trimmings.' My mum wasn't much of a cook either – the reason the men never stayed, she used to joke. But we didn't want turkey anyway, it was so hot and humid that seafood was our Christmas Day menu.

'Are you going to marry him?' she asked.

'Hell. I don't know. Can we talk about something else?' I said rudely and took my cup to the sink. 'Actually, no!' I turned back to her. 'Let's talk about it, about your divorces, and the defective marriage gene you've given me.'

'What are you talking about? And don't take that tone with me – I'm still your mother.'

'You were married three times and divorced three times, Mum. Why would you want me to get married when it obviously never worked for you? All your marriages failed.'

'Firstly, three divorces out of three marriages means I have a hundred per cent success rate. And that's how I'd prefer to look at it.' Mum poured herself another cup of tea. 'Secondly, they didn't really fail. They gave me four beautiful children, and many years of happiness when the times were good. And that's the way I choose to look at it.

Always look on the bright side is what one of those husbands used to say to me.' She smiled and sipped her tea.

'But they didn't stay!' I was confused.

'No they didn't, but it's not because they didn't want to. I didn't want them to.'

'What? Why? I don't even know my own father.'

'Your father . . .' My mother paused, 'had an affair with his secretary for the first two years he was married to me and while I was pregnant with you. He was not the kind of man I wanted my first-born child to know. He didn't respect me, or you in my belly, and I couldn't have that. I was short-tempered and perhaps a little short-sighted at the time, but I knew my mind and I told him to leave and never come back. And he left and didn't come back, which tells you what kind of man he was. I'm so sorry that you didn't have a decent dad, it was my fault I chose a bad man.'

'But what about Gerry? He was a good father to Ben, Matt and Gis. He was lovely. Why did he leave? I know it wasn't your cooking, because he did all the cooking.'

'The others don't know this, but Gerry is gay. Of course he wasn't when he married me, but then one day, I don't know, he woke up and was gay. What was I supposed to do? Should I have told my children, "Gerry's your mum *and* your dad?"'

'Gay? Gerry? Oh my God, that's harsh to deal with when you've been married and had kids together. I'm sorry, it must have been hard for you.'

'Yes, when your first husband is having sex with another woman and your second husband tells you he wants to have sex with men, it doesn't make you feel very good about yourself at all. And so I vowed never to have sex again.'

'But then you married Kevin?'

'I married Kevin because I wanted companionship, not sex, which in fact we ended up having anyway, but only after we went to the club and drank too many middies of beer. I realised Kevin was an alcoholic when I woke up with a hangover every day for six months. It was too much. I vowed off the booze and the bed and I've been happier ever since.' Oh God, I got the celibacy gene from Mum also – but that was not a conversation I was going to have with her, not now.

'Wow, why haven't you ever told me this? Or Gis at least?'

'Because as kids I told you to stop asking me questions that I couldn't answer and then you just stopped asking all together. I'm sorry, but I did the best I could. Now I'm trying to just live the life I've got. No point in living in the past, is there?'

'You're so right.' My mum had wisdom and a history I had never appreciated or known.

'And the only defective gene you might have is the gene that makes you pick the wrong men. It's got nothing to do with marriage, though. Not if you pick the right one. Is James the right one?'

'Well, he would never cheat on me, he certainly isn't gay, and he doesn't even like me drinking too much, let alone him drinking too much.'

'Sounds like the right one to me.' Mum poured another

cuppa for both of us and we sat looking into the back garden, where Kyla was wrestling with a bone.

Mum and I went to midnight mass and at nine the next morning my siblings arrived with all their kids. Ben dressed up as Santa, Matt cooked the barbecue and Gis and I sat back and she told me all about life on the coast. Aunty Nell rang from Melbourne after lunch to say Merry Christmas and as Mum chatted with her I could finally see the similarities between them. They were both happiest with their kids and grandkids around them. It was the best Christmas I had ever had, and I had to tell James about it when he called.

'I've had the most wonderful day. Mum and I had a great talk, the kids were so much fun and they made me cards, and it was great to see Ben, Matt and Gis. I'm so glad I came up here.'

'Sounds like you didn't miss me at all today.'

'What?' I was stunned. 'It's not always about you, James. I just had Christmas Day with my family for the first time in four years. I learned things about my mother and my father that I never knew. And somehow, it's turned into a discussion about whether or not I miss you. I just called you, didn't I?'

'I'm sorry.'

'I've got to go.' I hung up.

Later that night as I got into bed, I checked the messages on my phone and he had called to apologise. I didn't have the energy to talk, so just sent him a text:

I'm sorry 2. It's been an emotional 24 hrs 4 me. Cya soon n we can make up! Px

At midnight my mobile sounded with a message:

> Merry Christmas Peta! Hope Santa was good 2 u. Mike

The message made me smile and I texted back:

> Merry Xmas 2 u 2! On Gold Coast with fam. Was Santa kind 2 u? P

He texted back immediately:

> I asked Santa 2 put me in ur stockings, but he said I wouldn't fit. LOL.

Mike was funny, and it was just so easy to be his friend.

> Perhaps I shoulda taken them off first. Hehehehe!

It was harmless flirting. Next he asked:

> When r u back?

I texted him back:

> Jan 4 back @ work. Finish up end of month.

My phone buzzed again straight away:

> Can I buy u dina b4 u leave?

I smiled again.

> That'd b nice. Will let u know date of departja. Off 2 bed. Nite.

♥

I'd had a great time in Coolangatta, but I was looking forward to New Year's Eve in Sydney. I'd well and truly made up for my time away from my family and now I could relax at the beach with my friends.

I stayed with James in the inner west and discovered he'd already started packing boxes, assuming he'd be moving in with me when I returned to Sydney, although we hadn't discussed it properly at all. He'd gone to a lot of trouble to make the place pretty for me: lots of flowers and Christmas decorations. He took me to Cafe Sydney for my belated birthday dinner and prepared a dinner for us at home to celebrate Christmas. He also gave me some lovely gifts: diamond earrings from Dubai, perfume, lingerie and a double-sized beach towel for us both to lie on.

On the inside of the pantry door hung a calendar and he'd been marking off the days until my return, like a prisoner checking the days until parole or release. It was sweet, but I couldn't help thinking that my perfect James was a little obsessive. Still, I couldn't fault his commitment. He loved me, he wasn't shy about saying so, and he'd never leave me. James was a known quantity – something my mum had never found in a man – so I tried not to think too hard about his flaws. I didn't have time, anyway – we were going to enjoy the fireworks from Alice's balcony, and had to get ready to go.

It was one of the best New Year's Eves I'd ever had. Alice and Gary were so at peace in their little home, glowing with the preparations for their wedding in March. Dannie and George were both glowing with the thought of their new baby due in April. Liza and Tony were back together and he was booking dinners out at restaurants and taking a basic cooking class and getting naked as often as Liza wanted him too, so they were glowing from lots of sex without socks. And then there were James and I. It seemed like all the old friends back together. But *we* weren't getting married or having a baby, and we weren't even having lots of sex any more. James didn't seem to care, though, as long as we were all together.

'This is how it should be, babe,' he said, as we watched the fireworks and celebrated the beginning of another new year.

forty-three
Heavy hearts

In January I was so busy analysing the impact of the first six months of the implementation of some of our new policies and programs that I didn't have time to think about James and what was waiting for me on my return back to Sydney.

My time at DOMSARIA had clarified my absolute commitment to forging a career in arts and culture, but I was heading back home to my old job in education. Although I was worthy of a promotion I knew there wouldn't be one until a position became available, so I felt like I was going backwards. I still wanted to be Minister for Cultural Affairs one day, and that meant I'd have to start looking at vacancies in other departments almost immediately in order to keep moving in the right direction. I was only now beginning to realise how much I would miss my job here in Melbourne – and my colleagues.

'You got a minute, boss?' Sylvia and Rodney were at my door.

'Yes, well I won't be boss for much longer.'

'That's what we wanted to talk about,' Rodney said, following Sylvia into the office and closing the door behind them.

'Oh, come right in and close the door behind you, please,' I joked. We had a good rapport, the three of us, and they took charge when they needed to. 'What's wrong?'

'Nothing's wrong, Rodney just had something he wanted to run by you.'

'Well, speak now or forever hold your peace,' I joked, trying to hide my heavy heart.

'You've heard of that new Centre for News on Email, Radio and Downloads?'

'Otherwise known as the Centre for NERDs? Yes, I've heard of it, it's the joke of the bureaucratic world. Why?'

'They're looking for a CEO, and I've got the inside that they love what you've done here, what with policy and setting up a strong foundation for the team.'

'So, you're suggesting I be the CEO of NERDs. Is that what you're telling me? I'm not quite sure how to take that.' I thought it was hilarious, but neither Sylvia nor Rodney laughed.

'He's serious,' Sylvia said.

'Oh, right. Look, I'd love to be in charge of NERDs,' I giggled, 'but I wish you wouldn't give me these teasers on the eve of me leaving. It's hard enough to say goodbye and go without you giving me options to stay. How hard would it be to manage NERDs anyway?' I couldn't help myself, and they both finally cracked a smile.

'We just don't want you to go is all,' Sylvia sniffled.

'We've loved working with you – just wanted to thank you for being such a considerate, kind and always-there-for-us boss,' Rodney said earnestly.

'Aw, gee, thanks,' I didn't mean to sound corny, but I was touched.

'And it's not because we don't really like the dragon lady who's starting in your position next week,' Rodney added, trying to lighten the mood.

'Aw, gee, thanks again – I think?' I told him and looked towards Sylvia, who was blotting her eyes, no doubt hoping not to smudge her expertly applied kohl. 'You do realise that I would poach you both and take you with me, if I could. A manager is only as good as their staff. And as management goes, I've had a very easy run with you two on my team. So, in actual fact, I should be thanking you.' And tears started to fall from my own eyes as Sylvia passed me a tissue.

'Right – can't be seen to be crying in front of the rest of the staff. Let's fix ourselves up and head out to that luncheon I know everyone's been waiting to have.'

We all went to lunch and there were more tears all round. Sylvia made a speech on behalf of my team before announcing she'd written something poetic for me. I started to cry before she'd even started reading.

'I was going to write you a haiku, but haiku are not my strong point. Then I thought a sonnet, or an ode, but I decided on a limerick, because it just seemed the best way to sum you up. Here goes:

'There's a girl from Sydney called Peta
She's your friend the minute she greets ya
She's the world's best boss
Now the department's at a loss
So if you get the chance you should meet-a.'

I sobbed unashamedly while the rest of the table laughed and cheered loudly. I blew my nose, took a deep breath and stood up.

'Right, well, I don't have a prepared speech, because my

speechwriter has been busy writing Nobel Prize–winning limericks. Thank you, Laureate Sylvia.' And there was another round of applause.

'But I did want to take a moment to let you all know how much I've enjoyed working with you the past twelve months. I've had an amazing year both professionally and personally, I'm very sad about leaving Melbourne and the department and all the friends I've made here. And I'd like to make special mention of my wing-woman, diarist, bodyguard, travel agent, driver and now, personal limerick-ist, Sylvia.' I looked directly at Sylvia, who smiled through black-ringed eyes. Her attempts to remain smudge-free had failed. 'I'd like to thank you for making my job at DOMSARIA not only manageable, but pleasurable as well. Finally, I'd like to make a toast to you all, and wish you well in all your goals. Cheers.' With that everyone raised his or her glass, and I knew that one of the most important parts of my life in Melbourne had come to a close.

I'd agreed to meet up with Mike for a quick farewell at the George before heading home, but I was feeling emotionally drained by the time I got there.

'Hello, beautiful,' Mike said when I arrived. 'Sorry, I'll start again – hello, *Peta*.'

'Hi.' I looked into his blue, blue eyes and I was suddenly overwhelmed. If I stayed there feeling as vulnerable as I did, I'd say or do something that I knew I'd regret immediately. I was leaving Melbourne tomorrow morning and James would be waiting for me at the airport at the other end. My year was up. I'd met the challenge I had set myself professionally, and it was time to go home. Kissing

Mike at the eleventh hour would only knee-cap me, Mike and James at the same time.

I tried to swallow the lump rising in my throat. 'I'm really sorry, but I feel completely wiped out and I don't think I can stay. I'm sorry.'

Mike looked disappointed, but he nodded.

I started to walk off.

'Hey, aren't you forgetting something?'

I turned around confused. 'What?'

'Me!' Mike stood up. I didn't know if it was just another of his cheesy lines or if he was serious. I gave a crooked half-smile and kept walking.

'Wait!' Mike called out but I didn't stop. By the time I got to the corner he'd texted me:

If I followed you home, would you keep me?

I didn't know what to say. I wanted him to follow me home. But then what? I texted him back:

I'll call u from Syds when I've settled in. Take care always. Pxx

forty-four
Should old acquaintance . . .

The day of my departure arrived and I was counting down the hours I had left till I returned to Sydney. My thirteen months were up and I was due to go back to my little flat in Coogee, to Sauce Bar and the beach and the Ladies Baths and my coastal walks with Alice – that is, if Liza and Gary hadn't now permanently filled my spot. And I was going home to James.

I felt empty as I packed up my sunny room in my comfortable house in Eildon Road. I would miss Shelley and all her shoes and drinking Pimm's and the house and St Kilda. It had been an amazing year. Shelley's parents would be home in two weeks and she'd be moving out again too.

'You must have these.' Shelley walked in holding a pair of red pumps and a matching bag, neither ever used.

'I can't take them – you love them. I was with you when you bought them, remember?'

'Yes, I do remember. I bought them because you raved about them so much. I don't use them. Red's not even my colour really. And I bet your friends would love to see your Melbourne style back in Sydney. Red's a very *Melbourne* colour, you know – and it goes so well with black!'

'Oh, you're wicked,' I laughed. Shelley knew how the girls had given me a hard time about the Sydney

vs. Melbourne thing. And yes, they would love my little
red numbers. Alice would want to borrow them for sure.

'Thanks, darl – I'll wear them the first night we go out.'

Shelley and I crammed everything into her little black
Alfa and she took me to say goodbye to Josie. We cruised
along Jacka Boulevard until we saw Josie doing her beat.

'Hey, hottie!' I sung out the car window.

'I always knew you wanted me,' Josie called back as she
made her way to the car. I got out and gave her a hug like
sisters do.

'I'll miss your crazy ways, sis,' I told her.

'Yeah, I know, but don't miss me too much, okay?'

'Okay.'

'I'm coming to Sydney later in the year so we can catch
up for sure, eh? Maybe you can take me to some bars in
Newtown or Erskineville.'

'Sure thing. Would love to. Gotta run now, no tears,
okay?'

'No tears, love. Now move along, Shelley—' Josie leaned
in the car. 'Or I'll have to give you a ticket for stopping in a
no-stopping zone.'

'She would too!' I said as I climbed back in the car.

'See ya . . .' I screamed out as Shelley took off at
lightning speed.

On the way to the airport we swung around to say
goodbye to Aunty Nell, Joe, Annie and the kids. Aunt
put the kettle on and Joe had made some lemon-butter
muffins. They were to die for. I'd miss the cuppas with
Aunt and the delicious creations that I'd come to expect
from my cousin. I'd even miss suburban East Bentleigh,
which served my family well.

'Now, you write to me, Peta, and you know I love photos, so please send me some photos, okay? You will, won't you?'

'I will, Aunt. I promise.'

'Sorry, Peta, but we better run if you're going to make your flight.' Shelley was pointing to her watch.

'Right, can't miss it. James will be waiting and if I didn't get off the plane, he'd freak out for sure.'

They all walked me to the car and Will and Maya gave me huge hugs.

'I'll write to you and send you photos,' Maya said.

'I would love that.' I kissed her on the top of her head and got in the car, fighting back tears and a massive lump in my throat.

'Bye . . .' I said, weeping as we drove off again, and we hardly spoke all the way to the airport.

Shelley had always refused to use Skype or Facebook, but we'd become such good friends I knew we'd keep in touch. 'I'll call you,' she said as she helped me lift my coffin-like suitcase out of the car.

'Well, that'll mean you'll have to turn your mobile phone on.' And we both laughed in a sad kind of way. We were girls who liked to talk, not text or email. We hugged goodbye.

As I walked up the gangway off the plane, I had no idea what would happen between James and I. It had been an intense year for both of us. James was a good man and deserved good things. And so did I. Whether or not those good things would happen with each other, I just didn't know. All I knew at that very moment was that I could rely on James: he loved me, he missed me when I was away, and he wanted to give me a great lifestyle. He would never leave me and he would never change. James was the ultimate safe bet.

As I walked through the opened glass doors I saw him. A man with a smile that filled my heart.

He strode towards me as I pulled my cabin trolley through the crowd and crushed me in his arms. 'Hello, babe,' he said.

epilogue

Six months later I ironed the blue shirt carefully. I'd never believed I would feel so comfortable in a domestic relationship. Aunty Nell knew what she was talking about when she said that when you met the right man it would all fall into place.

What I felt with Mike now I never felt with James. I'd never felt that sense of ease, the sense that things were 'right'. With Mike it was different – I wanted to be around him. I didn't want to send him off with his mates on Sunday, although it wasn't a drama if either of us wanted space.

I'd moved back to Melbourne and was in a full-time position at DOMSARIA, doing what I was best at. And Mike was still reading books I brought home and reports related to anything on Indigenous issues and policing. He attended Klub Kooris with me, and art openings and book launches, and he loved it, but he didn't do it just to support me. He said he did it for himself, 'to be a better man'. That was the difference. Everything James did, he did *for* me, not with me. James did things to make me happy, but I didn't know if he was ever happy doing them.

I realised also what Dannie had been trying to tell me about marriage and sex. The one thing that was never a problem for James and I was physical intimacy, and it had been the only thing that kept us close when we were separated. Mike and I had great sex, too, but we shared intimacy in so many other ways: laughing over his stupid lines, which didn't end when we got together; going to rallies together and feeling the power of protest; and talking about how we both wanted the same thing out of life – to make the world a better place. In Mike, I'd found my soul mate. He had been my Mr Right all along.

I didn't have the fancy lifestyle that James would've given me, but I had the kind of mutually supportive relationship I'd always thought was beyond me. In return for helping Mike become 'a better man', he taught me unconditional love. And he never, ever, ever called me 'babe'.

Acknowledgements

For inspiration with characters, scenes, key phrases and funny lines, my thanks go to: Josef Heiss, Michelle Wong, Ali Smith, Rachel Berger, the boys at Sauce Bar and Grill, Prue McCahon, Paul Galea, Michael McDaniel, Paula Maling, Bernardine Knorr, Julie Reilly, Ray Kelly, Richard Frankland, Angela Gardner, Kerry Kilner, Phillipa McDermott, Scott Weber, a certain muso friend and the entire Sydney Swans footy team.

For a research base in Melbourne, thanks to: Mark Olive, Greg and Lola the cat.

For ideas on the Melbourne vs. Sydney debates, thanks to: Prue Adams, Michelle Crawford, Jeff Hore, Nicholas Birns, Josh and Danielle Goodswin and Kevin Klehr.

For the essentials on how to research 'properly' in Melbourne, thanks to: Marianne, Pete, Maya and Will, Doug and Steve, Wesley, Rayce, Dianna, Stella, and everyone else who sat in bars, cafes and restaurants with me.

For inspiring Peta's astral travelling, thanks to: the Greek waiter, the Italian security guard, the American tour guide, the Spanish customs officer, the Japanese limo-driver, Buddy Holly, Robert Redford and Barry Manilow.

To the Random House Dream Team, Larissa Edwards, Elizabeth Cowell and Claire Rose – Thank you! Thank you! Thank you! – for making the dreams of a girl from the burbs come true.

A massive serve of appreciation to Tara Wynne from Curtis Brown for being so wonderful.

To the lovely ladies at Matraville Newsagency – for making a Matto girl feel like a local celebrity, and for keeping newspapers and magazines for me – I pay my respects and gratitude.

To my friend and confidante, Robynne Quiggin, for making me laugh on the bad days, and keeping everything in the cone of silence. To Terri Janke for making me want to be a better human being. And Geraldine Star for teaching me how to be. Thank you all!

As always, a heartfelt thanks to my mum and all the family, who tolerate me like no-one should ever have to. They constantly demonstrate unconditional love, the kind that Peta Tully feels she will never know or be able to give.

www.anitaheiss.com

Dr Anita Heiss has published poetry, non-fiction, historical fiction and social commentary. Her first chick lit novel, *Not Meeting Mr Right*, won the 2007 Deadly Award for Outstanding Achievement in Literature. In 2004 she was listed on the *Bulletin*/Microsoft 'Smart 100'. Anita is a member of the Wiradjuri nation of central New South Wales, lives in Sydney and enjoys her research trips to Melbourne.

Not Meeting Mr Right
Anita Heiss

Alice Aigner is successful, independent and a confirmed serial dater – but at her ten-year school reunion she has a sudden change of heart. Bored rigid by her 'married, mortgaged and motherly' former classmates, Alice decides to prove that a woman can have it all: a man, marriage, career, kids and a mind of her own.

She sets herself a goal: meet the perfect man and marry him before her thirtieth birthday, just under two years away. Together with her best friends Dannie, Liza and Peta, Alice draws up a ten-point plan. Then, with a little help from her mum, her dad, her brothers, her colleagues and her neighbour across the hall, she sets out to find Mr Right. Unfortunately for Alice, it's not quite as easy as she imagines . . .

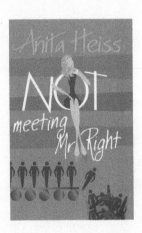